He sucked a little at her lips and she shivered.

And as his tongue slowly entered her mouth it felt like warm, sweet cherry sauce sliding through layers and layers of her skin, making her drunk as dormant desires awoke and raced through her veins screaming for more of him. She liked the feeling going through her and never wanted it to end as she drank from the velvet cup of forbidden sensations, making her knees weak as her heart pounded an erratic rhythm. She'd never been kissed like this before.

She laid her head on her chest and listened to the thumping of his heart.

"I missed you," he said.

The Other Side of the Mountain

Janice Angelique

Genesis Press, Inc.

INDIGO LOVE STORIES

An imprint of Genesis Press, Inc.
Publishing Company

Genesis Press, Inc.
P.O. Box 101
Columbus, MS 39703

All rights reserved. Except for use in any review, the reproduction or utilization of this work in whole or in part in any form by any electronic, mechanical, or other means, not known or hereafter invented, including xerography, photocopying, and recording, or in any information storage or retrieval system, is forbidden without written permission of the publisher, Genesis Press, Inc. For information write Genesis Press, Inc., P.O. Box 101, Columbus, MS 39703.

All characters in this book have no existence outside the imagination of the author and have no relation whatsoever to anyone bearing the same name or names. They are not even distantly inspired by any individual known or unknown to the author and all incidents are pure invention.

Copyright © 2011 Janice Angelique

ISBN-13: 978-1-58571-442-1
ISBN-10: 1-58571-442-9
Manufactured in the United States of America

First Edition

Visit us at www.genesis-press.com
or call at 1-888-Indigo-1-4-0

R0431902174

Chapter 1

Pamela stood listening to the huge waterfall and looking over at the twin mountain that her daughter was not allowed to visit. She shook her head, closed her eyes and opened her arms to welcome the wise spirits of her ancestors.

There was no organized religion in the Rahjah Rastafarian culture, but Sunday was their day of worship and everyone wandered all over the mountain meditating and communing with nature. They always gave thanks for every blessing bestowed on them. Today, Pamela gave thanks for her daughter and asked for guidance for her in her quest for peace among their people.

"We'll all be a family again, you know," Tim said, quietly coming up behind her.

She knew the sound of his voice, the curve of his bearded chin and the beautiful, unusual blue ring around his gray eyes. Tim had been her best male friend almost all her life. She smiled, finished her prayer and looked at him. He put his arms around her shoulders. "It bothers you, doesn't it?"

"What?"

THE OTHER SIDE OF THE MOUNTAIN

"Dissension among the tribes. I know what the children are saying, especially your little one." His voice was deep and almost always somber.

She shrugged. "Gracie and the other children have been talking about someone they call the ogre. What's your take on all this?"

"Pam, children make up stories about things they don't really know about."

Pamela sighed. "I guess you're right, but I want to know exactly what happened to separate us like this." She pulled at her twisted brown locks.

"Why don't you know about all this?" Tim asked.

"I think because when all this was going on, I had lost a husband and was busy with a toddler. I heard but didn't hear, if you know what I mean."

"But it's been years, Pam." He began walking with her.

"I know, I suppose I didn't really care before."

"And now you do?"

"Yes." She looked at him with querying eyes. "Are you following orders by not talking about it? Somehow, I think you know all about what happened."

He laughed but still said nothing as they crossed the small bridge and walked back to the village.

As with all Rahjah residences, the cottages were built in a circle with wraparound verandahs. The village was painted in an array of colors. The roofs were either dark brown or green, blending in very well with the flora of the island.

Before going to the circle for breakfast, Pamela left Tim's company and walked to her cottage to collect her cushion. The meal circle was established by the first Elders when they'd conquered the Blue Mountain on the island of Jamaica. It was their way of communicating with each other what they intended to do during the course of the day. At supper, they'd talk about what they'd actually accomplished. It was also family time for everyone.

Mary, Pamela's neighbor and closest friend, walked beside her to the circle. A very long, low table was set on reinforced dirt in the meal circle. Everyone ate and drank with coconut and bamboo utensils and flatware.

Sitting in the circle, Pamela kissed Gracie's cheek as her father, Ishmael, a tall, lanky man with long gray locks flowing down his back, stood and gave thanks for the meal while everyone held hands.

Huge platters of ackee and codfish, fried dumplings, boiled bananas, fruit and vegetables were passed around, then set on the table for anyone who wanted a second helping.

Pamela noticed that her daughter ate slowly, as if deep in thought. "What's on your mind, little one?"

Gracie shrugged.

Pamela smiled at her daughter's pretty little round face. She had her mother's freckles across her nose

THE OTHER SIDE OF THE MOUNTAIN

and the same colored hair. She hugged her. "Come on," she said. "Tell me what you're thinking."

Gracie looked up at her mother's face. "The Elders teach us that all Rahjahs are related, all are from slaves and we must be honest and not judge, right?"

Oh boy. "Right."

"Well, why do we judge the ogre on Misfit Mountain without talking with him?" She kept looking into her mother's light brown eyes.

Pamela took a deep breath. "Why do you say we judge him?"

"I've always heard that he was a bad person and we shouldn't talk about him or even go close to his mountain. I've never heard of anyone giving him a chance to clear his name." Again, she held her mother's gaze. "And why do we call him an ogre? Isn't an ogre an ugly, horrible creature? And why do we call the people on that mountain misfits? Do you know there are children like me living there?"

For the first time in her life Pamela felt dumb. She didn't know how to answer her daughter without letting her know that she'd been too busy being a mom to pay attention to what was being said of the man they called the ogre. "Yes, an ogre is a horrible creature, but sweetheart, who told you that he was an ogre, and that the mountain was called Misfit Mountain?"

"My friends. Are they lying, Mama?"

"No one is perfect, honey, but I don't think the man you speak of is an ogre. As to the villagers being called misfits, we are all Rahjahs on this island, sweetie. No one is a misfit. The mountain is called Jahyah Mountain, everything on this mountain is identical to that on Jahyah Mountain."

Gracie nodded. "Then may I visit them?"

Pamela thought that was where the conversation would lead. She laughed and squeezed her daughter's shoulder. "No."

"Why, Mama? You just said…"

"I know what I said, but I can't give you permission, honey, only the Elders can."

Gracie smiled and leaned into her mother's embrace. "Then I will ask the Elders tomorrow when I go up for history lessons. Thank you, Mama."

Pamela held her daughter close. She was not going to let this go anytime soon. "Oh, Gracie." A horrible rift had been made and the Rahjahs turned against their own. It was time to repair the rift, and her daughter was determined to be the one to do it, even if she had ulterior motives.

Saul slowly walked from his cottage on Jahyah Mountain to the small bridge close to the waterfall. This was his favorite thing to do after being away from home for a long time. For him, no place on earth compared to this island.

He leaned against the wooden rail with one foot propped against the post and listened to the soothing sounds of the waterfall mixed with the sound of the slow rhythmic beating of the drums. The Rahjahs were steeped in tradition; no motorized vehicle was to be found on their island. Saul thought of his two beautiful children playing in the meadow on the other side of the mountain and smiled. Suddenly his ex-wife crossed his mind in a violent rage. His eyes flew open as his back stiffened. His mood became dark as he ground his teeth. Wanting desperately to rid himself of her image, he crossed the bridge, quickly stripped himself of his clothes and took the deep plunge off the cliff into the cool river water below.

∞

The morning had become quite warm. The sun slowly burned the mist from the forest. At the end of breakfast, Pamela realized her daughter had awakened her interest in the lives of her family, whom she had not seen or spoken with in years. She, too, needed answers. She watched as her mother walked away from the circle, and then she got up and followed her to the community kitchen.

She caught up with her mother and touched her shoulder. Esther turned and hugged her.

JANICE ANGELIQUE

Unlike Pamela's slightly darker skin, Esther had very fair skin, with hazel eyes and long, salt-and-pepper locks that hung loosely down her back. Her full lips almost always smiled.

"Gracie asked me at breakfast about the people on Jahyah Mountain." She moved from her mother's gentle embrace and looked into her eyes. "Do you know that the kids call the people misfits and one of the men an ogre?"

Esther laughed. "We never speak of them, so I'm not surprised that they would make up stories about them."

She held her mother's hand. "We really need to talk. Let's go to my cottage."

Esther allowed Pamela to lead her towards her pink and white cottage with roses, daffodils and crotons growing on either sides of the walkway. Like all the Rahjah cottages, there was an encrusted emblem on the front door that read *The Lion of Judah shall break every chain.*

Pamela walked through the verandah, pushed open the door of her two-bedroom cottage, and stepped into her living room with her mother in tow. She sat on a huge green cushion on the highly polished wood floor. Her mother sat beside her on a yellow cushion.

There were four huge green and white cushions on the floor, and a mahogany center table with cut flowers in a coconut vase. No other furniture was in

THE OTHER SIDE OF THE MOUNTAIN

the living room. The windows were open and bare of curtains. On the walls were paintings done by different artists in the village, including Pamela, who was considered one of the best on the mountain.

"So, Mama, refresh my memory of what caused the rift."

Esther smiled her motherly smile and leaned back into the cushion. "We promised long ago not to speak of them, but I can tell you this: the man they call an ogre is far from being one." She shook her head. "You know that no Rahjah is tied to these mountains but encouraged at the age of sixteen to see the world if they so wish."

"Yes, I know all that."

"Well, Saul—by the way, that is his name—Saul went away for a long time. He attended university in Jamaica and then went to the United States, where he got his doctorate in geology."

"Why geology?" Pamela interrupted.

"Is that important?" Esther asked with a frown.

"No, not at all. Go on, please." She rolled her eyes at her mother.

"Anyway, he got himself a foreign wife, which was the greatest mistake he'd ever made. There's nothing wrong with marrying out of our culture, but he barely knew her before he moved her into his home. She talked a lot and smiled a lot, but behind closed doors she was the devil. I don't know much because he's an extremely private man, but she almost drove him crazy even after the twins were born. She was extremely jealous and made mischief on his sister. It was after she'd turned on his parents that he sent her packing. There are many holes in my story, but as I said, he is a very private man."

Pamela leaned forward, her elbows on her knees and her hands under her chin. "That doesn't tell me why there's a rift between the two mountains."

"You weren't following the story, were you? The woman told lies on everyone. She wanted him to send everyone away and keep a few as servants. She'd never had a real family life, so she didn't know what it was like to be a part of one."

"Oh, Jah," Pamela whispered to herself.

"As I said, the rift came when Saul actually tried to please her by keeping himself from his people and believing all the lies she'd told him. Some were so angry with him they left and came to this mountain. To cut a very long story short, by the time her lies had reached his parents, things had gone beyond repair. Have you ever spoken to Myah about it? After all, she is his sister."

Pamela shook her head. "No, I've never spoken to her about any of this."

"She's the only one who can fill in the holes in my story, and she hates talking about it. The lies that woman told…"

THE OTHER SIDE OF THE MOUNTAIN

"Why don't you say her name, Mama?"

Esther sighed, and the smile left her entire face. "Her name is Raquel. Anna Raquel, but she loves to be called Raquel. When Saul finally got rid of her, the hurt was so deep that we…" She stopped talking.

"But it wasn't his fault, Mama."

"Rahjah men are supposed to be strong. They are supposed to make good decisions. He should have asked questions instead of believing everything that woman said."

"Oh, Mama, he's a man. Rahjah or not, they are weak. You once told me about the power of a woman's thighs and…"

"Never mind that. He didn't come to us. His Elders didn't meet with our Elders, so we just went on with our lives."

"Did it ever occur to anyone on this mountain that he might have been too embarrassed? All that is expected of a Rahjah man is too much, Mama."

The smile was back on Esther's face. "Pride in who you are, love, trust, and self confidence is not too much to ask. It doesn't matter what they do as long as it's honest. We have a strong family tie, you know that."

"He sent her away. If he sent her away, then the marriage is finished. Wasn't that enough?"

"Pammy, I didn't start this."

"How can you talk of family ties being strong when we don't speak with the other half of our family? If communication breaks down between each mountain, the Elders step in. Their main responsibility is to keep the people together. The hierarchy is not only because of age but wisdom." She shrugged. "So, basically, they are partly to be blamed for this thing going on so long. Mama, is there more?" Pamela looked into her mother's eyes.

"You will have to speak with his sister. I've said enough," Esther said, not very pleased that her daughter had laid blame at the Elders' feet.

Pamela nodded. "Okay, Mama."

Esther smiled at her daughter, got to her feet and walked to the door. She turned. "The Elders are really not to be blamed, you know. After all, they try to stay out of people's business as much as they can. Then again, the good book says a child shall lead them." She left Pamela to think of what she'd said.

Chapter 2

The next day, after a hearty breakfast, the work began. The farmers went to the fields while others packed hampers on their donkeys to go to the markets in Jamaica to sell their wares. The boats from the island were usually full to capacity.

Fishermen would go fishing and weavers would go to their stalls where they'd lay out vines, dried bamboo and palm leaves to begin their day.

The women, who did nothing but cook, began preparing each meal, one after the other.

Mondays and Wednesdays the Elders taught history in their village. This was the day that Gracie would make her big speech about reuniting the Rahjahs. She sat in the front of the class, taking in every word her great-grandmother spoke. She never got tired of hearing how the slaves on the Blue Mountain held off the British soldiers, preventing them from ever setting foot up the mountain. She also loved to hear about how they came to live on this tiny island outside of Jamaica. The island was founded by a Rahjah woman from Blue Mountain named Water, who thought the Blue Mountain was getting overcrowded. She bought

JANICE ANGELIQUE

the tiny island from the Jamaican government only months before she'd died.

When the class was over, Gracie didn't move but engaged her great-grandparents in conversation.

From afar, Pamela, Mary and her daughter, Shaela, stood listening.

"She's a brave little girl," Mary said.

Pamela nodded. "She's taking on a very big job."

"Do you think they'll allow her to go and visit the children on Jahyah Mountain?"

"I don't know. The Elders have always been fair, and maybe I'm a little partial to those two because they're my grandparents, but we'll see."

They heard Gracie laugh and knew the meeting was over. Jane motioned for Pamela to come to her. "I told little Gracie that we will have a meeting with the Elders of Jahyah Mountain to have this thing resolved, and reunite our people." Jane looked at Gracie. "I thank you for bringing this to our attention, but as I said, wait for us to reach out to the Elders."

Gracie nodded. "Yes, ma'am, but if I see them, is it all right to say hello?"

"Of course. It would be rude not to."

That was all Gracie wanted to hear. "Of course, ma'am."

"But Gracie?"

"Yes, ma'am?"

13

THE OTHER SIDE OF THE MOUNTAIN

"I don't want you to ride into their village and shout, hello, I'm here. You must wait to hear from us." Jane and her husband Solomon laughed.

"Of course not, ma'am," Gracie said and got to her feet.

"Thanks for taking the time to speak with her, Grangran and Grampa," Pamela said.

Solomon held his wife's hand as they got to their feet. "Pam, you must visit for tea soon," Jane said, walking beside her husband to their cottage.

"Yes, Grangran."

Gracie hugged her mother.

"Were you nervous?" Pamela asked.

"No. Is it okay if I go riding with Shaela?"

"Of course."

As they walked down the mountain together, Pamela decided that she needed to be by herself. While Gracie, Shaela and Mary went home, she went to the stables to get her horse.

◈

Pamela didn't know how long her eyes had been closed when a shadow fell over her. She opened her eyes and focused on the tall figure in front of her. She noticed his very white shirt tucked into blue jeans, his milk chocolate complexion and his clean-shaven face. His intense brown eyes revealed featherlike laugh lines when a half smile formed on his beautiful and expressive mouth. She didn't move.

"Do you always travel by yourself?"

"Do you always sneak up on unsuspecting women?"

As his gentle laugh rippled through the air his lips parted, showing white, crooked teeth in the upper front of his mouth. He held her gaze. "May I sit with you?"

"I don't see why not. Where is your horse?"

"I walked." He sat down, pulled his feet toward his chest and casually placed his elbows on his knees.

"From where?"

He smiled again. "You ask a lot of questions."

"So do you."

"Maybe I shouldn't be here, but I've glimpsed you a few times and wanted to see you up close."

"And now you have. Who are you?" she asked with an inquisitive look. She'd never seen him before and he certainly didn't dress like a farmer or fisherman.

"I am from Jahyah Mountain." He kept looking at her, wondering why she didn't recognize him. Granted, it had been years since he'd seen her, but he sure had not forgotten her beautiful face or the distinctive freckles across her nose. "I love your freckles."

She nodded and transferred her gaze to the open ocean. "Too much sun. It's been a long time since I've seen anyone from Jahyah Mountain who is not actually living in my village."

"I know. It's a shame. It should never be, but we are human beings and we make mistakes."

"You're Saul?" she said coolly, observing him through lowered lashes.

He smiled. "You have me at a disadvantage. Am I famous or infamous?" He'd decided that the time wasn't right to tell her that many years ago he'd had a crush on her. Still, he couldn't remember her name.

"The latter."

"Am I banished forever?" His brown eyes were hooded.

"I don't think so. Just today two Elders spoke to a little girl about you and the people of Jahyah Mountain."

"Were they trying to decide my fate? And on whose side was the little girl?"

"She wants to meet your children."

"What's my fate to be?" His voice held a hint of laughter.

"Hard to say. You know how Elders are. They have to talk and reason everything to death before they come to a conclusion that they know they'll make from the start."

He threw back his head and a peal of laugher escaped his throat. She found his crooked teeth fascinating and beautiful.

"The little girl is yours?"
"Yes."
"I'd love to meet her." He peered into her face.
"I don't think you and I are supposed to have met yet."

He shook his head. "Yet? Well, I don't think we can unmeet each other."

"Why haven't I seen you before? I mean, I come here all the time, but…"

"I've never wanted to be seen before. I'm not always good company for anyone." He got up and extended his hand to her.

She looked at his outstretched hand and shrugged, then allowed him to pull her to her feet. "You're moody, unapproachable sometimes?"

"I have a feeling that you know my entire life story."

"Not really." She slid her hand from his and walked towards her horse. "It was a pleasure meeting you." She was wearing a dress and had forgotten to wear the long, loose fitting pants under it.

"I'll turn so you can get on your horse," he said, turning away from her with a crooked smile.

Pamela pushed her sandal-clad foot into the stirrup and pulled herself onto the back of her horse.

He turned when he heard the horse's hooves thunder away from him. "I don't know your name," he said

THE OTHER SIDE OF THE MOUNTAIN

haltingly, softly. He leaned against the coconut tree and prayed that they were not first cousins.

❦

At supper, Pamela was quite preoccupied. She kept seeing Saul's face in her mind's eye, especially his crooked teeth. His mouth was so beautiful that just that imperfection made him even more handsome. She'd become as curious about him as her daughter. Well, maybe not. Her daughter wasn't interested in knowing about Saul; she was interested in knowing about his children.

"Where'd you go this evening?" Mary asked, sitting beside Pamela.

"Down to the beach. I needed to clear my head."

"Remember, we have a guest after dinner. Your cottage or mine?"

"Mine's all right." She turned to Myah. "Are we still on for tea after supper?"

"Of course."

"We haven't talked in such a long time," Pamela said.

Tim, who was sitting not too far away from Pamela, coughed.

"Sorry, Tim, do you want to be included?"

He smiled and nodded.

Unconsciously Pamela kept looking at Myah to see if there was any resemblance to her brother. Then she remembered she hadn't told Saul her name.

When the main meal was finished, the three women and Tim picked up their desserts and walked to Pamela's cottage to have tea.

While Mary, Tim and Myah settled on cushions in the living room, Pamela prepared a herbal blend in her tiny kitchen. Even though there was a community kitchen, each cottage had its own personal kitchen equipped with a small Dutch stove with oven and a chimney to carry smoke from the house.

"Do you need any help?" Mary called.

Pamela walked in with a tray and placed it on the center table. "No, it's ready." She filled each cup.

Mary brought the cup to her face and inhaled. "Mmmm. This smells wonderful." She added a teaspoon of honey.

"I'm so glad you invited me," Myah said leaning into her cushion.

"Me, too. It's been too long." Pamela took a sip of her tea and came straight to the point. "Today my daughter spoke with two of the Elders about the rift between our people, and I can't help but wonder why it took a little girl to do this." She quickly looked at Myah in an apologetic manner. "I don't mean to pry. If you…"

THE OTHER SIDE OF THE MOUNTAIN

"No, it's all right. No one has really asked me about Jahyah Mountain in a very long time. It's as if it's taboo. I loved living there until my brother's woman came." She ate and sipped, then talked.

"Saul and I were very close, and the first thing Raquel did after a month of moving in was tell him that my husband and I should leave the house. As a geologist who visited many different countries, he brought material from almost every country he traveled: marble, satin, brass. We helped him build the house. When it was finished it was as big as four normal cottages in one. He said his job required so much concentration that working on the house was his way of relaxing. Every time he went away he brought back something for everyone. Raquel stopped him from giving away the things he'd brought back, so he stopped bringing things back after the house became cluttered with stuff they didn't really need.

"I was disappointed and ashamed that he'd allowed her to come in and destroy our relationship, so we came here. She was like a hurricane or a tornado in the village. Unfortunately he didn't realize or see what she was really doing until the children came. She didn't want to share them, not even with him. When he would come home from a long trip the children would run into his arms and she would pull them from him and slap their faces, telling them their father was tired. His greatest joy was seeing and being with his children. She was jealous of the attention he gave to them." She took a deep breath and looked away from her friends.

Mary and Pamela gasped and put their hands to their cheeks. "He was that in love and blinded by her?" Pamela asked.

"He was bewitched by her. Some said she gave him something to drink or eat that caused him to change completely. She'd brought her own herbs from her country and wouldn't allow anyone to help her plant or reap them. She kept them in clay pots in her kitchen." Myah took a cleansing breath. "You have no idea how long I've wanted to talk about that. I really miss my brother."

"But it's been years since she left. Why haven't you gone back to speak with him?" Pamela asked.

"I don't know. I suppose I'm still waiting for him to come and apologize again. I'm waiting for him to tell me how much he's missed me. He knows where I am."

"You said *again*. Did he ever come here?" Pamela asked.

"Yes, once."

"He must be so embarrassed."

"We're all Rahjahs, Pam, we always forgive."

"Apparently not, since you're here and he's not."

"It's hard for me to go back to Jahyah Mountain knowing that I left because of *her*." She began crying.

THE OTHER SIDE OF THE MOUNTAIN

"You weren't the only one who left and came here." Pamela moved closer to Myah and hugged her. "I'm sorry you still feel this way."

"No. It's been a long time since I've felt this good. Thank you for inviting me over. I try to stay busy so as not to give myself time to think about it all."

"Gracie would love to meet your brother's children."

"Really?" Myah said, laughing. "I could take her to meet them but I suppose the Elders have to mend fences, right?"

"You know it. Frankly, I think a few of us should just go over with fruit and vegetables and make nice, but traditions hold us back, I suppose. So we'll let them do their thing." Pamela looked at Myah. "It's still your home. You can go there any time you wish without the Elders' permission."

"I know, but…"

"Pride," Mary said.

Myah nodded.

"Why do you think the children think Saul is an ogre?" Pamela asked.

Myah laughed so hard she fell back on her cushion. "The poor man."

Pamela covered her face with her hands. That was not exactly how she'd wanted to ask the question.

"Is that what they say?" Myah said.

She nodded.

"He's taken to brooding, but he's not afraid to speak his mind. He's bold and intelligent and gentle and resourceful…"

Pamela and Mary watched Myah talk about her brother. She positively beamed.

"Now I know why you're still so hurt. You really love your brother."

Myah blushed. "I miss seeing my niece and nephew, and he doesn't even know my daughter. I miss my parents, too."

"Then we must put some fire under the Elders to bring peace back to our people," Mary said.

For the first time since they'd sat down, Tim spoke. "You know the Elders, they go at their own pace. That's why they live so long, but if someone were to keep talking to their grandparents…" He looked over at Pamela.

She shook her head. "No, not me. Plus, I think Gracie will bug them if they don't go fast enough."

It was getting late and tomorrow was another work day.

Outside, Gracie and Shaela, Mary's daughter, were sitting with Isha, Myah's daughter.

"You followed me?" Myah said, scooping up her four-year-old.

"Miss Maud said I could follow you," she told her mother.

"Next time we'll walk together."

THE OTHER SIDE OF THE MOUNTAIN

They both waved and walked the few yards to their home.

"Okay, ladies," Pamela said to her daughter and Shaela. "Bedtime."

⟡

On Jahyah Mountain, Saul thought about Pamela's beautiful face and prayed once again that if they were related, they were fifth or sixth cousins.

He'd sent his children to the circle for supper, but had remained in his home to brew himself some tea. He didn't feel like being with anyone.

Of course that didn't sit well with his mother, who'd sent his supper to him. She didn't want him to begin brooding again, and a sure sign of him brooding was not eating. He sat by the window and ate.

After the children had gone to bed, he took a second cup of tea and walked down the mountainside to sit in the cool night air. He closed his eyes and saw Pamela's face and relived each word she'd uttered. He'd noted her skepticism and her boldness. It had been such a long time since he'd given a woman a second look that he'd forgotten how bewitching women could be, this one more than others.

He thought of his sister and wondered if the woman he'd met on the beach knew her. He wondered if they were friends and if Myah had told her anything of him. He flinched at the thought. The first thing he'd do when he saw her again would be to ask her name.

Chapter 3

A week had passed since Gracie had spoken to the Elders about going to Jahyah Mountain. Every evening after school she went riding by herself.

Curiosity got the better of Pamela one day when she noticed that Gracie had gone riding by herself a few days in a row, which was unusual since she loved Shaela's company so much. Today, after Gracie left alone, she followed at a distance. At the top of the mountain, hidden by huge shade trees, she watched as Gracie got off her horse and sat beside a cluster of grape bushes. After a while two children rode up to her and got off their horses. After hugging each other excitedly, they sat down and pulled out books. Gracie gave her rabbit to the little girl and Pamela laughed. *So that's why she comes alone.* She instantly knew that these were Saul's twins. She turned her horse and rode back home, thinking of Saul.

―――

Saul still couldn't recall her name, but he didn't have to wonder why she'd been occupying his mind. He was intrigued by her. He'd gone back many times to the very spot he'd met her, hoping she'd be there, wondering if she ever thought of him. This evening he got off his horse and walked, all the while looking behind him and up toward her village.

He sat on the cold sand and wondered what her likes and dislikes were. He remembered her being very outspoken, but that was a long time ago. He'd been so focused on his work and children that he'd forgotten the protocol of dating. On the other hand, he'd never really dated on the mountain. He'd gone to college in the States, met Raquel, brought her home and married her. He shook his head, got to his feet and walked to his horse. He didn't want to think about that part of his life. He wanted to see the woman who had him riding to the beach every chance he got. He was determined that once he saw her again and found out her name, he would never let her go. *Am I being stupid?* he wondered. He got on his horse and rode hard back to his village.

In bed with the lights out, Pamela decided she would go back to the beach the next day after supper to see if he were there. She closed her eyes and saw his handsome face, saw him laugh, revealing his crooked teeth in his otherwise perfect face. He was handsome and funny. How could such a funny person not be nice? She'd not thought of any one man so much since her husband died. When her husband was alive she'd not thought of him this much. She pushed her head into her pillow. *Oh Jah, what am I doing? What if this man isn't even thinking of me? Why should he think of me?*

She got out of bed and walked to the verandah with an afghan thrown over her shoulders and looked up at the stars. In the quiet village a few lamps were still lit. In the distance men were banging dominos on wooden tables. She walked down to Gracie's thinking rock and sat down. There she could see Jahyah Mountain. Fireflies were in abundance on both mountains, twinkling like the stars above. She closed her eyes and inhaled the night air. Was he asleep? She stayed there for a little while longer, listening to the waterfall.

Finally she got up and began walking back to her cottage.

"I could have sworn I saw your lamp go out a while back," Tim said. He was walking from where they were playing dominos.

She jumped, placed her hand over her heart and laughed. "Tim, you shouldn't do that. You scared me half to death," she managed.

"Sorry, I didn't mean to scare you. Where were you?" He slipped his arm around her shoulder and continued walking with her.

"I couldn't sleep, so I thought I'd take a walk."

JANICE ANGELIQUE

"You're thinking about our friends across the way, aren't you?"

"I have to admit that I am." She could have been specific, but she knew how protective Tim was of her. He was like the brother she never had but wished for.

"I too think of them every now and again. It's really too bad."

"I know." She looked up at him. "Tim, you teach at the university in Jamaica. Don't you ever run into people from there?"

He nodded. "Yes, I do."

"Don't you talk with them?"

"Sure, but we never talk about what happened." He squeezed her shoulder.

"Are you friends with any of them?" She pushed her arm around his waist, listened to her bare feet squish against grass wet with dew.

He laughed. "Yes."

"But you'd never go there, and they would never come here?"

"That's what it boils down to."

When they reached her cottage, she smiled up at him and stood on the step. "Thanks for the company."

"You know, whenever you want to go for a walk, all you have to do is ask me to come along."

"I know, but tonight I just felt like being alone."

"You mean I intruded on your alone time. Why didn't you tell me to go away?"

THE OTHER SIDE OF THE MOUNTAIN

"You didn't intrude. I welcomed your company, plus you answered a few questions that were swirling about in my head."

"Glad I could help." He kissed her forehead. "Have a good night." He stayed until her door was closed, then walked away.

The night air was all she'd needed. Without lighting a lamp or candle, she got into bed and fell into a peaceful slumber. "Goodnight, Saul," she whispered.

※

In the Rahjah culture there was never homework, but the children had to get together in groups with a teacher for at least half an hour after school and talk about what they'd learned. If there were any questions concerning the day's work, that's when they would be answered.

The next day after school, she and Mary answered the children's questions, then Pamela walked to Gracie's thinking rock and stood gazing at the twin mountain. She sighed. The island was so beautiful. Why had they allowed one outsider to mar its beauty? She turned and walked back to the kitchen to begin making supper with the other women.

Esther noticed the somber look on her daughter's face. "What's wrong?"

She smiled. "I've been thinking of Gracie's request to mend fences with the Jahyahs."

Esther nodded. "Me, too, but it'll take a while."

"Why? Why can't we just go there? If they walked into the village now, we'd all break out the food and drink and music and welcome them, so why can't we just go there thinking they'll do the same?"

Esther didn't have an answer for her daughter just then. She'd taken her by surprise. "Your daughter is just like you. Or is it the other way around? What's gotten into you two? We went through this with Gracie last year and the year before, remember?"

"Yes, I remember." What she should have said was, *Yes, but I just met the most gorgeous man who lives on Jahyah Mountain and he's not an ogre.*

Just before supper, she went to the waterfall with Mary and bathed.

All through supper she couldn't get Saul out of her mind. And as her preoccupation continued, her mother kept watching and wondering if she were all right. She would do anything for her only daughter and wondered if she should cross the Elders and tell her to allow Gracie to go to Jahyah Mountain.

Pamela glanced at her mother and smiled.

"Are you all right?" Esther said.

"Of course I am. You worry too much." She leaned over and kissed her mother's cheek, patted her hand and then had dessert. After supper, with a full moon lighting her way, Pamela led her horse out of the stables and down the mountainside, then got on its

THE OTHER SIDE OF THE MOUNTAIN

back and rode down to the beach where she'd first met Saul. She had not expected to see him, but there he was, on horseback.

Her heart skipped a beat. She reined in her horse and sat looking at him, wondering what she should do. He saw her and turned his horse toward her but didn't make an attempt to move to her.

Why doesn't he come to me? she wondered.

Is she afraid of me? Saul wondered. *Why is she just sitting there? Should I make the first move?*

Pamela wet her lips and, on impulse, nudged her horse toward him. "What are you doing here?"

"What's your name?" he immediately asked.

She laughed. "Pamela."

He nodded. "You're not going to run away again, are you? You looked a bit scared when you came down and saw me waiting here."

"Why would I run away? And no, I'm not afraid of you. Should I be?"

"You ran away the last time. And no, I won't harm you."

"No, I left. There's a difference."

Saul got off his horse and held up his hands to help her down. She smiled and accepted his help. They began walking. "So, Saul, tell me about yourself and why you're here."

"I'm here because I wanted to see you again. More than anything I wanted to know your name."

"Well, now you do."

"Yes." He cleared his throat. "You may not believe this but I have been to this very spot every night since we met." He didn't look at her.

"Now why would you do that?"

An awkward silence fell. Pamela laughed. "You don't seem anything like an ogre."

"Huh?"

"The children call you an ogre."

He stopped walking and looked at her. "Why?"

"They don't know you, but they hear bits and pieces of things and make up stories. You don't look anything like an ogre to me."

He smiled and continued walking. "If you'd met me a while back maybe you would have thought me an ogre. I was moody and very impatient."

"Did you bite people's heads off?"

"A little."

"Didn't hear anything about cannibalism, so maybe it wasn't that many heads."

He laughed.

"What happened to make you moody and impatient?" she asked, as if she didn't already know his story.

"You don't know me." He kept smiling.

In the bright full moon she could see the crinkling at the corners of his eyes as he smiled. "You're right. Are the people on Jahyah Mountain the same as they were years ago, or have they changed?"

THE OTHER SIDE OF THE MOUNTAIN

"They're the same loving people they've always been…" He stopped talking and looked at her. "Do they really call me an ogre?"

"Just the kids." She laughed at him.

"Maybe I've been a little bit of an ogre, but I'm trying to be a better man. I don't see my children enough because of my work. I'm a geologist. I take my boat off the island to Jamaica, then fly out of Jamaica to different parts of the world. I love what I do. I think if I'd had my children before I started working I would never have left the island."

"And maybe you would have. There are some things you just have to do. You studied in Jamaica and the United States and instead of coming back home you began contracting in different countries. You love doing what you do."

"You know a lot about me."

"You're telling me a lot."

"Your turn. Have you ever left the island?"

"Only once, to go to Jamaica."

"That's all?"

"Yes. You seem surprised."

"A little. Once most Rahjahs leave the island, they want to know about other parts of the world. Didn't you want to fly or walk into history?"

"I got a bit turned off when I went to Jamaica. The difference was overwhelming."

"Of course, but you shouldn't have stopped there. Do you like to read?"

"I teach English. I love to read."

"If you could wish for anything right now, what would you wish for?"

She laughed and took a deep breath. "I would wish for lots and lots of books. I've read almost all the books in our library. I've never read a world history book."

He stopped walking, gasped and touched her hand. "You have never read a world history book?"

She shook her head. "Our own history is so fascinating and the Elders are so good at telling it that I never thought of it. I've read British and American history."

"African history?"

She shook her head. "Again, I get bits and pieces from the Elders."

"I can help you there. I have a library with both."

"Don't tease me, sir." She was grinning from ear to ear.

"I can go for them right now and bring them to you, but how will you explain them?"

"Maybe tomorrow. The Elders cannot actually tell me what to do. I am a grown woman." She bit her lower lip. "We just met and you're complicating my life already."

He laughed and wet his lips.

"I'll meet you here at this time tomorrow night."

THE OTHER SIDE OF THE MOUNTAIN

She didn't have to look at him to know he was laughing. "And all because I remembered that I am a grown woman and can do whatever I want to do."

"You do realize that you can come home with me, don't you?"

Now it was her turn to laugh. "No, I will not come to your home."

"Then I will come to yours…"

"After all these years you're willing to ride into Rahjah Village just to deliver a bag of books?"

"To you, yes."

"I must have made a great first impression." She looked down at her sandaled feet.

"And second. I don't want anyone to come looking for you. You've been gone long enough. I will meet you here tomorrow, at this time." He motioned to help her on her horse.

"Thank you, but I am used to being on my own at all hours of the night. In case you've forgotten what I just said, I will repeat it. I am…"

"I know, you're a grown woman. You live on your own?"

"Of course I do. Should I repeat that I have a daughter?"

"No. Sorry. I don't want you to leave."

She laughed. "So you want me to leave but you don't want me to leave. Make up your mind, sir."

"I don't want you to leave."

JANICE ANGELIQUE

She looked into his face for a long while, watching his smile gather and fade and his eyes moving from her eyes to the top of her head to her chin and back to her eyes. She knew she was being forward staring at him like that, but she couldn't tear her eyes away. She wanted him to laugh again. He laughed.

"What are you doing?" he finally asked.

"I don't know, but I have to leave." She was still looking at his face. She saw a flash of nervousness.

"Should I help you on your horse?"

"I've been jumping on this horse almost all my life…"

"And here I come…"

"You may help me."

He shook his head, smiled and helped her on the horse. "I'll go a different way, just in case."

She laughed. "I love this cloak and dagger business."

He kissed her hand. "Have a good night. I'm glad you came. By the way, are we related?" He held her hand.

She laughed and shook her head. "We may be very distant cousins."

He gave a devilish laugh.

"Is it relevant?" she asked, turning her horse around.

THE OTHER SIDE OF THE MOUNTAIN

He didn't answer. "I'll see you tomorrow." He watched her horse gallop away and saw her wave as she began climbing the mountain again.

"You have no idea how relevant it is," he said to himself as he got on his horse. He heard her coming back. She reined in her horse next to his. "Not that I'm not glad to see you back so soon, but is everything all right?"

She laughed. "You have your own boat?"

It was his turn to laugh. "Yes. It's not uncommon for someone who travels a lot to have their own boat or plane."

"You have a plane?" Her eyes lit up.

"No, but a few other Rahjahs who live on Blue Mountain do."

"I'm so impressed. Not that I'm materialistic, but to be able to fly a plane is an enormous achievement."

"Well, I'm not the one with the plane. I only have a boat."

"That's great, too. I'll see you." She turned her horse and rode away once more.

He stood still waiting for her to return, but this time she was actually gone. He rode slowly home. "She could have asked for anything and she asked for books," he repeated to himself and shook his head. "Who does that? Okay, so me having a boat didn't impress her that much." He didn't know if he should have felt insulted by her saying flying a plane was an enormous achievement. Then he thought about it and agreed that it *was* an enormous achievement. What was it about her that fascinated him so much?

He'd traveled the world and met many different women, some powerful, some simple. He'd made a big mistake by marrying someone outside of his own culture. Despite the education he'd had, he was still a stupid man making stupid mistakes. Jah knows he'd paid dearly. He'd lost the one person he'd been close with all his life, his sister. He didn't know how to get her back. He'd almost lost his parents.

He was twittering between dark and light. He'd forgotten to ask if Pamela knew his sister. He would have loved to ask how she was doing.

∞

Pamela tiptoed into Gracie's room, kissed her on the cheek and blew out her lamp. "I love you," she whispered.

She walked to her room, took off her clothes, got into bed and blew out her lamp. She lay there looking up at the ceiling. She didn't know what excited her more, getting new books or seeing Saul again. *What am I doing?* A little sliver of excitement ran through her. She'd read enough romance novels where the protagonist had to hide to see her man. She closed her eyes and turned on her side. *I am not in a romance novel, and Saul is not my man.* Then what was that

THE OTHER SIDE OF THE MOUNTAIN

feeling she was feeling? Maybe it was the imaginary danger. What danger? Nothing exciting ever happens here unless it rains hard and someone's home washes down the side of the mountain. She laughed at herself. She could have waited on the beach while he fetched the books. No one would have seen her return home with them. She turned over and closed her eyes.

Chapter 4

Gracie was so excited about being with her new friends, she wanted to keep them to herself a little longer before she allowed them to meet Shaela.

When she met with her great-grandmother, Jane, for history lessons, she was all smiles. Jane called her to her side and said. "You look very happy today. Have you given up the idea of meeting the twins from Jahyah Mountain?"

"Oh, no, ma'am."

"Good, because tomorrow all the Elders from here and Jahyah Mountain will meet and talk about this thing. You're a very smart child. We should have done this a long time ago." She held Gracie's hand and got to her feet. "As a matter of fact, we should not have allowed this feud to happen at all." She let go of Gracie's hand and laughed, then motioned for Pamela to come to her.

"The Bible says 'a child shall lead them,' and I think that child may be yours."

Pamela smiled and nodded. "This is a very good thing, Grangran."

"I know my child," Jane said.

THE OTHER SIDE OF THE MOUNTAIN

It was Jane's nap time, so, as usual, she and Solomon walked hand in hand to their cottage.

Pamela wasn't surprised when Gracie asked if she could go riding by herself. She'd scarcely given her permission before Gracie turned, laughed and waved. Pamela shook her head and waited for Mary and Shaela to walk down the mountain with her.

"What's that little girl of yours up to?"

"You've got me," she replied, wanting to keep her daughter's secret.

Little Isha ran up and pushed her tiny hand into Pamela's. Pamela looked down and laughed. "How are you, little one?" She scooped her up and looked behind for Myah.

Myah caught up to them. "She wants to play with Gracie."

"Will Shaela do? I think Gracie wants to be by herself for a little while today. Maybe Isha can come over before supper and stay a little bit after. Will that be all right with you?"

"Of course. I'll come for her after."

"Or I can walk her home, it's no bother." How could she tell Myah that she had a date with her brother? She was hoping he would understand if she was just a little late.

Pamela, true to her promise, walked little Isha home twenty minutes after supper. Gracie, who'd sat cross-legged on her bed with her head buried in a new book, hardly nodded when her mother told her she'd be back soon. She looked around to see if Tim or anyone else was watching, then walked casually to the stables and jumped bareback onto her horse.

Saul was patiently waiting for her. He stood up as she approached and caught her as she slid from her horse. "I'm so sorry. I'm never late for an appointment, but I had to wait while a little one played with my little one."

He laughed at her. "I'm not in a hurry to go anywhere. You said you'd be here and I knew you'd be here. Being a little late is inevitable sometimes."

She sat on the damp sand. "Thank you."

"Do you care to translate what you were saying into plain English?"

She laughed. "Myah's daughter…"

He stopped her. "Myah… My Myah… My sister. You were talking about my sister?" He held her hand. "Tell me all about her."

She looked at his hand holding hers and felt the softness and warmth that it exuded. For a second she couldn't speak. Composing herself, she said, "Yes, your sister. She has a four-year-old daughter named Isha." She slowly curled her fingers over his. "She played with Gracie after supper and I took her home."

THE OTHER SIDE OF THE MOUNTAIN

He let go of her hand and rested his hands on his knees. "I have a niece that I don't even know. I miss being a part of my sister's life."

She balled her fingers to keep the essence of his touch within her. "She misses you a lot, Saul. She speaks of you so lovingly." She nodded. "I think Isha has your eyes."

He smiled. "I have to come to your village, Pam. I don't care if everyone looks at me as if I'm mad. I don't care if I'm *persona non grata*." He waited for her to say it was a bad idea.

She nodded. "You should."

His eyes brightened as he turned and spoke in an excited tone. "Tomorrow. I'll come tomorrow. I won't let anyone know that I know you. I'll ride into the center of the village and you can take me to them."

"Tomorrow is Friday," she said.

"I know. Is that a bad idea?"

"No, it's a great idea. Perfect, actually." Great because there's always an evening of merriment after supper, she thought. "When will you come?"

"When should I come?"

"Before supper, and bring the children."

He nodded. "Thank you. The children will be very excited." He, too, was keeping Gracie's secret. He'd seen the children together today and had stayed out of sight.

"Are you scared?"

JANICE ANGELIQUE

He laughed as his earnest eyes sought hers. "Should I be?"

"I don't know. I think I would be scared."

"But I'm a man, not to mention a Rahjah. I'm not supposed to be scared."

She laughed at his bravado, but then became serious. "Being a man or a Rahjah, as you so bravely put it, does not stop your apprehension or it shouldn't. You're human. Men don't hesitate to show their anger, why not their fear or love or…" Realizing how preachy she sounded, her voice trailed off. "Sorry, I do go on." She lowered her eyes to her lap and saw that her fingers were still curled. She opened them, hoping he would take her hand again before he left.

He looked at her face in the moonlight and noticed the concerned crease in her forehead. "Okay, but you can't say anything to anyone. Actually, I do feel a bit apprehensive. These are my people and I don't want to be rebuffed again. I will definitely come, and I promise I won't show any fear."

She laughed. "You're not being condescending, are you? I was kidding when I asked if you were scared."

"I know, but conversing with you about anything is so much fun, I'd do or say anything to prolong it."

He reached behind him and pulled four books from his saddlebag. He would have brought more but he didn't think she could carry them. He handed her the books and she peered at them in the moonlight.

THE OTHER SIDE OF THE MOUNTAIN

"Thank you so much. World history, African history..." She looked up at him, then at another book. "And a dictionary." She shook her head and laughed. "These are great. But don't you think I'm smart enough to know the meaning of the *big* words in these books? Don't answer, that's rhetorical. I have a small dictionary with tiny writing, but this is great, thank you." On impulse she kissed his cheek.

He smiled. "I'm leaving for two weeks in a few days. What should I bring back for you? Don't tell me more books."

"We just met and you want to give me gifts already?"

"Is that all right?"

She shrugged. "I'm not sure."

He laughed and shook his head. "I have to go to France for a few days. I'll bring you back a book of famous artwork."

"You know that I paint!" she gasped.

He shook his head, "No, I didn't. You're very busy, aren't you? I bet you're very good."

"Not always. I haven't painted in a while, but it relaxes me."

"I have to admit that while I can build an entire house, I cannot make a stroke on canvas."

"Not everyone can. I won't see you for two weeks?" She kept looking at the books in her hand.

"Will you miss me?" he teased.

"Yes. After two meetings, I was just beginning to enjoy our secret rendezvous." She laughed and touched his hand.

"When I come back we can pick up where we left off. I'll miss you."

She laughed and reiterated, "We just met."

"Really?" He gave a conspiratorial wink.

"Are you being sarcastic?"

"Yes."

She caught his infectious laughter and once again his eyes held hers. "You're beautiful in the moonlight."

To cover her embarrassment, she said, "Maybe we should only see each other by moonlight."

He got up and pulled her to her feet, took the books from her and placed them back in his bag. "Walk with me a bit." He dropped the bag on the sand.

As they walked, he talked. "I've been to so many places, but no matter where I go, after two or three weeks I yearn for this place, this island. There's no place like it. It's my safe haven."

"You can let your hair down, so to speak. Do anything, say anything without fear of recrimination," she said.

He stopped and, with a smile on his face, nodded. "Yes, that about sums it up. And tomorrow will be the great test." He laughed.

So did she. "I think I should go now."

THE OTHER SIDE OF THE MOUNTAIN

"Okay." They walked back to her horse, and he slung the saddlebag over its back. "You felt like a daredevil tonight?"

She glanced at her horse and laughed. "Bareback? You might say so."

Saul helped her onto her horse, then got on his. Tonight he'd ride with her until she took the path up the mountain. He had to admit the anticipation of seeing his sister and niece was almost overwhelming. He couldn't wait. They rode side by side along the shore. The ocean seemed dark and mysterious when a thin cloud passed over the moon. She touched his hand and turned onto the path for home.

"I'll see you tomorrow. Don't be afraid." She laughed softly.

"I can't wait." He watched her go up the mountain, her long skirt billowing in the wind. She gave a backward wave. Then he nudged his horse into a gallop.

Chapter 5

The men began bringing out their drums and guitars and the women their tambourines. This was everyone's favorite day; the work week was done, and everyone was dressed in yellow and white.

Pamela stood at her door dressed in her long yellow dress with a white wrap on her head. She heard the horses' hooves coming up the mountain.

No one paid any attention. When the horses and riders came into view, Pamela stepped from her home, waited, and greeted them as they got down off their horses.

Saul handed Pamela another bag of books and squeezed her hand. She looked at him, smiled confidently and gave a slight nod.

Gracie came to the door and, with a shout, immediately ran to David and Ruth. She hugged them tightly and accepted their gifts of more books. And as if by magic, grand Rahjah style, they were surrounded by Rahjahs running from their homes to welcome their prodigal son back into the fold. They touched him and hugged him and cried and leaned their heads against his shoulder. Saul looked at Pamela as she gave each person a chance to greet him and he grinned.

THE OTHER SIDE OF THE MOUNTAIN

She'd felt his hesitation before, but now she saw the true man, the vulnerable man.

Then came the best part of all. The crowd parted as Myah walked towards them with her child and husband at her side. Tears streamed down her face. She ran into his outstretched arms and they both cried and talked and apologized to each other.

Pamela stood and watched them. She knew he was handsome, but now she saw how devastatingly handsome he was in the full light of the many tiki lamps around the village circle. With tears streaming down his cheeks, an unchecked grin on his face, his emotions all out in the open, she thought he was the sexiest man she'd ever laid eyes on. She moved away from the crowd to give them a chance to love him and banish his insecurities at being there.

Myah's husband, Samuel, who'd known Saul his entire life, brought their daughter Isha to finally meet the uncle she'd never known she had. As if she'd always wanted to meet this man, Isha hugged Saul's neck and wouldn't let go. Tim was among the crowd of greeters, and noticed the connection between Pamela and Saul. How did he know to bring books? Why did he give them to Pam and not to his sister or anyone else, and why was she now in the back with this satisfied smile on her face? He went to her and folded his arms. "Did you have anything to do with this?"

"This warm, exciting gathering? Not at all."

"This is the beginning of the healing," Tim said.

She nodded. "This is beautiful."

The band never played before supper, but tonight it did. The Rahjahs celebrated everything with food and music, tonight was no different. While the food was being brought out, Samuel handed Saul a guitar.

Samuel broke into a song of the prodigal son returning from far away and, with much nudging, Saul joined in.

Pamela stood looking at him. He hadn't told her he had the voice of an angel. She placed a finger to her lips and smiled. Myah hugged her and whispered, "Why do I think you had something to do with this?"

She smiled innocently. "Me?" She shook her head. "I don't think I've ever really seen him before."

Myah kept looking at her, but Pamela wouldn't give her secret away. She loved seeing Saul secretly and wasn't ready to give that up just yet.

Before they all sat down to eat, Myah finally got to hug her niece and nephew. Gracie hugged her mother and said, "Is this the power of Jah, or did you have a hand in it?"

Pamela laughed. "Okay, why do you and Myah think I had something to do with Saul and his children coming here tonight? Maybe he was tired of being away from his family, maybe he thought it was time. Remember, he and his sister were once extremely close. Maybe he longed for that closeness. And don't

THE OTHER SIDE OF THE MOUNTAIN

forget, the Elders have been talking. And you, my little one, maybe your thoughts influenced it. Who knows."

"Uh-huh," was all Gracie said.

Saul ended up sitting beside Pamela with Myah beside him. Tim sat at the far end of the group looking at the exchanges between Saul and Pamela. Even if they'd never met before and she happened to be the first one he'd seen on entering the village, he still didn't like what he was seeing.

The children were all curious about David and Ruth, but they couldn't help looking at Saul and listening to his constant laughter. No, he didn't look anything like an ogre.

Saul wanted to hold Pamela's hand. He wanted to thank her again. He wanted to say a lot of things. His knee touched hers and neither attempted to change positions. No one noticed but Tim, or if they did, no one said anything.

Esther gave the prayer and thanked Jah for bringing Saul and his children back to them and for once again reuniting the island.

The platters came around. The fishermen had had a good day at sea. Escoviched and brown stew fish were passed around. Bammy, boiled bananas, yellow yams, white yams, fried plantains and of course, what would fried fish be without fried dumplings made from their own corn and flour. Then the vegetables and fruits were passed around.

Myah asked Saul about their parents.

"They miss you," he told her.

"I'm so glad you came. You have no idea how long I've waited for you to ride up here and hug me the way you did." She leaned her head against his shoulder and tears came to her eyes once more.

He placed his arm around her shoulders and leaned his head against hers. "A little voice asked me if I could do this without apprehension, and I wasn't sure how to answer. I didn't know what to expect. As a Rahjah, I know the past is the past. As your brother who loves you very much I didn't know how ready you were to welcome me back into your life. I did a foolish thing…"

"Don't," she said. "Don't go back. The past is the past and I'm… I'm, I can't tell you how glad I am that you're here."

Saul's hand brushed against Pamela's when she passed him a bowl of fruit, and their eyes met. He thanked her without words and she understood.

The music began again, but the evening of dancing didn't quite begin until three Elders from the village came down by buggy to welcome Saul back to the fold.

"How did they know?" Myah whispered to Pamela.

"How do they know anything? They are the Elders. They would like us to think they know and feel all, but

THE OTHER SIDE OF THE MOUNTAIN

I think one of our mothers or fathers went for them."
She looked and saw Mary's father leaving the buggy.

Myah laughed. "I don't really care who had a hand in it. I'm the happiest I've been in a very long time."

The music got louder. Saul danced with his sister and his niece, then with Pamela. If he hadn't, some would have been suspicious. After all, she was the first one to greet him. There were no slow songs, but very upbeat pocomania that didn't stop him from holding her hand just for a little while. Unable to help himself, he leaned close to her and whispered in her ear, "Thank you so much."

"I didn't do anything at all. You rode in like a knight in shining armor and swept us all off our feet."

Without warning, the music slowed. Pamela looked over at the band and saw her grandmother and grandfather standing there. Pamela shook her head, but Jane just smiled.

Saul did what any red-blooded Rahjah would have done. He pulled her close to him. She didn't resist, and their bodies touched for the first time in front of Jah and everyone. That was too much for Tim to take; he walked away.

In order not to embarrass the couple too much, Jane and Solomon walked beside them and began dancing. Everyone joined in.

"What are they doing?" Saul whispered.

"Let's pretend we have no idea. Just enjoy."

He smiled. "Did I ever tell you that you're the smartest woman I've ever met?" he whispered in her ear.

"No," she said.

"You are."

She didn't answer, but bit into the corner of her lower lip.

Pamela excused herself from him and took the tambourine from her cousin. Slowly the women took over the band, allowing the men to enjoy a dance or two with their wives or girlfriends. Mary played steel drums, and Myah surprised everyone by playing the guitar and singing.

As the night wore on, the Elders said their goodnights and were taken back to their village the way they'd come, by buggy, this time driven by Samuel.

Ruth left her friends and came to tug at her father's shirt sleeve while he played dominos with the other men. "May I stay with Gracie for the night?" she whispered in his ear.

"If Gracie's mother says it's all right then you may stay, but what about your brother?" he replied, distracted by the game.

"He wants to stay, too."

"With Gracie?"

"Of course. We can all sleep in the same room. It's okay, Dada, he won't see us naked."

THE OTHER SIDE OF THE MOUNTAIN

He didn't know whether to laugh or scowl at her. He pointed to Pamela. "Ask Pamela."

The children were trusted to do almost anything and go anywhere on the mountain they wished, but not at the imposition of another family. At an early age they were taught to make decisions for themselves, but with consideration for others.

Gracie was standing by her mother. She had already asked if the twins could stay and received the same answer Saul had given Ruth. When Ruth asked the question of Pamela, she glanced at Saul. He gave her an "it's up to you" look.

Pamela quickly sized up the two girls. They were the same size, but it really didn't make any difference because the clothes they wore were never form-fitting. David would have to wear the same clothes tomorrow that he wore today. "It's fine," she told the children. Looking into those innocent, happy faces, there was nothing else she could have said.

Pamela watched as Gracie, the twins, and more than six other children filed into her cottage. She smiled and shook her head. She looked around for Tim but he was nowhere to be found. It wasn't like him to go away like that or miss a domino game. After saying goodnight to her parents, Pamela walked to Mary's cottage with Myah.

Myah was still so excited about her brother's visit she could hardly contain herself. Sitting in the living room sipping a calming brew, she still thought Pamela had something to do with him being there. "How can you explain it? Your daughter begins asking to go to Jahyah Mountain. She meets with the Elders. We three sit and talk, and then he shows up after so many years."

Pamela shrugged. "Does it matter how he got here?"

"I guess not." She took a sip of the brew, but still kept looking at Pamela.

"Are you going to visit your parents soon?" Mary asked Myah.

She sighed. "I have a feeling they don't know that he came. Maybe he wanted to test the water so he could tell them that he'd made peace with the rest of his family."

"That's all right. I think he did the right thing. I think it's our turn to visit them," Pamela said.

"Should we just show up like he did, or should we send a note of our intended arrival?" Myah asked.

"Somehow I think they'll be very glad to see us, especially you and your little family. Mary and I will come with you when you're ready."

Myah nodded. She wasn't afraid to go back to see her family, but was a bit embarrassed that she had not been in contact with them over the years. "Why don't we go on Sunday?" She looked from Mary to Pamela.

They both nodded. "We'll take the children with us," Pamela said.

THE OTHER SIDE OF THE MOUNTAIN

"I'm so excited. I have a feeling Saul will apprise them of his actions tomorrow. I'll tell him to say we'll visit on Sunday." She again looked at the other women.

"Good idea," Mary replied.

Pamela suddenly remembered that Saul would not be there on Sunday. As if being summoned, he showed up at the door.

Pamela beckoned him in. He came in and sat on the floor. "Are you having fun? Can we get you some tea?" Pamela asked.

He smiled and nodded. "Yes, and no. I can't tell you the last time I've ever felt so comfortable. Coming here was the best thing I've done in a very long time." He held his sister's hand. "I should have come a long time ago. Pride is a horrible thing. We shouldn't keep ourselves from the people we love."

Myah shook her head. "If you go on like that you'll make me cry again."

He hugged her. "Sorry, I can't help it. I'm just so damned happy."

She laughed and kissed his cheek. "We want to visit on Sunday. Will you tell them?"

He nodded. "This is good, very good. Unfortunately I won't be there to celebrate the continuation of the reunion. I'm sorry."

"Why?" Myah asked with a sad face.

"I have to travel."

JANICE ANGELIQUE

Pamela chose her words carefully. "That's a shame, we'll miss you. Will you be gone for long?"

He looked directly at her. "Just a couple of weeks. I wish I could be there to entertain you all, but I can't get out of my commitment."

"No, it's all right," Myah said. "I'll see you when you get back, but I think it's important now for me to reach out to them the way you did to us." She nodded as she spoke.

"Yes. I'll try my best to hurry back." He got to his feet, and so did Myah.

Pamela walked with them to her cottage so that he could say goodnight to his children, but they were already asleep. Quietly he pushed open the door to Gracie's room and saw both girls in bed while David slept on a blanket on the floor. He tiptoed in, kissed Ruth and pulled the sheet up to her chin, and then knelt and kissed his son's cheek.

"They won't give any trouble. I'll come back for them in the morning," he whispered.

"After breakfast," Pamela said, smiling at him.

Looking directly into her eyes, he touched her hand. "Thank you for welcoming me back."

She smiled shyly and looked away from his gaze. "Anyone would have done what I did."

"But you did it." This time he held her eyes until he saw that he was making her uneasy. "I'll see you tomorrow."

THE OTHER SIDE OF THE MOUNTAIN

"Yes." She walked out the bedroom door with him still holding her hand. She gently eased her hand from his as they entered the living room.

He touched Mary's hand and said goodnight, then walked with his sister to where his horse stood grazing. He would have loved to take that walk with Pamela but it wasn't appropriate or the right time. He looked back and waved to the two women standing on the verandah.

They both waved and didn't turn away until he hugged his sister and mounted his horse. Myah walked back to the two women. "I thank you, Pammy." She smiled. "I haven't seen him so relaxed in a very long time. Of course I haven't seen him in a long time." She hugged the two women and walked the short distance to her cottage.

Mary went to her cottage, and Pamela closed her door and quickly went through the bag of books Saul had brought for her. She sat on the floor in her bedroom and looked at each book. Among them was an American magazine with the caption *The Sexiest Men Alive*, but to her the sexiest man had just left her house. Not having seen a magazine like this before, she flipped wide-eyed through the pages and laughed softly at the half naked bodies.

She remembered when boats used to come to the island with foreigners. They were forbidden to climb the mountain, but they did bare themselves as they swam in the ocean. After it was declared scandalous, the boats stopped coming. The council of Elders had complained and banned the boat owners from bringing the foreigners. "It's bad for our community, especially the very impressionable children, to witness such behavior," they'd told them. Out of respect for the Rahjahs, no more boats of that kind ever came back to the island.

Pamela opened a novel written by Ian Fleming, *From Russia with Love*, and didn't put it down until her eyelids began drooping. Even then she still persisted until the book fell from her hand and she crawled into bed.

She fell asleep with Saul's image etched in her brain.

Chapter 6

It was Saturday. At the break of dawn Pamela woke from a peaceful slumber. She sat up in bed, wrapped the cotton sheet around her shoulders and walked to the window. She took a deep breath, closed her eyes and allowed the cool breeze to slowly wash over her face.

She turned and went to the children's room, knocked on the door and peeped in. They were all awake. "Get ready for breakfast, you three, you have all day to read."

"But their dada is coming for them after breakfast. May I go home with them?" Gracie gave her most winning smile.

Oh, boy, Pamela thought, taking a deep breath. "Yes, you can go home with your new friends providing their dada agrees."

Pamela went back to her room and did her toiletries in a beautifully decorated enamel basin filled with water on a polished wooden stand that Peter had made. She had painted the basin white, with yellow, green and red flowers. She changed into a blue and yellow dress and wrapped her hair with a yellow scarf.

Mary was waiting for her when she came to her door. "You look pretty in yellow," she commented with a smile. "Are you ready for the day?"

"Why wouldn't I be?" Pamela replied. Then, before Mary said anything, she said, "I would like to make a sorrel drink today. What do you think?"

Mary gave her a quizzical look. "You've never made sorrel before except grinding it for tea."

"I know, but I feel like doing it."

"You do know that it takes twelve hours to make, don't you?"

Pamela made a face and looked at Mary. "Really? I thought you just boiled it and mixed it with ginger and sugar."

Mary laughed. "What's your hurry?"

She shrugged. "No hurry. I still want to make it."

"Then go ahead. All the ingredients are in the kitchen. I can't wait to taste it."

Pamela made another face and glanced at her. "Me, too. Hopefully I won't poison anyone."

"In that case, you should drink it first."

Both women burst out laughing as they entered the kitchen. Myah was already there kneading the dough for dumplings. They greeted her, and while Mary took the fresh vegetables from the basket, Pamela began gathering the ingredients for her sorrel drink.

It was still cool, but the sun had begun showing its face, stripping the mountain of the lingering fog, casting its prisms through the huge trees. Some of the boys had begun playing cricket and soccer while others got water from the well.

Pamela poured boiling water on her sorrel and covered it in a big clay pot.

Breakfast was ready to be set on the table.

Unfortunately, as soon as the first platter was put on the table, it began raining. Mary quickly grabbed the platter and ran back to the kitchen as the men picked up each cushion. There was always a contingency plan. Although the kitchen was quite large, it was not set up for eating. But this was in no way an unusual occurrence. They'd try to wait out the rain or take covered platters to their cottages and have breakfast there.

Eventually, each family took a platter with food and tea from the kitchen for an intimate breakfast in their cottage.

Pamela prepared a platter of food while Gracie took the teapot back to their cottage. Because Shaela's parents couldn't drag her from her new friends, they joined Pamela for breakfast.

After breakfast the rain slowed to a drizzle and the children went back outside to play. The rain had fallen hard enough to create a muddy environment, but that had never stopped them before.

Giving the children time to play, Saul had taken his time in picking them up. David and Ruth saw him before he saw them. They rushed to greet him as he dismounted from his horse. "Dada, may Gracie and Shaela come home with us now?" David asked.

He hugged his children and laughed. "Why did I suspect something like this would happen?"

"I guess you know your children," Pamela said, coming towards him. She took a deep breath and let it out slowly to ease the quickening of her heart.

His eyes quickly appraised her. He smiled approvingly. "Good morning. Were they any trouble?" He spoke in a tone filled with awe and respect for the woman who now stood before him. But that didn't stop him from gazing at her lips and almost tasting their sweetness in his mind.

Trying not to be caught staring at him, she quickly averted her eyes and straightened her shoulders. "Not at all. They were like little angels. You've done a good job with them."

"With a village like ours, I can't take any of the credit." He let go of the horse's rein and followed her with the children trotting behind. "Did you hear the request?" He left his muddy shoes at the door and walked barefoot into the house.

"I heard it before you did." She entered her cottage and turned. "May I get you some tea?"

"Yes, I would love some." He seated himself on a plush cushion on the floor.

"So, Dada, can they?" Ruth persisted.

THE OTHER SIDE OF THE MOUNTAIN

"Yes," he said.

They disappeared outside.

"You sure know how to clear a room," Pamela said, placing the pot of tea, along with two cups, on the center table.

"It's a gift."

She poured the tea in his cup and set it on the table instead of handing it to him, then sat on the cushion beside him.

"I can't thank you enough for yesterday. I couldn't think of anything else all night. The best part was dancing with you." A seductive look came into his eyes as he remembered their closeness. Before his body could react, he took a deep breath and glanced outside, then back at her.

"You're trying to embarrass me, aren't you?" She dropped her eyes from his steady gaze.

"Sorry, I really didn't mean to embarrass you. I can't help saying what I feel sometimes. It has gotten me into trouble a lot of times." He crossed his legs, picked up the cup, and rested it on his knee.

"In another society you would probably be the boy who got beat up on the playground."

He laughed. "You do read a lot."

"That, plus I've seen a few squabbles between the boys on the playing field." She excused herself, got up and came back with the magazine in her hand.

"Somehow I have a feeling that this wasn't meant for me." She gave it to him and sat down.

"Did I give you this?" he asked, surprised.

She nodded.

He flipped through the pages as one corner of his mouth twisted upward. "You're right. This wasn't meant for you. As a matter of fact, I don't remember how this came into my possession. Could be reading material from one of my flights." He continued flipping through the pages.

"You mean you actually bought it?" she asked, looking at him in amused wonder.

He shrugged. "I might have. Magazines pass the time quickly while sitting in an airport waiting for a flight. I can read a serious novel or flip through the pages of one of these things," he said unapologetically.

"You're honest. Some people would have come up with some kind of excuse."

"I'm not embarrassed to read these things. They're drivel, but I actually find them quite entertaining. There are some good articles in here."

They expected the children to come running in when the rain started again, but they didn't. Pamela figured they'd gone to Myah's cottage. She smiled to herself, wondering whose idea it was to leave her and Saul by themselves.

Saul looked up at the paintings on the wall. "These are wonderful." He got to his feet and walked over to

THE OTHER SIDE OF THE MOUNTAIN

one showing a cluster of villagers. "These look as if they should be hung in a museum."

She turned but didn't get up. "You mean for people to look at?"

"Of course." He glanced back at her.

She shook her head. "No, they would laugh at their amateurish appearance. I do this for fun. I told you, painting relaxes me."

"These are not amateurish at all. These would put some paintings I've seen in museums to shame."

She flushed. "You really think so? You think they're good?"

"And you say I'm modest. They're beautiful. What about this one of you. Did you do this?"

"No, Mary did. It's well done, isn't it?"

"It's very beautiful. But one could never go wrong with you as a subject." He didn't look at her because he knew his comment would make her blush.

She didn't answer. "This rain is going to continue for a while. I can run out and get us something to eat from the community kitchen."

"If you're hungry, I can go." As he sat back on the cushion, a drop of water dampened his hair. He looked up to see where the leak was.

"I'm not hungry. I was thinking of you." She walked casually to her kitchen, embarrassed that her roof had to leak at this very moment.

He shook his head. "I'm not hungry, either, but I could use some more tea. Did you mix the herbs?" He leaned over and poured himself another cup of tea.

She came back into the room and placed a pot under the leak to catch the water. "I'm really sorry about this. Yes, I mixed the herbs, and you're still alive to ask that question." There was a trace of laughter in her voice.

He stared at her, then burst out laughing. "I bet you're a good cook. And don't apologize, I'll get the roof fixed before the real rain starts."

A momentary look of discomfort crossed her face and she said, "You don't have to, really. I can do it myself."

"I won't have you going up on the roof while I can do it. I'll do it."

"Okay."

"That was easy."

"Did you think I'd wrestle you for the job?"

Amusement flickered in the eyes that met hers. "You're good for me."

She arched her brows and gazed into his eyes as if to say, *"Really?"*

⚘

Tim sat in his cottage, bewildered. It seemed that in the blink of an eye he was being replaced by Saul, a man who'd made a mess of his own life and now had come to infringe on his. He walked to his window and looked out at the rain. He had not told the other men last night that he wouldn't play dominos with Saul because they would have thought he was jealous of the man. Of course, he *was* jealous of him. For years Tim had been Pamela's closest friend. He'd seen her through sad times when her husband died and joyous times when her daughter was born. He'd been patient, thinking that eventually she'd come to know how he really felt about her and come to feel the same way about him. But here comes Saul, a man who didn't deserve her, and she seemed to be taken with him. He'd seen the way Saul looked at her when they danced. He didn't think they'd just met, either. Pamela had not been straight with him. Why?

He couldn't see Pamela's house from his, but he knew Saul was still there. He felt like going over there. Just being there would prevent Saul from making a move on Pam. Somehow, he didn't think Saul had made his move yet, but love was a tricky thing. One didn't have to make a move to fall in love. He'd never seen the look Pamela had in her eyes last night when she looked at Saul before.

The cup cracked in his hand and the warm liquid leaked to the floor. He still didn't move.

JANICE ANGELIQUE

"Apart from this magazine that should not have been included in the bag, have you had a chance to look at the other books I brought?" Saul asked Pamela.

"I began reading *From Russia with Love*. Fascinating," she said. "I guess you've been to most of these places I read about." She looked at him expectantly.

"Most, but I've never been to Russia." In her eyes he could see that little girl wonder. Someone who would drink in all the wonders of history jumping off the pages of the books she'd read.

"Would you love to visit the places you've read about?"

She hesitated and looked through the open door at the rain making puddles in the mud. The wind picked up and she got up to close the door. He got up and picked up the shutters from beneath the window and put them in place, making the room dark. She bumped into him. For a brief moment neither one moved as the heat of their bodies passed from one to the other. Saul bent his head and inhaled the perfume from her hair without touching her. His heart raced.

Pam's breath caught in her throat and she closed her eyes as their fingertips touched. Quickly, she moved away from him and lit the lamp.

They sat back down together and as if to cool his body, his eyes moved around the room. He saw the bow and arrow in the corner. Her eyes followed his.

THE OTHER SIDE OF THE MOUNTAIN

"That belonged to my husband. I don't think he ever used it."

"Peter?" he questioned.

She didn't quiver at the pronunciation of her dead husband's name. "My deceased husband. Remember, I told you about him?"

He nodded. "Tragic."

Sounds of the rain had stopped, and she got up, took one shutter from the window. There was still a drizzle. Saul got up and took the rest of shutters from the windows and extinguished the lamplight. "I enjoyed being alone with you." He stood behind her. His arms raised to touch her shoulders but instead just hung in the air above her.

She could feel his warm breath on the back of her neck. "Me too." She saw the children as they came running back. Her daughter was anxious to go home with her friends.

Saul touched Pamela's hand, as he'd become accustomed to doing. "I'll see you when I get back." He bent toward her ear. "I'll miss you."

She smiled and waited for her heartbeat to slow from the nearness of him. "I await your return," she whispered.

He walked out in the drizzle to his sister's cottage, and Pamela stood at her cottage door until he left Myah's home. She watched him and the children mount their horses and slowly ride away from the village.

Tim walked to her verandah. She smiled at him. "I missed you last night and this morning. Where did you go?" she asked.

He didn't answer her question. "Did you have a good visit with Saul this morning?"

She heard the anger in his voice. "Did I do something wrong? Is everything all right with you?" She stopped and looked at him.

A muscle quivered at his jaw. "It seems Saul has taken an instant liking to you."

"You didn't answer my question."

"Nothing is wrong. I just don't want you to get hurt, that's all."

Her brows furrowed. "Why would I get hurt?"

He shook his head. "Just be careful. Don't be taken in by his act."

Now she was annoyed. "Timothy! How can you say something like that? He's your cousin."

"I don't know what the bloodline is, I haven't checked, but that has nothing to do with what I just said."

"I don't like what you just said, Tim. You and I have been friends for too long for me not to feel embarrassed about the implication of your words. Maybe you should leave."

THE OTHER SIDE OF THE MOUNTAIN

He frowned, then walked toward where a domino session was in progress.

Chapter 7

Saul brought the children back to Pamela's home and left before anyone saw him. The children were filled with excitement as they got off their horses and ran to Pamela's cottage. Gracie burst through the door. "Mama, you should have been there. They welcomed us almost like we did Uncle Saul. They hugged us and called us cousins and asked about you and Aunt Mary and Aunt Myah and everyone. They gave us coconut juice and sorrel and made our favorites."

"And which of your favorites was that?" Pamela asked, marking the last page she'd read and looking past the girls to see if Saul was with them.

"Fried dumplings rolled in sugar," she said, laughing.

"Ahhh, I see." Pamela smiled.

"Uncle Saul's cottage is huge." She opened her arms wide. "It would make four of ours or more. Oh, and Mama, they have lots and lots of books and paintings and stuff from all around the world."

"Stuff from all around the world," Pamela mused, nodding, disappointed that Saul had not stayed.

"Yes, and there was a picture of Miss Raquel."

THE OTHER SIDE OF THE MOUNTAIN

It was interesting to Pamela that her daughter had not referred to the woman as Aunt Raquel or described her looks or offered any other comment.

"They have all the animals we have and they're just as friendly."

Pamela listened to Gracie and then looked at Shaela and asked, "What did you see that was different from here, Shaela?"

"All the things that Gracie said," she replied.

Gracie had not given Shaela a chance to speak, but Pamela was sure that when Shaela saw her mother she would speak with the same fervor as Gracie.

"I'm glad you children had a good time. Why don't you get ready for supper. Shaela, your mama's in the community kitchen. You should go and let her know that you're back."

The meal area was still wet from the afternoon's rain, so everyone had supper in their cottage.

After supper, Pamela wanted desperately to go back to the place she'd met Saul on the beach, but the ground was wet and slippery. She could walk down, but it would take too long. Then she thought if Saul and the children could ride up the mountain and down, why couldn't she?

She got her horse and rode carefully down the mountain to the beach.

When she reached the spot where she'd met Saul, she got off her horse, left him there and began walking toward the rocky area. The stubborn horse walked slowly behind her.

"I thought you'd never come," Saul said, quietly coming up beside her.

Startled, she turned quickly and grinned at his smiling face. "I didn't think you'd be here," she said.

"I wanted to see you again before I left. My eyes can't seem to get enough of you."

She glanced at his face. There was that look again. She laughed. "You can't help yourself, can you?"

"The truth always sounds perfect when it comes back to my ear."

"Does that mean you like to hear yourself talk?"

He laughed. "Boy, do I love your wit."

It was getting cool and he placed his arm around her shoulder, stirring up feelings that weren't appropriate at this moment, but certainly felt good. She smiled and put her arm around his waist. For the first time she felt his muscles move under her hand. He pulled her closer as they walked and she laughed nervously and let go of his waist.

They could hear the drums from the mountain and she began walking to the rhythm. He laughed. When the rest of the band joined in with a reggae beat, she danced. Then she ran across the rocks, almost fell, and he caught her in his arms. They were so close that she could feel his breath on her face. She looked into his eyes. "I'll miss you. It's only been a short while since we met but I've become accustomed to seeing you."

"I'll hurry back." He hugged her tight and she rested her head on his chest, closed her eyes and felt the warmth of his body seep through his shirt. She could hear his heartbeat. His smell was warm and woodsy.

He didn't want to move away from her. Inhaling the lavender perfume from her hair, he closed his eyes. His body became prickly, as if her skin were penetrating his senses. He caressed her arms and she moved away from him to look in his eyes.

"You're not going to do that thing you do with your eyes again, are you?" he asked.

"You mean look away or roll them?"

He nodded.

She laughed. "No, I just want to commit every part of your face to memory until I see you again."

He allowed her to look at him, all the while wanting to kiss her and mold her form to his. His body warmed again and his muscles grew tight. His loins ached and his member took on a life of its own. Abruptly he broke away, then held her hand and walked off the rocks to their horses. He didn't want to let go of the small, soft fingers that wrapped around and occasionally tightened against his.

She let go of his fingers, smiled, mounted her horse and so did he. "You're quite a woman, Pamela."

"And you're quite a man, Saul. From an ogre to a very gentle man." She laughed. "Children, where do they get these things?" She shook her head, waved and rode up the mountain.

He stayed until she was out of sight. He could still feel the warmth of her hand on his skin. He took a deep breath. *Why am I going away? Because I love the travel and the challenges work gives me. But meeting Pam makes all that pale.* He shook his head. He still had to go. He kneed his horse into a gallop, then suddenly reined him in. He got off his horse and, with the smell of her perfume still lingering in his nostrils, walked home.

⸺

Sunday morning Pamela opened her eyes, rolled onto her back and knew Saul was already on his way to the airport in Jamaica. As she had done the morning before, she glanced at the books on the floor. Among the books was a poetry book. *Butterfly Unmasked.* She'd read all the poems last night and looked through her window at the moon and wondered if Saul had wanted to kiss her goodbye. She knew she'd distracted him with her constant jabbering, but that's what she did when she got nervous. She closed her eyes and kissed him in her mind.

Now looking out her window, she noted that the mist was so thick she could hardly see the kitchen. "I

THE OTHER SIDE OF THE MOUNTAIN

hope he has a good flight," she said to herself, offering a little prayer for his safety.

Lazily, she swung her feet off the bed. This was the day she, Mary and Myah would visit Jahyah Mountain. Out of respect, she'd allowed the Elders to play catch-up. After breakfast, they'd make the short trip from one mountain to the next.

Braving the cool mountain air, she met Mary at her door to go to the waterfall to take a bath. "Today is the day," Mary said.

Pamela nodded.

They got to the waterfall and Pamela hesitated, dreading the cool water. Mary looked at her and laughed.

"This is no time to stand and shiver."

"I know, but I was thinking of my sorrel drink."

"You didn't make it?"

Shedding her gown, Pamela nodded and braved the cold river water.

A short while later, fully clothed with their night gowns tucked under their arms, they dropped their clothes at their respective cottages and went to the kitchen. Pamela took the cover off the sorrel and strained it through cheese cloth, wrung it until no more of the liquid bled through, and then sweetened it. She looked at the blood red drink, then slowly, timidly, poured some in a cup and held it to her lips. The cinnamon and ginger gave it a very powerful but mouthwatering aroma.

JANICE ANGELIQUE

She took a sip and stood with the cup in her hand, waiting to die. She didn't feel lightheaded, nauseous or giddy. She smiled and handed the cup to Mary. "I didn't die, so it's your turn."

Mary took the cup from her and drank. She nodded. "Not half bad, Pammy, dear." She nodded again. "I think you outdid yourself this time."

"I may not be a good cook, but this proves I'm not a dud in the kitchen. I should save some of this for Saul." She slapped her hand to her mouth. She couldn't believe she'd said it out loud.

Mary looked at her, then around the empty kitchen. "What did you just say?"

"Oh, Jah. Please don't say anything. I'm begging you." She stared at her friend.

Mary stared back. "Are you…? Are you and…"

"Please, Mary."

"I'm your friend. We've been friends since we were babies. We drank from the same bottle…"

Myah entered the kitchen and they both began taking down pots and looking into cupboards. "Big day today," Myah said. "Do you think I should take my family with me?"

"Of course," Pamela said without hesitation. "Everyone will want to see the baby." After a quick glance in Mary's direction, she joined in making the first meal of the day.

81

THE OTHER SIDE OF THE MOUNTAIN

Myah looked at the prepared sorrel drink, then back at Pam.

Pam smiled. "You must taste it. I'm still standing, so is Mary." She touched her stomach.

Myah drank from the cup Pamela offered and grinned, then waited for a second. She laughed. "I feel fine, and it's really good."

Pamela rolled her eyes, laughed and left the kitchen.

During breakfast, while the fruit was being passed around, Gracie asked her mother, "Mama, will it be all right if Shaela and I go with you?" She didn't wait for her mother's reply. "I think it would be nice for the children to make the trip, too. We already know the way and the children…"

"The children?" Pamela said.

"I mean Shaela and me."

"Oh, okay. I guess it would be all right, but we don't want to overwhelm them on our first visit, even though you guys were there yesterday."

"Oh, no, Aunty Pam. They won't be overwhelmed. They love us and they want to see us again," Shaela said.

Pamela and Mary laughed.

"Why do I feel ganged up on?"

"I think it was intentional," Mary said.

"I would love to make the trip, too," Tim said, looking across at Pamela. "After all, I have a few friends that I would love to visit."

"Male or female?" Mary said, laughing.

"Ahhh, I'll never tell." He wagged a finger, then slyly glanced at Pamela, who was busy talking with Myah. He'd hoped for a reaction from her.

After breakfast the girls took their bath and eight people from Rahjah Mountain made their way past low-lying green and purple ferns, huge fruit trees, dwarf coconut trees, huge coconut trees, streams, guava trees, pastures with grazing horses and sheep and over the river by way of the bridge to Jahyah Mountain.

They passed through much the same flora and fauna on Jahyah Mountain as on their own and, as soon as their horses came into view of the village, they heard the sound of steel drums, tambourines and guitars. This was an exact replica of their village with the exception of Saul's enormous cottage. The way Gracie had described it, it could not be missed or mistaken for any other.

The children rushed out to greet them. Gracie and Shaela nudged their horses ahead and jumped off to be once again welcomed by their friends and relatives. The adults followed and got off as throngs of Rahjahs came to greet them.

Myah and Samuel immediately saw their parents. With tears in her eyes, Myah's mother took Isha and kissed her face all over. Then it was Samuel's mother's turn, then the fathers'. They didn't shake hands but gave their children great big bear hugs. Isha was passed

THE OTHER SIDE OF THE MOUNTAIN

around like a little doll and she kept giggling while hugging everyone who hugged her. As Pamela tried to back away gracefully from the crowd, Nanuk, Saul and Myah's mother, caught her by the hand and hugged her. "Welcome, my dear. Welcome. I am Nanuk, Myah's mother."

Pamela was a bit surprised that she had been singled out by Nanuk, but nonetheless, she was her charming self, determined not to give away the relationship between herself and Nanuk's son. "Thank you. It's good to be here."

Nanuk would have loved to say more to Pamela, but was summoned by Eve. "We must talk later," she said before she squeezed Pamela's hand and walked in the direction of the Elders.

The music began again and great big bowls and platters of fruits, small bammys and sweet flour dumplings were passed around. Knowing that they had to eat even a little of what was provided in their honor, Mary whispered in Pamela's ear, "We shouldn't have eaten."

As they sat in the circle, Jane and Solomon came out with two other Elders. Pamela smiled and nodded as they took their places in the center of the circle. The huge dining table had been replaced by four Victorian chairs, not unlike the ones the Elders on Rahjah Mountain used when there was a function.

The crowd hushed when Jane and Solomon kept standing. Both smiled and clapped their hands. "It took a long time getting here," Jane said in her soft voice. "It is written that a child shall lead them, and this proves it. It took young Gracie, Shaela, Ruth and David to bring us all back together. Gracie was very determined that this day should come, and, on behalf of everyone, I'm glad she was. We must not let this ever happen again. There is nothing stronger than family bond. We must not allow strangers to break that bond, but should welcome them into our midst, into our culture if they so wish." She sat down.

A great big cheer went up from the crowd. Eve and Jeremiah, two of the Elders of Jahyah Mountain, got up. Eve spoke. "I have to agree with everything my sister Jane has said. We made a pact when we fought those soldiers for the first Rahjah Mountain that no one would drive a wedge between us. We made our village in circular patterns to show solidarity. We allow and encourage our offspring to go out into the world and come back to us if they so choose. Our peaceful way of living, our beliefs, and our love for each other have seen us through for more than a hundred and fifty years. We are thankful each day that Jah has seen fit to give us another day on his land. We must never forget the struggle, the fight, but more importantly, we must always show kindness to those who do not know our way and teach them, but never forget our bond."

Another cheer went up when Jeremiah held Eve's hand and they both sat down. Pamela wondered why

THE OTHER SIDE OF THE MOUNTAIN

none of the men spoke, but nevertheless the message was one of strength and solidarity. Then she thought of the role of the Rahjah men and smiled. They held their women in high esteem, which didn't mean they thought any less of themselves. There was no division of power.

Food was passed around and the merriment continued. Pamela found herself staring at Saul's cottage. She wanted to see his library, but, as bonded as their culture was, one did not enter another's cottage unless invited. While she stood there staring, Gracie grabbed her hand and led her out of the crowd towards the cottage.

"It's all right, Mama," she said as she kept pulling her closer to the cottage.

Ruth took her other hand. "You have to see our home, Auntie," Ruth said.

Trying to hide her excitement, Pamela followed the children into Saul's home. On entering, she stopped and gazed at the décor, which was unlike anything she'd ever seen. And before she could take everything in, she was dragged to the library. With her mouth agape, she stood looking in awe at the huge number of books that lined the walls of the room. There were no paintings on the walls, just books. In the middle of the room was a huge desk. There were big colored cushions thrown on the floor and a ladder in the corner.

"You can take any book you want," David said. "Dada won't mind."

"Wow!" was all Pamela could say as her eyes took in the entire room.

"You could read to us like Grampa and Grangran, only they get tired. Dada loves to read to us."

Pamela ran her hands along the covers and spines of the books. "I could lock myself in this room and never come out," she said.

The children laughed.

"But I think I'll wait until your father comes back before I borrow any. Plus I have a few that he gave me that I have to finish reading first."

"May I stay here, Mama? Can I stay here and read everything?" Gracie said.

"I would never see you for a very long time." She looked at Gracie and laughed. Her fingers ran over a first edition Makabé Bible. She took it out and carefully turned the very delicate pages. She read a few lines, then replaced it.

Interestingly, the children didn't show her their father's room, but they did take her to their room. There were two beds in the room and, again, cushions on the floor. One section of the room had shelves lined with books for the children, and this time there were paintings on the wall.

"Who paints?" Pamela asked.

"I do," David said.

THE OTHER SIDE OF THE MOUNTAIN

"Beautiful." She looked at Ruth, who shook her head, then showed her a sculpted bust of David. "I did this."

Pamela nodded and took a good look at the sculpture. "Wonderful. This is beautiful."

"Mama, can I learn to do that?" Gracie asked.

"Of course you can." Gracie had never shown any interest in sculpting before. She and Shaela loved to paint. "You can do anything you want to do."

Sensing the children wanted to be with each other, Pamela made her way back to the verandah without seeing any more of the cottage. There was much more to be seen, but this was not the time.

As she stood on the verandah, Jane and Solomon walked towards her. She walked down the steps. "I know you've denied this, but I know you did this. There's no denying Gracie lit the fire, but you fanned the flames," Jane said, taking Pamela's hand.

Pamela smiled. "Then I won't say anything more."

Solomon laughed. "It is a wise women who knows how to pick her battles."

Pamela shook her head and stood between her grandparents. They each pushed their hands through hers and began walking slowly away from the crowd. "Pammy," Jane said.

"Yes, ma'am?"

"You're not related to Saul, you know."

"I thought we were distant cousins…" She stopped talking. "Why are you telling me this?"

"Oh, no reason, just wanted you to know."

"Grangran…" She shook her head again. "Stop matchmaking." Then she remembered, there were paintings of the children and of Saul in the cottage, but none of their mother. Gracie said she'd seen one. She wondered if Saul still kept a painting of Raquel in his bedroom. Then she wondered if she felt jealous of the woman. She shook her head. Why should she be jealous? He was no longer married to her.

"But he is a wonderful fellow," Solomon said in his baritone voice.

"I'll take your word for it, Grampa."

"This was a great day, and a great deed," Jane said. "Now everyone can go and come from one mountain to the other and we can give this mountain back its rightful name of Rahjah once more."

Pamela stopped when they got to a bench under a lignum vitae tree. They sat down. "Where have I been? You mean this mountain was renamed because of the rift?"

Jane nodded. "It was a sad thing, my dear. Things were said that should not have been said. Words are very powerful. We should have gotten together and talked, but instead we allowed things to escalate out of control."

THE OTHER SIDE OF THE MOUNTAIN

"My Jah." She didn't want to ask exactly what was said; her mother had told her enough.

Eve and Jeremiah came to sit beside them. They didn't speak of the past, but of the future and each other and how happy they were to be as one again. After a while Pamela could tell that they were getting tired. Eve smothered a yawn and apologized. Jeremiah beckoned to one of the men and he immediately left the crowd. "Will you get the buggy for us, please? I think Eve is getting a bit tired.

"Who's getting tired?" Eve said.

"I am, dear." He corrected himself to the man, then turned to Pamela and introduced the man. "Pammy, dear, this is my grandson, Peter."

Taken aback a bit, Pamela looked into the man's face. He was young and handsome with a bearded face and gray eyes. His locks were tied in a ponytail and the hand he pushed into hers felt soft. His voice was equally soft. She'd had no idea Saul had a brother.

"Peter will be leaving us for Germany in a few weeks. I don't know why he chose Germany as the first place to visit, but we never ask why. I think it's Saul and his books."

"Now, Grampa," Peter said.

"Germany," Pamela said, "that's very interesting." She'd read a lot about Germany, but would not have picked it as the first country to visit. Who was she to say anything, though. She'd spent only a few minutes in Ja-

90

maica and hated it. She suddenly realized that she was staring at him. She let go of his hand and said, "Sorry. It's very nice to meet you."

He went for the buggy and helped all four Elders aboard. "We will see you tomorrow," Jane said, waving to Pamela.

"Yes." She waved back and watched Peter turn the horses toward the upper village. She rejoined her friends and the other villagers.

"That's an unusual Rahjah cottage," Mary said with a smile on her face.

Her smile told Pamela that she already knew it was Saul's home. "You promised," Pamela said.

"I'm only pointing out the obvious." She snickered.

Pamela shot her a look as Myah joined them. "Did you expect this?" Myah said to Pamela.

"No, but in keeping with what Gracie said and the reception Saul got from us when he came to visit the first time, I'm not surprised. This is our way of doing things. We welcomed Saul back into the fold and you were welcomed back into the fold. The prodigal son and daughter, so to speak."

Myah hugged Pamela. "I'm so happy."

"We are, too," Mary said.

"Why didn't Judiah come with us?" Myah asked.

Mary smiled. "He wanted us to pave the way."

"I think we live in the most beautiful place in the world," Pamela said, and began walking away from the villagers with her friends. The children seemed to have charmed everyone and were now the center of attention.

"I think you can only say that if you've at least been to a few other countries," Myah said. "You know, a long time ago tourists visited this island by way of Jamaica."

"What happened?" Mary asked. "Not that I'm sorry that they stopped coming."

"I think there were too many disruptions. There was a building on the beach where they sold liquor. Some would bring picnic baskets and try to climb the mountain. When they were told that it was forbidden they became outraged. So the Rahjahs petitioned the Jamaican courts."

"And?" Pamela encouraged when Myah hesitated.

"Well, this island belongs to the Rahjahs, so they had to stop the tourists from coming. The building was torn down. There was also an old fort of some kind. Rastafarians, not like our kind, used to use it as a hangout. That, too, was stopped after there was an altercation involving one of our own and a foreigner who was the fiancée of the same man. That part of the island was wiped clean of any building, and no unauthorized boat was allowed to ever dock off our shores."

"That should have been put in our history books," Mary said.

"It is," Myah replied. Her daughter called her name and she turned and walked back to the circle.

JANICE ANGELIQUE

Mary looked at Pamela. "You've read all our history. Who was it?"

"His name is James, his wife Angel."

Mary nodded. "I'd love to meet them sometime."

"Me, too."

Pamela cast another look at Saul's home and secretly wished he were here today. No one saw Tim until it was time to go. He came back the same way he vanished, but on his return there were men and women with him laughing and talking.

Even when they were ready to go and their horses were brought to them, the excitement at their visit had not waned. They said their goodbyes with hugs and kisses, then made their way back along the path. The gates of friendship between relatives had once again been opened. One couldn't tell who was happier, the children or the adults.

At supper that evening, the excitement seemed to have been transferred from the Jahyah Village to the Rahjah Village as Pamela's party talked about their visit. Tomorrow, the boats that carried the Rahjahs and the Jahyahs would no longer be separate and the name Jahyah would be stricken from the records and replaced with the right word, Rahjah, one people.

Chapter 8

Raquel Tanquez thought of the way she'd left her children and shrugged. Her marriage to the wealthy landowner Velaz Tanquez had failed. He'd cut up her credit cards and told her to go to work. Well, that wasn't going to happen. Now, with five suitcases and four bags, she took a limousine from Kingston airport to Portland, where she took a boat to Rahjah Island. The boat owner had protested. "No one is allowed to go to that island," he'd said.

"I live there. My family is there. I was on holiday," she replied.

"You don't look like them."

"I don't have to look like them," she said with disdain.

"I will not take you up the mountain," he said in an angry tone.

"All you have to do is get me to the island." She cursed at him in Portuguese.

He demanded payment, tossed her suitcases on the sand and left.

Raquel stood on the beach and looked toward the mountain. It was an unforgivably hot and humid day. She sat on one suitcase and fanned herself with a folding fan. She pushed the hat down on her head, opened a suitcase, took off her heels and exchanged them for a pair of flat shoes. She began walking. Her suitcases were safe. She would have someone come down to collect them.

Gracie and the twins were taking their evening ride. They dismounted and began walking. Ruth stopped and pointed. "Who's that walking up the mountain?" she said to her brother.

He turned and looked for a long time without answering. Then a hard look changed his entire countenance and he said, "It looks a lot like Raquel."

The woman had taken off her shoes and was swinging them in her hand.

"Who's Raquel?" Gracie asked, noting a look on her friends' faces she'd never seen before. "Is something wrong?"

"Raquel is our mother," Ruth replied.

"Should we run to meet her?" Gracie was just about to run down the mountain.

Ruth caught her hand. "We never told you the story about why our mother left us."

Gracie shook her head.

"She's not a very nice lady," David said.

"But she's your mother. All mothers…"

"We know, you've said it many times, but believe me, our mother is different," David said.

THE OTHER SIDE OF THE MOUNTAIN

Gracie ignored her friends and began leading her mare toward the woman.

Raquel saw the children and, almost out of breath, waved. "My children, Mother is home," she shouted. Breathing hard, she stopped to rest.

Still the children lagged behind Gracie as she waved and said, "Welcome."

When they finally reached her, Raquel said, "You're not glad to see your mother, children? It's been a very long time. Have I changed that much?"

"No, ma'am," they both replied with their heads down and their hands at their side.

"Then give your mother a big hug." She opened her arms but neither of the children moved into her embrace.

She looked over at Gracie. "And who might you be? I've never seen you before."

"I'm Gracie. I live on the next mountain. Where did you go?"

Raquel took a deep breath and looked at Gracie. "Oh, I see, you people have made nice."

"Yes, ma'am," Gracie said.

"Well, you run down and get my things. They're down there." She pointed behind her. "The boatman was a very nasty person. He refused to bring them up."

Gracie looked in the direction she pointed. "What kind of things, ma'am?"

"My suitcases. Now go, shoo."

JANICE ANGELIQUE

Gracie got on her horse and rode down the mountain, but when she saw the many suitcases, she shouted back, "I cannot carry all these things, ma'am."

Raquel ignored her. The children looked at their mother and mounted their horses. "We'll go and help," David said.

"No, she can carry them. Those people are stronger than they let on."

The children ignored their mother and pushed their horses into a gallop down the mountain. There was no way they could have carried the heavy cases. They had no way of hooking them onto the horses. Plus, they were too heavy for them to lift. Gracie took up a make-up case and began walking up the mountain with the case while Ruth and David took up two other bags that weren't very heavy.

"Maybe she's changed," Gracie said to the twins.

They didn't answer. They didn't want to tell Gracie that they were more afraid of their mother than anything else.

Hoping for a rousing welcome, Raquel had walked ahead and left the children. When she got to the village, she said in a loud voice, "I'm home."

"You've come back." Ludy had been her only friend in the village. It was more of a question than a statement of joy.

"Yes. Are you glad to see me, my friend?"

THE OTHER SIDE OF THE MOUNTAIN

"I guess...I guess so," Ludy said. "We didn't know you were coming. You should have sent word. Where are your things?"

"They're on the beach. I told someone named Gracie to bring them."

"Gracie is a child, Raquel. She cannot carry your heavy suitcases and, if I know you, and I do, you have a lot."

Raquel waved her hand impatiently. "Well, send someone to fetch them then. Where is my husband?"

"Who?" Ludy cocked her ear as if she didn't know of whom Raquel spoke.

"My husband Saul." The pleasantness disappeared from her voice.

"Oh. He's away until next week."

Raquel was disappointed. "Well, it will give me a chance to make amends with his people." She looked around and saw that everyone was busy doing something. She looked towards Saul's parents' cottage just as they came out. She waved to them.

Nanuk and Daniel looked at each other and walked to Raquel. "You shouldn't be here," Nanuk said.

"Why not? My children are here, and so is my husband."

"You don't understand the ways of the Rahjahs, do you? We tried to teach you our ways, my dear," Nanuk said softly.

"No, it is you who do not know my way. Send someone for my things. They are on the beach." With that, she turned and walked toward Saul's home.

Daniel shook his head and sighed. "Just when things had become whole again. Just when we are one people again, the very cause walks in. Is the devil that strong?" He turned to his wife.

"Not this time, Dan. Not this time." She shook her head. "Saul will be furious when he sees her."

"What can we do?" Daniel asked.

"We have to contact the Elders from both mountains. We have to do this thing together." She saw the children walking up with three small bags and smiled. "Oh, my children." She took the bags and handed them to Ludy. "We'll send someone for the rest after supper."

Ludy nodded and took the bags to Raquel.

Raquel turned when she saw Ludy come into the cottage. "Little has changed," she said, looking around. Her portrait was not on the wall. In its place were paintings of horses and mountains. She scowled at Ludy. "Put them in my room."

"You can say please," Ludy said.

She was sad to see that reminders of her had been removed from Saul's home as if she no longer existed. Then she smiled and turned to Ludy. "I know he still hates me. Heck, everyone hates me."

THE OTHER SIDE OF THE MOUNTAIN

"You did a lot of damage when you were here," Ludy said.

"Will you help me get him back on my side? He loves you. You're his cousin."

"We're all cousins and brothers and sisters and aunts…"

"I get it," Raquel said impatiently. "But you'll help me?"

"I don't know what I can do, Raquel. You have to show him that you've changed. I can't tell him to love you, and you can't tell him to love you."

"Is there someone else?" she asked point-blank, looking directly at Ludy, knowing that she didn't lie.

Ludy shook her head. "Not that I know of."

"He still travels a lot?"

Ludy nodded.

Raquel heaved a sigh. "Not if I can help it. He needs to be here so that I can show him that I've changed."

Ludy shook her head and left the cottage. Her friend had not changed at all. But just maybe, if she kept telling herself that she'd changed, she would.

Gracie saw the sadness on her friends' faces. She'd never seen them like that before. "Do you want to stay with me until your dada comes home?"

They both looked at her and nodded. "We'll ask our grandparents."

Of course Nanuk and Daniel said it was all right. Saul had left them in charge of their grandchildren.

The children went inside and packed quickly, but not quick enough. Raquel came into their room. "What are you doing?"

"We're sleeping over at Gracie's," David said.

"No, I just got here. You cannot go anywhere unless I say so."

"But Grampa and Grangran said it was all right," Ruth protested.

"I'm here now. They cannot tell you what to do, that's my job."

"But…" David said.

"No buts. Go get washed up for supper."

"Can we at least tell Gracie we can't go with her?" Tears came to Ruth's eyes and her brother hugged her.

"I'll tell her." Raquel marched out of the room and stood on the verandah. "You." She pointed to Gracie. "You can go home; Ruth and David are not coming with you." She turned and walked back inside the cottage.

Gracie looked weepily at Nanuk.

"It's all right, Gracie, you can come back tomorrow, or they will come to see you. We promise."

"Really, you promise?" She looked into Nanuk's eyes and wiped the tears from her cheek.

"Yes."

Gracie mounted her mare and rode sadly home.

THE OTHER SIDE OF THE MOUNTAIN

Pamela immediately noticed something was wrong when Gracie got home and went directly to her room. She slowly pushed the door open and sat on the bed. Gracie was crying. "Gracie," Pamela said, knowing her daughter didn't cry unless there was a very good reason. "What's the matter, my little darling?"

Gracie got up and hugged her mother. "Their mother came back, Mama. She wasn't very nice to me. Ruth and David wanted to come and stay with us but she said no."

Pamela hugged her daughter. "Their mother is back?" she said, feeling a dull ache crawl up her shoulders.

Gracie nodded.

Pamela searched for words to comfort her daughter. "Maybe she wants to spend time with them, sweetie. She hasn't seen them in a very long time."

Gracie nodded.

"You know how much I'd miss you if I went away for a long time?"

"But you won't ever go away for a long time, will you?"

Pamela shook her head. "No, my little one, I won't."

Gracie looked into her mother's eyes. "You like Uncle Saul, don't you, Mama?"

Wondering why Gracie had asked the question, Pamela met her daughter's gaze. "Of course I do, dear."

"Then you can send her away."

"Oh, my little one, I can't do that. She came to see her children. She'll leave soon."

"Are you sure, Mama?"

Pamela couldn't say yes. "I believe so."

Gracie nodded. "Can I rest for a little while before supper?"

"Of course, dear." Pamela felt Gracie's little forehead, kissed her cheek and smoothed her hair. "You're not feeling ill, are you, dear?"

"No, Mama, just a little tired." She crawled up to her pillow and lay down.

"Okay then, I'll come get you in a few minutes." She left the room.

She couldn't believe that Saul's woman was back. She walked in a daze to Myah's cottage and knocked on the door. Myah opened the door and frowned at Pamela's face. "What's the matter? You look as if you've seen a ghost. Come in."

Pamela walked into the living room. "No, I didn't see a ghost, but you may think one has come back." She sat on a cushion. "Raquel is back." She looked up just as Myah seemed to fall onto the cushion next to her.

"Are you sure? Who told you? When did she come back?"

"Seems as if she arrived not too long ago. Gracie came home very upset. The twins wanted to sleep over but Raquel wouldn't let them."

Myah sat staring at Pamela. "Oh, Jah. Not again. We're one. We just mended fences."

"Is she that bad?"

"You have no idea."

"Will Saul take her back?" The question came out before Pamela had a chance to think. She hoped Myah wouldn't read anything into it.

Myah shook her head. "Absolutely not. She made him extremely unhappy in every way. It took a long time for him to heal after she'd left."

"But wasn't he the one who sent her away?"

"Yes. Although he told her that she could come back and visit the children whenever she wanted to, he hoped she would never come back."

"Maybe she doesn't have an ulterior motive. Maybe she just came to see the children."

Myah nodded, but she didn't really believe it. She thought of the things that Raquel had done and said to cause the rift between her people and shook her head. "Oh, Jah," she said again.

"Saul will be back next week," Pamela said. "Maybe she'll be gone by then."

"We can only hope."

⊸⊶

Word of Raquel's arrival spread quickly, and at supper that was all the Rahjahs spoke about. For the first time in a long while, Pamela was quiet. For someone who almost always had a ravenous appetite, she didn't seem to be very hungry this evening. Mary patted her hand. "Everything will be all right, Pammy. You know the saying, *what a fi you cannot be unfi you,*" she said in Patoi.

Pamela placed a finger to her lips. "I told you not to say anything."

"And I haven't, but still one has to wonder if she came back to beg him to take her back."

"Then so be it. There really isn't anything between us. We saw each other a few times and talked…"

"And he brought you presents."

"He brought me books, Mary. He brought me books from his library."

"Because he knew you loved to read."

"Yes, but that doesn't mean anything. I bet he doesn't even remember me."

"Phooey. You should have seen the way he looked at you when you two were dancing."

"Stop reading signs that aren't there." Frustration seemed to take hold of her. She didn't know exactly what the relationship was between her and Saul, and now she may never find out.

Myah came to sit with them and Mary stopped talking. "Devon came to my cottage right after you left," she said to Pamela. "He had to go down and haul up five suitcases. She is in no hurry to leave. She began ordering the men around once more. And here's the

THE OTHER SIDE OF THE MOUNTAIN

worst part: She ordered supper to be brought to her cottage and didn't allow the children to eat with the others, either."

Mary nodded and Pamela shook her head.

"Oh, Jah," Pamela said. "Maybe she was just tired after her long trip and wanted to talk with the children. You know how we mothers are." She smiled.

"I know that you're not naïve, Pammy," Myah said.

"And I'm no fool. We have to give her the benefit of the doubt."

Myah nodded. "Okay, I'll try to see things your way. I'll think positive. But, frankly, I'm positive she's come to start some kind of trouble again."

"I like the first part of your sentence," Pamela said, smiling. "We could invite her up for tea tomorrow. What do you think?" Pamela looked at Myah.

"Okay." She didn't feel very optimistic. "We'll invite a few of the other women, too."

They all agreed.

Gracie didn't eat much supper and afterwards crawled into her mother's bed.

"Read to me, Mama," she said.

"Should we take turns?" Pamela asked her.

She shook her head. "No, I just want you to read to me tonight. I'll read to you tomorrow."

They heard a light knocking at the door. Pamela got up and opened the door to see two children standing there in their nightgowns. She smiled and hugged Ruth and David. "How did you get here?"

"Grampa brought us," David whispered.

"But I thought your mother said you couldn't come."

"Grampa is more powerful than our mother," Ruth replied, laughing.

"Let's surprise Gracie," Pamela said. "Why don't you go into her room and I'll get her."

They nodded, giggled and did as they were told.

Pamela looked out and saw Daniel on his horse. She walked out to speak with him. He got down off his horse as she approached.

"Thank you, Daniel."

"The children were very sad, so their grandmother and I thought it best that they come to be with Gracie."

She nodded and looked away for a moment. "If you don't mind, will you extend an invitation to Raquel for me?"

He smiled and nodded.

"Will you tell her I would like it if she would have tea with us tomorrow after the children's discussion."

"Yes, I will." He gave a short bow. "Have a good night."

"I will, and thanks again."

He nodded, got back on his horse and rode off.

When she got back into the house, Ruth had become a bit restless. She stood at the door and tried to stifle a giggle.

Gracie heard her friend's laughter and jumped out of bed. "You came."

Ruth and David rushed to her. She hugged them both. "I'll sleep in my room now, Mama."

"I thought you might." Pamela lit the lamp and gave it to Gracie. "Don't stay up too late. Remember, you have school tomorrow."

"We can go to school with Gracie tomorrow," Ruth said, showing Pamela her knapsack.

"Very good." She kissed all three children as they laughed and went to Gracie's room. Gracie was back to her old self again. There was another knock on the door and Shaela appeared with her pillow. Pamela laughed and pushed her head out to see Mary standing at her door. She waved and closed the door. She took a deep breath and went back to her room. Her daughter was happy, and so was she. She picked up a history book Saul had given her and slipped her feet under the covers.

For some reason she couldn't concentrate. Why did Raquel have to come back? Did she come to visit her children, whom she had not seen in years? Pamela sat upright. Why had she not seen her children in over four years when the invitation had been extended for her to return whenever she wished? The entire village had resented her, but that was her own fault.

She took a deep breath, flopped backward and picked up a different book. It didn't take very long for her to fall asleep.

Chapter 9

When Pamela woke the next morning, she went down to the river, took a bath and got ready for the day. By the time she'd decided what her day would consist of, the children were ready for breakfast.

During breakfast Pamela asked her mother if she would join them for tea in the afternoon. "I've invited Raquel to tea," she told her.

Esther shook her head. "Be careful. You've never dealt with an outsider before. They're different."

"You'll be with me. What kind of trouble can I get into?"

Esther shook her head again and began walking away. "I'll be there. I'll bring Nana and Phyllis along if you don't mind."

"Not at all." Pamela and Mary walked up the mountain with the children. She had not expected Jane to monitor her class, but there she was in the back of the class listening to her speak of another country's history. The children were fascinated, and before Jane left she smiled and gave a little bow of approval, which greatly pleased Pamela.

It was another hot, humid day, and instead of having tea indoors, Esther, Pamela and the other women spread a blanket in the midst of two big shade trees that seemed to kiss each other overhead. They set out trays of tea and finger food.

The time that Raquel should have arrived passed without even a message declining the invitation. Being late for an occasion was frowned upon by the Rahjahs, and Raquel didn't have an excuse since she did absolutely nothing in the village. They began without her. "I'm sorry," Pamela said. "Maybe I wasn't specific enough about the time."

"Yes, you were," Myah said. "That's just how she is."

Esther didn't say anything.

They looked up warily when, half an hour after the appointed time, Raquel rode slowly into the village, escorted by one of the men from her village. Pamela and Esther went to greet and welcome her. She wore a tight-fitting cotton blouse, long pants and riding boots. Her long, shiny hair glistened in the sunlight. Her painted lips and nails intrigued Pamela. She wondered what she hid under the paint on her eyelids, face and lips.

Pamela glanced at her mother but didn't say anything about the woman's attire. It was different, and not as dreary as the clothes they wore. Of course she would never admit that to anyone. As far as she was concerned, the war paint on Raquel's face could go,

THE OTHER SIDE OF THE MOUNTAIN

but the clothes could stay. "Welcome. It is very nice to meet you," Pamela said with an extended hand.

Raquel shook her hand. "Thank you," she said in a quiet tone. She handed Pamela a bottle wrapped in gold cellophane paper. "It's wine," she said. "I brought it with me from Brazil." She stopped talking.

They walked to where the other ladies were and sat down. Pamela offered Raquel a seat on the pillow reserved for her. She sat down and poured herself a cup of tea and began talking. "I'm sorry Saul isn't here. I know he misses me, but I couldn't find the time until now to come back."

"What about your children?" Myah asked, not able to keep the hatred she felt for the woman out of her tone.

Pamela shot her a warning look. She didn't withdraw the question.

Raquel looked at her and laughed. "Now I remember you. You're Saul's little sister. You were the one who ran away." She looked around at Esther and Mary. "This one would cry every time Saul and I had an argument." She turned to Myah. "I could never figure it out. Why did you always cry?"

Not appreciating that her friend was being made fun of, Pamela came to Myah's rescue. "So tell us about Brazil, Raquel. The only place a lot of us have ever been is Jamaica, so it's a treat for us to hear about other countries." She glanced at her mother. "Well, that wasn't quite accurate. Mother has visited other countries, but she never visited Brazil."

"Is that where you were born?" Mary asked.

"No, I'm from Spain, but I have relatives in Brazil."

Pamela had to admit she was enjoying the woman's accent, her mispronunciation of many words and her constant repetition of, "How do you say."

In spite of her being rude in many ways, Pamela didn't hate her. She didn't quite like her, but hate was not a word she would use to describe the way she felt about her.

"So when are you going back to Brazil or Spain?" Myah asked, ignoring the look Pamela gave her.

"Oh, I don't know. I brought enough clothes to stay for a very long time." She laughed boisterously.

Pamela swallowed the lump that came up in her throat. She liked seeing Saul. What would Raquel's being here do to the friendship between her and Saul? When two people were committed to each other in Rahjah tradition, the man or woman could dissolve the relationship by walking away, which was what Saul had done, not only by sending Raquel away but by not visiting her or acknowledging her at all. Raquel spoke as if she had rewritten that particular Rahjah law.

"There's one thing I don't understand," Raquel said to Esther. "You've left the island and seen what the outside world is like."

Esther nodded.

THE OTHER SIDE OF THE MOUNTAIN

"Why aren't there motor cars or electricity on the island? When I came back I had to walk all the way up to the village. If there was a car on the island I could have been driven up the mountain."

"We like the way our life is, Raquel. There is no pollution here. Our people are healthy…"

"No electricity, no running water…" Raquel muttered under her breath.

"That would spoil all that we've worked so hard to preserve, my dear. If you split the word Rahjah you will find that the Rah, which stands for the raw earth that sustains us even though we spell it r-a-h. Of course you know Jah stands for God. Polluting our air would destroy everything that our ancestors worked so hard to give us. We have to maintain to show our appreciation. We're working on piping water into each cottage, but that's as far as we will go. No electricity, no motor cars."

Raquel leaned back into her pillow and threw one leg over the other. "Well, I like the modern conveniences. I hate going to the river to bathe in cold water. I hate that I have to light a lamp instead of throwing a switch. I hate walking on mud and gravel."

"This island really isn't for you, is it then?" Myah said.

Raquel shrugged. "We could at least bring a car over and pave the path."

"No," Pamela said coolly. "We enjoy riding horses; plus, we don't miss what we never had."

"I love riding horses, too, but they smell," Raquel said as she ate heartily and spoke as if she'd known all the women for a very long time. They, or at least Pamela, wanted her to feel welcome. Myah looked as if she wanted to cut a switch and thrash Raquel within an inch of her life, but at the end of the tea, she smiled at her.

"I enjoyed this very much, Pamela. Do you mind if I invite you to my cottage for tea sometime?"

"Of course. I would love that."

"Good. I think we're going to be good friends. I never really had a friend when I was here." She walked to her horse, which had been grazing close by, then waved and flung her leg over the horse's back.

The women watched Raquel ride back down the path to her village. Myah touched Pamela's hand. "Now do you see how much trouble she can cause?"

"What do you mean?" Pamela answered.

"Were you listening to her suggestions: She wants cars and electricity and pollution."

Pamela shrugged. She was thinking of other things, like why she suddenly missed seeing Saul. "Well, I wouldn't worry about that. She can't change the way we live. No one wants that sort of thing here. We've enjoyed living this way for more than a hundred years. Don't even give it a second thought. She'll get tired

THE OTHER SIDE OF THE MOUNTAIN

of the things that are a nuisance to her and eventually leave."

Mary had been watching the interaction between Pamela and Raquel the entire time. "Are you sure you want to get close to that woman?" she asked Pamela.

"Why do you ask?"

"Just watching out for my friend. I don't want you to get hurt."

Pamela looked into Mary's eyes and shook her head. "There's nothing to worry about. No one will get hurt."

"Are you sure?"

"Yes."

"What are you guys talking about?" Myah asked.

As Esther and the other women left to go to the weaving hut, Esther threw a backward glance at her daughter and waved.

"Thanks, Mama," Pamela said waving back.

Myah repeated her question.

"Raquel wanting to be friends with Pamela," Mary said.

Pamela looked at her and smiled. Nice cover.

"Pammy's an intelligent woman. Raquel can't put anything over on her the way she did to so many of us who were not as wise to her as we now are."

Pamela had not gone night riding since Saul left. Now, walking down to the beach in the late afternoon, she watched the quiet waters slip onto shore as seagulls landed and took off from the rocks.

Taking off her sandals, she walked at the water's edge and kicked at the cool water. She thought of Saul and why she had not entered into another relationship since the passing of her husband. It wasn't for lack of opportunity or suitors. The problem was that they all came up short when compared to Peter. At least, they had until she met Saul. He was in a class all by himself. He was interesting and beautiful and intelligent. She thought of his smile and saw the imperfection of his slightly twisted front teeth. His voice was smooth, and when she looked into his eyes there was a certain something, a wanting or a willingness, maybe, or a need to please. Magnetism, yes, that's what it was. But there was something else, a kind of loneliness. The sun was sliding downward. She was about to start home when she saw Tim.

"I haven't been following you," he said, walking along the shoreline with his pants legs hiked up.

She laughed. "Hi, I haven't seen you in a while. Where have you been hiding?"

He didn't answer the question. "Did you hear that Saul's wife is back?" He sat down.

"You know better than that, Tim. She's no longer his wife. The commitment has been broken for a long

THE OTHER SIDE OF THE MOUNTAIN

time now." She sat beside him. "Why have you been so distant these days?"

"I haven't been distant. I've been a bit busy. You do remember that I work in Jamaica, too, right."

"Yes, I know."

"Anyway, the talk is that she's come to try and win him back."

"You mean she wants to remarry him?" She looked up at him.

"I knew he was bad news, and that's why I told you to be careful."

She shook her head. "Timothy, what are you going on about? Saul isn't here. He doesn't know Raquel is on the island. You seem to be blaming him for something that he hasn't done."

He knew that she was upset when she called him Timothy. "If it weren't for him there wouldn't have been a rift in our relationship with our neighbors."

"Why do you hate him? He's not the bad guy in this story." Her voice held a bitterness that made him look at her with a frown.

"Because you don't know him, Pam. He brought this woman to the island. Did he think he was too good for the Rahjah women?"

"What's wrong with you? He made a mistake. It could happen to anyone."

"Not to me. When I commit, it will be to someone who respects my culture. It will be for life."

JANICE ANGELIQUE

She shook her head. *You need to be committed.*

He looked at her angrily. "Is there something going on between you two?"

"Like what?"

"You tell me." He stood, his face distorted with anger.

"Where is this coming from, Tim? Saul is my friend, just like you are my friend."

"How far will the friendship between you and Saul go?" he demanded.

"That's my business. How dare you speak to me like that? I don't have to answer to you for my actions."

"He will hurt you, Pam. Don't start anything." He walked away without so much as a backward glance.

Whatever she did with her life was none of Tim's business, but she didn't want to lose his friendship. She took a deep breath and wished Saul had never left for work. She wanted him here to tell Raquel to go away.

She whistled for her horse and waited for him to come to her. He galloped to her and she jumped onto his bare back and rode him hard up the mountain to the village.

It was suppertime and there was a full moon. She stood on her verandah and stared at the moon wondering if Saul was staring at the same moon and thinking of her. She glanced at the flowers in her garden and their colors looked more vibrant in the moonlight.

THE OTHER SIDE OF THE MOUNTAIN

She didn't hear the children when they ran up to her to lead her toward the circle.

Gracie had promised the twins that she would share her mother with them, so, on their way to supper, they lovingly held Pamela's hands while Gracie walked ahead of them.

"We must have both villages celebrate our reunion," Pamela told her mother after she'd sat down.

"That's a wonderful idea," Esther said.

"When do you think?"

"Next week, Saturday."

"Okay."

They loved to celebrate anything at the drop of a hat, and this was a very big hat. Pamela had thought of the time and factored in Saul's return. She laughed. "This is going to be a lot of fun," she said, glancing at Mary and Myah.

She couldn't wait to dance with Saul again. Her thoughts were interrupted by the sounds of approaching riders, as they looked to see Myah's mother and father approaching. Myah quickly got up to greet them.

Two more cushions were added to the circle and Nanuk and Daniel joined them for supper. Esther told them Pamela's idea and instantly they began planning the festivities. Soon the entire circle was abuzz with the news of the upcoming celebration. Everyone wanted to have a hand in it. Myah leaned over and whispered into Pamela's ear, "Do we have to invite you-know-who?"

Pamela whispered back. "Yes, we do. You don't have to forget what she's done, but it would do you good to forgive her. Be the bigger person."

"I don't feel like the bigger person right now," Myah said.

Pamela leaned over and hugged her. "I know." She took a deep breath and smiled. "Let's eat."

"We always have something to look forward to, don't we?" Mary said.

"If we don't, we make it happen," Pamela replied.

∞

The next evening after supper, Pamela encouraged David and Ruth to spend some time with their mother. Seeing the sadness on Gracie and Shaela's face, she said, "You can go with them, Gracie, but Shaela, you'll have to ask…"

For the first time since she'd met the twins, Gracie didn't seem enthused to go home with them. She looked at Ruth. "Please, Gracie, for me."

Pamela stood and listened.

Gracie took a while to answer then she nodded. She looked at Shaela. Shaela nodded and trotted off in her mother's direction.

THE OTHER SIDE OF THE MOUNTAIN

It didn't take long for her to get back with an answer. "If Gracie is going, then I can go, too," an out-of-breath Shaela relayed to Pamela.

Pamela smiled, but the smile vanished when she remembered what Gracie had said about Raquel. Nevertheless, she got the children packed and rode with them to the village.

Raquel was more excited to see Pamela than her children, but they were none the wiser. David and Ruth rushed into the cottage, hailed their mother and proceeded to their room with Gracie and Shaela.

"Does he always follow Gracie around?" Raquel asked Pamela.

She laughed and leaned against the white verandah railing. "No, he plays a lot with the other boys, but he keeps close to his sister."

Raquel nodded. "I'm having a glass of wine, would you like some?"

Pamela looked at Raquel's long black hair moving slightly in the gentle evening breeze and her rich, red lips. Her body was more slender than that of any other young woman in both villages. She wore a fitted pink blouse and equally tight pants. Actually, her shape was that of a young boy.

"No, thanks. What else do you have?"

"Some kind of a fruit drink they made and sent up for me." She walked back into the cottage. Pamela followed her.

"Don't you eat with the others?"

Raquel shrugged. "They don't really like me, so no. But they bring my meals to me."

Pamela took the drink Raquel offered. "You know, if you try to associate with them they may change their opinion of you."

Raquel shrugged. "Maybe. I've asked if there is anything they want me to do, but they always tell me no."

"Don't ask, just do whatever they're doing. You talk about all the different meals you can prepare, so why don't you prepare some for them?" She began walking back to the verandah. "Start with small things. There must be someone in the village that you talk with."

"Yes, her name is Ludy."

"Okay, start with Ludy. She'll spread the word of your cooking. The villagers don't want to be mean to you. They would like to forgive you if you just show them you're open to forgiveness."

Raquel leaned against the rail and looked at Pamela. "Have they been talking about me?"

"No."

"Then how do you know I need forgiveness?"

Smiling, Pamela held her gaze until she looked away.

"Okay, so I did some stuff."

"I don't need to know what, but try going to breakfast with the children tomorrow." She finished her

THE OTHER SIDE OF THE MOUNTAIN

drink and walked inside with the glass. "Do you drink wine all the time?"

"Almost every evening. I like the taste."

Pamela nodded.

The children had gone out to be with the other children, so Pamela went to kiss them all goodnight. Ruth and David both hugged her tight. "Do you have to leave?" David asked, looking into her eyes.

"Yes, but I'll see you tomorrow."

He seemed reluctant to let her go. She bent and kissed his cheek. "It will be all right."

He nodded, released her and went back to playing the Scrabble game his father had brought for them. There were three sets of Scrabble being played under the bright tiki lamps.

Pamela walked to the rocky edge of the mountain with Raquel and listened to more stories before she said goodnight.

Chapter 10

Days had passed since the announcement of the festivities, and preparations were in full swing for Saturday night. There was even talk of people from as far as Rahjah Blue Mountain attending. The village pathway was already brightly decorated with tiki lamps and candles placed in colored paper bags just waiting to be lit. The menu was planned. Even the Elders were excited.

Thursday after supper Pamela went riding down to the beach. She got off her horse and began walking to the rocky side of the beach where she'd never been before. She climbed the rocks, sat down, placed her elbows on her knees and her hands to her chin. She'd finished the book by Ian Fleming and the history books. She'd looked at the books in Saul's library but knew she couldn't borrow any without his permission; at least that's what she told herself.

The sun had already hidden its face and darkness was descending, but she didn't feel like going back to the village just yet. She leaned back on the rocks and closed her eyes.

She felt the presence of someone and hoped to Jah that Tim had not followed her. She thought it was probably Mary. She slowly opened her eyes, then suddenly sat upright. "Oh, Jah! Is it you? Is it really you?"

Saul held her hand and pulled her to him. "It's really me, my princess." He hugged her tight.

His shirt front was open, exposing his beautiful, almost hairless chest, and, as her arms went around his neck, her face brushed against his chest. She buried her face in his neck, inhaled his scent and hugged him. "You're not supposed to come back until Saturday. But I'm so glad you're back. I missed you." She breathed a kiss on his neck.

He laughed and held her at bay to look in her face. "Really? Because I thought of no one else but you every day that I was away." He gently held her face in his warm hands. "I would like to do this. I must, please."

She closed her eyes. "Yes, please," she breathed shakily.

He kissed her forehead, her eyes, her nose, and, finally, his mouth moved thoughtfully over her lips. Her lips were soft and warm and sweet and without his tongue penetrating her mouth he lingered, enjoying her sweet breath upon his face, the sweet taste of guava jam on her lips. He sucked a little at her lips and she shivered.

And as his tongue slowly entered her mouth, it felt like warm, sweet cherry sauce, slowly going through layers and layers of her skin, making her drunk as dormant desires awoke and raced through her veins

JANICE ANGELIQUE

screaming for more of him. Suddenly, being afraid that her body would betray her, she backed away.

Not knowing what he'd done, he whispered her name. "Pam."

She turned and raised a shaky finger to stop him from talking. She liked the feelings going through her. Actually, she loved them. She wanted more. Before he could say another word, she ran back into his embrace and recaptured his warm mouth, drank some more from the velvet cup of delicious forbidden sensations that made her knees weak. Never before had she ever been kissed like that.

His lips moved hesitantly from her mouth to the pulsing hollow at the base of her throat and her head swam with need as she clutched him to her.

"Where did you learn to do that?" she whispered breathlessly.

He smiled and lifted her in the air. "I've wanted to kiss you from the very moment we met and sat together."

"Why didn't you?" She felt lightheaded. She sat and pulled him down beside her.

"Would you have slapped my face?" He looked into her face and smiled warmly.

"I don't think so."

He laughed.

"How did you know I'd be here?" Her voice was just above a whisper.

THE OTHER SIDE OF THE MOUNTAIN

"I went to the village and asked Mary."

She gasped. "Did anyone else hear you?"

"No one else saw me in the village. I wanted to surprise you. I haven't even been home yet."

"You came to see me first?" Her eyes opened with wonder.

"Yes." He nodded. "I came to see the one person other than my children who brought me back home."

She laughed. "Of course." Then she took a breath. She still held his hand. "Then you don't know that Raquel is in your village." She felt him tense. Suddenly his face went grim as a cold expression settled there. She'd spoilt the moment. She waited for him to say something, but it took him more than a minute to speak. When he did, his tone was serious and his contempt for Raquel unmasked.

"Do you know when she got here?"

"The day after you left."

He nodded, took a deep breath and looked at her. She smiled at him and the light in her eyes made him smile. "I told her that she could visit the children anytime she wished. She came to see the children. They don't ask about her anymore, but I'm sure they've wondered about her." And that was the end of that conversation. "Have you finished the books I gave you?" He placed a hand around her shoulders and pulled her closer to him.

"Yes, I have."

In spite of the news he'd just received, just being with Pamela melted the anger he felt over Raquel being in his village. "Your thirst for knowledge is more than that of anyone I've ever known." He kissed the top her head, leaned over and produced a wrapped gift.

She tore the paper to see the book he'd promised her and two poetry books. "I love them. Thank you so much. I don't have anything for you."

He laughed. "Yes, you do."

She blushed and fidgeted.

"I want to go places with you and do things with you. I want to show you the world. Will you let me?"

He laughed and she knew it was from his heart. It sounded like the best music. "Yes."

He hugged her.

"Where exactly did you go this time?" she asked.

"I went to Italy and America."

"No Australia this time?"

"Not this time." He couldn't stop himself from laughing as he buried his face in her hair. "You smell so good." He got up and pulled her to her feet. She swayed against him as if dancing to her own music.

"We have a big celebration, or should I say reunion party, planned for Saturday." She let go of him, turned and took up her gift.

He stepped down off the rock and held out his arm. She smiled and went to him. He held her to his warm

THE OTHER SIDE OF THE MOUNTAIN

Suddenly his face went grim as a cold expression settled there.

"What?"

She was still in his arms, her arms around his neck with her feet dangling freely.

"Kissing you and holding you like this."

"I thought of you constantly, but I don't know why I missed the kissing part. If I'd known it would make me feel so happy and strange, I would have thought of it all the time."

She was back on her feet but their eyes were still locked. "I read enough so I should know how to express the way I feel." She was silent for a while as the wheels in her brain spun. She shook her head. "I can't find the words."

The strong hardness of his lips claimed hers and the delicious sensation spread through her entire body once again. Then his lips moved away like a whisper.

Her eyes were still closed and her face still turned up to him. "It's getting harder to describe," she breathed. "But do it again."

He laughed and reclaimed her lips. His body hardened against her and lust ran through him like an open flame. He moved slightly away from her and she opened her eyes, held his hand and walked to her horse. He kissed her again and lifted her onto her horse. "This was the best night. Thanks again for this." She held up the books. "And for coming back to me so soon." Then she remembered the drink she'd made. "I have something for you. It's in the river close to the village." Seeing the gleam of interest in his eyes, she laughed.

"I can't wait to see it or taste it."

"Taste," she said.

"Then it will be the best thing I've ever tasted in my life."

"I think you should taste it before you say that." He was making her nervous with his gaze fixed on her.

He bowed gracefully. She laughed and galloped away. He had walked all the way to see her, and now he resumed his walk with a smile on his lips, a gladness in his heart and a lilt in his step until he thought of what was waiting for him when he got home. Just when he'd begun seeing the sun again, Raquel had to appear like a black cloud.

⊰⊱

Neither had seen Tim standing close to the beach watching. He was shocked to see her and Saul together like that. As a matter of fact, he'd never seen her with anyone before except her husband, and it made him angry. His face was marked with loathing for Saul and his expression turned vicious. He didn't think Saul deserved a woman like Pamela. He'd thought himself too good for the Rahjah women so he'd married Raquel and brought disgrace to his people and himself. The

THE OTHER SIDE OF THE MOUNTAIN

more Tim thought of Saul, the more he felt hatred for him and the more he wanted to protect Pamela from him. Pamela was his. He took a deep breath and angrily stomped away before Pamela rode up the mountainside. He could no longer watch the interaction between her and Saul.

※

In bed, Pamela licked her lips. She closed her eyes and there he was. She felt his kiss on her lips and she breathed, "Oh, Jah." Just the thought of him made her body come alive and her hand brushed her taut nipples. Surprised at the sensation going through her, she rolled on her side and took a deep breath to clear her head but, as she exhaled slowly, there he was again holding her, smiling at her, not letting up on the wonderful feeling going through her. "Oh, Jah," she said again and closed her eyes.

※

With his suitcase in hand, Saul hesitantly climbed the steps to his cottage. It wasn't that late, so he knew the children weren't asleep and he needed to see them before he saw Raquel. He pushed the door open and the first thing that greeted him was his ex-wife staring at him. She smiled broadly, but didn't move toward him from her perch on the cushion. "You're back. I thought you'd be back on Saturday."

"Hello, Raquel. How are you?" His voice was calm, controlled.

"I'm great. You're not glad to see me? You said I could…"

"And I meant it. It's good to see you. Are you enjoying your visit with the children?" Now his voice took on a more casual tone.

"Yes." She was surprised at his casualness. She'd thought their meeting would be more touching, a little romantic even.

Saul placed his suitcase on the floor in the living room, smiled and tiptoed to the children's room. He slowly pushed the door open and poked his head in. David was the first to see him. He jumped off the bed and rushed into his arms. "Dada, Dada, you're home."

Ruth followed. Both children were in their father's arms talking over each other. Gracie and Shaela were still sitting on the bed. He beckoned to them. "My arms are long enough for everyone."

The twins made space for Gracie and Shaela. Saul thought he was a strong man, but with all four children pulling at him purposely, he fell to the ground, laughing and listening to them scream in his ear. This was a perfect homecoming. "I have gifts for everyone," he said.

"Even me?" Gracie said.

THE OTHER SIDE OF THE MOUNTAIN

"Even you, Gracie, and you, too, Shaela." He sat cross-legged on the floor, answered everyone's questions and listened to them talk about the upcoming festivities. Gracie opened a bottle of guava jam and gave him a huge spoonful. He ate it and laughed. That was what he'd tasted on Pamela's lips.

"We made it," Gracie said. She pointed to everyone. "We all made it. We were saving this one for you alone." She sat on one leg while the twins sat on the other. Shaela sat on the floor in front of him.

"Do you want to see your gifts now?" he asked.

They jumped off his legs and he went out to the living room. They didn't follow. Raquel was sitting with a glass of wine in her hand. "I'm just going to get their gifts," he said to her.

She nodded. "Then will you talk with me?"

He stopped and looked at her. "Of course." He was still smiling. He reached into his suitcase and then walked back into the children's room with a handful of gifts. He'd gotten books and chocolate candy for everyone. He'd brought enough sweets for all the children in the village, but now there was a flaw in his gift-giving. There was another village of children. He would go to work tomorrow making chocolate. He couldn't cook as well as his father or the other men in the village, but he could make chocolate better than anyone.

After the children had settled down, he walked out into the living room to talk with Raquel. She patted the cushion beside her and he could tell she was intoxicated. Her drinking had been one of their biggest problems. Every time she went away, she'd bring back a lot of wine. Even though he occasionally took a glass of wine, he'd refused to drink with her. No other woman that he knew in the village drank, so she drank by herself.

He sat beside her.

"Pour me more wine, please." She held out her glass.

He shook his head. "Don't you think you've had enough?"

"I've had enough when I say I've had enough. Now pour."

He looked at her, then touched her hand. "That's fine, you can drink, but I won't give you any more."

"That's the problem. You always force me to do what you want me to do."

He could have sat there and listened to her drunken ranting, but he didn't want to. He knew she'd soon fall asleep. He got up and carried his suitcase into his room. He opened the closet door to see all her clothes hanging in his closet and most of his clothes on the floor or pushed to the corner. He sighed and closed the door. He changed into jeans and a t-shirt and walked back into the living room. She was stretched out on two cushions. He threw a blanket over her and walked down to the river. He peeled off his clothes and

THE OTHER SIDE OF THE MOUNTAIN

jumped in. The cold water felt refreshing against his skin. He swam for a while, then went back home to see Raquel in his bed. He picked up a blanket and his night clothes and made himself comfortable on cushions in his library. There were four bedrooms, but he felt like sleeping in the library.

⊗

The children were so excited that their father was back from his trip that as soon as they awoke they ran to his room. They saw their mother lying alone in his bed. They backed out noiselessly and began to look for him all over the house. They found him asleep in the library. Gracie knelt and peered at him and when they heard him snore, they laughed.

Saul took a deep breath and opened his eyes. He pushed back his hair from his face and grinned when he saw the children.

"We're going to get ready for breakfast. Are you up?" David said.

He sat up. "Of course I'm up. I dreamt of fried dumplings with ackee and codfish. Is it Friday?"

Ruth nodded.

"Then it's ackee and dumpling day. Are you going to wake your mother?" He looked at his children, who seemed to shrink in size at the mention of Raquel, as did their friends.

"She's mean when she drinks," Ruth said.

He was surprised that she'd again drunk in front of the children, but he said nothing. He patted her cheek. "Okay, you go get ready for breakfast."

The children left the library and he got up and pulled on his jeans and shirt. He walked to his bedroom. Raquel was still asleep. He had not noticed the empty glass on the floor last night. She'd had another glass of wine before she'd climbed into his bed. He pulled the door closed behind him, walked to the verandah and breathed in the sweet mountain air. Every time he came home, he appreciated it more. But, more than anything, he wanted to take Pamela for a trip around the world, one country at a time, starting with the one she feared most, Jamaica. He smiled and bit into his lower lip. Jah, he could still taste her. He closed his eyes for just a second and saw her face, her eyes gazing into his. He felt his muscles tighten in places they shouldn't and he took a deep breath and opened his eyes. He had to be very careful how and where he thought of this goddess who could put him in a tailspin without even trying. That slow kiss would not leave his thoughts. Somehow, he really didn't want it to.

The smell of frying dumplings drifted through the air. He pushed his hands into his pockets and walked to the kitchen, snuck up behind his mother and hugged her waist. She didn't even turn but reached behind and patted his cheek. "Welcome home, son."

THE OTHER SIDE OF THE MOUNTAIN

"Can't you even act surprised?" He picked up a dumpling and bit into it.

"I could, but then I'd be faking it. I saw you on the verandah last night."

He leaned against the iron stove and looked up at the black chimney. The heat from the stove quickly seeped into his skin and he jumped away and leaned against the table.

His mother shook her head. "I'm sorry you had to come home to her."

He laughed and pushed the entire little dumpling into his mouth. "It doesn't matter."

She took a good look at his smiling face. He was genuinely happy. "Is there something you want to tell me, son?"

He took a deep breath and reached for another dumpling. She slapped his hand. "It's Pammy."

"From the village?" She stopped chopping the callaloo and turned and leaned against the table.

He nodded. "She's wonderful. She was right under my nose all the time and I didn't know."

"And now you do."

"Yes."

"She's a very intelligent woman."

"I know."

"Does she know how you feel about her?"

"Judging from last night, I think she feels the same way about me."

She motioned toward his cottage. "She came back to be with you again."

"That book has been written, Mom. We all know the ending. It cannot be rewritten."

Nanuk nodded. "You may have to shield Pam from Raquel. She can be violent, we all know that."

"Don't say anything to anyone, not even Dad."

She smiled. "My lips are sealed."

He kissed her damp cheek.

It was still cool outside. The sun's rays were shining through the trees like an airplane bursting through dark clouds. He walked to his cottage while the food was being brought to the table. He didn't have to go inside, the children came out.

At breakfast, his thoughts were only of Pam and their kisses. He'd never wanted to stop holding or kissing her. His fingers lingered on his lips and his eyes held a faraway look.

Nanuk watched him. "Are you eating or dreaming, son?"

He looked at her and laughed. "Both."

Since it was the day before the festivities, everyone in the village was busy with the preparations. Saul wanted very much to see Pam but he knew she'd be busy, so he did his part by making chocolate for the children and stayed away from the cottage all day.

THE OTHER SIDE OF THE MOUNTAIN

Pamela tried her best to stay away from the kitchen as much as possible, which wasn't hard since all she did was daydream about Saul. She could still smell his scent in her hair, and every now and again she would catch a lock, slide it across her nostrils and inhale.

◈

Saturday morning at breakfast, Mary leaned toward Pam and asked, "Did he find you Thursday night?"

"Yes. Thank you."

"That's it?"

She laughed and looked at her plate of fruit. "Do you want the details?"

"I guess not."

Pamela nodded. "It's been a long time since I've been this excited about anything."

"Today's festivities?"

"What else." Pamela glanced at her friend and smiled.

"If I didn't know you, I'd say you were trying to hide something."

"You know me, do you?"

Chapter 11

After breakfast everything went fast. The steel drums once again were in their places. Musicians climbed the mountains with their instruments and were met with hugs and good-hearted slaps on the back. Horse-drawn buggies brought highly polished tableware from which to eat, and vessels of food, drink and spices for the finishing touches. People who'd not been to the island in years came in from Jamaica's Blue Mountain to hugs and tears. The kitchen wasn't big enough for all the preparation, so a makeshift kitchen was set up outside with iron stoves and wooden tables.

The delicious smell of cakes and puddings wafted through the air. Pamela wished she could cook like the older women. Her mother laughed at her as she went around picking at the food. "By the time the festivities begin you'll be too full to eat a proper meal," she said.

"That's what you think," Pamela replied.

Even the children joined in the making of bread. Under the supervision of her mother, Pamela made two cornmeal puddings, poured a cherry sauce mixed with coconut milk on top and pushed it back in the oven for a few more minutes. For the past couple of

THE OTHER SIDE OF THE MOUNTAIN

weeks she'd been spending more time in the kitchen watching the other women cook and bake. One of her aunts had asked her, "What's your sudden interest in cooking, Pammy?"

"If I get hungry in the middle of the night, it's nice to know that I can make something without thinking I'll poison myself."

She laughed. "No one ever gets hungry in the middle of the night after one of our huge suppers, except a pregnant woman." She looked suspiciously at her niece.

Pamela shook her head. "Don't even think about it."

She pulled her puddings out of the oven, placed them on the table and smiled at her mother. "How do they look?"

"Great, but you know the taste…"

"Is in the eating," she finished. "You're so funny. They will be excellent. I can't wait to taste them myself."

"Me, either," Mary said.

"Do you think you can get along without me, Mama? I think it's time for me to start getting ready."

Esther nodded. "I think we can, and I promise no one will touch your puddings. By the way, where have you been hiding your sorrel drink?"

Pamela froze in the doorway of the kitchen. She'd thought everyone had forgotten about her drink. Her eyes shifted from Mary to her mother. "Ahhh, I..." She let out a breath of air and smiled again.

"Pammy," her mother said. "What's going on? Have you drank it all already?"

She squeezed her eyes shut and breathed again. "No. Didn't you have any?"

Esther shook her head, folded her arms and leaned against the table.

"I'm saving it."

"For what?"

"For tonight." Thinking that was enough, she shrugged and left the kitchen.

Pamela looked in on Gracie and Shaela getting ready. They were wearing the new clothes that had been made for them, and Pamela had to admit that they looked very pretty in blue and white frocks. "Try not to get dirty before the festivities begin," Pamela said to both girls.

"We'll stay in the room until you tell us to go outside," Gracie said, sitting with the rabbit in her lap.

"You and these animals," Pamela said. "Your aunts and I are going to get ready now." She walked to her room and looked at the dress she'd made, which was laying on the bed. It was slightly more form-fitting with a belt to match. She wondered if any of the women would think it was too form fitting, but Myah and Mary had made theirs almost the same way with dif-

THE OTHER SIDE OF THE MOUNTAIN

ferent colors. She made a face. Was she trying to look like Raquel? She sat on the bed and stared at the dress.

Mary called to her. "Are you coming?"

"Yes." She picked up the dress, placed it over her arm and walked with Mary and Myah to the river. "Do you think our dresses are too tight?" she asked no one in particular.

A resounding "No!" came from Myah.

She felt better knowing that Myah had no idea of her feelings for Saul.

They carefully placed their dresses on a nearby tree and stripped. This part of the river where they always bathed was off limits to men. Pamela took her time washing her hair with lavender oil, and then dove under the water and came up shaking the water from her thick, long locks.

They sat on the rocks and gently patted their locks dry. Pamela pulled her hair into a pile on the top of her head and held it in place with a turtle-shell comb, then got dressed. Without a mirror, each woman appraised the other. It was time to present themselves.

"By the way," Mary said, "where did you hide the sorrel?"

Pamela smiled. "At the top of the waterfall."

Mary nodded and smiled. "I have a feeling we won't be getting another taste."

"Only if I feel generous. There are two bottles left."

"I didn't get much," Myah said.

"I'll have to see to that," Pamela said.

They broke through the trees to see the village filled with people. One thing about the Rahjahs, they were extremely punctual. Pamela scanned the crowd for Saul, but didn't see him.

"Wow!" Mary said under her breath. "If I wasn't married I would certainly have my pick of gorgeous men tonight. I don't think I've ever seen some of these people before."

Myah saw and recognized James, a very handsome, famous architect from Rahjah Blue Mountain. She pointed him out to the women and began telling them about him. "He could be all yours if he wasn't already committed to the woman beside him," she said to Pamela.

But Pamela was more interested in the woman because her hair wasn't locked. "How many of our men marry outside of our culture?"

"Well, they leave to attend the university or just to travel and inevitably fall in love," Myah said.

"Saul didn't meet Raquel on a university campus. I think they met at a function," Pamela said, then bit her lip.

"No. Boy, was that union a huge mistake," Myah said.

Pamela shrugged.

The steel drums began playing and the tambourines and guitars joined in to make a reggae beat.

THE OTHER SIDE OF THE MOUNTAIN

There was an array of colors and hairstyles and sandaled feet. Pamela smoothed her dress with her moist palms, looked at her friends and walked toward her cottage. She knew Gracie would still be in her room.

She peeped in and saw Gracie and Shaela with the twins. "You can go and mingle anytime you wish," Pamela said.

Gracie nodded, pushed off her bed and led the children outside. Pamela walked back out to Myah and Mary. Myah broke through the crowd to introduce them to James. She said something in his ear. He turned and looked directly at Pamela. He smiled and Pamela understood why Myah thought he was such an awesome catch. His hair was pulled back in a ponytail and his face was clean-shaven. He was a handsome man, but still not as handsome as Saul. She shook his hand and he said his name in her ear. "I am your first cousin," he said.

She nodded and saw his wife coming towards her. Angel hugged her. "So you're the one responsible for all this," she said in her ear.

"I only suggested it," Pamela replied.

"You're being too modest." Angel stood very close to Pamela and held her eyes. "You did a wonderful thing for your people. I would love to talk with you some more, maybe tomorrow. I don't have to fly back to New York for a while."

Pamela's eyes lit up. "You flew from America just for this?"

Angel laughed and nodded.

"I would love to talk to you. I can come to see you…" Then she remembered that Angel and James were staying on Rahjah Blue Mountain. "Maybe you can come back here before you go back to America."

Angel nodded. She looked at James and he nodded. Then Pamela's eyes met Saul's and her entire demeanor changed. She was so nervous she was afraid everyone would be able to discern her feelings for him. He looked more handsome than ever with his hair pulled back from his face. He smiled and she melted.

Angel's eyes followed Pamela's and she smiled and moved away as Saul came to Pamela.

Saul kissed Pamela's cheek and whispered in her ear, "You're the most beautiful woman here."

She blushed. "Have you seen everyone?"

He gazed into her eyes and laughed. "You're doing something to me."

"What?"

"I'm not sure, but don't stop."

She shook her head and turned him towards Angel and James. He laughed and slapped James on the back and then turned to Angel. "How are you? I'm so glad you could make it. How is Hildie?"

THE OTHER SIDE OF THE MOUNTAIN

"She's great. She sends her regrets. She would have loved to come but had a prior engagement."

He nodded. "I'm sure I'll see her on my next visit to New York."

"You know each other?" Pamela asked.

Saul chuckled. "Are you joking? Angel is the most outspoken woman I've ever met. She made history on the Blue Mountain." He glanced at Pamela and Angel laughed.

The laugh disappeared when Raquel walked over. "Aren't you going to introduce me to your relatives, Saul?" Her painted eyes seem to drink in James. Her face looked flawless under her makeup and her straight black hair, as long as it was, didn't seem to move with the evening's soft breeze.

"Of course." He introduced her to Angel, then James. Ignoring the fact that his wife was beside him, she held James's hand in an overly familiar manner and laughed when he told her she was beautiful. He slowly removed his hand from hers and smiled just as he saw Tim. He turned and greeted him with a slap on the back, ignoring Raquel. Tim hugged Pamela. "Save a dance for me. You look wonderful."

"Thank you," she said casually, treating him the way she always did. Like a brother. He touched her hand and walked away with Saul and James as if they were his dearest friends.

The women turned and made way as the evening's festivities began with the children coming into the center of the circle to dance. They were all in white with orange scarves tied to their hair. The band played pocomania and the children danced an African dance taught to them by their teacher Hildigarth. When the dance was finished and the children ran from the circle, Hildigarth sang a rendition of an old Jamaican folk song. When she was finished, one of the band members sang a Bob Marley song, which turned again into pocomania.

Finger food was passed around on huge trays. Tiny fried dumplings with jam for dipping, seasoned fish balls, roasted potato balls, berries, sliced mango, pineapples, nesberries and an array of vegetables were quickly snatched off the platters.

The circle closed as the entertainers left the center and the floor opened for dancing.

"I think we should dance," Raquel said, taking James's hand. He'd come back to dance with his wife.

James glanced at Angel and she smiled. "Why not?"

Pamela had never met a more confident woman. She looked at Angel and smiled. Angel shrugged. "I trust him with all my heart. I've heard about her."

"He has eyes only for you?" Pamela asked.

"Yes."

THE OTHER SIDE OF THE MOUNTAIN

Pamela glanced at Saul, he smiled and for a moment, She wished she could capture the entire evening on canvas.

She saw flashes of light within the crowd. "What's that?"

Angel smiled. "You've never seen a camera?"

She shook her head. "What does it do?"

Saul came close to her. "It makes pictures of people on film, which is then transferred to paper."

Pamela was quiet. She didn't want to seem foolish next to Angel. With Raquel hanging off his arm, James made his way back to where they stood. She laughed, glanced at Saul, and laughed some more as they got closer. "He's a wonderful dancer," she said.

"I know," Angel said.

"Aren't you going to dance with me?" Raquel asked Saul.

"Why not? This is such a wonderful evening." He glanced at Pamela and she smiled. Raquel dragged him to where a few people were dancing.

"I thought he was with you?" Angel said.

Pamela smiled but didn't say anything.

"We do know their story, you know," Angel said.

"I only know they're no longer married," Pamela said. "Saul didn't speak much of her until she showed up more than a week ago."

Tim seized the moment and caught Pamela around her waist. He whispered in her ear, "Do you want to dance?"

She laughed and nodded.

"I'm your guy." He moved her onto the dance floor, only once glancing at Saul. Even though the music had a fast beat, he drew her close to him. She looked up at him, laughed and gently pushed away from him.

When the music stopped, she purposely guided them back to where Angel stood with Mary. "Thanks for the dance," she said, smiling up at him.

Pamela glanced at Angel as Mary began talking about the food.

"You have to taste your pudding before it's all gone. It's your best yet."

"I thought Esther said she wouldn't cut it until I did."

"She didn't, Myah did. And speak of the little devil…"

Myah handed a plate to Pamela and one to Angel. "I thought I'd snag these before it was all gone."

They laughed and Pamela tasted her handiwork. "Yes, I really outdid myself."

Angel agreed. "I have to tell you, I didn't know how to cook until I met the Rahjahs. And this was about ten years ago."

"Then it's not too late for me," Pamela said.

The women shook their heads.

Before the music stopped, Saul made his way back to Pamela and asked her to dance. "But I wasn't finished dancing with you," Raquel protested.

Saul ignored her. "I want to put my arms around you," he said in Pamela's ear.

"I'm not too comfortable dancing with you in front of her."

"Pam, we're no longer married. She's moved on and so have I. She came here to visit her children, that's all."

She nodded. "Sorry."

"Don't be, it's all right."

When they got close to the band, he nodded to the drummer and the music changed to a waltz. He held her close and moved his cheek against hers. "I waited all day to hold you," he said, gazing at her. She smiled up at him wordlessly. She didn't want to admit to him that she'd also waited all day just to be close to him.

Raquel stood fuming. She had danced with James just to make Saul jealous. Now he was dancing with Pamela. She stood staring at them, wondering if that was why he'd been so nice to her. He had found Pamela. She made her way back through the crowd. Angel glanced at James and he shook his head. "The things I do for you," he said and hurried towards Raquel. On reaching her, he caught her hand and began dancing with her at arm's length. She smiled and he threw his

JANICE ANGELIQUE

wife a look. She smiled back and blew him a kiss. His eyes seemed to say, "You owe me big for this."

Tim was standing beside Angel. She looked at him and laughed. "I know you're not going to stand there and let a good song go to waste. Ask me to dance."

He laughed. "It is true what they say about you."

She took his hand and led him to the dance floor. "Of course. I never let a good song go to waste."

He laughed but secretly wished he could snatch Pamela from Saul's arms.

Saul saw Raquel and moved farther away from her, holding Pamela close. "Will tomorrow be too soon for us to begin our travels?" he said in her ear.

"As soon as that?"

"Are you busy?"

"No, but I wanted to visit with Angel and…"

"Perfect. I'll take you to Rahjah Blue Mountain first then."

"I…"

"Don't be afraid. I won't let anything happen to you in Jamaica."

"I don't think I have the right clothes for Jamaica, or any place outside of Rahjah Village for that matter."

"I'll buy you clothes."

"I have my own money."

"I know you do, but I would like to do this."

She didn't want him to see the fear of traveling in her eyes. She nodded. "Should I pack?"

"No, just come away with me. Mary or your mother won't mind looking after little Gracie."

"What about your children?"

"They'll be fine. I'll talk with my mother."

"I haven't said anything to my parents."

He slid a finger under her chin and brought her face up. "Are you afraid of what they'll say?"

She looked into his smiling eyes. "No, but I have to let Mama know my plans so that she can have one of the other teachers fill in for me."

"That won't take long." He studied her thoughtfully for a moment. His eyes drank in her beauty, her well-formed lips rouged by cherry juice, her high cheekbones and her liquid brown eyes. "You're making excuses."

To ease her nervousness, she laughed. "What's the hurry?"

"I want to have you all to myself, not just to see you for a few minutes before you run away."

"Are you dying?"

"I may die if you say no."

She looked for a smile, a wink, but all she saw was the softness of the night he'd kissed her. "You'll take care of me?"

"With my whole heart and soul."

"Okay. I'll come to the boat tomorrow evening after supper."

His entire face lit up and he hugged her.

Raquel tried to move James towards Saul, but he was too clever for her. He glanced once more at Angel dancing with Tim and shook his head. Then he looked at Raquel and smiled. This time she didn't smile back at him, so he stopped dancing. "Is everything all right?"

"Where are they?"

"Who?" he asked innocently.

"Saul and Pamela."

He turned around. "Oh, I don't see them. I'm sorry." He came face to face with a smiling Angel.

Tim had also left the circle.

"Do you mind if I have my husband back now?" Angel said to Raquel, who quickly moved through the crowd looking for Saul and Pamela.

"Good job, darling," she whispered in her husband's ear.

"I feel so used," he said in her ear.

"Oh, stop it. You were having fun protecting one of your own. You knew how much those two wanted to be together."

"You won't ever stop matchmaking, will you? How did you catch on so quickly?"

"I don't get the big bucks in New York as a shrink for standing around."

"I guess not." He spun his wife around the dance floor and kissed her.

THE OTHER SIDE OF THE MOUNTAIN

Everyone, including Raquel, stood still when they heard Saul's voice singing a love song. Pamela stood beside her grandmother, away from Raquel's eyes, and blushed because Saul was staring straight at her, singing to her. His voice echoed softly through the mountain, through the trees, carried back by the soft breeze. Jane patted her granddaughter's hand. She would certainly approve of the relationship if she knew there was one.

"I had no idea he could sing," Angel said to James.

"There are a lot of things people here don't know about him."

"I thought your people knew everything about the family."

James smiled. "We do, but not everyone knows everything about everyone."

"What?" Angel said.

"Oh, come on, Angel. We hardly bring the outside to the inside."

"But this."

"That's what I mean. They know, but you don't."

"That's a lot of double talk," Angel said.

"I know." He kissed her forehead.

Saul finished his song and walked into the crowd of cheering Rahjahs. Raquel hurried to where she thought he was but found it difficult going through the crowd and she lost sight of him once more.

Chapter 12

With two cups in her hand, Pamela led Saul to the waterfall. She pulled the bottle of sorrel from the cool water, uncorked it and poured it into the cups. "It's my first attempt at making this stuff, so be kind." She watched him take a careful sip, then another.

"And you're still alive." She laughed, causing him to almost spill the drink.

He coughed twice, then threw back his head and let out an uproarious peal of laughter that almost drowned out the sound of the steel drums. She couldn't control her own laughter. He took out a handkerchief and wiped the liquid from his face. She sat beside him on Gracie's thinking rock.

"I haven't been this happy in a very long time." He shook his head. "Thank you."

"Don't thank me. I didn't do anything, but I did have you in mind when I mentioned this reunion of the villagers."

"We could leave tonight."

She looked at him. "You *are* impetuous."

"Just lightheaded." He took another swallow of the sweet liquid and placed the cup on the ground.

"Where were you all those years when I grieved for my life?"

"Grieving for my own, I guess."

"And now here we are consoling each other in such a wonderful way."

Her hand brushed his face. "Am I really consoling you?"

"You're making tiny stitches in my heart."

The night sky was filled with twinkling stars and reggae music floated through the air. His hand brushed a loose lock of hair from her face and each moved toward the other's waiting lips, warm and inviting, seemingly hungry for a promise made not too long ago on a beach on the other side of the mountain. His lips pressed gently against her mouth, more persuasive than she cared to admit. Her hunger built, igniting a fire that soared through her body. Her breasts pressed against his hard chest, tingled, reawakening a sexual need long suppressed. She wrapped her arms around his neck and heard him groan. She wanted more of the delicious feeling going through her, and as her head swam, she was sure her entire body wanted all of him.

He pulled away, looked into her eyes, leaving her mouth burning and tingling; then he stood and drew her to him. His hard body pressed against her and as his mouth moved over hers, devouring its softness, a glowing heat traveled from her tender nipples to the softness below her belly and she shivered and clung to him. "What's happening to me?" she whispered.

He looked into her upturned face.

"I'm scared for us," she said breathlessly, holding his cheeks and planting urgent kisses on his eyelids, his cheeks and his forehead.

"Don't be afraid. I won't do anything you don't want me to do," he said, fighting his own lustful demands.

"That's the problem. I want you to do everything, but as much as I do, I don't want us to rush."

"I'm a big boy. Don't worry about me."

"Who's going to worry about me?"

He chuckled. Swaying her in his arms, he took a cleansing breath. "I'll be strong for both of us."

"Oh, Jah. And you want us to go away together, alone."

"Would you prefer a chaperone?"

"I think we'd eventually ditch them."

He laughed. "Once again I ask, where have you been all my life? Why did I have to go through all that unhappiness to get to heaven in your arms?"

"Is that rhetorical?"

He nodded. "I don't want to leave the warmth of your body, but maybe we should rejoin the others."

"Yes, we should."

He picked up one bottle of sorrel, and put the other back into the water. She drained her mug. Walking

THE OTHER SIDE OF THE MOUNTAIN

with their arms around each other they made their way back towards the party only to be met by Raquel. She was in a state.

"I came back to be with you and here you are with her." She pointed to Pamela and swayed with a glass of wine in her hand. "I thought you were my friend," she said, glaring at Pamela.

Raquel swayed again and Saul reached out and caught her. "Let go of me." She pushed him and threw the drink in his face.

He took a deep breath and wiped the liquid from his face with his hand just as Raquel lunged at Pamela. He quickly placed a hand between them. "Don't," he said in a stern voice, holding her hand. "Don't ever try that again." He turned to Pamela. "I'm sorry, Pam. Will you wait for me with the others?"

Embarrassed and angry, she nodded and hurried away, but she could still hear them.

"Why shouldn't I do that? Are you sleeping with her? She's your people, just across the river. Well, Saul, are you sleeping with her?"

"That is none of your business. I haven't asked you about your whereabouts…"

"I never loved you," Raquel interrupted. "but I came back to this land of ignorant people to see if we could start again."

Pamela froze.

"You're not making sense, Raquel. If you never loved me why did you come back?"

"Because you owe me."

He shook his head. "What do I owe you?" His voice was low and mocking.

"I left here with nothing, without alimony, without…"

"Alimony," he repeated. "You came back for money?" His voice held distaste and resentment.

"Why else do you think I'd come back to this backward place? For your children?" She laughed scornfully.

He stared at her, but wasn't as surprised at her words as he should have been. "If it's money you want, Raquel, give me a figure, then never come back here again. The children will be better off not being confused by your presence."

"Ten thousand American dollars."

"Done. And you'll leave this island forever."

That was too easy, she thought. "We're still married, you can't stop me from coming here."

"What is it about the word *divorced* that you don't understand, Raquel? We were married on this island, by my people. We made a promise to each other and the day you broke that promise was the day our marriage ended. We are divorced. We have no ties to each other except for our children. We stopped being man and wife a very long time ago."

THE OTHER SIDE OF THE MOUNTAIN

"We are over when I say so," she said, lunging at him, pulling her long nails across his cheek.

He caught her hand. "You love saying stuff like that, don't you? I won't fight you, Raquel. I won't hit you." His eyes flashed with controlled anger.

"Why not, you coward?"

He could feel the warm blood running down his face. He let go of her hand. "Go back to where you came from, Raquel. I can't be the type of man you're used to. I can't be who you want me to be." It was not the first time she'd hit him, begging for him to retaliate.

Pamela had turned just as Raquel screamed at Saul and lunged at him. Tears came to her eyes. She trembled with rage as her fists balled at her side. She wanted to go back and defend Saul, to defend her people, but her feet wouldn't move.

Raquel stumbled and Saul reached out his hand to prevent her from falling. She slapped his hand away and fell on her rear. He reached out to her again but she screamed, "You're weak. Get out of my sight."

Once again he reached out to help her up. "Did you hear me? Get away from me. You disgust me," she screamed at the top of her lungs. Fortunately her words were drowned out by the loud music.

Pamela stood and watched him walk towards her, leaving Raquel sitting on the damp grass.

"I'm sorry," he said.

She took the handkerchief from him and touched it to the scratch on his face.

"I should go home."

"No, please don't go. It's dark, no one will see it."

He smiled. "My family knows of the fights. She's done this before." He smiled. "She once scratched my neck so badly I had to wear my hair down until it healed just to hide it from the children." He showed her the scar and she ran her fingers along the lines of remembrance. He held her hand and kissed it.

"I'm sorry. I didn't know."

"Come home with me. I'll bring you back after the party, or when it starts breaking up. My parents will be the first to leave," he said.

They took her horse and he rode slowly home to dress his wound before it became infected. He sat on a chair in the lamplight and Pamela realized that the scratch was deeper than she'd thought. He gave her a dark powder of dried herbs and she made a paste out of it and spread it on the wound. "This will work fast," he said. "By tomorrow it will dry and form a scab." He saw the concerned look on her face. "Don't worry. It'll be fine. You're not changing your mind, are you?"

"Not at all, but I think we should wait. You should resolve everything with her before we start a relationship." She could feel her anger rise again as she thought of Raquel.

THE OTHER SIDE OF THE MOUNTAIN

He shook his head and looked up at her. "Our relationship has already begun, Pam."

She nodded. "I know, but I don't think that woman really understands the ways of our people."

"She understands, she just refuses to accept." He shook his head and placed his elbows on his knees, looking down at his hands. "She wasn't always like that."

"I believe you. After all, you fell in love with her and married her."

"I was young and foolish. If I'd waited maybe I would have known the real woman."

"Then you would not have had those two beautiful children."

"That's the only good thing."

She nodded. "Let's walk outside. I feel that I shouldn't be here."

"This is my home. I built it with my own hands. Of course you should be here." He got up and walked to the verandah with her. "I'm sorry you met her, but Pam, you have to believe me, our only attachment is the children."

She could see the sadness and regret in his eyes. "I know. I'm not running away." She'd planned a party of merriment and within a few minutes Raquel had changed it to a bitter memory for Saul. She not only saw his pain, she felt it. "Will you be all right?"

"Yes."

"Men never talk about the abuse they suffer from women. You're all supposed to be strong and buoyant enough to bounce back from pain no matter how brutal. You're supposed to swallow and digest, but the scarring is always there deep inside, isn't it?"

He sighed deeply and nodded.

She turned to go and he caught her hand. "Don't go."

She looked at the scar on his handsome face and again felt the rage rise within her. "I have to, because if she comes here and even points a finger at you, I know you won't hit her, but I swear to Jah I will. I've never been in a fight before in my life, but I am prepared to make an exception."

He inhaled deeply, then smiled and held her trembling body to him. He didn't know what to say. He'd had no idea how deeply her passion ran. She was proving to be smarter and more understanding than any woman he'd ever met. She could see his scars even through his laughter. He'd been right. She was making tiny stitches in his heart. "I think I came to terms with everything a long time ago. I met her in New York. I was at a convention. She was one of the waitresses. She was so nice and pleasant. As our friendship developed she told me she didn't have a green card. I didn't know then that she wanted to marry me. But she pushed and pushed. She purposely became pregnant and said I had to marry her because of the pregnancy. I wasn't

THE OTHER SIDE OF THE MOUNTAIN

ready. I was only two years out of college. She lost the child. She never stopped pushing. I was supposed to go to Kuwait for a job. She hid my passport." He shook his head. "I lost the contract." He shrugged. "I think somewhere along the line I fell in love with her in spite of herself. There were so many red flags, but I ignored them all. She lived with her sister. Her sister told me she was a horrible person, but I just laughed. I thought she was kidding."

"You're an American citizen?"

"Yes, but I have dual citizenship."

"Why?"

He shrugged. "I wanted the freedom to go and come as I please." He looked at her.

"Go on."

"Her sister wasn't kidding. But instead of marrying her in the States, I brought her here and had a traditional Rahjah ceremony."

"She couldn't go back to America, am I right?"

He shrugged. "No, I could have filed the papers in Jamaica. She became pregnant with the twins. She kept insisting that I file her papers so that she could have the children in America, but after knowing the type of person she was, I refused. She became a devil and began making trouble. That's when things began happening in the village." He stopped talking.

"It's okay, you don't have to say anymore. I've got to go. If I don't put Gracie to bed she'll be up all night." She touched his face.

"Will you keep my children tonight?"

"Of course." She kept looking into his pained face. He couldn't have harmed Raquel, not even in anger. He had a temper, she could tell, but he knew how to control it.

He took her hand and kissed her palm. "Thank you for everything. Give my excuses to anyone who asks. Tell them anything. I know you'll think of something."

"You're not only handsome, you're beautiful, inside and out."

"Even with a scarred face?"

"It will heal."

"It will leave a mark."

"It doesn't matter."

He pulled her to him. "What can I say?"

"Just kiss me."

His lips caressed her mouth as she hugged him with a strength that told him of her true character. Despite the pain from his cheek, his arousal reminded him of the man he was and made her aware of the strength he held within. He lifted her off the floor and buried his face in her neck, then slowly let go of her. Their fingertips touched as she walked away. She turned. "You can stay at my house, you know. I could stay with my parents."

THE OTHER SIDE OF THE MOUNTAIN

"I'll see you tomorrow as promised." He didn't want her pity.

"Yes." Mounting her horse, she realized she didn't want to leave him. She gazed at him and sighed then turned her horse around and rode slowly back to where the music and merriment had not ceased.

Ushering her horse into the barn, she walked slowly back towards the crowd of people, smiling deceptively at everyone until she saw Raquel laughing with another glass of wine in her hand. She was drunk.

The smell of ganja assaulted her nostrils as she gathered up the children for bed. "Did you have a good time?" she asked them.

"Did my dada go away again?" Ruth asked.

"No, but he had some work to finish up, so he went home. Would you like to stay with Gracie tonight?"

"Yes, please."

Pamela was relieved not to have come up with an excuse. David asked to stay with Rodney's two sons so that they could finish up their game of chess and Pamela agreed. She made sure the girls were in bed, then walked with David to Rodney's cottage.

Pamela walked back with Rodney's wife, Cherry, to the party and met up with Mary and Myah. "Look at her. Just look at her," Myah said, staring at Raquel.

Pamela looked away from the woman who'd caused physical pain to a very gentle man. She'd tried to emasculate him and Pamela wanted nothing to do with her. "Why don't we talk about something more pleasant?"

"Where's Saul?" Myah asked.

"He had some work to finish up so he went home."

"But he didn't even say goodnight." Myah looked at Pamela. "It's her, isn't it? She did something. It's because of the way she's behaving that he left. She embarrassed him."

Pamela didn't answer. She smiled when she saw Angel and James.

"This was one of the best parties I've ever been to," Angel said, "and believe me, I've been to a lot." She looked around. "Did Saul leave?"

"Yes, but he says he'll see you both tomorrow."

James leaned in and spoke only to her. "Will we see you too?"

She nodded.

"It may not seem that way all the time, but we Rahjahs always stick together."

She nodded. He kissed her goodnight and so did Angel.

Pamela turned and smiled at Mary. "I'm going to Rahjah Blue Mountain, then Jamaica for a week. Will you look after Gracie for me?"

"You don't have to ask." She respected Pamela's privacy enough not to ask the reason. "When will you leave?"

"Tomorrow evening."

THE OTHER SIDE OF THE MOUNTAIN

She nodded. "Have a good time."

"I'll look after her, too," Myah said.

"Thanks." Pamela wondered if Mary had said anything to Myah about her and Saul, but thought not. She excused herself from Mary and Myah to find her mother. She pulled her aside. "I am going to Rahjah Blue Mountain tomorrow to visit with Angel and James, Mama. I'll be away for maybe a week or so. Can you have one of the other teachers fill in for me?"

Esther looked at her daughter. "Does this have anything to do with Saul?"

"You don't beat around the bush, do you?"

"Have I ever?"

"Yes, it has to do with Saul."

"You're going to spend time with him?"

"Yes."

"I can't say I approve at this time, Pammy."

"I know you have reservations about him, Mama, but I'm a big girl and he's a good man."

"I know, but he went away and brought her back with him." She motioned toward Raquel. "Are you sure you're his type?"

"Mama!" she gasped.

"I'm sorry, Pammy, but…"

Pamela shifted her eyes from her mother. "I would like to get to know him better away from the village. Away from her."

"Pammy, he's Rahjah, but…"

170

JANICE ANGELIQUE

"When I come back we can talk more."

Esther sighed and hugged her daughter. "Okay."

"Thanks, Mama." She walked back to her cottage and looked in on the girls. She had to tell Gracie she would be away for a few days. She'd never left her before. The band played softly, as if playing a lullaby, and people still stood around smoking, talking and dancing.

The girls, including Shaela, were playing Scrabble. She sat on the bed and made a word for Shaela, then said, "Gracie, I have to go to Rahjah Blue Mountain for a few days."

"Then you'll come right back?" Gracie hardly looked up from her game.

She smiled. "Maybe a week, but no more, I promise."

"It's okay if you stay a little over a week as long as you come back."

"Of course I'll come back. You'll stay with Aunt Mary. Okay?"

"Okay."

Pamela kissed the girls and left the room. Still thinking of Saul and the occurrence of the night, she walked to her room and sat on her bed. Then, overcome by a strange, sorrowful feeling, she began crying. Saul had been so gentle even through Raquel's insults. She couldn't understand why Raquel had been so malicious. She didn't understand Raquel at all.

THE OTHER SIDE OF THE MOUNTAIN

She got into her nightclothes and slipped under the covers. Thinking of the coming week, she felt conflicted. Was this the right time to be going away with Saul? Jah knew she wanted to be with him with all her heart. If the incident hadn't happened tonight she wouldn't have thought twice about going. She closed her eyes. Maybe this was the perfect time to go. He needed to get away; he needed her. Things would look better in the morning.

Chapter 13

Raquel was still at the party but didn't seem to crave much attention anymore. She held onto Ludy and drained her cup, then threw it to the ground. "Go down and get me another bottle of wine." Her words slurred as she swayed.

"No more wine. Let me get a cup of tea for you. Then I'll take you home," Ludy said.

Raquel didn't seem to care one way or the other. Both women moved to the table close to the kitchen and Ludy poured a cup of hot, steaming herbal tea. Raquel drank it and sat down on one of the cushions. Ludy sat down beside her.

"He never gave me any money when he ran me from the island, you know. He never gave me anything but plane fare to wherever I wanted to go."

Ludy shook her head. "Didn't he set up a bank account for you?"

"It wasn't enough. It's almost gone. My husband used almost all of it."

Ludy gasped. "What?"

"He used it, then threw me away."

"Who? What are you talking about?" Ludy inquired.

THE OTHER SIDE OF THE MOUNTAIN

"My husband," she emphasized.

"You got married again?"

"Of course. You didn't expect me to stay single all my life with no man to take care of me?" She looked at Ludy and placed a finger to her lips. "Shhh, don't say anything. Swear." Her eyes closed and she swayed.

Ludy caught her and nodded, still not sure of what Raquel was telling her. "I'll keep your secret," she said slowly, thoughtfully. She got up, pulled her to her feet and motioned for Boyd. "We need to go down in a buggy," she told him. "She's too drunk to ride."

"No problem," he said, lifting Raquel as if she were a feather and carrying her to the buggy. Ludy climbed in beside the sleeping Raquel.

On reaching the village, Boyd carried Raquel into the cottage. Ludy showed him to the room and he set her down on the bed and left. Ludy undressed Raquel and pulled the sheet over her, then looked at her. Even in sleep she didn't look innocent, or even nice. She turned and went to her own cottage.

⦅⦆

The sun was hardly up when Saul walked to the small kitchen in his cottage to make himself a cup of tea. He didn't look into the bedroom as he passed even though the door was wide open. He brewed his tea, then stood on the verandah with the cup in his hand. The cool breeze washed over him and the steam rising from the cup shifted in the wind. How had it all come to this? How had his life again become such a nightmare? He breathed deeply and shook his head. He was so sorry that Pamela had seen and heard all that she had last night. If only he could turn back the hands of time.

"You loved me once," she said, leaning against the doorjam. She brushed the hair from her face and stared at his back.

He didn't turn. He didn't respond.

She walked out and stood beside him. She placed an arm on his back and he shifted.

"Yes, but that was a long time ago. All that's gone now."

"It can come back again. I can bring it back. I can change."

"I can't." He still didn't look at her. She'd driven away the love he had for her a long time ago. He could tolerate her. He could even be civil to her, but it was all for the children. "I will put the money in your bank account, but that will be it. No more."

She touched him and he moved away. With the cup in his hand he walked off the verandah into the mist.

"I'll make you regret this," she shouted. "I won't leave."

He turned and walked back to the verandah. His eyes were dead cold as he looked at her. "What is it you want from me, Raquel? What do you want from this family?"

"I need a place to stay."

"Not here. You can't do this to the children."

"I'm sorry I said I don't love you."

"It doesn't matter. My love for you died a long time ago. I'm going away for a while. Be gone before I get back."

"Where are you going? You just got back."

This time when he walked away, he didn't come back.

Raquel held her pounding head and walked back to the bedroom. She threw herself on the bed and fell back to sleep.

⁂

Pamela sat on the cushion in her cottage as Mary twisted and oiled her hair. "What happened last night?" Mary asked. "Why did Saul go home so early?"

Pamela sighed. "He had a fight with Raquel."

"Physical?"

"She's like one of those hungry African lions you read about. She attacked him."

"Did he fight back?"

She turned and looked up at Mary. "What do you think?"

Mary shook her head. "I guess not. You know, the children thought he was an ogre because he often stayed in his cottage for long periods of time, but she is the ogre."

Pamela sighed again. "Does anyone know about us?"

"I haven't said anything to anyone."

"I like him a lot, but I don't want to be a part of the drama. I don't want Saul and Raquel. I want just Saul. He has to do something, I don't know what, but he has to straighten her out as to where they stand."

"They're no longer committed to each other."

"She seems to be under the impression that they still belong together, for what reason I don't know."

"The way he looked at you last night..." Mary shook her head. "Everyone knows that he really likes you."

Pamela nodded.

Gracie came into the room rubbing her sleepy eyes. She sat on her mother's lap and hugged her. "Don't let me miss you too much." She yawned and placed her head on her mother's shoulder.

Pamela laughed. "I won't. I'll be back before you know it."

"I wish you were going with Uncle Saul." She yawned again.

Pamela opened her eyes wide and glanced up at Mary. "Why do you say that, dear?"

She shrugged. "I don't know. I like Uncle Saul, and I like Ruth and David. They're like my sister and

THE OTHER SIDE OF THE MOUNTAIN

brother, so maybe if you marry Uncle Saul, he'll be my dada."

Oh, Jah, Pamela thought. At this point, if she told her daughter Saul was just her friend she'd be lying to her. She kissed her daughter's cheek and her forehead.

She nodded and got off her mother's lap. "I'll get dressed for breakfast."

Mary chuckled. "Out of the mouths of babes."

Pam didn't say anything.

~~~

The day went fast and Pamela tried with every step to avoid her mother.

With a small bag under her arm, she rode halfway to the boat. Then she got off her horse and sent him back home, walking the rest of the way. As she walked, she wondered if she would like Jamaica this time. Going to Rahjah Blue Mountain didn't scare her because she would be with her people, but she had to go through Jamaica to get there.

Saul was waiting for her. He held her hand, took the bag from her and smiled as they got into the boat. He sat beside her and placed a protective arm around her shoulders. "Is everything resolved?" she asked finally.

"Yes," he said pensively and hoped it was true. He had no intention of hurting Pamela or allowing anyone to hurt her, least of all Raquel.

Pamela stayed by his side all the way into Jamaica, and his arms never left her shoulders.

At the dock, James and Angel waited for them. Knowing that Pamela must be quite apprehensive about her visit, Angel ran to greet her. "I'm glad you came." She hugged Pamela.

"Me, too." Pamela returned her hug, then received James's hug.

"We have some talking to do, my friend," he said to Saul, who just nodded. "Cheer up," he said, glancing at Saul as he pulled away from the curb in a BMW. "You're gonna like what I have to tell you."

They drove for fifteen minutes, then parked the car in a garage at the foot of the mountain and took four horses that were tied to a hitching post. James and Saul rode in front while the women rode behind.

"The first time I came up these mountains, I have to tell you I don't think I even liked Rastafarians," Angel said, laughing.

Pamela glanced at her and smiled.

"I had never met people so strong, intelligent and gentle before. At first I resented them and thought they were very condescending. It took me a while to understand their way." She glanced at Pamela. "Your way."

"Yes, we take some getting used to." Pamela laughed.

THE OTHER SIDE OF THE MOUNTAIN

"You can say that again. For a while I had to forget what I knew to learn about the Rahjahs. You guys are not just Rastafarians. You're the first, the original." She looked over at Pamela. "Sorry, I'm going on and on. This is your first visit here, isn't it?"

Pamela shook her head. "I don't think so." She switched subjects. "Why haven't you locked your hair?"

Angel laughed. "My daughter asked me that question when she was about sixteen. I'll tell you the story later, but I wanted to keep some of my identity. One could get lost in the ways of your people. Everything seems so right here."

The air got cooler as they got higher on the mountain. As the village came into view, it almost took Pamela's breath away. It was the same as her village, but yet not the same. It was much larger, with more colors and more trees and flowers. Each cottage had a verandah with hanging flower pots. All the roofs were green with grass and flowers.

"No planes flying overhead can see the village, just like yours," Angel said.

They came into the circle and the first person who came out was Clara, James's mother. The four dismounted and Clara greeted her niece warmly.

"It's good to meet you," Pamela said.

Clara smiled. "You were born on this very mountain, my dear."

She looked at Clara and tried to remember. No one had ever spoken of her birthplace. Maybe her parents thought she was old enough to remember when she'd left the island.

"Esther left the mountain when you were only six years old."

"Why don't I remember?" She tilted her head to the side, really trying to remember.

"Maybe because everything here is the same as on the island. It really doesn't make a difference."

Pamela smiled and nodded. "You're right."

The village came alive as everyone greeted Saul and Pamela. *Just like home*, Pamela thought.

And after all the salutations were over, Angel snatched Pamela away to her favorite place, a rock close to the waterfall. They both sat down and didn't say anything, even when the wind blew the spray of water into their faces.

"I can't believe I wanted to be like her," Pamela finally said. She looked at Angel, then looked away. "Like Raquel, I mean."

Angel nodded.

"She seemed to just sweep into the village with her brand of style. I had never seen anyone dress the way she did. She wore pants and threw her legs over a horse like a man and…"

Angel laughed. "And you wanted to do that?"

"It seemed so free, you know."

"The way you guys ride a horse is more free than anyone I've ever seen."

Pamela looked down at her dress. "I guess I wanted to be different. Don't get me wrong. I love my people, our way of life, but…" She looked again at Angel. "Like the way you dress. You're pretty. You dress pretty."

"Have you ever looked at yourself in a mirror?" Angel said, looking directly at Pamela.

"Not really."

"You are drop-dead gorgeous. Your brand of beauty is hard to find in the outside world. You don't wear a drop of makeup and you have the most flawless, beautiful skin."

Pamela blushed.

"You have an innocence about you."

"I'm a teacher. I was married and I have a child," she said, not being used to compliments from a woman.

Angel shook her head. "Yes, you are intelligent, that's not what I meant. I mean…" She stopped talking and looked away. "I mean, you're unspoiled by modern society."

"Maybe I should have said I wanted to look like Raquel, not be like her."

"I knew what you meant. When I first came here, I thought the Rahjahs were backward for not using modern medicine or machinery, but I quickly learned that modern medicine could take a lot of pages out of the Rahjah's book of medicine. Clara taught me a lot in the way of patience, of getting what I want without saying a word. Saul loves you, Pam. He's free of entanglements, if you know what I mean. Let him love you."

Pamela turned and looked at her from under lowered eyelids. "How do you know…"

The beating of the steel drums floated through the air.

"Come, let's go talk with Saul and James." She took Pamela's hand and they walked back to the village.

Saul and James were sitting on James's verandah with James's brother Devin. Saul smiled when he saw the women approach.

"Did you tell her?" James asked Angel.

"No."

Pamela looked at Angel. "Tell me what?"

Suddenly everyone, except for Saul, seemed to have something else to do. "I'm going to raid the kitchen for something to eat," James said.

Pamela sat in the chair beside Saul. "Tell me what, Saul?"

He took a deep breath and shook his head. "Raquel got married again." He glanced at her. "She went to Brazil, got married to a wealthy landowner and left him after he refused to maintain her wasteful lifestyle. Before she met him she'd gone through all the money

THE OTHER SIDE OF THE MOUNTAIN

I'd given her. She was broke. He showered her with gifts and she partied and traveled all the time. He came to his senses and cut up her charge cards, so she came back to the island."

"You mean she's still married to the man?"

He nodded. "Yes. She pretended that she didn't know the way of the Rahjahs, but she does. She only wanted money." He looked at her and smiled. "You see, Pam, everything is all worked out."

She smiled and took the hand he offered. She wrinkled her nose. "Forgive my ignorance, but what's a charge card?"

He threw back his head and laughed. "You're not being ignorant. You have no way of knowing what a charge card is. It's a card that allows you to buy things on credit and pay later."

"Wait, back up a bit. How did James find out all these things so quickly?"

He chuckled as he looked at her. "It wasn't done so quickly. Remember when James whispered in your ear that we take care of each other?"

"Yes."

"Well, he and Devin began investigating Raquel the day she showed up again in the village. And before you ask how they knew when she came back, Devin had made a quick visit to find out how my job went. He was the one who'd talked me into the contract with the company I'd worked for. Anyway, when he saw Raquel, he knew no good could have come from her visit."

"So he took it upon himself to find out what she'd been up to all these years?"

He nodded. "In a nutshell."

"We certainly do take care of our own."

"We have people all over the world, Pam, in many different positions."

She nodded. "I know." Holding his hand, she sat back in the chair. She'd felt as if she were hurting Raquel. She'd thought that Raquel didn't understand the rules of commitment and letting go in her culture. Now she knew that they'd been taken for a ride. Saul was free of entanglements. They were free to have a relationship. She looked at him. "I will go to Jamaica with you now."

He laughed and stood. "Come here." He pulled her to him. His lips pressed against hers and gently covered her mouth. His mouth slid from hers and he looked into her face. His eyes glowed with a savage inner fire. She chuckled and gave him a shy smile as his lips recaptured hers, more demanding this time, almost taking her breath away.

"Oh, you've never done that before," she breathed once he'd taken his mouth away from her lips.

"Is that okay?"

His voice sounded boyish and uncertain. She laughed and hugged his neck tight. "That's okay."

THE OTHER SIDE OF THE MOUNTAIN

Then she looked seriously into his eyes. "Are you going to tell her what you found out?"

"No, I told her I'd give her more money and that's what I'm gonna do. Then I'm really done."

"But now you don't have to give her money. She's extorting money from you and she doesn't even have the children to use as an excuse."

They looked at each other.

"You're right," he said. "You're so right. If I keep giving her money it will never end. Thank you." He kissed her lips.

As if by magic, James, Devin and Angel appeared. Saul looked at them and laughed. "You're all a bunch of cowards," he said.

"Hey, man," James said. "There are some things that you just have to do by yourself. Now that all that's out of the way, let's go play some dominos. Ladies, don't wait up." He threw a backward glance to his wife and she shook her head and ushered Pam inside the cottage.

"I went shopping for you today before we came to get you."

"Really?" Pamela could hardly hide her excitement. No one had ever bought her anything except books before. Actually, she'd never wanted anything else before.

Angel took her into the room, showed her the packages, then sat back and watched her reaction. At first she was timid. "Go on," Angel encouraged. "They're all yours. We're about the same size, so they should all fit."

Pamela withdrew the dresses with an amazed look on her face. Again Angel encouraged her to try them on.

"You look amazing," Angel kept saying as Pamela tried on form-fitting blue, green and yellow dresses.

Pamela looked at one of the tags on her dress. "Size fourteen. Why do they all have numbers?" She looked at Angel.

"Beats me. If you ask me, we can all do without the numbers. As you know, there are no mirrors here, but take my word for it, you look amazing."

"I feel amazing. You've turned the ugly duckling into a swan."

"I wouldn't exactly put it that way. You do more for the clothes than they do for you." She gave her one more package.

"Oh, no, you've done enough, Angel. I couldn't accept anything more. I insist on paying you for all this."

"I wouldn't hear of it. They are a gift. Now open the other package."

Pamela smiled and opened the package. She pulled out two pairs of sandals, a pair of jeans and a pair of slacks. "Oh, Jah, My people would kill me if they saw me in this."

"They aren't here. Do you like them?"

THE OTHER SIDE OF THE MOUNTAIN

She took off the blue silk dress and slipped easily into the pair of jeans. "I love them." She ran her hands up and down her hips. "They feel so soft." Then she tried on the sandals. "How did you know my size?"

"I took a look at your feet last night. Sandals are easy. Shoes are a bit harder."

Pamela hugged Angel. "You must allow me to repay you for all this."

"Not with money. Just promise me you'll have a wonderful time in Jamaica. I want you to write to me in New York and tell me all about it."

"Maybe I'll just visit you in this New York of yours one day. I'd love to visit you and your daughter. The girl with the blue-green eyes and flaming red hair."

Angel laughed.

"You're in the history books."

Now it was Angel's turn to be surprised. She placed her hand over her face and laughed some more. "I hope they were kind."

"Your passion, fire and rebelliousness were the talk of our village once the books were updated." She laughed and sat beside Angel.

"This is the first time I'm hearing about this. Why didn't you say something last night?"

"I'd forgotten until Myah gave a snippet of your story. You know our people."

"Yes, I do." She laughed again and lay back on the bed. "I can't believe my little family made the Rahjah history books." Then she sat up and looked at Pamela. "Does that mean someday you'll be in the history books?"

She shrugged. "If I leave the village to live on the outside. Saul and Raquel will. I think it will be labeled 'Get to know who you marry before you marry.'"

They both cracked up and lay back on the bed.

"What was mine?" Angel asked.

"Strength, morality and challenge."

"Just like that. They thought I was challenging."

"Yeah."

That night Saul and Pamela didn't sleep in the same room, or the same cottage, for that matter. Talking with Angel almost half the night was a welcome distraction. Not once did Pamela or Saul think of Raquel. Saul's domino session went into the wee hours of the morning.

Chapter 14

After breakfast, it began drizzling, but not hard enough for any plans to be changed. James and Angel would be staying on the mountain for another week and Devin had to fly back home to upstate New York.

Pamela wore one of her old dresses for the trip to wherever Saul was taking her. Angel had wanted her to wear her new pair of jeans, but she wanted to wait. She wanted the new Pamela to be for Saul's eyes only. Plus, she didn't want anyone on the mountain to see her in any clothes but theirs.

Their trek down the mountain was a quiet one. Saul seemed to be in a world all his own, and Pamela didn't interrupt his thoughts. At the bottom of the mountain, Saul packed their belongings in the trunk of the small BMW and smiled when he saw the new travel case that Pamela now carried. He ushered her quickly into the car when the drizzle turned into a steady downpour.

"I hope our vacation doesn't get rained out," she said as they drove onto the road.

"Never," he said, changing gears and flashing her a reassuring smile. "We're going to Devin's beach house in Manchioneal. It's fully stocked with everything we may need."

"Have you ever been there before?"

"No, but I know the way." Again he became pensive.

Pamela's eyes took in everything along the way, women dressed in short dresses or skirts and sandals walking with baskets on their heads. Every car that passed, she'd ask, "What kind is that?"

He'd laugh and tell her.

"Does Jamaica make these cars?"

"Not to my knowledge." He glanced at her, then back to the road ahead. He reached over and held her hand, laid her hand in his lap, changed gears, then held onto her hand, again caressing her fingers with his thumb.

She observed the homes. Some were unappealing to her and some made her eyes open wide because of their beauty. They were all different from the Rahjah cottages. He drove through streets with splendid sprawling homes and she whistled and laughed. Every time she'd point to a big house with well-dressed women or men, she'd say, "Jamaica is richer than I thought."

They finally got to the beach house, and the reward of seeing Devin's place was worth the trip from Rahjah Island.

THE OTHER SIDE OF THE MOUNTAIN

"Wow!" she said, opening the car door before Saul could reach it. "I love it. It's beautiful." She ran ahead of him and bypassed the front door to run around through an arch made of roses to the back of the house onto the beach. The water was calm and inviting. There were no homes to be seen for at least a mile. "How did he ever find this place?" She opened her arms and twirled, falling right into Saul's arms.

He held her and smiled. "I never asked him, but I do agree with you. It's a very beautiful place. Should we take our things into the house and see if we like it?"

Her nervousness only lasted for a minute. "Oh, I do, I do." She grabbed his hand and ran back to the car.

He wanted to tell her to slow down, but to tell the truth, he was enjoying every minute of her exuberance and laughing right along with her. When they went into the house, she bypassed the expensive furnishings and went to the lanai. Saul dropped the bags in the foyer of the three-bedroom house and went out to sit by her as she rocked in the lounge swing. The rain had stopped and now they watched as it slowly moved over the ocean towards them. They didn't move.

Pamela felt so comfortable sitting there in Saul's arms that even the rain coming into her face couldn't disturb her. "You know, when I met Raquel…" She caught his furrowed brow. "I'm sorry, if you'd rather not speak of her…" She turned back to the rain and wind now making the palms and young coconut trees bend to the beat of their own drum.

"What did you think of her?" he asked.

There was a hint of something in his voice, but she couldn't tell what without looking at him and she didn't want to look at him. "I saw the way she dressed and jumped onto her horse and wanted to be like her. Well, not to be like her, but to dress like her."

His smile was bleak and tight-lipped.

She changed the subject. "My daughter talks with animals."

His smile was more of a 'thank you for changing the subject' smile. "Mine, too. And I know what you mean when you say with. She can hold a conversation with any animal."

She pulled her feet onto the seat and faced him. "What do you think of that? Do you think our girls are lonely?"

"I don't know. The village is filled with children her own age. Her brother is constantly with her. I really don't know."

She inhaled deeply and looked out at the raindrops massaging the ocean. "How can they be lonely?" She wrinkled her brows thoughtfully. "You know, I never seriously thought of it before. As you say, the village is filled with children the same age, yet they choose to talk with animals." She looked at him. "Is Ruth more commanding or more conversational?"

THE OTHER SIDE OF THE MOUNTAIN

"More commanding, I think." He kept looking at her. "Why?"

"Gracie never really had a father, and Ruth's mother went away." She shifted in her seat and gestured with her hands. "I mean, ninety-nine percent of the children in the village have both parents; some parents don't live together but they're there anyway. Gracie's father died tragically and I'm assuming Ruth saw her mother…well." She looked away from him and down at her feet.

"She's seen us quarrel, I'm afraid. She once saw her mother slap my face." He didn't look away from her.

She looked back into his eyes. "I'm sorry."

"It's all right. You know, I was never one to fight. I'd walk away before I lost my temper." He laughed now as he remembered. "James and I used to have some real fights, though, and about the stupidest things."

"Now you're best friends."

He nodded. "Yes, and I see what you're getting at. I never dominate my children, and I'm assuming that you allow Gracie to make decisions all her own."

"It's the Rahjah way."

"They don't dominate the other children but they do the animals, and I may add, not in an angry way."

"Yes. I know sometimes Gracie will say, 'Keep quiet' when the animals are making noise and they'll stop immediately. Am I being foolish?"

He held her gesturing hands. "If you are, then so am I because I swear they respond to Ruth. But since she's begun coming to you, she doesn't talk with the animals as much."

She threw up her hands, taking his with hers. "Same with Gracie."

He laughed, pulled her to him and kissed her mouth hard.

"Are you trying to tell me to shut up?"

"Not at all. But I still can't believe you won't be running away from me for an entire week."

She didn't respond.

He pulled her to her feet, slipped his hand around her waist and walked inside. "Should we share a room or…" The word got lost somewhere in the air when he saw the look on her face.

"Let's just let nature take its course. We won't plan anything."

He nodded and they walked back into the living room. She'd run right through and had not looked at the walls to appraise the paintings or seen the television set or radio standing in the corner of the room. He didn't have to call her attention to them, as she went from one to the other nodding and mumbling. "Water's paintings are all over the Rahjah community. I never met her, but I hear she was the nicest Elder you'd ever want to meet. She was 105 when she died?" She glanced at him.

THE OTHER SIDE OF THE MOUNTAIN

"I think so. She loved Angel."

"What did she love about her?"

"Angel has a knack for calling it as she sees it, so to speak. And by the way, the lady has a temper that even burned Aunt Clara."

"Oh, Aunt Clara scares me. It's as if she knows what you're thinking. She speaks without hurry and is authoritative without being authoritative."

He smiled. "Yes, that's Aunt Clara." He picked up the remote and turned on the television.

Pamela jumped at the sound. "What is that? How did you do that?" She walked up to the screen and touched it. There was a pause and she jumped away from it. "Did I do that?"

"No." He switched the channels to something he thought she'd like. *Animal Kingdom.*

She sat and stared at the screen. "Oh, my Jah." She patted the empty seat beside her. "Sit for a while."

He'd known this would be her reaction. She was his blank slate, ready to absorb everything of interest. He also thought he knew her filter system. She took the remote from him and began switching channels until she got to the History Channel. She gave him back the remote and leaned back into his arms. "I can't believe I'm seeing what I've read."

"Wait until you actually see it for real."

"Are you going to take me to these places: Italy and France and America?"

"If you'll let me."

"Oh, Jah, yes, yes."

She pulled her feet off the floor and he threw his arms around her and could feel her heart beating a mile a minute. "You do get excited, don't you?"

"I never have before, but all this, and with you, yes, I'm really excited. If I forget to thank you, thank you."

He kept his hand close to her heart until it went back to normal. Then he took a breath. "Would you like to walk into town this evening? It's a small town, but you'll at least see some of the people you've been afraid of."

"I'm not afraid of them, just a little wary of them."

"That was careful sidestepping."

"You liked that?"

He laughed and leaned his head against hers and closed his eyes. Would he be able to live up to her expectations, however simple? She was so easy to please.

When she'd had enough television, she got up and went to the bedroom and the adjoining bathroom. She looked at herself in the mirror and smiled as she saw her reflection looking back at her. She touched her hair, her face.

Slowly, she took off her clothes and took a shower, then wrapped the big soft towel around herself and walked back into the room. He'd carried her travel case in and set it on the bed. She searched through and took out a yellow silk dress. She dressed then walked

THE OTHER SIDE OF THE MOUNTAIN

to the standing mirror, took a good look at herself and ran her hands down the length of her dress.

She walked out to see him standing by the window. He turned and smiled as his eyes swept every inch of her. He took a deep breath and exhaled. "You are beautiful."

"Thank you." She touched the length of her dress. "I have legs."

He laughed resoundingly. "And what beautiful legs they are."

She blushed and tried to pull the dress past her knees.

"Don't do that. It's not too short."

"Really?"

"Really."

They drove into town, parked and walked the quiet streets. She held his hand and, smiling brightly, nodded to everyone she saw. To her amazement even the meanest looking person smiled back at her and nodded. People were going to or coming from work. She laughed. It wasn't so bad after all. "I love second impressions," she said in a low voice.

He smiled and gave her hand a little squeeze. Devin had told him about a little Ital restaurant and when he suggested it, Pamela thought for a while. She wasn't quite ready to poison him with her cooking, so she agreed.

They walked into the restaurant and sat down at a table. They were waited on by a pleasant Rasta woman with beautiful dark skin, scarf-wrapped hair and a bright smile. She gave them a menu. Pam read the choices and made her selection.

After supper, they walked some more and drove back home.

Then she remembered something Raquel had told her. She turned to him and said, "I would like to see a movie."

"A movie? Who told you about that?"

She smiled.

He thought Angel had told her. "I don't know any theaters around here, but we can drive into Kingston."

"Is that far?"

"A little."

"Then we can come back here?"

"Well, if we leave now, we can catch a nine o'clock movie, I think. Since it's so far, we can stay in Kingston for the night and go west tomorrow."

"Okay, let's go to Kingston."

"And you call me impetuous."

They packed and drove into Kingston. It took her breath away. The houses were bigger, perched on top of mountains. The streets were crowded with buildings and vehicles and lots of people. They checked into a hotel and although she said nothing, he could tell by the look in her eyes and the way she looked at

THE OTHER SIDE OF THE MOUNTAIN

everything and everyone that she was now taking it all in stride.

"Two rooms or one?" he asked her.

"We are together. Why would I want to be away from you in another room?" she asked, looking into his eyes.

He nodded. "Silly question, but I just wanted to be sure."

"I'm sure."

After checking in, they went directly to the Harborview drive-in. Tonight was oldies night. She watched *Ben Hur* in silence, taking in every word and action of the actors on the screen, jumping every now and again at the loud bangs and booms.

Tuesday, she wore her jeans and wiggled in them when he complimented her shape. He couldn't believe she could eat so much and still have a flat stomach.

He took her shopping, and she bought very little for herself, just for her mother, daughter and the twins. "I took you shopping to buy things for yourself," he said.

"I don't need anything," she replied.

He laughed and they went walking in Trafalgar. She ate ice cream made from almond milk, vegetable and ackee patties, more ice cream, and then pudding and fish and vegetables and fried plantains when they had supper. That night he held her hair while she threw up in the toilet. "I guess I ate too much. I should pace myself."

He smiled and nodded. "I was just as bad my first time in Jamaica, but I'm used to all these things now and I'm bigger than you."

She laughed and washed her face.

They lay side by side in bed that night talking and laughing until he asked what kind of man her husband was. She got serious, turned onto her back and smiled.

"He was wonderful. I don't think he ever left the island except to go fishing. He loved fishing. He went fishing every day and always came back with something. He always laughed, even when I got upset with him."

"I can't imagine you getting upset with anyone," Saul said, pulling her into his arms.

Her head lay on his arm and she laughed. "Oh, yes, I can. I got angry with Raquel." She slapped her hands to her mouth. "Sorry. I didn't mean to…"

He shook his head. "It's okay. Was he a big guy?"

"Not big like you, but he was tall and lanky. Is that a good word?"

"I suppose so." He inhaled the lavender in her hair and kissed the top of her head.

"We made all kinds of crafts together. He knitted an afghan for me all by himself. He made a spread for our bed out of finely cut scraps of cloth." She turned in his arms and clasped her hands as if praying.

He faced her and pushed a stray lock from her face. "You loved him very much?"

"With all my heart. Gracie was our second child. The first one died before he was born." She laughed nervously to keep from crying. "I know we aren't supposed to speak of the dead, but sometimes there are exceptions. I never saw him. Mama took him away immediately. I became pregnant again three months later. Everything went so quickly when Gracie was born. He'd gone fishing. Gracie took only four hours to be born. She was determined to take as little time as possible." She stared into his face until her eyes burned with unshed tears remembering the joy of childbirth and the horror of death. The tears rolled down her cheeks and she looked away.

"Don't, don't, darling," he said, pulling her close and cuddling her.

"I guess this is one of the reasons we are not allowed to speak of the departed or utter their name. It's too hard. But the memories are always there, you know. Deep down inside you suffer. It's better to talk about it, to cry aloud and get it out. I cried when he left. I cried a lot. I felt lonely. I felt angry, then sad, even though I had little Gracie and the entire village."

He held her close and she pushed her face into his neck as tears blinded her eyes. He rocked her back and forth, caressing her soft cheek and whispering into her ear, "It's all right, I'm here."

"I'm sorry," she whispered. "I don't know why I'm crying. I think I'm a little bit happy and a little bit sad."

He looked into her eyes, clouded with unshed tears, and then kissed a salty tear as it slipped down her cheek. He placed a finger under her chin. "I didn't want you to cry."

His face was sad, his eyes at half-mast. She smiled. "I know." Her hand reached up and caressed his cheek where the scar from Saturday night stood as a bright reminder. Then she ran her fingers over his hair.

He pressed his lips to her mouth and she closed her eyes and savored the sensation of want running through her.

He needed to wrap himself in her warm body. She looked into his smoldering eyes and he touched her face. He shifted his body away from her. The blood pulsing through his veins made him very aware of his own needs, but something was saying, "Not now. The time isn't quite right." He should not have asked about her husband. He squeezed his eyes shut briefly. She was staring at him.

"Are you all right?" she asked in a quiet voice.

He smiled, turned her around and cupped her body into his, creating a delicious warmth between them. His lips pressed against her neck and she took a deep breath and closed her eyes.

"I want you to relax and just enjoy us."

THE OTHER SIDE OF THE MOUNTAIN

She nodded.

⁂

She kept looking at him and loving him. She'd thought he'd make love to her last night even though she'd been sad, but what they'd shared was more than physical. She would not have hesitated to give herself freely to him, but he didn't want her to be sad and still thinking of her dead husband. He'd listened to her and held her at the appropriate moment and now she thought he was the most understanding, thoughtful man she'd ever met. She didn't realize he was awake and looking at her until she heard his soothing voice.

"What do you want for breakfast?" he asked.

"Are you cooking?"

He smiled. "We're in a hotel in Kingston. There are no stoves in the room." His fingertip played with her chin.

She kept staring at his face, his mouth, his eyes. *I want you for breakfast*. She tilted her chin in thought. "I don't know what I want."

Knowing she probably wouldn't like the hotel food, he kissed her forehead. "Come on, get ready. I'm gonna take you to a nice little restaurant not far from here."

She didn't move. She kept staring at his half-naked body as he moved out of the bed.

He went into the bathroom and ran a bath. Then he came back, pulled her into his arms and carried her to the bathroom. He would have taken off her clothes, but that would have been asking too much of him. He didn't want to rush their lovemaking. He wanted to spend hours exploring this very fine body.

She grinned at him when he shook his head and left the room. She'd read his mind. *You're mine.*

After a leisurely bath, she got dressed and met him in the room. He wore a pale yellow cotton shirt tucked into blue jeans and she wore a red sundress and sandals.

"You look so relaxed," he said, taking her arm and pulling her to him. "And you smell delicious."

"And that's a good thing, right?"

"That's a very good thing." His hands slipped the length of hers. Then he brought her hands up to his shoulders and left them there. He kissed her deeply.

She swayed against him. He smiled and shook his head. "Let's go. Is there anything special you want to do today?"

"Eat until I get sick again." She laughed.

So did he. He was enjoying every moment of getting to know her. He was pretty sure he was head over heels in love with her. He slipped his arms around her shoulders and they walked to the elevator together.

Stepping out into the bright sunlight, Pamela breathed in the cheap gasoline fumes and coughed.

THE OTHER SIDE OF THE MOUNTAIN

At least the weather was the same as on her island. She shaded her eyes. He turned, guided her back inside the hotel and told her to wait for him. "I'll be back in a little while."

She nodded, sat down and began looking at everyone walking through the lobby. Some ignored her completely, some smiled. She was becoming very self-conscious. *Where's a book when I need one?* She could have been ignoring all the people who were either ignoring her or looking at her.

Saul was back with a pair of sunglasses for her. She stared at him, then at the glasses. He slipped them on her face and she kissed him. "Thank you. Now no one will know if I'm staring at them or not."

He laughed and guided her back outside. "I bought them for you yesterday while you were shopping. You'd tried them on so I thought you'd like to have them."

She hugged his waist. "Thank you."

After breakfast he took her to Port Royal. He knew she'd love this particular historical site. Then he took her to the airport, where they sat in the car for a while just watching the planes take off.

"You're so good to me," she said, leaning her head against his shoulder as they listened to oldies music on the radio.

"I'm having as much fun as you are. I can't think of any place I'd rather be than right here with you."

"Me, too."

It wasn't until they'd had supper that he decided to take her to see a musical at The Little Theater. Although she loved the movies, he thought she'd love this side of the arts even more. After all, they put on plays all the time in the villages, but they were almost always historical. This was different.

⁂

Dressed in a royal blue sleeveless dress that she'd picked out for herself when Saul had taken her shopping, Pamela looked like a completely different woman. "If Gracie and Mary could see me now," she said, looking at herself in the full-length mirror in the bathroom.

"They would agree with me when I say, princess, you're a knockout." He pulled her to him and pressed his lips to hers.

She took a deep breath after he'd released her lips. "And that's a good thing, right?"

"Oh, baby," he groaned.

They both laughed and headed out the door.

He was right, she enjoyed the play immensely, not only because of her artistic nature but because this was her first non-historical musical. It was light and comical and she laughed loud and heartily, unaware of how enthralling she was to him when she laughed. Her happiness was his delight.

THE OTHER SIDE OF THE MOUNTAIN

"What do you want to do now?" he asked after they left the theater.

She looked into his face and laughed. "You'll do anything I want to do?"

He nodded. "Yes."

"Are you sure?"

He nodded.

"Let's go back to the hotel and make love."

He laughed at her boldness but couldn't hide the pleasure he felt at her request. "I'll do anything you ask."

She pulled him to the car and opened his door for him. "Get in."

She slammed his door and ran around to her side. He leaned over and opened the door for her. All the way back to the hotel, he never stopped laughing.

She pulled him through the lobby, not caring who stared.

Off the elevator, she pulled him to the room and unlocked the door, but when she got inside, she just stood with her back braced against the door.

"Are you all right?" he asked, sensing something had changed in just a few minutes.

She looked into his eyes. He wrapped her in his arms. "Are you afraid?"

She nodded. "But not for what you think."

"What?"

"What if you don't like the way I make love?"

He lifted her off her feet and took her to the bedroom. "You know, I wondered why you never remarried for all those years," he said as he gently placed her on the bed.

"I guess I was waiting for you."

"And I for you, it seems." His fingertips touched her cheek. Then he switched on the light.

She stood and turned for him to unzip her. When he did and her dress fell to the floor, she turned in his arms and began unbuttoning his shirt. He allowed it to fall to the floor.

He pressed her to the bed, lay beside her and thoughtfully claimed her lips. His fingertip gently caressed her chin, drawing a line to her cheek. Her body responded to his touch as her breasts pressed against his chest through the thinness of her bra, tingling and trembling as she closed the gap between them and pressed hard into him.

His hand fished for the bra closure and it easily came loose. He let it slip to the bed as she fumbled with his pants. Grudgingly, he stood and quickly got rid of his pants, then stripped her of the rest of her clothes.

His moist warm mouth hungrily reclaimed hers, demanding and giving. She tingled in places she'd forgotten existed and groans escaped from deep within. Her hands fumbled for the light switch without moving her mouth from his. She turned out the light.

THE OTHER SIDE OF THE MOUNTAIN

"I want to see you," he said.

"Not yet." She pulled him down on her. There was no waiting. Their bodies were starved for each other and his hands roamed over her breasts.

His kiss was hard and bruising and she wanted his entire body inside her to put out the blazing fire that raged within. His lips moved from her mouth to the base of her throat. His body moved on top of her, imprisoning hers in a web of growing arousal.

He felt her body tremble as he locked himself fully into the soft folds of her inner thighs. He could tell by her whimper that he'd touched her pleasure spot. She pressed closer and they were as one, moving in sync.

Hot tides of passion raced through her and she wantonly pushed him to a sitting position. She felt him deep inside her as she lost herself in the pleasure of his kiss. Her thighs tightened around his waist as passion pounded the blood through her heart, chest and head.

Feeling the intensity of her hunger, he released her lips and watched the emotions play out on her face, felt her impatience as her body jerked and clung to the hardness of him, pulling, draining.

She gasped in sweet agony as her body lit up and shattered into a million glowing stars. The strong hardness of his thighs pressed hungrily against hers as he gave her all the fiery release she needed, they needed.

Still clinging to him, he allowed her to pull him back against the damp sheets. He rolled off her and gathered her to him. Her gentle understanding ways had certainly belied her fiery passion. He turned on the light and she grabbed the sheets and covered her body.

"You are the most beautiful woman I have ever known. You have the body of a goddess," he said, gently lowering the sheet from her body. "Please don't deny me the pleasure of seeing the body that just brought tears to my eyes."

She slowly let go of the sheet and his hand wandered over her body, taking in all her curves. She closed her eyes to his touch and bit her lips.

"I love you. I love every single thing about you. Every curve of this wonderful body." He inhaled deeply and shook his head.

"Everything?" she said in a small voice as she opened her eyes to look at him.

"Everything."

She ran her hands over his muscular body, the scars on his neck and cheek. She gently kissed each scar and whispered, "I love you."

She watched him grin, showing his uneven white teeth. "You're beautiful on the inside, and handsome and…"

He blushed.

THE OTHER SIDE OF THE MOUNTAIN

"It's true." She turned and fitted her body into his. He ran his finger down the small of her back and she trembled and moaned. Quickly aroused, she claimed his mouth savagely, sending currents of desire running through him. He groaned and was ready for her. She slipped on top of him and massaged his body with hers. Her breast to his made him tingle and he pulled her up and took a ready nipple into his mouth. She gasped and moved against him as he willingly gave his entire body and soul to her. She took him inside her and made love to him in a way that his body would never forget. Wave after wave of pleasure radiated and pulsed through him. Every nerve ending in his groin became sensitive as his breathing became erratic. *If this is how I should die, Jah, I'm willing,* he thought.

His senses reeled as if short-circuited when she moved her body, expertly bringing him to a fiery pitch. He allowed her breast to slip slowly from between his teeth and hungrily claimed her mouth. She felt him and waited and squeezed as once again they exploded together. He held her there, on top of him. She rested her head against his damp chest, feeling the rapid beat of his heart until it slowly went back to normal. "If I didn't know then, I know now," he said.

Her eyes opened, then slowly closed.

She fell asleep on top of the man she loved.

Chapter 15

Dawn in Kingston was so unlike dawn on Rahjah Mountain. There was no waterfall, no mist to burn off as the morning wore on, no breakfast with the entire village. It was just her and Saul in this hotel room. The sun wasn't quite up yet, but she was awake. She turned to see bright brown eyes looking at her. She smiled.

"Good morning. Sleep well?"

"Like a baby."

With the events of the night before permanently etched in his brain, he grinned and wondered how this docile, beautiful, woman could be such a tigress in bed. That was not the right thing to think about because he could feel his member become hot and pulsing.

It had been nine years since she'd had a man, but she had not forgotten a man's needs. She grinned back at him and pulled herself into his waiting arms.

Her body was as hot and wanting as his and he didn't hesitate to enjoy every inch of her as they made love.

All insecurities about her body had slipped through the open window and when he got out of bed and reached for her, she took his hand and followed him to the shower stall. She tried not to look at his naked body, but the temptation was too great. She grinned and bit into her lower lip as she took in every rippling muscle.

"Am I okay?"

Looking at him, she'd been in a world of her own and in that world she was once again touching him, setting off sparks as a hot ache grew in her throat, moving down to the surge of blood between her thighs. His low voice startled her. She screamed and covered her face with her hands. She'd had no idea he was watching her. "I'm so embarrassed."

"Why? I can tell you where your dimples are and how long your legs are."

"I have short legs," she said between her fingers.

He pulled her to him, turned on the shower and ran the liquid soap all over her body. "I love those short legs." Her flawless body under his caressing hands almost made him go into overdrive again. *Control yourself, boy, or she'll think you're an addict.* Allowing the cool water to run over his body, he half turned away from her. She began rubbing the soap on his back. He laughed and shook his head. "Don't do that. If you do we'll never leave this room today."

She returned his laugh. "Is that so bad?"

He looked at her and shook his head. "Not at all." He pulled her to him, washed the soap from her body and buried his face between her breasts. Then he lifted her off the tiled floor. She wrapped her legs around him and once again allowed him to make delicious love to her.

After an hour, they ordered room service, made love, slept, awoke and made love some more.

James had reserved a villa for them in Bluefields. So after a morning of enjoying each other, they left Kingston for Bluefields. As a child, Saul and James had visited Bluefields with their fathers, but James had warned him that this was no longer the Bluefields he'd known way back when. The drive took roughly an hour and a half and when they got to the Cottonwood cottage, Saul understood what James had been talking about. The place was breathtaking. When they'd visited Bluefields as kids, there were no hotels at all, just the beach and private homes; now these splendid structures made him grin.

"Wow," Pamela said. "This is beautiful."

He had to grab her hand for her not to get out of the car before he could get a chance to open her door. She laughed. "Have I been that bad?"

"No, but you're so enthusiastic that it's hard to keep up with you."

"I know, I'm a little like Gracie would be if she were here. And I know I said the same thing in Portland, but Jamaica is really beautiful."

THE OTHER SIDE OF THE MOUNTAIN

"I wouldn't go as far as to say you're childlike. Don't get me wrong, I'm not complaining. I just want to be able to keep up with you." He opened his door. "Now don't go away."

He ran around to her side and opened the door for her. She took his outstretched hand and laughed. "More of a lady?"

"You've been nothing but."

She kissed his lips. "No, I haven't, but thanks for saying that."

While the headman had someone take their suitcases to their villa, she pulled Saul to the overlook and laughed. She coughed. Although this place was far from the maddening crowd of Kingston, it wasn't exactly Rahjah Mountain; there had to be a little pollution. "Jamaica is really so beautiful," she said. "I don't know what I was afraid of."

He shrugged. "No matter where we go in the world, there's going to be someone who gives the wrong impression. But there are some really nice people in this world away from Rahjah Mountain."

She nodded, slipped her arm around his waist and leaned her head against his chest. "Or maybe I was just waiting for you to bring me here."

He waited a moment, then walked her to their room. She stood at the door and smiled at the dark, richly polished floors and four-poster king-size canopy bed draped with soft white embroidered material. The headboard had very intricate carvings and she ran her fingers into each crevice, remembering her own mahogany bed at home that Peter had made for them. It just wasn't this big or elaborate.

The heels of her sandals clicked on the floor as she walked out to the terrace where a sumptuous lunch awaited them. Saul had chosen everything for their lunch, even the freshly prepared banana bread.

Pamela slipped off her sandals, poured them black tea and sat back while Saul made a plate for her. "You did all this for me?"

"Yes, but I can't take all the credit. James made all the necessary arrangements. I haven't been to Bluefields in years. He warned me that it had changed but I never expected anything like this."

"Better than before?" She ate a piece of the banana bread and shook her head. "This is almost as good as my mother's. Don't tell her I said that." She laughed.

"I won't, and yes, this is extremely different from the Bluefields I once knew. When I came here there were no hotels, just private houses." He shook his head. "I can't get over how beautiful this place is. The transformation is remarkable."

"I love it, too. And thank you so much for bringing me here."

He gazed into her eyes and smiled. He'd become conscious of her looking at his teeth every time he laughed, so he hardly showed them anymore.

THE OTHER SIDE OF THE MOUNTAIN

"Why do you do that?" she asked.

"What?"

"Hide yourself from me."

He knew what she meant. "Sorry, I won't do it anymore. What would you like to do after lunch?"

"I would like to do that snorkeling thing you spoke of. I mean, with the plastic thing on my face. You did say the fish and coral appear much clearer with it on."

He laughed, showing her what she wanted to see. She happily caught his laughter.

"Yes, you are truly a gem, extremely rare, extremely exotic."

She didn't say anything but averted her eyes from his and looked out at the crystal clear water. "Are you sure we can't swim without our bathing suits?" She giggled.

"Yes." He looked out at the dense tropical foliage. "This might be very private, but the beach is not. I promise when you go back home you can go back to swimming in the nude." He took a deep breath and closed his eyes for a second as the alluring sight of her beautiful body swam before his eyes. "I have to learn to control myself," he said, opening his eyes.

"Do I have anything to do with it?"

"You have everything to do with it."

Her eyes glowed with enjoyment as they sat in silence and finished their lunch.

JANICE ANGELIQUE

She picked up her glass of guava nectar and leaned against the white railing, looking out at the people boating, kayaking or just lying on the beach. She walked inside, got her book and came back out to just sit in the lounge chair and read for a while. He sat beside her. In only a few minutes her eyes closed. Try as she may, she couldn't keep them open. She had not gotten much sleep the previous night and before long she fell into a peaceful slumber. The book slipped from her hand to the floor. Saul picked it up, gazed at her for a moment and then brushed a kiss on her lips. As the ever-present balmy breeze persisted and the fan overhead spun, they both slept.

He woke to find her in his arms, one foot flung wantonly across his leg. He inhaled the lavender perfume from her hair and caressed her cheek. Her eyes fluttered awake. "Hi," he said.

"I guess we both needed the rest," she said.

He nodded, but he knew the rest was not for long. She got to her feet, went inside and came back dressed in a black one-piece bathing suit. He sat there just gazing at her, taking her in frame by frame: her collar bone, her breasts, her flat belly, her hips, and her thighs. Oh, those thighs that had held him in place while she made love to him. He took a deep breath and thanked his lucky stars that she was his.

She attempted to cover herself with her hands. He laughed and shook his head. "You're funny."

THE OTHER SIDE OF THE MOUNTAIN

"Get ready. The water awaits."

He did as he was told and soon they were both walking on powder-white sand to the warm inviting ocean. It didn't take him long to teach her how to snorkel. She was not only an excellent swimmer but a very strong one, used to looking at marine life without the help of goggles.

※

Pamela had told the very efficient staff exactly what she wanted for supper.

Sitting in lounge chairs under an umbrella, they welcomed the tropical drinks a member of the staff brought them.

"Do you miss home?" Saul asked.

"Not as much as I thought I would, but I do miss Gracie."

"Next time we come back we'll bring her."

"Along with Ruth and David." From her chair, she touched his outstretched hand.

He looked at her and smiled. "Yes."

She kept looking at him. The scar on his cheek had begun taking on his complexion. She closed her eyes.

"Are you sleeping?" Saul asked.

She laughed and didn't answer.

"Was that a stupid question?"

JANICE ANGELIQUE

She opened her eyes and looked at him. "Who was it that once said there are no stupid questions, just stupid answers?"

"Water."

"Then I will choose my words carefully. No."

He brought the glass to his lips and almost spilled it on himself as he began laughing. "You are the light and dark of my life." He wiped the drink from his belly.

"Why dark?"

"I don't know. I guess I mean you are my entire life. Does that sound sappy?" He held her gaze.

"Sappy? Let me think about that for a while." She shook her head. "You, sir, are a romantic."

He kept looking at her. He hadn't always been a romantic. She'd done this to him. In just a short while, she'd changed him for the better. With all his heart he hoped this feeling would never leave him. He nodded. "Yes, I think I am."

"What keeps you safe when you're all alone in the big, bad world, Saul?"

He thought that a strange question. "You've been thinking."

"I'm always thinking of you. I mean, who protects you from, you know…"

He laughed. "The last time I went away, I couldn't stop thinking of you. You kept me safe."

"I mean all those years when you traveled, you must have met some very nice women?"

THE OTHER SIDE OF THE MOUNTAIN

He studied her thoughtfully for a moment. "Believe it or not, I grew up a lot after my marriage failed. I kept seeing Raquel in every woman's eyes until you."

"Am I that different?"

"Yes," he whispered. He got out of his chair, lifted her and carried her back into the water. They swam out to where his feet could still touch the sand without the water covering his head. He looked around and there was no one else to be seen.

Her feelings for him were intensifying as she became more and more a part of him.

He held her face and drank from the soft lips that awakened his senses and sent shock waves to his loins. His tongue traveled the fullness of her lips, sending waves of desires racing through her.

She hugged his neck, wrapped her legs around his waist and whispered in his ear. "Am I being bad?"

He laughed. "You're everything I want and need."

"Are you sure?"

"As sure as my feet are on the sand." He couldn't help himself. She got under his skin, welcomed him into her body and made love to him.

Slowly, hesitantly, they pulled apart, swam back to the place they'd snorkeled before then went back to the cottage to have supper.

After supper they walked on the beach barefoot. "What makes this different from walking on the beach on Rahjah Island?" she asked.

JANICE ANGELIQUE

"You're not running away. And, when I wake in the morning, you'll be in my arms."

She nodded. "Yes."

Under the moonlight, as the balmy breeze caressed their bodies, he lay her on the sand and once again took her in his arms. She laid on his chest and took a deep breath. "This is better than the big lovely bed."

He nodded.

Chapter 16

The next day, in the privacy of James's beachfront cottage, Pamela got her wish to skinny dip in the ocean outside of Rahjah Island. A day later, Saul drove to the Blue Mountain and James's uncle drove them to their boat.

A few minutes before they docked on the island, Saul cut the engine for her to see how beautiful her home was.

She looked up at him and smiled. "Thank you. It is a very beautiful place."

"You have to stop thanking me. I did this as much for you as me. A little bit of you at a time is better than none at all."

She looked into his beautiful eyes and didn't know what to say. Jamaica was very beautiful, but he'd reminded her of how precious and beautiful her island was.

But when he offered to take her to her village, she refused.

"Pam, we've been with each other for a week. Your mother knows you were with me, my mother knows we were together, and now you don't want me to take you home?" His earnest eyes sought hers. "Pam, we're adults. We have a right to live our lives as we see fit."

"And we are." She glanced down at her clothes. She'd purposely chosen a palazzo pants outfit to wear back home because it wasn't form-fitting.

He laughed. "You're turning back into a Rahjah."

"Did I seem to change?"

"Oh, yes," he growled, pulling her to him with a big grin on his face.

She laughed and blushed under her dark skin.

Saul pulled the boat up to her side of the island and anchored close to the other boats. She picked up her bag and he guided her out of the boat. "I loved every minute of being with you. I wouldn't change a thing even if I could," she said.

"I love you." He pulled her into his arms and kept her there.

"I love you. Saul, let's keep this a secret a little while longer, please. You changed me a little this week. You awakened something inside of me that I didn't think existed anymore. You pulled me into you and showed me that I don't have to be afraid of anything." She hugged him then gave him a long and promising kiss.

He touched her cheek in a profound gesture. "I'll do anything for you. Although I'm sure your friend Mary has her suspicions, I'll try to keep our relationship a secret a while longer. I'll walk half of the way with you."

THE OTHER SIDE OF THE MOUNTAIN

She nodded. They walked until they got to the path leading up to the village. She whistled for her horse and he laughed.

"When will I see you again?" he asked.

"You know you can always visit me in the village, right?"

"Oh." She certainly knew how to confuse him. "Yes, right."

"But I still want to keep our relationship a secret."

He laughed and shook his head. "Won't they guess what's going on if I show up at your door every day?"

Surprised that her horse wore a saddle, she smiled, took hold of the reins and jumped onto his back. Saul placed her bag in front of her. "I love you," she said, then urged her horse into a gallop.

He watched until she was out of sight, then shook his head and chuckled. "You're doing it again, but as long as I have you I'm not complaining." He walked back to the boat and got in.

Pamela reined her horse in when she saw the children riding towards her. She got off when they got close and gathered Gracie in her arms as she jumped from her horse.

"I missed you. Did you have a good time? Did you see Uncle Saul? We knew you were coming back today so we made sure your horse had his straps on." She hugged her mother's neck and wouldn't let go even when Ruth, David and Shaela hugged her.

"Yes, thank you. I had a wonderful time but I missed you a lot." She looked at the other children. "I missed all of you."

"Did you see our dada?" Ruth said. "He went to Jamaica, too."

She couldn't lie. "I know. And yes, I did see him. As a matter of fact we came home together."

Eight little eyes seemed to stare at her at once. "You did?" Gracie said, laughing.

"Yes. What's so funny?"

Gracie glanced at her friends and they all shook their heads together.

Then Ruth said in a quiet tone, "Our mama is still in our village."

Pamela's heart leapt to her throat and she swallowed and slowly stood up. She smiled nervously. "She is?" She looked at the twins. "You guys should go and welcome your father home."

"Yes," the twins said in unison. They got up onto their horses. "We'll see you later." They waved, then galloped away.

Pamela, Gracie and Shaela rode their horses into the village, then took them into the barn. Pamela had not said anything much about the fact that Raquel was still in the village, but she wondered how she would react when Saul revealed her secret.

"I love your new bag, Mama. Did you bring me anything from Jamaica?"

THE OTHER SIDE OF THE MOUNTAIN

Pamela laughed. "Yes, I got something for you and Shaela.

"I'll take your bag in for you."

Mary stood on her verandah grinning as Pamela walked up to her. Both women hugged, but Mary still grinned.

"What's so funny?" Pamela asked.

"Seeing you back here safe and sound. Apparently the Jamaicans didn't gobble you up."

"Yes. You are funny."

"What are you wearing?" Mary asked.

"Do you like it?" Pamela spun around, showing off her new attire.

"Yes, I do, and I want one like that."

"It's very easy to make." Both women walked into Mary's cottage.

She followed Mary into her small kitchen and watched as she brewed tea.

Mary placed two cups and a pot of tea on a tray with a few slices of banana bread, then walked back to the living room.

Pamela sat down and took the cup offered to her.

"Okay," Mary said, sitting opposite Pamela. "I want to hear everything about your little escape with the gorgeous Saul. Did he sweep you off your feet? Did you fall in love? Did he sweep the cobwebs from your heart?"

JANICE ANGELIQUE

Pamela laughed. "You sure are nosy. But yes, and yes." She kept the cup to her face a bit longer.

"He didn't sweep the cobwebs from your heart?" Mary seemed a bit disappointed.

"I think he did, but…"

Mary giggled and made a face. "Why the hesitation? Ahhh, let me guess. The children told you that the lady never left the island."

Pamela nodded. "Mary, I really don't want her to be here any longer." She sighed and lowered the cup to the floor.

"I know. No one wants her here. We are all aware that she's trying to push herself back into his life, but it's not going to happen. And before I go any farther, Myah suspects that her brother is sweet on you. Actually she has her fingers crossed that something will develop between you two."

"Mary!" Pamela gasped.

Mary placed her cup on the floor and held up her hands. "I have not said anything to anyone. I swear. But come on, Pammy. He's not hiding his feelings for you. I would go as far as to say he cannot hide his feelings for you. They're right there in his eyes, the way he looks at you when he thinks no one is looking." She shook her head. "My dear friend, I wish my husband would look at me like that."

Pamela sighed. "I don't feel comfortable with her there in his home."

THE OTHER SIDE OF THE MOUNTAIN

Mary offered her a piece of banana bread. "I know how you feel, but when the woman gets intoxicated she spills everything and doesn't remember a thing the next day. Of course no one reminds her of what she's said…"

Pamela shook her head. "What are you talking about?"

"She got married to someone else." She looked at Pamela, thinking she'd be shocked at the news.

Pamela nodded. "I know."

"You know? Who told you? Does Saul know?"

She nodded. "Of course. As soon as Raquel showed up in the village, James and Devin put their spies to work and found out what she'd been up to all those years," Pamela said.

"What do you think Saul is going to do?"

Pamela shook her head. "Your guess is as good as mine. I know he's a very sweet and gentle human being, but…" She hated thinking of Raquel with Saul in the same room. She'd seen firsthand what the woman could do. But knowing what he knew, how was Saul going to handle her still being there?

Mary touched Pamela's knee. "Hey, are you here or back in Jamaica?"

"Why?"

"I've been talking to you for the last few minutes and you haven't responded. You just had this spacey look on your face."

"Sorry, what were you saying?"

"What exactly did you do in Jamaica?"

Pamela smiled. "I went to the movies and to a pantomime in Kingston. Then Saul took me to a place called Bluefields Bay." She had a dreamy look in her eyes. "It was beautiful."

"So you really had a good time then?"

"Up to now. How's my mother?" Pamela asked.

"She's been a little down since you left. She won't say why."

Pamela finished her tea and got to her feet. "I'll go see her."

"Aren't you going to change first?"

She laughed. "Oh, yes. Come with me. I brought you a new hair comb." She fished into her bag and gave the pearl comb set to Mary, then proceeded to change her clothes. "I think after a certain age, the grown-ups should stop dressing like the children, don't you agree?"

"Ummm, absolutely," Mary murmured, sticking the comb into her hair. "Judiah will love me in this." She touched the comb and looked back at Pamela.

"I'm sure he will," Pamela said.

"You're right. This is only for special occasions."

They both walked outside together. Pamela made the short walk to her mother's cottage and quickly embraced her when she came to the door. "I missed you," she said, noting her mother's smile.

THE OTHER SIDE OF THE MOUNTAIN

"So why didn't you come here first?" Esther held her daughter by the hand and led her to the living room.

"Oh, Mama. Anyway, I hear you've not been yourself since I left. Why?"

Esther sat down on a cushion and shrugged. "I don't know." She looked at Pamela. "Yes, I do. I know we raised our children to be independent of us, but when your…you know…"

"Please say it, Mama." Pamela's eyes pleaded with her mother.

She nodded and held her daughter's hand. "When your husband left, you were heartbroken for a very long time and I don't ever want to see you like that again."

"Mama, Saul is healthy and gentle and so loving. He's not going anywhere. He's not going to die. Not for now, anyway."

"We all die sometime, dear."

"I know, but I have a feeling you're not really fearing his death. You're fearing his life, my life, our life together. What's really bothering you?"

Esther heaved a very big sigh. "Does he seem to be very taken with you, Pammy? Did you have a good time with him?"

Pamela laughed. Thinking about Saul in that loving way did something for and to her. "Oh, Mama, he's wonderful and attentive. He allows me to be myself. He never tells me what to do. Actually, he went along with everything I wanted to do. He loves me, Mama."

"He told you so?"

"Yes."

"So I suppose at this point he can do no wrong."

"Oh, Mama." She wrinkled her nose and squeezed her eyes shut.

"And you?"

"It didn't take long for me to realize that I love him."

"It never does, my dear. I've always said you can't try to love or like someone. Either you do or you don't. They turn you off or they turn you on. It goes for a lover or a friend."

Pamela laughed. "You are hip, aren't you?"

"You got that word from that Angel."

"It's not a bad word."

"No, it's not."

"I know Mary told you that Raquel is still in the village."

Pamela nodded woodenly and looked down at her fingers laced in front of her.

"Don't worry. His mother and I had tea a few days ago. He's a very smart man. He's all you said he is and more, so don't worry, he'll make himself properly available for you."

THE OTHER SIDE OF THE MOUNTAIN

Pamela looked up at her mother with a quizzical smile on her face. "Is this the woman who was once so doubtful of us?"

Esther shrugged. "Well, you know, a mother never stops being a mother. Even when you're ninety, if I'm still alive I'll still worry about you, and it has absolutely nothing to do with trust."

Pamela leaned her head against her mother's shoulder. "Thanks, Mama. I love you, too."

The women got to their feet and walked to the verandah. "So what did you think of Jamaica?"

"It's not as warm and beautiful as here."

"No place is, dear."

⁂

Saul had just stepped onto his verandah when he heard his children call, "Dada, Dada." He laughed and gathered them in his arms. "You're home. We heard you had a good time in Jamaica," Ruth said.

He wrinkled his brow and laughed, then kissed her cheek. "Now where did you hear that?"

"We saw Auntie Pam and she said she came back to the island with you." David shot his sister a conspiratorial look.

"Oh, right," she said.

"So tell me, how have you both been behaving?"

"Grangran said it was all right to stay with Gracie's grangran until you came home, so we did. Mama didn't come for us," Ruth said.

His brow furrowed. "What do you mean?"

"Mama is still here," David said.

"Oh." His smile was tight. "I brought something for you kids, it's in my bag." He handed them the bag. "You can carry it into the library and search for your gifts. You'll know them when you see them. I have to speak with your grandmother. I'll be back in a few minutes." He stood up, took a deep breath and went straight to his mother's cottage. She wasn't there, so he went to the kitchen.

Nanuk rushed out of the kitchen to welcome him as soon as she glimpsed his head through the kitchen window. "Son, how are you? I'm glad you're back." She wiped her hands on her apron and walked away from the kitchen with him. "So was it all you expected it to be? Does she feel the same way about you that you feel about her?"

"I have a feeling she's being asked that same question at this very moment," he said, smiling. "Yes, it was, and more." His attitude changed. "Why is *she* still here?"

They stopped under a shade tree. "I don't know, son. She keeps saying you owe her something and you're still her husband. Unfortunately, she doesn't realize that we all know her secret."

THE OTHER SIDE OF THE MOUNTAIN

"So everyone knows?"

"My dear son, when she drinks she talks and we listen."

"So she still doesn't know that we know she's married to another man?"

Nanuk shook her head.

"I can't deal with her anymore, Mama. I've asked her to leave as nicely as I can."

"And as a gentleman you're not allowed to lose your temper."

"I'm at the edge. I really am."

"I know you are, my son."

He left his mother, walked inside his home and sighed loudly at the mess before him. Raquel's clothes were thrown all over the place. The kitchen was filthy with wine bottles in the sink. He wondered if she had brought a suitcase of wine with her. He feared to look in the bedroom. This time, he would not pick up after her. He walked into the library, which was the only place untouched by Raquel's mess. He sat and talked with the children. "Is Mama sick again?" Ruth asked.

"I think so," he said, not sure what to tell them this time. He kissed the children. "I'll be back soon." He walked outside and stood on his verandah, remembering the wonderful time he'd had with Pamela. Lost in his thoughts he walked to the stables and got onto his horse. He was angry with Raquel for bringing her lifestyle into the village, into the home of his children.

He didn't know where he was going until the horse walked across the bridge toward Pamela's home. He reined the horse in outside of the village and sat there for a while. He needed Pamela. He allowed the horse to take him to her home, then dismounted.

Pamela saw him. The look on his face was the look of a beaten man. She opened the door and he walked through. He sat down and she sat beside him. She didn't say anything. He looked into her eyes and smiled. "You're so beautiful."

"You didn't come here to tell me how beautiful I am. What's going on?"

He sighed, shook his head and explained the mess he'd seen in his home.

Pamela leaned back and scoured the paintings on her walls. "Put her in the hospital."

He looked at her with furrowed brows.

"She's sick, Saul. There is an area in the hospital that deals with these things. It hasn't been used for a while, but it's there and so are the means to help her."

He knew what she was talking about. Detox. That area of the cave hospital was once used to help people work through anger issues. There had been a few Rahjahs that had gone into the outside world and come back addicted to alcohol and asked for help. They had a 100 percent cure rate. The men and women who'd helped these people get over their addiction were still there in the village and would be very willing to help even Raquel.

"I'm glad I came to you," he said, smiling. "Do you think they'll be ready after supper?"

"I don't see why not. Can you get her there?"

That was the other thing. If Raquel wasn't willing to go on her own, they'd have to force her, which was not the best thing to do.

"I'll get her there. Have the practitioners standing by." He got to his feet. "Where's your little one?"

"At your sister's."

He pulled her to him and kissed her hungrily, then hugged her. "Thank you." He walked out of the cottage, then stopped and turned before he mounted his horse. "Thank you." Then he got on his horse and rode away.

She should have told him that there were practitioners in his village, too, but knew he would find that out once he made his intentions known. Myah was one of the practitioners, and Pamela wondered if she would be willing to help Raquel for Saul and the twins' sake. She walked over to Myah and told her of Saul's intentions.

Myah looked at her with resentment in her eyes. "I don't know, Pammy."

"Myah, you took an oath when you became a practitioner to help everyone who needed your help."

"I know, but my heart will not be in my work this time."

"For your brother and his children, Myah, please. Help her to get better so that she can leave the island a healthy person."

Myah was still hesitant, but she nodded. "When?"

"After supper."

"We need four people to work in shifts. She has to have someone there all the time." She took a deep breath. "I'll tell Tiney."

Pamela hugged her. "Thank you, Myah. You're a good person. I'll help Samuel with Isha."

"I know you will."

⁂

It was more difficult on Saul's end. When he told his mother of his plans to get Raquel into detox, she got the two practitioners in the village ready to go to the hospital. But getting Raquel to agree to do this was something else entirely.

When Saul went back to the cottage, Raquel was up and searching through all the drawers for her wine. Saul stood at the kitchen door watching her. "I threw them away," he said.

She turned and glared at him. "You threw away what?" she shouted.

"The wine. I will not allow you to submit these children to your drunkenness any more. You need to

THE OTHER SIDE OF THE MOUNTAIN

go to the hospital for at least a week to get the liquor out of your system."

She laughed in his face. "And if I refuse?"

"Then I will take you bodily."

For the first time in her life she saw coldness and contempt in his eyes. But still, she advanced toward him and raised her hand. He grabbed her hand and shook his head.

"No more, Raquel. Your reign of terror is over. I will not allow you to hit me, degrade me, or degrade yourself in front of the children."

She spat in his face and turned to leave. He calmly wiped his face, reached out and swung her around to face him. "That will be the last time you do that." He glared at her. "Get dressed. Either you do this willingly or I will send for your husband and allow him to see you as you are."

Shocked, she gasped and closed her mouth.

He let go of her. She stood with her chest heaving. She was angry, but seemingly afraid of her husband and maybe a little bit afraid of Saul at the moment. "How did you find out?" Her voice shook.

"You have no idea who we are, do you?" His eyes bore into her.

Raquel now saw the side of her husband she had never taken the time to notice before. He stood intimidating and strong with his shoulders pulled back and his eyes cold.

JANICE ANGELIQUE

"Before you go, clean up this place. I will be back for you in an hour." Saul strode to the library, got the children and went to supper.

Sitting with his children, he ate very little. He smiled as he thought of Pamela. She could have told him to just ship the woman off the island. Knowing what they all knew, it would have taken no effort at all. Instead of being vindictive, Pam had unselfishly thrown Raquel a lifeline and him his self-respect.

His mother touched his shoulder. "Will she be ready, son?"

He nodded.

Nanuk was skeptical, but she trusted her son.

After supper, John and Lila escorted Raquel out of the village toward the caves. They would meet Myah and Tiney there. Raquel would be required to eat with everyone else in the hospital and could not see the children or Saul until she was well.

Chapter 17

After school the next day, Pamela had a meeting with Jane in her cottage to talk about the new class. "So how do you think it's going?" Jane asked. "Do the children seem to like this new class of yours?"

"Absolutely. Grangran, we are not the only ones occupying this great big world of ours. This great expanse of dirt and water."

Jane laughed but didn't interrupt.

"You have traveled all over the world. Why do you think we shouldn't teach about the outside world? Why should we restrict ourselves to just our history? We encourage the children to leave and learn about the world, but we really don't prepare them for it. I would like to think this class will prepare them for that, whether they wish to leave the island one day or not."

Jane looked at her and smiled understandingly. "You will have to teach all Rahjahs about the outside world, not just our village."

Pamela nodded. "I see what you mean. Okay, Grangran, I'll write a book of my work and send it to the other villages. Then I will ask Saul to get us more books of the same kind for the other villages."

"That's a very good idea. Is there anything else you would like to change?" She was still smiling at her granddaughter.

Pamela shook her head. "If I think of anything I'll let you know."

Jane smiled. "I may have to elect you as an honorary Elder."

Pamela ignored her grandmother's comment. She put her finger to her cheek. "You know, we should have more parties, more dancing in the villages. We've been so consumed by work and the woman Raquel's displeasure that we've forgotten to celebrate why we are on this earth. We need to celebrate life every day of our lives and thank Jah for giving us another day. Every day is someone's birthday in this village. We must celebrate always. You should remind the Rahjahs of that."

"No, not me dear, but you. You and your little girl are subtly making changes in the village, changes that affect everyone in a positive way. You and Gracie have demonstrated such extraordinary positivism that people are beginning to talk."

"I don't think I've done anything…"

"Pish posh, of course you have. The first Elders should not have placed responsibility of the tribes upon just the old, but the young who inspire and do things for the betterment of our culture. You know, Pammy, when our ancestors made the long, danger-

THE OTHER SIDE OF THE MOUNTAIN

ous and arduous trek up the Blue Mountain, it was decided then that women would be treated equally. The making of the home and preparation of the children was left to us. Our men were satisfied providing for us and coming home to rest and play with us. We were and still are the force behind our home. We make it pleasant for each other. Some women craved more control and tried to manipulate their men to their every whim; other women, well, they tried the balancing act and found it more rewarding. The Elders never intervened unless asked to do so. They preferred that Rahjahs learn from each other. Not everyone likes to be told what to do, but if they see something good happening, they'll follow."

Pamela didn't respond and Jane smiled and touched her cheek to her granddaughter's cheek. "Modesty is a very good virtue, my dear." She changed the subject. "Your grandfather felt a little under the weather so he chose to stay in bed today."

"Is he all right?"

"Oh, sure."

They sat and had tea and biscuits before Pamela left.

Passing the schoolhouse, she noticed Saul leaving. She stopped and waited for him. "What are you doing here?" she asked. "Not that I'm not glad to see you, but I didn't know you'd be here." She looked into his smiling eyes.

"Remember me telling you that I actually taught geology to the older children in my village?"

She nodded.

"Well, I've decided to do for all the villages what I do for mine."

"That's wonderful." She laughed. "And a lot of traveling, hopefully not on the same day."

He began walking with her. "Not at all, but I will go to the Blue Mountain twice per week." Still smiling, he glanced at her.

"I'm so glad you're doing that. I wish all the other professionals who live outside the villages would think of doing the same."

"Your wish is my command. I have contacted the Rahjah professors in Jamaica and those on other Caribbean islands who can afford to come in to give a workshop at least once per month."

She glanced up at him. "Wow, how innovative of you. We thank you."

"No, we thank *you*. You actually inspire us to give something back to a community that gave us everything."

"You do know that I don't sit and contemplate the things I do, don't you? I come up with ideas and pass them along or act on them."

He stopped, took her hand and looked in her eyes. "You have to learn to take a compliment or an award."

"Who would give me an award?"

THE OTHER SIDE OF THE MOUNTAIN

He laughed and shook his head. "There you go again. Give me a chance to say thank you, just this once."

She wanted to object but clamped her mouth shut.

Saul began walking, still holding her hand and intertwining his fingers in hers. She eased her fingers from his.

"I forgot. To the world, we are still just friends. But I have to tell you, there are people who will not be fooled," he said.

"I know. Did Raquel go to the hospital?"

"Yes." He didn't want to speak of her.

"Was it a difficult task?"

"Not after I told her that if she didn't get the alcohol out of her system I would send for her husband."

"That was easy." Pamela laughed. "You are so bad. Would you have done that? Sent for her husband, I mean?"

"I wouldn't have threatened her if I couldn't back it up. Yes, I would have sent for him. I'm sure the poor chap is worried out of his mind."

"Or not."

"Or not," he echoed. "After all, we're not exactly on the map and I'm sure she didn't tell him of the children or me."

They got to her cottage and she invited him in. He sat down and she went into her room to change her clothes.

"Will you spend some time with me tomorrow?" he asked.

She came back out and sat beside him. She observed him thoughtfully. "That can be arranged."

"Okay."

She kept looking at him.

He laughed. "I'm not saying anything more. I hope you like surprises."

"I think so."

"Okay."

"Again with the okay."

He leaned back against the cushion and winked at her, then got to his feet. "I'll see you later." He looked to see if anyone was in sight, then lifted her off the cushion and kissed her passionately. He released her and she stood there breathless with her eyes closed. He gently kissed each cheek. "Later, then."

As if she were in a daze, she nodded.

The door closed and she opened her eyes, adjusted her dress and walked to the kitchen. *You can kiss me like that any time you wish.* She had a very seductive smile on her lips.

⁂

Just after supper, when it was time for dessert, Saul arrived with his children.

THE OTHER SIDE OF THE MOUNTAIN

Jane must have gotten the message across because halfway through dessert, the drums and tambourines began making music in celebration of life.

While the dishes were cleared and everyone sang and danced on a Monday evening, Saul and Pamela slipped away past the Elders' village to the top of the mountain.

Standing there with Saul's arms around her waist, she felt a bit light-headed. "I can see Jamaica from here," she said, a bit out of breath. She sat on a huge white rock. He sat beside her.

"Some of it at least," Saul replied, looking at the twinkling lights of somewhere in Jamaica. He thought Kingston, she thought Port Royal. The ocean was frighteningly dark without the moon, though the stars twinkled in abundance as if to the rhythm of the drums.

Saul took a deep breath and kissed Pamela's hands. "I have a confession to make, but please don't be angry with me. I was but a young boy."

"What is it?" She looked into his eyes and feigned being serious as her lips trembled with the need to laugh.

"I met you a long time ago, before I left the island. I fell in love with you, but you were with Peter at the time and you seemed quite unapproachable." He looked at her, not knowing what to expect.

"Unapproachable?" she echoed, losing the urge to laugh.

"Yes. Okay, you were always giving advice." He laughed. "And people gladly did what you told them to do."

"Did I steer them wrong?"

"That was the intimidating part. You gave good advice, but got a bit peeved if they didn't do as they were told. Frankly, half the time you were right on. Apart from Peter being around you all the time, you were never by yourself."

"And you were shy?"

"Yes, I was shy."

She looked away from him. "Why did you pretend not to know me when we met on the beach that first time?" Her voice was bland.

"I didn't know if I should tell you. When we went away, the things you said, the way you acted. You are so genuine and unpretentious." He stopped talking and looked out at the vast ocean. "I left for Jamaica at age seventeen. I thought of you a lot and wondered what you were doing and if I should have approached you, but as I said, Peter was always with you." His thumb gently caressed her hand. "Would it have made a difference if I'd approached you at any time back then?"

"I don't know. Peter and I grew up together. I was fond of him before I fell in love with him." She turned to look at him. "Unapproachable?"

THE OTHER SIDE OF THE MOUNTAIN

"Okay, maybe not unapproachable. Formidable?"

"That's not any better than intimidating and unapproachable." She shook her head and smiled as her voice became soft and alluring. "Are you trying to say if we'd known each other then maybe your life would have turned out a different way?"

He laughed. "Yes, but as I said, Peter never seemed to leave your side."

"Then this is our time. Nothing ever happens before its time."

He nodded. "This is our time. But for me, some regrets." He leaned over and pulled her into his arms. She laid her head on his shoulder and looked into his earnest eyes. His lips pressed against hers, gently covering her mouth. Her thoughts spun and her mind burned with the memory of their lovemaking as she kissed him hard. Slowly, before her body could betray her anymore, she released his lips and relaxed in the safety of his arms. He gently laid her on the rock and looked appraisingly at her as he propped himself up on his elbow. She drew his face to hers in a renewed embrace and pressed her open lips to him, causing her body to react in a way she wasn't ready for at the moment. She moved her mouth from his and pressed her thighs together.

When he was about to protest, she placed a finger on his lips. "I have a favor to ask you."

"Anything," he breathed.

"Do you mind if we don't make love again until Raquel leaves the island?"

He wasn't ready for that request. His body had already begun to rise in temperature. He gently pulled her to a sitting position.

"I'm sorry," she said.

"No, don't be. I'm trying to understand you. And right now I'm trying to understand your request."

She didn't say anything.

"Why?" he asked as if he were in pain.

She almost regretted her words. "I… I don't want to think of her being here, of you trying to do something kind for her. Of you going to the same house that she is in. Is that selfish of me?"

He held her gaze and shook his head. "No, you're not selfish at all. And, by the way, you've done something kind for her, too."

"What?"

"If it weren't for you, she would not be getting the treatment that hopefully will save her life."

"You asked for my help."

"Will you please allow me to compliment you?" He shook his head and his fingers intertwined with hers. "And although she was in my home, we never slept in the same room. Actually, we were hardly civil to each other. Just don't tell me I can't kiss you because that will just drive me mad. If that's all I can do, then that's all I will live for…for now. Should we hurry her treatment?"

She laughed and hugged him. "No, we can't. I have a feeling she will want to get out of there as quickly as she can, though. After all, she's not really allowed to see anyone she can antagonize. And her seeing Myah for the duration is not the most pleasant thing for Myah."

"Why?"

"Myah hates her."

"Oh, yes, I forgot, but Myah is a professional and knows how to hide her feelings." He laughed.

They sat there looking at the twinkling lights of Jamaica. "Did I make an unreasonable request? I mean we just cemented our relationship with the most sacred act, and now I want you to stop that act…for a while, at least."

He put his arm around her shoulder and pulled her close to him. He didn't look at her. "You know I want what you want. I want only your happiness. You've been inside me from the first day we met. Not making love for a while will not in the least diminish my feelings for you. As a matter of fact it makes me love and want you more. It's wonderful to share the flesh, but to nourish the soul is the most important thing." As he said the words he knew it was hogwash. He wanted her flesh every day of his life, but it sounded good.

She looked up at him and, for a second, she regretted her request because she wanted him to make love to her right there, right then. To bury her own feelings she laughed and squeezed her eyes shut. "Sorry."

"No, I mean…" He shook his head. "You know what I mean. I don't have to make love to you to show how much I love you. Am I making any sense here?"

She nodded. "Yes, and I love that you understand and will do this for me."

"Are you sure there's no way we can hurry her treatment?" He laughed and squeezed her shoulder lovingly. "I'm joking."

"I know, but I think the herbs they'll give her will help a great deal."

He got to his feet and pulled her to him. His body was hard against her and she slipped her hand around his waist to feel the rippling muscles in his back. Unconsciously, she ran her fingers down his spine and he smiled and shook his head. "No fair."

"Sorry. I don't really know the rules. I just know that touching you gives me a lot of pleasure."

"Me, too." Again he laughed.

"But…"

"Never mind."

They began walking down the mountain and he bent his head to touch hers and smell the lavender perfume in her hair. He slipped his hand around her waist. "I can do this."

THE OTHER SIDE OF THE MOUNTAIN

She didn't say anything.

When they were almost to her village, he spun her to face him. He lifted her off her feet and brushed her brow with his lips. "I love the way you smell," he said, kissing her forehead.

She clung to his neck and he allowed her to slide down his front, touching every part of him. He shivered inwardly, summoning all the strength he could not to ravish her. She was beautiful, enticing, and the sexiest woman he'd ever been with. He had to refrain from making love to her for the period of time she wanted them to be celibate. Starting later. "Every time I think of the first time we made love, I want you," he whispered in her ear. "I can't do it."

"Yes, you can. Try not to think of it for a while." She opened her mouth and welcomed the kiss that she had to have right at that moment. There was a dreamy intimacy to their kiss now, and neither wanted to stop. They both grew hot together in the cool mountain air. Finally their lips parted and she whispered, "I know what you mean." She felt desire racing through her.

They parted awkwardly. "Do you trust me?" he asked.

"Yes, I do," she whispered.

He nodded. "I have to live up to that trust."

"You've never let anyone down, have you?"

"Only myself."

She looked up at him and instantly knew what he meant. "Don't," she said in an almost commanding tone.

He took a deep breath and they walked back to the village in silence. Every now and again he'd caress her fingertips with his thumb.

Other people from his village had come to be with their friends or relatives and, after a while, they all left together.

Saul helped his children onto their horses, kissed her cheek and mounted his horse.

She waved.

Mary stood beside Pamela. "What was all that about?"

"What?"

Mary rolled her eyes and shook her head. "Myah's still guessing, and she's real close to calling you sister-in-law. She's paying very close attention."

Pamela turned and looked into Mary's eyes. "Don't you encourage her in any way."

"You know I won't, but do you think these people are stupid?"

"Oh, Mary, people will be people. Let them believe what they will. I am not saying anything yet. I want my fun."

"And you can have it."

Chapter 18

Saul and the twins met Pamela and Gracie just as she got to her cottage.

"Remember what I asked yesterday?" Saul said.

"Yes."

"Okay, let's go."

She tried to search his face but he was giving nothing away. "Okay."

They walked toward the stables. "We're riding?" Pam asked.

"No."

She looked at the children but they shook their heads. He'd not told them anything either.

He walked toward the caves. When he saw the serious look on Pam's face, he shook his head. "No, we're not doing that."

"I didn't say anything."

"I know, but the thought crossed your mind. I would not subject you to visiting Raquel at any time at all."

They silently walked through the bat-infested caves on to the beach. Still leading the way, he crossed the rocks, and suddenly his boat came into view. Pamela said nothing but got into the boat.

"Okay, now I'll tell you what we're doing," he said. "Pam, I thought you wouldn't mind visiting Port Royal again."

"No, it's a wonderful idea." She looked at Gracie, who was now very excited. This was her very first trip off the island and her first boat ride. The twins had actually visited Jamaica a few times, but at a younger age.

As the kids sat down, they could hardly contain their excitement. Pam looked at Saul and smiled as he slipped the key into the ignition and powered the boat.

"Thank you for doing this for the children." She stood beside him and he was careful not to put his arm around her, which was very hard because he really wanted to hug her.

"What's in Port Royal?" Gracie asked. Pamela turned and explained that a very long time ago Port Royal was swallowed up by the ocean and spat out. Gracie laughed. "Maybe it didn't taste good to the ocean."

"Only you'd find the humor in that," Pam said, laughing. In the open sea, she kept watching Gracie for sea sickness, but she kept grinning from ear to ear as the boat sped across the water.

"Where's bunny rabbit today, Gracie?" Pam asked.

"She's with her family, just like I'm with my family."

THE OTHER SIDE OF THE MOUNTAIN

Pam nodded slowly and glanced at Saul. She didn't know what to say. Neither did he. Pam wished she knew what was going through Gracie's mind.

When they got to Port Royal, Saul stopped by one of the vendors and ordered fish and bammy before they toured the small city, and as the children ran ahead, he held Pam's hand. "She is with her family, you know," he said, gently squeezing Pam's hand.

She looked at him, smiled and nodded. "Yes."

Stopping by the old cannon, Gracie asked, "Can you tell us about this place and why the sea thought it so bitter?"

Pam nodded and they sat under the flagpole. "Do you want to take this one?" she asked Saul.

"You start," he said as the children looked at them expectantly.

"This was once called the wickedest city on earth," Pam said.

"Why?" Gracie said.

"Port Royal was one of the largest towns in the English colonies during the late seventeenth century. Unfortunately, it was a haven for pirates and bad people. After 1670, Port Royal became very important because of the trade in slaves, as well as sugar and other raw materials."

"Did our ancestors come to Jamaica through Port Royal?" Ruth asked.

"That's very possible," Saul replied. "It was designed to serve as a defensive fort, but over time became extremely important because of its location and the fact that it was well protected. Jamaica's economy grew because of Port Royal."

"Did anyone die when it sank?" Gracie asked.

"Don't you ever listen when the Elders give their history lessons? I'm sure they talk about Port Royal. Anyway, yes. History reports that more than two thousand people were killed instantly and another three thousand died of injuries and disease. After the earthquake Port Royal was rebuilt but was once again destroyed by fire. After being battered by hurricanes and earthquakes, Port Royal disappeared into the ocean," Pam said.

"But it's here again," David said.

"This is just a shell of what it once was. Picture this as a port with huge ships docked and all kinds of people, including dignitaries, trading and living here. The over two thousand buildings were made of brick, a sign of wealth in those days." Pamela looked out at the woman walking toward them. "Remind me to have the Elders go over the history of Port Royal. It's a fascinating story."

Their fish was ready. They got up and walked toward the table containing their food.

By the end of the day, Saul was holding Pamela's hand without even thinking of what he was doing. She

THE OTHER SIDE OF THE MOUNTAIN

didn't try to remove her hand from his as they made their way back to the boat and home.

It was late when they got back to the island, and, as they walked back to Pam's cottage, the children remarked that they'd had a wonderful day. "I'm glad you had a good time," Pam said, hugging the twins.

Saul hugged Gracie before he hugged her, then got onto his horse. "Thanks for making this a very special day," he said, then turned his horse and set off with his children.

"I had the best time," Gracie said.

"Are you tired?" Pam asked.

She nodded.

Pam kissed her cheek and patted her behind. "Okay, wash up, then go to bed." She had to admit she'd had a good time, too, and now she was tired.

Sitting on her bed, she went over the day's events in her head. The afternoon had seemed perfect, but what Grace and Saul had said kept swirling around in her head. "They were a family."

She laid back on her bed and stared at the ceiling. *Did the twins think of her and Gracie as a family?* She nodded and pulled the covers to her chin. "A family," she repeated and fell asleep.

The next day Saul began working on Pam's roof. When he saw her, he waved. She waved back and began planting flowers and weeding her garden.

"I can help you with that," he said.

She laughed. "Freddie told me that you promised to help him make a push cart. I think you have enough to do for the time being." She shrugged. "Plus, I love doing this."

"Okay."

As long as you don't take off your shirt I'll be fine, she thought, secretly glancing at him. But as the day wore on, it got considerably hotter and he took off his shirt. She glanced up and found herself on her bottom. She looked up again at the sweat glistening on his well-defined chest. As he moved, so did his muscles. She bit into her lip and took a very deep breath. "You need to put your shirt back on," she said, digging her finger in the dirt where there were no flowers or seeds.

He looked down at her and laughed. "Am I distracting you from your gardening?"

She could hear the laughter in his voice and shook her head. She took another deep breath and abandoned her gardening for the weaving hut. As she entered the hut, she noticed the women snickering, including Mary. "What?" she said.

"Naked chest too much for you?" one of the women asked.

THE OTHER SIDE OF THE MOUNTAIN

She glanced at Mary, who shook her head. She cut her eyes at the woman and began making a kite.

Within a few hours, Saul had finished his work on her roof and was helping the boys build their cart.

That evening Pamela and Gracie would have supper with Saul and his family. To tell the truth, she was a bit nervous. Mary met up with her and shook her head when she saw the smile on her face. Myah joined them.

"What are you doing here?" Pamela asked.

"I had to get away from that woman. Even though I'm only on the day shift, she's getting on my nerves. She's changed from the woman who loved to dress up to someone you'd never believe."

"What do you mean?" Mary asked.

"She doesn't even want to take a bath. She says she's not trying to impress anyone so she doesn't have to smell good. Can you imagine anyone saying that?"

Pamela shook her head. "I think she did the same thing while she was at the cottage."

"How do you know that?" Myah asked.

She shrugged. "Your brother told me. She drank and neglected the children. That's why they stayed here while Saul and I were away." She closed her eyes and shook her head.

"I knew it. I knew it," Myah shouted. She laughed and hugged Pamela tight. "I knew there was something between you and Saul. Why were you keeping it a secret from me?" She stood in front of Pamela and stared inquiringly at her.

Pamela stared back. What should she say? She needed time with Saul for their relationship to grow without interference from the Rahjahs, or that she loved sneaking around with him? Or… "I…I wanted to be sure of my feelings for him before I told anyone."

Myah looked at Mary, who didn't seem surprised at her revelation. "But you told Mary and not me."

This was what she had been trying to avoid. "Myah, I didn't tell Mary anything. She snooped and found out. I told her not to tell anyone."

"Thanks a lot," Mary said, sighing and shaking her head.

Pamela ignored her and focused on Myah. After all, it wasn't really a lie.

"Are you telling me that you haven't really told anyone?" Myah said.

"Not really."

"Not really?" Myah said.

"Right, and please don't spoil it for us. We aren't ready to tell everyone. I don't want anyone making a fuss."

Myah and Mary laughed. "I have news for you. There already are knowing smiles, but you two are so gaga-eyed that you never see them," Myah said. "But I just had to confirm. You both have been by yourselves for so long that everyone just wants to see you both

THE OTHER SIDE OF THE MOUNTAIN

happy. Look at what Saul's going through with this mad woman." She cleared her throat. "Oh, by the way, speaking of the mad woman, she wants to see you."

"Who, me?" Pamela pointed to herself.

"Yes."

"Why?"

"Don't know, but I think it has something to do with Ludy's visit last night."

"But Raquel is not supposed to have visitors."

"Yeah, we know, but that little sneak snuck in, and I'm sure she did a bit of gossiping."

"Did she give her liquor?" Pamela gasped.

"No, she knows better than that. She won't break the rules, but it's human nature to blab. I think she also suspects that you and Saul have a thing, and I think she told Raquel."

Pamela thought for a moment. She knew that Raquel already knew about the relationship between her and Saul. Was she pretending not to know? Why? Pamela shook her head. "No, she shouldn't have visitors yet, so I'm not going to see her."

"We'll be there to protect you if she gets violent," Myah said.

"I know, but why should I break the rules and visit her just because she wants to see me? Is she dying?"

"No."

"Then there you are. Tell her I will come to see her when it's time for her to have visitors. By the way, is there someone watching her at night?"

"Of course. In cases like these the men take turns watching the patients, especially if they might harm themselves or others," Myah said.

"Please don't say anything to Saul." Pamela touched Myah's hand.

"Of course not, and don't worry. When you're ready to see her it's time enough. Taking care of this woman is like taking a horse pill." She turned to Pamela. "Saul's making something special for supper this evening."

"Now listen to you," Pamela said.

"No, I'm not gossiping. Mama told me when she brought snacks for us today. Does she know?" she said to Pamela. "Because if she knew about this before me, I will be very upset."

"Myah, I don't know if your mother knows anything. I don't live there. I don't know if Saul said anything to her." She was silent for a minute, trying to remember if Saul had said something about telling his mother. She began walking to the kitchen and the other women followed. Myah said goodbye just as they got to the door.

Pamela and Mary walked into a kitchen filled with action. Pots of soup were simmering and the oven was hot and ready for the different cakes and sweets. The

THE OTHER SIDE OF THE MOUNTAIN

Rahjahs always said a day without sweets was like a day without supper, but they should be eaten in moderation.

When they'd finished in the kitchen, Mary and Pamela went down to the waterfall to bathe while the children used the tubs in the bath house.

When Pamela was dressed and ready to go, she and Gracie took their dessert from the kitchen, placed it in a basket on the horse and made their way down to the twin mountain for supper with Saul and his family.

She was very surprised to see Saul coming to meet her. "You didn't have to," she said as his horse got close to them.

"I know." He turned his horse and trotted beside them.

As they approached the village, most of the villagers pretended to be doing something so they wouldn't be caught staring. It would have been less conspicuous if Saul had not gone out to meet her, but he really didn't care who knew that he was in love with Pamela. He was going along with her request to not tell anyone, but could not hide his feelings. Most of the villagers knew how much he resented his ex-wife and how much he loved Pamela. In the village center he got off his horse and reached up to gather her in his arms. He quickly released her and moved to help Gracie down.

But by the time he got to her, she'd already jumped off her horse. He laughed. "I'll be quicker next time."

As casually as she could, and so as not to arouse suspicion, Pamela smiled at him when they sat in the center and ate supper. She couldn't help seeing the smiling glances she got from a lot of her dinner companions. "What's going on?" she asked Saul under her breath.

"What do you mean?"

"They're all looking and smiling."

"Oh, that."

She looked at him. "Yes, that."

"They sort of know we spent the day as a family yesterday."

She wasn't very surprised, but she still had to ask. "How?"

"We weren't exactly hidden on the high seas."

"And when you and I went to Jamaica?"

He nodded.

Sheepishly, she smiled at his parents.

Saul gazed at Pamela. "You were right. Ruth is so busy with Gracie and Shaela that she has no time for the animals, either. Did I really cause her to do that?"

She looked at him with furrowed brows. It took her a while to realize that he was changing the subject. "Oh, no, you didn't and I didn't. It's just something children do. Plus, you're around much more now, it

THE OTHER SIDE OF THE MOUNTAIN

seems, and you're doing a very good job of being a father."

"I wasn't before?"

She bumped his shoulder. "Very funny. I think you're an excellent father and I'm glad that you include Gracie in things that you do with the twins."

"They're like a set. How can I break up a set?"

She laughed. "Thank you."

"Do you like coconut water?"

"Of course, who doesn't?"

He got up and went to where the jelly coconuts were stored, got one and chopped off the top with one swing of the machete. He handed it to her. He paid no attention to the whispers and the smiles.

She took it from him. "You wield that as if you were born with it attached to your hand."

"You can take the boy off the mountain, but you certainly can't take the mountain out of the boy."

The liquid slipped from the side of her mouth as she drank. He wiped the liquid from her chin and licked it from his finger. She gazed at him.

"What?" he said.

She smiled and shook her head. "Nothing."

At the end of the meal, Saul, Jacob and Ishmael began making almond milk ice cream for the children. The ice had been brought over from Jamaica early in the morning. As the ice cooled the canister inside, the men manually turned the handle of the wooden bucket while the children waited longingly.

Pamela sat beside Saul. "If you decide to see Raquel I would like to be there with you," he said, glancing at her.

"How did you know?" Then she shook her head. "Why do I ask stupid questions? I can't give Raquel the help she needs, so I've decided not to see her. By the way, I know she's talking to our shrink, but why don't we get Angel here to talk with her?"

Saul stopped churning and she immediately took over. "Angel doesn't like her very much. Plus she's not Rahjah."

"No one likes Raquel very much, but Angel's a professional and a Rahjah by marriage. Raquel is not a Rahjah, so they have that much in common. I think it would be better for her if she has someone from the outside world to speak with."

He took the handle from her and continued turning it, then shook his head and smiled. "I know I've said this, but it bears repeating. My degrees are quite worthless when you're around. You're so much smarter than I am."

She laughed. "Takes a big man to admit that a woman is smarter than he is, but I couldn't do what you do. As a matter of fact, I don't know the first thing about geology."

THE OTHER SIDE OF THE MOUNTAIN

He smiled. He knew she'd try to deflect his words. "I just love you so much."

"I love you a lot, too," she whispered. "But for me it's common sense to get Angel. Plus, I'd love to see her again. How do we go about doing that?"

"That's the easy part. All I have to do is go to Jamaica and telephone her office or her house." He used one hand to turn the wheel and on impulse used the other hand to pull her to him. He kissed her lips right there in the open before Jah and man.

Realizing what he'd done, he let go of her and whispered, "Sorry, I didn't mean to, but I couldn't help myself."

Biting down on her lower lip, she glanced toward where Gracie and the twins were playing. They'd not seen anything. "It's all right," Pamela said. "I was told by my friends that I've been only fooling myself. And if they weren't convinced yesterday, you've just openly confirmed their suspicions."

"I'm sorry," he said again, pouring more ice into the bucket. "But you think so quickly on your feet. It would have taken me hours or days to come up with what took you moments."

"How do you know that I haven't been thinking of it since yesterday?"

"Have you?"

"No."

He laughed. "And funny, too. Tomorrow morning I'll go into Jamaica and call Angel."

"Thank you."

He pulled a cell phone from his pocket. "This doesn't work here."

"That's a little phone, right?"

He nodded, then stopped churning and took the lid off the bucket. He spooned out a small amount and fed it to her. She tasted it and nodded. "Perfect."

As soon as she said it, bowls suddenly appeared attached to little brown hands, including her daughter's and the twins'. The other men had also opened their buckets and were spooning ice cream into bamboo bowls. Nanuk took over the sharing to give Pamela and Saul time with each other. She'd not missed their kiss.

Saul glanced at his mother's smiling face and shook his head. At this point he didn't want to take Pamela to his cottage at all. In the darkness they walked halfway down the mountainside and sat beside a stream. He began throwing pebbles in the water. "I have to say I'm sorry again for exposing our private life. But you know how the Rahjahs are, they keep each other's secret even when it's no longer a secret."

She sat down but said nothing.

"I have a question to ask."

"Okay."

"While I was on your roof I had an idea."

"Let's hear it." She looked at him and smiled.

THE OTHER SIDE OF THE MOUNTAIN

"Would it be all right if I added another room to your home? The children love staying with you and Gracie, but somehow I know they feel cramped."

She smiled and turned to look into his face. "I know little David would probably love his own room, and I do know he loves spending time at my home, but you would do that?"

"Of course."

She thought for a moment and wondered if he wanted to do it for her or for the children. "What about my vegetable plants? Because the back is the only place we have free land."

"I can build around the plants until it's time to put in the floor, or I can put everything in big clay pots."

Maybe it would be good to see him every day. Now that everyone knew the extent of their relationship there was no need to tip-toe or hide. Pity, she was quite enjoying herself. "Yes, but what about your job?"

"I'm taking some much-deserved time off. I can do that because I work for myself. I want to do this for you. I have the means and the opportunity. You do things so unselfishly for others, give me a chance to do something for you, please."

"Sure."

"Just like that?"

"Yep. I would love for you to build another room onto my cottage, but are you going to do this all by yourself?"

"Yes."

"But the rains will come soon."

"I promise I will not put any holes in your cottage that will cause the rain to come through. If it's taking too long to finish, I will get help, I promise."

"Okay. After all, you did fix my roof all by yourself." She knew that sometimes the rains could be brutal. Cottages were known to slide down the mountainside to be rebuilt only days later. She'd been one of the lucky ones. Her home was not on the side of the mountain.

She looked directly into his eyes and smiled.

"What?"

"Oh, nothing." She didn't want to tell him that the sight of his shirtless body on her roof had caused a stir within her. After all, she was the one who'd suspended their lovemaking. She looked up at the stars, then lay back on the soft grass. He lay beside her and their fingers touched and locked.

"Is this good for us?" he asked.

"What do you mean?"

"I mean us being here touching, having feelings we can't act on?"

"Yes."

"There's a lesson in here somewhere, right?"

"Yes." She turned her face to him. "May I ask you something?"

"Anything."

THE OTHER SIDE OF THE MOUNTAIN

"Judging from the tumultuous life you've led with Raquel, why haven't you become a misogynist?"

He looked at her with wrinkled brows. "How many women in this world are asking that very question to a man right now?"

There was probably a smile somewhere on his face, but she couldn't find it.

"Sorry, that came out wrong. I didn't…"

"…Mean to mock me?" she asked.

"No, no, please understand," he stuttered. "And I know you do. I live in a culture that is for all intents and purposes ruled by women. We as men don't admit it, but that's how it is. Pam, I've loved you all my life. I had to forget about you because of Peter, and I have to say I did a darn good job of it, too. The girl who'd seemed so untouchable, so unreachable, is now my whole world." Even though he was looking directly at her, he couldn't read her.

She turned back to look at the star-clustered sky. She knew he'd have said that. He'd touched her in a way no one had ever done, not even her dead husband. "You're handsome, intelligent, warm." She looked at him. "Stop me when you've heard enough."

"Okay." He kept looking at her.

She laughed.

"But seriously," he said. "You had a certain aura about you, a certain superiority."

"And again I say, no one is above the other."

"That's not what I mean. Don't take offense to this, but remember when Angel spoke of James's mother?"

"Yes."

"Well, I remember her saying that as educated as she was, one look from Clara would make her feel like a child and when she spoke, she did it with such calm and surety that it was as if she knew everything."

"Do I make you feel that way?"

"When we were younger, I think so. Even though I'm older than you are."

She turned back to face him. "Why would I take offense to being compared to Aunt Clara?"

Now he really couldn't read what she was thinking. He smiled with her. "See what I mean?"

She placed a cool hand on his cheek and kissed his lips, slipping her tongue slowly into his mouth. He closed his eyes and breathed deeply. He was calm even to a place of reverence as her lips remained on his. The heat that her kiss emitted rippled through his brain, scorching his senses. His lids felt heavy as he slowly opened his eyes then closed them. His fingers touched her face, her mouth as it slowly left his. He wanted her, in this place. Blood rushed to parts of him that were forbidden at this time. "Do you know what being this close to you does to me?"

"It does the same thing to me," she whispered.

"Is this a lesson in restraint? Because if it is, boy, it's a good one." Her sweet, warm breath on his face

THE OTHER SIDE OF THE MOUNTAIN

made him pull closer into her. His mind said stop but his body couldn't obey and he pressed into her and nuzzled her neck.

"We could go to my boat and make love in the middle of the ocean," he said. "The ocean is not a part of the island."

A part of her wanted to forget the request, but another part said no, he understands. She held him close and kissed his mouth hard. "Be strong for me," she whispered.

Abruptly, he pulled away from her. "I can't do this. I'm not strong enough. You're like a drug that enters my bloodstream with a look, a touch, a smile."

Trying to control her own urges, she pressed her thighs together and breathed deeply. "Should we forget our promise? It was stupid."

"No, I would like to honor your wishes. We just have to be more careful, more mindful, if you will." He got to his feet and pulled her to him.

She cupped his face. "You're so beautiful, so gentle and so willing to please me."

"My purpose on this earth is to please you."

She said nothing but held his hand and walked back to the village. She loved the moment. She was more than in love with this man. Spiritually, they were one; emotionally, they were tied and bound. "You've made me happier than I've ever been before," she said almost to herself.

Fingers intertwined, he gently squeezed. "You're really teaching me the meaning of control. If I can do this, I can do anything."

Chapter 19

The next day Saul got into his boat and made his way to Jamaica to call Angel. He would also pick up supplies from his relatives in Blue Mountain to begin building the extra room onto Pamela's cottage. In trade he had chocolate that he'd made himself, baskets his villagers had made and non-alcoholic blueberry wine that only the Eastern Rahjahs made.

Intending to use his cell phone, he pulled it out of his pocket. It was dead. There was no way for him to charge it on the island, and to try and charge it now would have wasted valuable time. He walked into a shop owned by a friend of his and asked to use his phone. When he put the call through to Angel and explained the situation, she agreed, with reservations.

"I would love to come and talk with Raquel, Saul, but years ago when I had offered my services, I was told that the Rahjahs had their own therapists."

"That you don't live here does not detract from the fact that you are truly one of us, making you perfect for the job. The request came from Pam."

Hearing Pamela's name immediately sealed the deal. "I will be on the first flight. If it wasn't for the Rahjahs I would not be as happy as I am today. Plus,

I would do anything for Pam. I'll be there before midnight. Give me your number and I will call you back with the details of my flight."

He gave her the number and a half an hour later she called back with the details. "I'll pick you up at the airport." He rung off, borrowed a truck from his friend, loaded the supplies and made his way to Blue Mountain.

Taking a break from writing the history lessons that she'd promised her grandmother, Pamela stood on her verandah looking at the children playing hopscotch and flying kites. The twins spent so much time with her that she'd come to regard them as her own. The more time they spent with her, the more she saw Saul. First, it was an excuse for them to be together because he'd pretend to bring them to the village even though they knew their way and didn't need a chaperone. Little by little he began spending more time with Pamela, doing things with her and for her. Now that the whole business had leaked out, well, they were on their own.

Pamela looked at her mother looking at her. She walked over and hugged her.

"You love those children, don't you?" Esther said, holding her daughter's hand.

"I do. They're so innocent."

Esther nodded. "What about the woman?"

THE OTHER SIDE OF THE MOUNTAIN

Pamela smiled. "Mama, you can say her name, she's not dead."

"I know, but I don't like her. I know we are supposed to love our enemies, but…"

"We don't hate her and she's not our enemy. She's just misguided."

"I would say strange."

Pamela shrugged. "I guess."

"When something different slips into a society, if we're closed-minded, we hate it without thinking or asking questions. If we're open we want to know all about it. We either embrace it or throw it out."

"Is it that simple?" Pamela asked.

"Sometimes. She didn't think enough of us to want to make a good impression, not even on Saul's mother. She thought of us as backward. She wasn't smart enough to know that she was the backward one."

Pamela looked at her mother, squeezed her eyes shut. "Ouch. Do you dislike her that much because you like Saul?"

"She hurt him and this community very badly."

Pamela kept looking at her mother. "You're warming up to him, aren't you?"

Esther glanced at her, then back at the children. "He's not a bad fellow. I can't chastise him for the mistake he made, no matter how big. But I want you to be very careful. If he begins to compare you to her…"

"Mother, no. He'll never do that. He knows he made a very big mistake. Oh, by the way, do you know that Saul and I had met when we were young?"

"No, but I'm not surprised. We've all met each other at some time or the other. Why didn't you become friends?"

"Peter."

Her mother looked at her angrily and immediately left her side. Realizing what she'd done, Pamela clamped her hands over her mouth. She'd committed the worst sin possible by uttering Peter's name. She ran after her mother. "I'm sorry, I'm so sorry." She held her mother's hand. "I never meant to say his name. Please forgive me. It won't happen again, I promise."

Esther stopped and gave her daughter a look that made it impossible for Pamela to look her in the eye. Instead, she looked down and shuffled her feet. "Never again," Esther said.

Feeling as if she were a child of ten, Pamela nodded. A time of silence between the two had to pass, so she went to the sewing hut to join Mary. She sat silent as Mary put the finishing touches to her skirt.

"Is something wrong?" Mary asked.

She shook her head.

Pam spent the rest of the day in silence. It was one thing to say her husband's name to Saul; he understood. Although he obeyed and mostly lived the customs of the Rahjah society, he was very open. He

THE OTHER SIDE OF THE MOUNTAIN

would even encourage her to say Peter's name if doing so allowed her to voice her feelings. It was a way for her to heal and move on even after so many years. He wasn't afraid to say Peter's name, either, but he wouldn't say it to anyone else. With Esther and the older people, saying the name of the dead was strictly off limits. Some believed in ghosts, some didn't.

After a satisfactory period of time had passed, Pamela sought out her mother. "Am I forgiven?" she asked in a quiet voice.

"Yes, you are. We will say nothing more of the matter."

"Of course." She hugged her mother, kissed her cheek and went back to Mary, who was waiting for her. They walked to the stables, climbed onto their horses and made their way to the beach where they sat under a tree and watched a ship miles off shore.

"Wouldn't you love to be on one of those someday?" Pamela asked Mary.

"I think you'll be on one before me, but it would be nice to meet people from many different backgrounds."

Pamela leaned back against the tree with her hands clasped behind her head.

"Are you going to see Raquel?" Mary asked.

"No, not until Angel has spoken with her."

"Is Angel on her way here?"

"I don't think she's on her way this very moment, but I asked Saul to get her. I don't think we're quite equipped to handle Raquel."

"You're right." Mary leaned against the tree and closed her eyes. "You mentioned your husband's name to your mother, didn't you?" She opened her eyes.

"Uh-huh."

"I figured that was the only thing that would get you in trouble with her."

"She gave me a look that sent me back into childhood." She sat up. "That's not supposed to happen. I'm an adult with a child. I teach children. I make decisions for myself."

"Calm down, don't take it personally. It's called respect."

Pamela looked over at Mary and smiled. "Yes, it is."

Chapter 20

Since Angel had come in on a very late flight, she stayed in Saul's cottage, but bright and early the next morning, right at breakfast time, they rode to Pamela's village.

When Pamela saw them, she didn't know who to hug first; Saul for doing her bidding so quickly or Angel for coming so quickly. Since Angel was the first to get off her horse, she received the first hug from a very excited Pamela. "You came. I didn't think you'd come so quickly. Actually, I didn't think Saul would make this happen so quickly. Thank you so much."

"Anything for love. I told you that I want to see you guys together no matter what I have to do." She hugged Pamela again.

Saul got off his horse and Pamela hugged him and thanked him. "You didn't have to work so fast. I could have waited."

"What my darling wants, my darling gets. There are two of us in this thing and I can't wait, you made sure of that. I want her off the island faster than you do, believe me."

Pamela laughed and shook her head.

"Plus, I had to get supplies for your cottage." He pointed to the horse-drawn cart coming up the mountain.

"You don't joke around, do you?"

"Well, it's either work or bug you all the while." He winked at her and she burst out laughing again.

Angel, who'd been talking with Esther, looked at them and laughed. "What do you think of those two?" she said.

Esther smiled but didn't answer.

Angel understood completely.

"Where are your bags?" Pamela asked.

"They're at Saul's place. We were in such a hurry to get here that I told him he could bring them later. Am I staying with you?"

"I don't have the space. Maybe if Saul doesn't mind you can stay with him. How long will you stay?"

"As long as you need me."

"Are you sure?"

"James will visit in a few days, if that's what you're worried about, and my partner will take over my cases until I get back."

Pamela laughed. "I wasn't worried. I know you guys are extremely solid."

Right through breakfast, Saul kept drawing sketches of the additions he wanted to make to Pamela's home. But he had a few things to do before starting the project.

THE OTHER SIDE OF THE MOUNTAIN

After breakfast, Angel sat down with Saul and Pamela. Saul told her about Raquel, and Angel sat in amazement at what he'd put up with over the years. But the fact that Pamela was the one who'd suggested that Raquel receive treatment before leaving the island was food for thought. Angel felt she had to ask. "Why did you want to do this for her, Pammy?"

"She's a drunk, and I love these children. I don't want them to lose their mother. I know she's not my responsibility, but she seems to have gotten worse since she's been here. Frankly, she could take a boat to Jamaica and get mixed up with the wrong crowd and get killed. I know I'm talking as if she's a child, but that's what drunks are. They're stupid children who don't realize what they're doing to their bodies and the people around them until it's too late."

Angel smiled. "And you need me for what?"

"You live in the outside world. You can better relate to her. You can help her because you can be impartial."

Angel looked at Saul, then Pamela, and smiled. "I love you guys. As I said, I'll do anything to see you two together and happy."

"We are happy," Saul said. "It's just a few things that need to be done for us to be truly together."

"Give me a week."

"That long?" Saul said.

The women laughed. Angel looked again at Pamela and Pamela gave a guilty laugh. "Okay then," Angel said. "take me to this place to begin my job. I have to tell you that she will absolutely hate the idea at first. After all, I am a Rahjah. Not one with locked hair, but one nonetheless."

"No one can do it but you, Angel," Pamela said, getting to her feet.

Then Angel said something with no idea of the consequences. "Saul, may I ask you something?"

"Anything."

She hesitated.

"It's all right, you can say anything in front of Pam. We have no secrets."

"Okay," Angel said, looking directly at him. "Have you ever hit Raquel?"

He didn't answer.

Angel could clearly see that she had stumbled upon an unexposed truth.

The length of time he took to answer shocked Pamela. Of all the things he'd told her, one thing he'd never admitted was hitting the mother of his children.

Saul sighed long and hard. "No, but I grabbed her hard and shook her once." He shook his head as both women stared at him. As a trained psychologist, Angel showed no emotion. He looked at Pamela and saw the shocked look on her face. He quickly added, "I grabbed her and shook her hard, then threw her out of

THE OTHER SIDE OF THE MOUNTAIN

my way…" Before he could finish, Pamela gasped and ran from the room.

"Please let me explain, Pam, please." But she was long gone.

Pamela was not really one to cry in front of anyone if she could avoid it. This time she could, and crying in front of him now was not an option.

Almost in a daze, Saul looked at Angel. "She didn't let me finish."

"That's why I wanted her to be out of the room," Angel said. "But before I tell you everything will be all right, will you tell me what brought that on?"

"I need to go after Pam and explain," he said impatiently.

Angel touched his hand. "No, you don't. Pam needs a bit of space and you need to elaborate." She kept looking at him.

He didn't sit down. "She was so angry with me one day that she abused Ruthie."

"What do you mean?"

"We'd gone to Jamaica with the children. I held David while she held Ruth. Ruth began screaming. Raquel wanted me to hold both children, I guess she wanted me to take Ruth without her asking. When I offered to take her, she said it was all right, but I could see in her eyes and actions that she was angry. While the baby screamed, Raquel pinned her little arms so that she couldn't move. She just sat there pushing down on the baby's arms and feet. I told her to give me the baby but she refused. Did I tell you that we were in a crowded restaurant?"

Angel shook her head.

"We were. I waited until we came home. I put David to bed, took Ruthie from her and put her to bed, then grabbed Raquel and told her never to do that again. Then I pushed her toward the bed."

Angel nodded.

"What do I do now? How can I get all that across to Pam before she begins to hate me?"

"She won't hate you. I don't think she ever can. You will find the words to explain and she will listen. Just give her time."

"Are you sure?"

"Yes, but I have to go to work." She walked outside with Saul and saw Pamela. She walked up to her and whispered in her ear, "Everything is not always as it seems."

Saul began walking toward Pamela, but the scowl on her face and her body language stopped him cold.

"You're not coming with us?" Angel asked Pamela.

"No, not this time."

Angel nodded and took the reins of the horse. Wearing a pair of khaki pants, she jumped onto the horse's back and rode away with Saul.

Pamela didn't know what to think. *How could he have done that?* She'd watched Raquel try to emasculate him. Was that his way of atonement? Did he allow her to abuse him because he'd abused her? Her head was spinning. Not once had she ever thought he'd do her harm. He was always so attentive, so eager to please her. Deep in thought, she began walking. There had to be an explanation for why he'd pushed her. And why on earth had she run away before he'd finished his explanation? That was the stupidest thing she'd ever done. Saul was gentle and kind. He wouldn't hurt a fly. She asked herself the question once more. *Why did I run away?*

She would be seeing him every day as he worked on her home. No, she would stop him from touching her house. She shook her head. *What's wrong with me? Why didn't I allow him to explain? He'd not finished the bloody sentence before I left. What's wrong with me?* She took a deep breath and walked slowly back to the village. She had a class to teach.

⁂

Saul accompanied Angel to the detox center but didn't go in. Apart from the fact that he had work to do, visitors were forbidden until the patient showed signs of improvement.

He rode back to Pamela's cottage and unloaded the supplies. Taking off his shirt, he began chopping lumber and preparing the material. He would work

JANICE ANGELIQUE

until it was finished. He would do this for Pamela and himself.

He worked tirelessly through the morning hours. He didn't know how long he'd worked when he heard the voice behind him telling him to stop. "What?" He turned to see Pamela.

Transfixed, she stood there staring at his naked torso, which was glistening with sweat. She shook her head and stuttered, "I don't want you to do this anymore. I don't want you to do anything for me."

He stopped what he was doing and walked slowly toward her. "Pammy, please let me…"

"No. I don't want to speak with you right now." She backed away from him.

"Pammy, you didn't let me finish."

"You didn't tell me."

"You never asked as point-blank as Angel did."

"You should have told me anyway."

"You still won't let me tell you. We trust each other. I would never do anything to hurt you."

"I said I don't want to speak to you about it right now. I want you to stop working on my house."

He shrugged. "That's too bad, because I said I would do this and I won't stop. I keep my word." He walked back and began working.

"I…I want you to stop." She didn't want to shout because the children weren't far away.

THE OTHER SIDE OF THE MOUNTAIN

"No. You don't want to listen to what I have to say, so I won't listen to you. I said I would do this and I will."

He sounded like a stubborn child, but Pamela was too upset to even notice. "Fine," she said and walked away. "I don't care what you do." She kept on muttering until she was away from him. Then she ran into Esther.

"I heard what happened this morning. Do you want to talk?"

"You know what I love about you, Mama?"

Esther didn't answer.

"I love the way you pry without prying. If I want to tell you, you'll listen but you won't insist and it's because you won't insist that I won't say anything. I'll deal with it."

"Did Saul say or do something?" Esther folded her arms in front of her.

Pamela smiled. "You raised me to handle things on my own so that you didn't have to worry about me. You talked and I listened, even when you thought I wasn't listening." She kissed her mother's cheek. "I was listening. You did a great job." She walked away, looked back and saw her mother smiling and shaking her head as she entered the fabric hut.

Pamela wanted to seek out Angel to ask her how Saul had finished the conversation, but pride prevented her; plus, Angel was still at the hospital.

She went to where the children were sitting with Mary and helped her with their questions.

But from the way Mary looked at her, she knew it wouldn't be long before she asked what was going on. One by one the children dispersed, including Gracie and Shaela. She knew they were heading for the stables to go to see Ruth and David. Gracie didn't even ask anymore. It was a given that if she was missing for a while, she was with the twins.

Mary sat beside her and Pamela got up. "Walk with me," she said. And as they walked toward the caves Pamela asked, "Am I selfish and stupid?"

Mary laughed and shook her head. "You are absolutely neither of those things."

"I think I'm stupid."

"What's going on with you?"

"Saul admitted grabbing Raquel and I ran out of the room like a stupid child without listening to the full story. Now I won't speak to him."

Mary stopped. "Do you know how evil that woman is? You're lucky he had the restraint to just grab her. If she were my wife I'd slap her a few times."

"So what you're saying is that I'm being overly dramatic?"

Mary gave her one of those "you said it" looks then began walking again. "Why on earth would you let him feel guilty without hearing everything that he had to say?"

THE OTHER SIDE OF THE MOUNTAIN

"I don't know." She shook her head. "I guess I wanted him to tell me before he told anyone else."

"Pammy, he was probably very embarrassed. You yourself talk about how gentle and attentive he is."

"But I'm not judgmental."

"Why did you run away from him?" Mary stopped and looked in Pamela's face.

Pamela didn't know what to say. They'd reached the caves and instead of keeping quiet, they kept on talking, waking the bats. They began screeching and flapping their wings. The women dropped to the ground and covered their heads until the bats went back to their perch, then they got to their feet and ran to the beach.

They both sat down on warm sand under a coconut tree. Pamela placed her hands behind her head and laced her fingers. "I wish I could speak with Raquel."

"She wanted to speak with you but you chose to put her in therapy instead."

"I thought it was the best thing for her and the children."

"It is, and you're being very gallant."

Pamela sighed. She closed her eyes and in her mind's eye could see Saul with his shirt off working on her cottage, the sun seemingly bouncing off his very trim body. She opened her eyes and looked over at Mary, who was looking at her. "Did I moan?" she asked, a bit embarrassed.

"A little."

Watching the water undulate on latté colored sand, she took a deep breath. Whether she liked it or not, she had to wait until supper to talk with Angel.

Chapter 21

It was close to suppertime when Saul decided to leave Pamela's cottage before she came home. All by himself, he'd gotten a lot done. He'd mixed concrete, broken rocks and laid brick on top of brick. He had not given himself time to think about anything but building. A few men had offered to help and he'd accepted, but for the next day.

The first thing he did after getting back to his own cottage was walk down to the beach for a long swim and then to the waterfall to bathe. As much as he tried, he couldn't help thinking about Pamela and her actions. She'd pulled a complete one-eighty on him. It was as if she were trying to start a fight with him, testing him. He was in the deepest part of the river, treading water. He dove and came up in the shallow end. He stood and began walking toward the river bank. He'd give her space if that's what she wanted, but he'd never give her up. Even if he tried he couldn't be angry with her. If he had to show her repeatedly how much he loved her, then that's what he'd do, but for now, he'd give her the space she needed.

Pamela sat with Angel at supper, but didn't ask her anything about the session with Raquel.

After supper, they had tea in Pamela's cottage. Angel spoke before she had a chance to ask any questions. "He never raised a hand to her, you know. She admitted she was always the aggressor."

"But why, why would she be like that?"

"Although everything ties into why she's so aggressive toward Saul, I can't divulge anything she's told me about her past," Angel said.

"I respect that. Can you tell Saul?"

"Not unless she wants me to, and she hasn't said so. But she has told him a lot of things about her childhood, the way she grew up. He was protecting his children, Pammy."

"From their mother?"

"You've met her. You've spoken to her. You've almost had an altercation with her. You've seen the way she treats him and the way he retaliates with kindness. It's not hard to do the math." Angel looked at Pamela and took a sip of her tea. "This is wonderful," she said.

"Thank you."

"Listen, in my world men are blamed for a lot of things, and very often they're guilty, but one out of a hundred is so gentle that he's taken advantage of by women. I'm a woman and it destroys me to say this, but there are women out there that are bigger bullies than some men. There are women out there that have had such tragic upbringings that they lash out at men. Why? Because men are supposedly the stronger of the sexes. When they meet a man that shows compassion, they mistake it for weakness and take advantage. Saul is one of those men. The things Raquel has admitted doing to him… A weaker man would have put her in the hospital or worse. But the more he showed compassion and understanding, the more he was misunderstood by her until she killed whatever feelings he had for her."

Pamela sat listening and digesting every word Angel spoke. She could run to Saul and ask his forgiveness, but she was stubborn and filled with pride, which was a dangerous combination. She changed the conversation. "How is your daughter?"

Angel looked at her, smiled and leaned back against the cushion. "You would like to change the subject?"

She nodded.

"I understand. Hildie is great. Still in college and working part-time in my office."

"She wants to be a psychologist, too?"

"I think so."

"I heard that she's so close to you she didn't want to leave you to go to college, so you had her attend the closest university to you."

Angel laughed. "Actually, she did that, not me. I would have preferred her to attend a university that was far from home, but she refused to be far away from me. She could have transferred after her second year, but not my Hildie. I notice Gracie is very close to you, too."

"Even though Gracie didn't know her father, I think we would still be this close if he were alive. It all depends on the kind of parent you are. I watch Saul with his children and he seems to love them both the same." She looked at Angel.

"Why won't you speak with him? You clearly adore this man. It's killing him that you won't speak with him."

Pam didn't answer.

"Okay, I know you'll tell me when you're ready." She looked at her friend, sighed, and shook her head. She got up from the cushion and followed Pam into the small kitchen with the tray. "Do you want to take a peek at what Saul's been doing?"

Pamela smiled but shook her head.

"You're a stubborn one. I'll see you tomorrow," she said, walking outside and mounting her horse.

Saul appeared from out of nowhere to ride with Angel. He sat atop his horse looking at Pamela. His eyes were soft and imploring, but he said nothing.

Pamela could feel his eyes rake over her body. She could almost feel his strength pulling her to him. Out of the corner of her eye, she saw him lift his hair from his shoulder and throw it behind him. His shirt was

THE OTHER SIDE OF THE MOUNTAIN

unbuttoned to his waist and she bit into her lower lip but didn't look directly at him. *What am I doing?*

Angel waved to her, and she waved back. Saul didn't wave but rode off down the path with Angel. They spurred their horses into a fast gallop. Pamela took a deep breath and exhaled.

Mary came to stand by her and shook her head. "Why are you doing that to him?"

Pamela lifted her head and saw her mother looking at her from across her verandah.

"I don't know," she said. She walked away from Mary, went to the stables and got on her horse. Bareback, she rode the horse hard to the beach. Before the horse came to a complete stop she jumped off, ran to the rocky edge of the beach and sat looking out at the dark ocean, wishing she'd never met Raquel or told Saul to help her.

━━━━━⁂━━━━━

Under cloudy skies the next day, Saul worked. The heavy rain wasn't far away now; he could smell it in the air. Without asking, men took time from the fields to help him. The building progressed quickly. Pamela never looked into the room so he could do whatever he wanted. He brought a gramophone from his home and placed it in the corner of the room. He knew what kind of music she liked and had brought a few vinyl records along. While the men secured the roof, he began making her a trunk, which wasn't hard until he began carving designs on the lid. It became a project, a labor of love, as he painstakingly carved her favorite flowers, waves and birds deep into the wood.

The sun finally showed itself. He stood on the roof shirtless, breathing hard, sweat glistening on his skin. He watched Pamela walk down the mountain with the children. He squinted and watched her hips sway. She smiled, but not at him. She didn't see him. He took a deep breath and closed his eyes for a few seconds. Being apart from her like this was killing him.

The rain began to drizzle, slowly soaking the dried palm, but he didn't notice. The sudden thunder jolted him and he turned quickly, only to lose his footing and slip from the roof. He tried to land on his feet but one foot gave way causing him to land on his arm and dislocate his shoulder. A tremendous pain shot through his shoulder and down his arm. He struggled to get up.

Pamela saw him fall and began running. "Oh, Jah," she kept repeating. When she got to him and knelt beside him, she could see the pain registering on his face.

He saw her and lay still, his teeth grinding together. She moved over him and called his name. "Speak to me," she said, but he said nothing.

Positioning his head to administer CPR, she held his nose and as soon as her mouth touched his, one

THE OTHER SIDE OF THE MOUNTAIN

arm came up, hugged her neck and pulled her mouth deeper into his. "Saul!" she gasped.

"You mean all I had to do was break a bone for you to notice me?" He was still holding her, but the pain had not in any way lessened.

"I never stopped noticing you. Are you hurt?"

He smiled and nodded. The pain soared through him as if someone were tearing off his arm. He tried to ignore it as he reached out his hand to touch her face, and winced as another wave of pain took hold. "It was my own fault. I should have climbed down as soon as it began drizzling."

"Can you move?" she asked, hardly listening to what he'd said.

"I think so." But when he tried, he couldn't. "Help me." He tried to get up, then looked at her face. "I never ever hit her."

"I know."

Within minutes he felt himself being lifted and carried. Before he realized what was happening, he was lying in Pamela's bed and one of the village doctors was leaning over him. Maura put a pinch of herb on Saul's tongue and in less than two minutes he was asleep.

When next Saul opened his eyes, there was no shoulder pain and his foot was bandaged. Pamela's fingers were intertwined in his and she was looking at him. She looked tired. "How long have I been out?" he asked.

"About four hours." She smiled. "How do you feel?"

"Like I fell off a roof." He looked down at his foot. "What happened there?"

"Bad sprain."

He moved his shoulder. "That works."

"You know you popped your shoulder, right?"

"Yeah, the shoulder pain was so excruciating I didn't feel the foot."

She shook her head and took a deep breath. "I've been an ass, haven't I?"

He nodded.

She laughed. "I deserve that. Any pain?"

He shook his head.

"You should drink this anyway." She held the cup to his head and he sipped the bitter brew.

He tried to pull himself up in the bed and she scoffed at him. "Will you help me?" he asked, enjoying the attention he was getting from her.

"No, you have to lie like that for a little while longer. What were you doing when you fell?"

"Looking at you."

"Why?"

"Because you're so beautiful. You took my breath away and I couldn't move. The thunder took me by

THE OTHER SIDE OF THE MOUNTAIN

surprise." He smiled. "I guess you could say I fell hard for you."

"Funny man. Maura popped your shoulder back in." She moved her hand to his cheek and gently caressed his soft skin, then moved slowly and placed her lips on his.

"Then I should be up in no time." Saul closed his eyes and allowed the gentle feel of her mouth to take him away. He knew he should have steeled his body, but he let go, enjoying each moment. His lips slowly parted. He gently held her cheeks and deepened the kiss, causing his body to react. Blood rushed to his lower extremities making his foot, among other parts of his body, throb. "I think I need more of that pain killer," he whispered, half smiling, half in pain.

"Okay. Maura says you should keep off the foot for a while. So you'll have to stay here until she says it's all right to get out of bed." She touched his face, looked into his eyes and shook her head, then put the cup to his head once again. "You are a stubborn man," she whispered.

"Yes." He lifted the covers and saw that if it weren't for his boxers, he would have been quite naked in her bed.

She looked at him and laughed. "I undressed you."

"I have to tell you everything," he said, holding up a hand to her protest as he told her exactly what he'd told Angel.

"I'm sorry, I've been such an ass," she said.

"A pretty ass, though."

She would have thrown a pillow at him, but she still felt sorry he was in pain.

Angel cleared her throat before she entered the room. "You'd do anything for her to talk to you, wouldn't you?" She sat down on the chair beside the bed.

"I try my best." He grinned.

Gracie and his children came in and Pamela went out to get him his supper. There was no bed in the new room, but the men had cleaned it. The twins were very excited to sleep on thick blankets on the floor, but Saul wouldn't hear of it. The bed he'd had specially made for the room was sitting in his home.

Not knowing how Tim really felt about him, when he came to visit, Saul asked him if he could arrange for the bed to be brought up so that the children could sleep on it. "Anything for Pammy," Tim said after inquiring about his health. He didn't stay long but went about getting the bed to the room.

It was still drizzling, and there was no doubt that in a couple of days the heavy rain would start. It was the same every year. Bags of sand were settled around the houses and new drains made for the run-off.

Pamela was accompanied by Mary, Myah and Esther as she brought food into the cottage. Until the

THE OTHER SIDE OF THE MOUNTAIN

rainy days were gone, everyone would eat in their cottages.

Saul pulled himself up until he was in a comfortable position to eat. Angel and the other women ate in the living room while Pam ate with Saul.

He glanced at her. "I was having amorous thoughts of you before I fell off the roof."

She almost choked on her food. She began laughing, and so did he. "That stuff can kill you, if you know what I mean."

He continued laughing so hard she had to take the tray from him.

"If I'd broken any bones it would have been your fault. You were driving me insane."

She stopped laughing and looked earnestly at him. "I'm sorry."

"I know." He took the tray from her hand. "This is one way of getting into your bed."

"Do you always take the hard way out?" She began eating again.

"With you, I do what it takes."

She shook her head.

When Saul was finished eating, Pamela took the tray from him and went into the kitchen. Angel walked in behind her. "Do you mind if I speak with Saul for a few minutes?" she asked.

"No, not at all." She turned and looked in Angel's eyes. "Is everything going well with Raquel?"

"Yes." Angel turned and left the kitchen with Pamela staring after her.

Angel sat on the bed next to Saul and smiled, then sighed.

He looked at her. "Spit it out." She pushed the pillows under his shoulder.

She shook her head. "This is not going to be easy."

He said nothing. He just kept looking at her.

"Did you know that your wife knows witchcraft?"

He gasped. "What are you talking about?"

"She brought powders and roots to this island and is keeping them where she thinks no one can find them. She plans to do harm to either you or Pamela."

At the mention of Pamela's name he jerked upright. "No! How do you know this?"

"I can't go into details..." Then she stopped talking and wrinkled her brows. "Well, in a case like this I think it best that I do. She knew of your visit to Jamaica with Pamela. A day after you left, she left the island for a couple of days. No one knew because she kept the room door locked. No one checked on her in those two days. She slipped away in the workers' boat. Everyone was so busy no one noticed a woman with a scarf tied to her head like everyone else. She flew from Kingston to Haiti and returned the same day. She's angry with you for throwing her over for Pamela and angry with Pamela for taking you from her..."

"But..."

THE OTHER SIDE OF THE MOUNTAIN

"I know. Here's the part that no one knows. She's not all there. She's tortured."

"You mean she's mad?" His eyes were large in his head as a million things ran through his brain. At the top of the list was the safety of Pamela and the children. "How long do you think she's been tortured?" He gestured with his hand.

She shook her head. "Hard to say. Did you notice her taking any drugs when you first met her?"

He shook his head slowly, trying to remember. "No, she never did anything like that in front of me. I only noticed the drinking, which she made very obvious."

"She was, and is, still quite clever."

"Back up. How do you know she has these things?"

"Saul, you and Pamela asked me to do a job, remember?"

He nodded.

"She's comfortable with me. She had a lot bottled up inside. And although she's told me about her present marriage, she's still under the delusion that you two belong together."

"But she isn't even in love with me," he said, baffled by Angel's words. "I found out after the children were born how much she hates our culture. This must never leave this room, but that's why the children's hair isn't locked. It's not because it can't be locked, it's because she didn't want them to be a part of the culture."

"Why didn't you have their hair locked after she'd left?"

He shrugged. "I'm letting them choose. If they want to, they can have their hair locked." He looked at her and knew she understood. After all, her daughter Hildie had cut off all her locks just to be like her.

Angel nodded. "I understand, but this has nothing to do with love. It has to do with possession and control. You allowed her to think for a long time that she could control you." Angel chuckled. "You know the saying 'don't take my kindness for weakness?' "

He nodded knowingly. "By not physically fighting with her and walking away from the mental abuse, she thought I was weak."

Angel nodded. "She still does." Somehow she knew that he knew Raquel had taken a lover in his bed to once again emasculate him. Raquel had laughed when she'd told her that he looked like a deer in front of oncoming headlights when he'd opened the door and seen her in bed with one of his distant cousins. "He just slammed the door and left the island," she'd said, still laughing. When Angel had asked her why she'd done it, she'd told her that Saul was always working and she had needs.

"Here is where I stop showing weakness because if she comes anywhere near Pamela or the children…" He stopped short of issuing a threat. "Do you know where she has these things?"

THE OTHER SIDE OF THE MOUNTAIN

"No, but she's not locked up, Saul. There's someone standing guard outside her door, but as I said, she's a clever woman." She took a breath and cleared her throat.

Saul looked at her. "There's more?"

"She's taken to smoking ganja."

Saul took a deep breath and looked down at his foot. "She traded one addiction for another. It's not a crime to smoke ganja in our culture, you know that."

Pamela came into the room and both Saul and Angel smiled at her. She scowled. "Okay, I think I know you two well enough to know that something's wrong. What are you guys hiding from me?" She sat on the chair beside the bed.

Angel looked at Saul, whose face was hard with anger. He shook his head and looked at Pamela. Just looking at her face softened his mood. Wondering if he should tell her, he took a deep breath. The ball was in his court. Angel would not say anything to Pamela.

"It seems that my ex-wife has knowledge of witchcraft and has threatened our lives."

Angel and Saul looked at Pamela, expecting to find her petrified. Instead, she laughed. "You must be joking."

The two shook their heads.

"And what does she intend to do, chop our heads off, invoke spirits, sprinkle scratching powder on our food?"

Knowing what Raquel was capable of, Saul took things more seriously than Pamela. His brows drew in and his hands washed over his face. His shoulder was still sore and he winced and dropped one hand. "I need to do something. I can't just sit here."

"Yes, you can, and you will. Just until tomorrow," Pamela said. "We are not afraid of Raquel. She is only one tiny foolish person, and when I say tiny, I do mean tiny. Whatever she has, whether it's herbs or roots, we can counteract it. Don't worry about what she'll do. There's nothing she can do to hurt us." She gave a sardonic laugh. "And she says we're backward."

She sounded so strong and confident that Saul had to smile. In the face of danger, she certainly was no shrinking violet. "I need crutches."

"For the rest of the day, you need to rest," Pamela insisted.

"I haven't finished the room."

"Your friends will take care of that. Everything will be done." She got to her feet. "Now you two can continue talking behind my back. I have some things to tend to."

Saul and Angel looked at each other. They knew that when she set out to do something no one could distract her, but what was she going to do?

Chapter 22

On her way up the mountain to the Elders' village, Pamela met Tim. "Thanks for taking care of the bed for the children." She touched his arm and was about to walk away, but he held her hand and walked beside her.

"What are you doing, Pam?"

"What are you talking about?"

"I mean with Saul. Why is he in your house? What's going on?"

She glanced at him. Everyone knew about the relationship between her and Saul. Was he pretending not to know? She gave an indirect answer. "Saul is in my home because he was injured, Tim. Not only that, he is my friend."

"I'm your friend. I've been your friend since childhood."

"So?"

"I can take him home. Heck, any one of us can help him home." His hand tightened around hers.

She tried to pull away from him. "Do you mind? You're hurting me."

He let go. "Sorry. It just makes me angry to see you two together."

"You're jealous?"

He didn't answer for a while. "Yes. You're supposed to love me, not him. He went outside the culture to get a woman…"

She stopped and looked up at him. "Are you in love with me, Tim?" She looked at his handsome face, but his beauty was different from Saul's. Saul was soft yet rugged. Flawed yet perfect. "You're right, we've been friends forever…" she didn't stop looking in his face. "I love the friendship we share, but there can be nothing else between us."

He was angry when he'd seen her with Saul on the beach. He was angry when he'd seen the way she and Saul looked at each other at the party, but now he was angry with her. He turned and began walking back down the mountain.

She looked after him but didn't call out to him. She would deal with him later. The ground under her feet was soft as the rain continued seeping deep into the soil. She pulled the wrap from her head and allowed the drizzle to dampen her hair. Outside Jane's home she brushed the water from her hair and knocked on the door twice before she heard Jane's walking stick clicking on the floor.

"Child, what are you doing out in this weather? You should be curled up with one of your books sipping hot cocoa." She laughed and moved away from the door.

THE OTHER SIDE OF THE MOUNTAIN

Pamela kissed her cheek and stepped inside. Jane sat in the chair and rocked while Pamela sat on the cushion.

"Okay, spill it. I know you didn't just come to say hello again."

"No, Grangran…"

"Where are my manners? May I get you some tea?"

"No, Grangran, I'm fine. Do you know about Raquel?"

Jane looked at her, then closed her eyes and rocked back and forth. "Yes, I know about Raquel."

"It's assumed that she has knowledge of witchcraft and has brought harmful herbs to the island."

Jane stopped rocking. "What kind of harmful herbs?"

"We don't know. She's hidden them."

"But she's not at the cottage. Someone can search her things." She looked at Pamela. "Whatever herbs she has, we have. We just use them differently."

Pamela smiled at her grandmother. "And prepare them differently. I suggested treatment for her addiction to alcohol, but I don't think it's working. She hates us too much. I'm afraid she'll hurt the children."

"What are you saying, Pammy?"

"I think she should leave the island, Grangran."

Jane nodded. "I think you should do what you think is best for our people. If anyone is threatened, then she should go, just as you suggest."

JANICE ANGELIQUE

Pamela sighed. "I wanted to help her." She looked down at her hands in her lap.

"Some people really don't want to be helped, my sweet."

"I can't risk the safety of the children. Saul and I can take care of ourselves, but I won't risk the safety of the children."

Jane nodded. "Do what you have to do."

She nodded. "Of course." She got up and kissed her grandmother. "Saul slid off the roof and hurt himself."

Jane smiled and looked at her under her lashes. "One could say he fell hard for you."

She looked at Jane and laughed. "Grangran, stop that." She held her hand, helping her out of the chair.

"You can't hide it anymore, my dear."

"I'm not hiding it anymore, Grangran."

"How is your mother?" she asked purposely.

"Still a bit reserved as far as Saul is concerned." Pam opened the door.

"When will we learn that not everyone gets it right the first time?" Jane said.

It was still drizzling. Pamela didn't bother to put the scarf back on her head. She kissed her grandmother again and closed the door behind her. She thought about Raquel. Witchcraft, voodoo, had no business on the island. It was barbaric and backward. She'd thought Raquel had some kind of intellect. She had

THE OTHER SIDE OF THE MOUNTAIN

never known anyone in her culture who'd used herbs to harm another. Not even through jealousy.

By the time Pamela got back home, Angel had left. She'd told Saul that she wanted to talk with Raquel a little bit longer.

⁂

Angel sat looking at Raquel smoking ganja and rocking herself. The rocking chair creaked with each movement. She offered Angel the weed.

Angel shook her head. "Doesn't do anything for me."

"You don't know what you're missing."

Angel shrugged. "Tell me why you want to stay here, Raquel. Why do you want Saul back?"

"He's my husband." She took a drag of the weed and slowly let the smoke slip from between her lips. Her eyes were red, as if she'd been smoking for a while.

"You can't have two husbands." Angel got up and went to stand at the open door.

"Why not?"

"It's not a part of this culture."

"I'm not Rahjah."

"What does that mean?"

"It means I don't have to abide by their rules. These people make up their own rules, so why can't I?" She stopped rocking and looked at Angel. "Do you have children?"

JANICE ANGELIQUE

"I have a daughter…" She stopped herself.

"What is she like? I mean, Saul doesn't want me to be with my children. He's turned them against me. I don't think they love me at all. You don't lock your hair. I bet your daughter doesn't lock her hair, either. It looks so dirty sometimes. I couldn't allow the children to do that to themselves. I see the Rasta people outside of the island and their hair looks horrible." She shook her head.

"Do you really think he turned them against you?"

"They all did. His mother…all of them." She gestured wildly with her hand, but held fast to the ganja between her fingers. "I can leave here any time I want to, right?"

Angel nodded. "What do you intend to do with the herbs you have hidden?"

She looked at Angel and laughed, then shook her head. "I can't tell you that. You're not supposed to tell anyone what we talk about, but I think you do." She kept looking at Angel. "Do you?"

Angel didn't waver. "Do you intend to harm Saul?"

"That Pam needs to back away from my family." She shrugged and took a long drag on the weed. "She's my friend, you know." She frowned and exhaled. "Friends screw friends over, don't they?" The weed burnt down to her finger and she dropped it to the ground and sucked on her finger. "Tell what's-his-name to bring me some more. I think I'm out."

THE OTHER SIDE OF THE MOUNTAIN

She attempted to stand up and plopped back in the chair and laughed. "Will you get me some more?" She didn't look at Angel.

"No," Angel replied.

Raquel began rocking herself.

"You wouldn't harm the children."

"The children are... They are... I should take them with me. He'd better give me the money he promised. You don't think..."

Angel waited for her to finish the sentence. "Think what, Raquel?" The next thing she heard was Raquel snoring. She turned around and saw Myah. "She's stoned out of her mind. She has a hard time holding a thought long enough for me to talk with her and make sense of what she's saying. Who gives her this stuff?"

"You know how it is. She asks and she gets."

"Her smoking just makes things worse. If she wants to leave don't try to stop her, but watch her. Maybe she'll lead us to where she has the herbs."

"We really aren't afraid of her herbs, you know. No one will eat from her."

"She's whacked out of her mind on this stuff, but don't underestimate her. She hardly eats, she just smokes. She's trying to get the same high she got from alcohol."

Myah nodded.

"I'm going to get some sleep. I'll see you tomorrow. I could say this session was a waste of time, but

I don't think it was. I think she's after Pamela, not the children or Saul."

"I'll kill her if she ever tries to touch one hair on my friend's head." Myah pursed her lips in anger.

"No, you won't. Just look out for Pam."

"Of course I will. John's waiting with your horse. He'll ride over with you."

"Thanks." Angel touched Myah's shoulder and left.

Pamela lay on the bed beside Saul and read by lamplight while he did the same. She looked over at him. "You know what we look like right now?"

"What?"

"An old married couple."

He laughed. "Talking about married couples…"

"No." She held his chin and kissed him. She kissed his forehead and both cheeks. "Goodnight. Sleep well." Her fingertips rested on his cheek for a while and she gazed into his eyes. "You are so beautiful." She smiled, rolled off the bed and left the room.

Saul smiled. He knew it was too soon to talk to her about marriage, but still, he had to say something to let her know of his intention. He shook his head and turned on his back. He stared at the ceiling, then turned and blew out the lamp when he was sure she'd reached her daughter's room.

THE OTHER SIDE OF THE MOUNTAIN

Pamela quickly changed into her nightgown and slipped into Gracie's bed. Gracie smiled and crawled into her mother's arms.

Pamela closed her eyes to a vision of Saul's face and fell asleep.

⁂

Pamela woke to rumblings in the village. She got out of bed and ran to the window. Smoke rose from the chimney in the kitchen and the aroma of breakfast wafted through the air, but more than that, Raquel was in the village. She dressed quickly and ran outside barefoot just in time to see her mother block Raquel from the kitchen.

"Pamela told me that I could help cook," Raquel told Esther.

Esther shook her head. "No, you're a guest in this village. Breakfast will be ready soon. Why don't you join the other women in…" She looked out at the rain-soaked earth.

"In what?" Raquel asked, looking at Esther.

"In my cottage," Pamela said.

Her mother looked at her as if she'd lost her mind.

Raquel turned and smiled. "Hi. I didn't mean to barge in, but…"

Pamela ignored her mother. She had to invite her into her home even though Saul was there in her bed.

Mary wasn't far behind. She was very casual and nonchalant. "It's my turn to host breakfast. Let's go to my cottage." She walked on the other side of Raquel.

Raquel looked at Pamela.

"Of course. I'll bring your children over so that you can spend time with them."

Raquel reeked of smoke and sweat.

"Would you like to wash up or anything? We're just about to go down to the river to bathe." Pamela glanced at Mary and Mary nodded.

"Okay," Raquel said. "But I don't have a change of clothes."

No one in the village except for the teenagers had any clothes that could fit Raquel, and somehow they didn't think she'd wear their kind of clothing. "I can get you something to wear, but it's not your style," Mary said.

"Sure. I'll wear your clothes," she said haltingly, looking at Mary's clothes and laughing.

Mary and Pamela exchanged surprised glances. What was she up to? She hated their clothes.

Mary nodded, left the women and went next door to get a frock and underwear for Raquel. They met back on the river bank.

Pamela and Mary stripped and walked quickly into the river while Raquel timidly undressed and skirted the water to sit on the riverbank.

"Don't you want to bathe?" Pamela asked.

321

THE OTHER SIDE OF THE MOUNTAIN

"Yes, but the water is cold."

"Your body will adjust. Come on in." Pamela swam up to the waterfall and Mary followed. They both looked back to see Raquel testing the water with her toes. They laughed, bathed and got out. They towel dried, got dressed and waited while Raquel washed and quickly got out. She used the towel they gave her and pulled the frock over her head but refused the underwear.

"What should I do with my clothes?" she asked.

Pamela wanted to tell her to burn them but said, "Why don't you wash them later when the sun is high. They'll dry quickly."

She nodded, folded the clothes under her arm and followed the women back to Mary's cottage.

Not allowing her in the tiny kitchen and watching her every move with the food, Pamela excused herself and went to check on Saul. He smiled when he saw her. "Did I hear…"

"Yes, she's with Mary."

He had his breakfast tray on his lap. "I see my mother is treating you well," she said.

"Actually, Gracie and the twins brought me breakfast."

"That's nice. I would love to eat with you, but I don't want any trouble from Raquel."

He shook his head. "Why?"

She shrugged.

"Pam, it's all right. You're my woman."

She laughed. "Am I now?"

"Yes."

"Makes me sound like a possession." She remembered she'd left her breakfast tray on the pillow next to Raquel and cursed at herself for being so careless. "I'll be back soon."

"Take your time. I'm not running away."

When she got back to Mary's living room, she looked on the cushion but her tray was not there. She twisted her lips and made a face. Mary shook her head.

Pamela mouthed, "Sorry."

"Careless," Mary mouthed back. "I didn't want your breakfast to spill so I put it on the table in the kitchen," she said out loud.

"Thanks." Pamela retrieved her breakfast and joined them.

"You didn't come to visit me, Pam," Raquel said, pouting.

"Sorry, I meant to."

"You're forgiven. Would you like to share with me? I think I took too much ackee."

"No," Mary said a little too sharply. She smiled. "Sorry. I didn't mean to shout. But Pam doesn't really like ackee."

Pam's eyes opened wide. She hoped Gracie wouldn't say anything; she loved ackee. Gracie wrinkled her brows but said nothing.

THE OTHER SIDE OF THE MOUNTAIN

Pam shrugged. "Sorry."

"Really, you don't like ackee? I thought everyone loved this stuff," Raquel said.

"I don't hate it, but I don't always eat it." She thanked her lucky stars that she'd not taken any. She continued eating the fruits on her plate.

Raquel placed her tray to the side and asked, "Does anyone want more tea? I'm going to get some from the kitchen." She looked at Mary. "Is it all right?"

"You can go to the kitchen, but all the tea is right there on the table." She pointed to the teapot.

Both Mary and Pamela watched as she poured her tea. Raquel's clothes had not left her side, and they wondered if she had anything in the small pockets.

"I would like to go back to my cottage after breakfast. I just came to say hello to Pam." Raquel stared at Pamela for a few seconds, then drained her cup. She ate a small amount of food, placed her plate on the table and sat back on the cushion with her arms folded. Her eyes darted back and forth across the room as if searching for something or someone. Her eyes settled on Pamela and she laughed. "You've been taking care of my children?"

"We've all been taking care of the children. It's something we do for each other."

"But they stay with you more than anyone else?"

"They are very close to Gracie."

Raquel had not hugged her children since she reappeared in the village, and instead of speaking to them directly, she asked about them. They looked at her but said nothing as they finished their breakfast and asked to be excused.

The drizzle did not in any way deter the children from playing outside. Punti came up in his go-cart to ask if David could come out and play. All four children left the cottage together.

Clutching her clothes, Raquel jumped to her feet. "I have to go, too. I'll change and bring your clothes back, Mary."

"Okay," Mary said.

"I'll come back and have supper with you. I'll make something special for you," she said to Pamela.

Pamela nodded, giving Mary a sidelong look.

Raquel left the cottage. She had a horse waiting in the stables.

Mary breathed aloud when she turned to Pamela. "I don't like it, Pammy. Whatever she brings for you, promise me you won't eat it."

"Of course." She got to her feet and helped Mary to clean up.

When Pamela went to her cottage, the first place she went was her bedroom to check on Saul. He wasn't there. The bed was made, the room was tidy. She peeped into the new room, but he wasn't there, either. Her brows furrowed as she walked outside and

THE OTHER SIDE OF THE MOUNTAIN

looked up to the roof, but there was no evidence of Saul anywhere. She shrugged and walked back inside to clean her cottage. She had not taken the time to look at anything in the new room.

Chapter 23

Saul had gotten out of bed while they'd been having breakfast. He had to see James. He hobbled to the stables, got on his horse and rode home.

He breathed deeply and smiled as he walked into his very clean home and saw James and Angel in his living room. After Raquel left, his mother and aunt had cleaned the place until it smelled like the outdoors. Saul gingerly took a seat on a cushion and stretched his legs.

"Fell hard, I see," James said with a chuckle, motioning to his leg. "Angel told me all about it."

"One way or the other they cause pain." He glanced at Angel. "I mean that in the most loving way."

"Of course," Angel replied.

He looked at James, and before he could say anything, Angel spoke.

"Raquel," Angel said.

"Right," Saul said.

She shook her head. "No, I mean Raquel is coming up the walk."

All three looked towards the walkway. Raquel's clothes had been packed by Saul's mother and placed

THE OTHER SIDE OF THE MOUNTAIN

in the guest room. All she had to do was pick up her bags and head for the open sea back to Jamaica.

Raquel stopped in the doorway and looked at the three people. She zoomed in on Saul. "I thought you'd still be in Pamela's bed." She gave him a hostile glare.

Saul didn't answer.

She walked to Saul's room, stood in the doorway, took one look around and turned back to him. "Where are my clothes?"

"Your suitcases are packed and in the guest room."

"Hmmm." She walked to the guest room and closed the door behind her.

Saul looked at Angel questioningly.

She shrugged.

Raquel came out dressed in loose-fitting pants and a silk shirt. She had her hands in her pockets as she walked to the kitchen.

The wind picked up and blew the leaves off the nearby trees as the rain began falling.

"What was the forecast?" Saul asked James.

"It's a small storm with a mighty punch coming straight for the island. It could veer off course and miss us completely, but I doubt it and it's too late to evacuate. The seas are too rough. I barely made it with my boat." He shook his head. "It's pretty brutal out there. If it hits the island it will also hit Jamaica, but they're prepared."

Saul got to his feet with James's help. His foot was starting to hurt, but he ignored the pain. "Well, the only thing to do now is what we always do this time of year. Lots of sand bags. The crops are in. Our only problem would be water. They had to stop laying the pipes because of the rain. The women are cooking enough food to last for a while." He motioned to James. "You can't go back to the Blue Mountain until after the storm."

"What about Pam?" Angel asked.

"I'm going back," Saul said.

James shook his head. "It's looking pretty nasty out there. If you're going, now is the best time or you'll lose this window. Angi and I will stay on the island and help in any way we can."

Saul nodded and motioned toward the kitchen. "Watch her. Don't eat or drink anything she touches," he whispered.

"We know," Angel said.

The sweet smell of brownies permeated the cottage and the three people looked at each other.

The wind had picked up even more and the rain was coming harder as Saul chewed on the herb he took from his pocket on leaving the cottage. He whistled for his horse and mounted. With ferocious winds and stinging rain pushing at him, he held his head low and nudged the horse into a full gallop.

THE OTHER SIDE OF THE MOUNTAIN

Pamela got the children inside as Tim came into the house to help her put in the shutters.

"Where's Saul?" he asked in a rough voice.

"You do know your resentment for Saul is making you into an ugly person? Where's my friend?" She scowled and shook her head.

He ignored her and continued. "He left you to fend for yourself in the middle of a storm." His face was stony.

"Tim, I've been doing this by myself for years…"

"With my help."

"Okay, yes, with your help. Maybe he went to his village to see to things there. It's all right."

"No, it's not. His children are here. This home should have been his number one priority."

She stopped what she was doing and put her arms akimbo. "You know what? If you're here to make me unhappy you can just turn around and leave. We each have to do our part, and if his part is to go to his village I can live with it." The water began blowing into the cottage, making it difficult for the shutters to fit into their openings.

Tim had to brace hard against the wind to get the shutters in. Pamela raced to the windows in her bedroom, but Saul had already begun placing the shutters in their place.

"When did you get here? How did you get in?" she asked, startled to find him there.

330

"I came through the window. Help me with this." She ran over to him and they both braced against the howling wind. "How is the new room holding up?" he asked.

"I don't know. I walked through but didn't take notice. The children have already covered their windows."

He moved past her with huge, limping steps and didn't even notice Tim putting the last shutter in. The new room was all secured and David was sitting on the bed. Saul looked up at the roof, praying that it would hold through the storm. He smiled at his son. "You're all right?"

"Yes, Dada."

"Good." He went to the girls' room. They were sitting on the bed playing board games. He nodded.

There was a commotion outside. Pam rushed to the door. Mary's roof had begun leaking. She turned to Saul, who was already out the door. Although Judiah was trying his best to repair the leak, he wasn't fast enough. Trying hard to ignore the pain in his foot, Saul ran back into Pamela's house for supplies he'd left in the new room and was back to Mary's house in a flash.

Tim was still fitting the last shutter in the living room for Pamela. She looked over at him. "I can do that. You go and help Saul and Judiah with Mary's roof."

He hesitated.

"Are you joking?" she shouted.

"Saul's helping."

THE OTHER SIDE OF THE MOUNTAIN

"So will you," she shouted. "Get over there and help. This is no time for jealousy or selfishness. I can handle this myself."

Judiah called out his name. "Tim, we need you over here."

Pamela shook her head at his back, took a deep breath and sealed her shutter into its opening.

Mary rushed in. "I need two more buckets. It's really bad. We thought the roof was all right." She grabbed a bucket from the kitchen.

"Didn't Judiah check this year?" She ran to get another bucket.

"I guess not. He was helping Saul with your room and forgot to check ours."

In Mary's cottage Saul and Judiah were on ladders trying to fight against the wind and rain. Both women placed buckets under the leaks and watched as the men hammered planks of wood and thatch. This was clearly a job to be done on top of the roof, but that was impossible.

"What can we do?" Pamela asked.

"We're almost done," Judiah said, putting zinc in place, then the thatch under it. Saul hammered and Tim held the ladders. The roofs would be properly mended after the storm.

The women dried up the water from the floor, giving the men a chance to catch their breath.

The heavy water began pushing the softened earth down from the Elders' village, but the sandbags were holding. They had placed the bags in a formation to force the water to run off over the mountainside.

At some places the river rose and overflowed its banks. Those who lived close to the river had to abandon their homes and pray that they would not be flooded.

Mary, Judiah and Saul sat in Pamela's living room talking. Pamela got up and asked if anyone needed anything. Saul looked at her and said, "Make brownies."

"Make brownies. What for?"

"Raquel is bringing you brownies that she baked herself." He stared at her.

She stared at him for a moment, and then caught her breath as she understood. "Oh, Jah, I'll bake brownies." She touched Mary's arm. "Help me, I'm not good at this."

Saul rose to his feet. "Sorry, I thought you could. The only thing I can make is chocolate and brownies. I do it quite well, if I may say so." He grinned and walked toward the kitchen.

"Does she make good brownies?" Pamela asked, following him into the kitchen.

He turned. "I don't know, she never cooks."

"Do you still need my help?" Mary asked from her sitting position.

"No, I've got it," Saul replied with a backward glance and a smile.

"If your brownies are better than hers, won't she know the difference?" Pamela asked Saul.

"At this point I don't think it matters because I don't think she'll eat any. She's bringing them for you."

Judiah leaned back on the cushion. "I'll just wait right here for you guys. One thing I can honestly admit is that I don't know anything about baking."

Saul gathered all the ingredients except the main one: cocoa. "Don't tell me you don't have any cocoa?" He turned and looked at her.

"The children might have had the last batch. I can go to the main kitchen for some."

"I'll do it. I would hate for the wind to push you up the mountain. Just mix these together." He showed her what to mix and hobbled through the door.

As soon as Saul left the cottage, Mary went into the kitchen to help Pamela. "I don't think she'll be able to make it back here in this weather. I hear the bridge is washed out."

"She can swim."

"Oh, come on, Pammy. Do you think she's so determined to kill you that she'll brave this storm to get back here?"

Pamela looked at her friend and sighed. "I have no idea what the strength of her hatred is. I have been nothing if not kind to her. Jah only knows why she'd want to harm me."

"Armed with all that we know, why would we let her back into the house?" Mary asked.

"We really aren't sure of her intentions."

Mary shook her head. "Why on earth do you see only the good in people?"

"That's not true. I can see both good and bad. I just choose to dig for the good rather than harp on the evil."

They'd just about mixed the wet ingredients when Saul came back with a bag of cocoa. Both women stepped aside and watched as he quickly made the brownies. The only time they interrupted him was to ask if he needed their help. The answer was always "no." He poured the mixture in an earthenware baking dish and pushed it into the small Dutch oven.

Pamela and Mary checked on the three children to find out if they wanted anything to eat and saw that they had a basket of dumplings on the bed beside them. Gracie's favorite rabbit was sitting on a folded blanket at the foot of the bed. Pamela smiled, nodded, and went back to join the men in the living room.

No sooner had they sat down when there was another commotion. The men jumped to their feet. Saul turned to Pamela, grabbed the timer and put it before her on the center table. "When the sand runs completely out, the brownies are done. Take them out to cool."

THE OTHER SIDE OF THE MOUNTAIN

Pamela nodded and got to her feet. A gust of wind almost knocked Judiah down as he opened the door. Looking outside, they could tell that although the men had worked on Esther's roof, it was no match for the gale force, howling wind.

"I told Esther that more work was needed," Judiah said and shook his head. "Ishmael should have listened."

"It might have been if the wind wasn't so forceful," Saul shouted as he hobbled onto the verandah. He looked back at Pamela and touched her hand. The rain was blowing straight into the cottage. He smiled and wiped the water from Pamela's face. "You look beautiful, even as a wet rat." He laughed, held her chin and kissed her pouting lips. "I'll be back as soon as we get things settled with your mother's roof."

The rain was coming so hard, they couldn't tell how many men had actually gone to help. Pamela turned her eyes to the upper mountain where the Elders lived to see mud rushing down against the sand bags. If the men had not made a run-off, no telling how many cottages would have been filled with mud. Just in case they needed help with anything, two young men were sent to each Elder's cottage to stay until the storm subsided.

Pamela turned and went back into the cottage. With Mary's help, they both pushed against the wind to close the door, then wiped the floors of the water. As the smell of brownies filled the room, Pamela inhaled. She sat on a cushion and was just about to say something to Mary when Gracie came out.

"I've been elected to ask if we can have some of whatever that is, Mama."

Pamela laughed. "Who elected you?"

"Everyone. We drew straws. I got the shortest one."

The women laughed.

Pamela glanced at the timer. "They're not quite ready." She pulled Gracie to sit by her side. "I'm surprised you don't have all the animals in your room with you."

"We put them in the barn. Rabbit wanted to stay with us, so we let her."

Pamela gave Mary a quick glance. "She still talks to you?"

"Now and again."

"But not as much as before Ruth and David got here?"

"Right."

Pamela nodded.

Pamela looked over at Mary. "How come Shaela doesn't talk to animals?"

Mary shrugged. "She's always had Gracie."

Pamela made a face. "But…never mind."

"They're done," Gracie said.

"What, baby?" Pamela asked.

"The brownies are done. The timer ran out."

THE OTHER SIDE OF THE MOUNTAIN

"Oh." Pamela got to her feet and went to the kitchen. She pulled the brownies out of the oven and put them on the counter to cool. "You can't have any until they're cooled." She ushered Gracie out of the kitchen.

"Will you come get me when they're cool then?"

"I'll do better than that. I'll bring some to you. Are you guys having fun?"

"Yes, but we'd rather be outside."

"Yeah. Me, too, but that won't happen until the storm eases up." She patted her daughter's bottom. "Go."

"Are you sure we should give them the brownies?" Mary asked, pulling yarn and hooks out of a bag she'd brought over.

"Why not? Saul made plenty. The children can have their brownies with plenty left over to switch with Raquel." She shook her head. "I don't believe she wants to kill me, though. I don't think she's that evil."

Mary shook her head and began making her blanket.

Pamela opened a footlocker in the corner of her living room and got out pieces of fabric to add to her quilt.

After allowing half an hour for the brownies to cool, Pamela went back into the kitchen to cut them into squares. She arranged six pieces on a plate and took them to the children.

"What about us?" Mary asked when she came back.

"I'm not hungry, but if you want a piece, I will get it for you."

"I do," Mary said.

There was an impatient knocking on the door. The women looked at each other. Pamela took a deep breath and walked to the door, Mary ran behind her. If both women didn't hold the door, there was a good chance the wind would push more rain into the cottage.

"It's me."

Myah's voice sounded like a breath of fresh air to the women on the other side of the door. They quickly opened the door to let her in.

"Why are you out in this weather?" Pamela asked, noticing that Isha was with her. "Come in, come in."

Myah was almost out of breath. "We got out with just the essentials when the house toppled down the mountain. It was knocked off the foundation."

"Oh, Jah. I was afraid of that. Your home was one of those perched precariously on the side of the mountain."

They pushed the door close.

Myah took off Isha's raincoat, ushered her into Gracie's room and then took off her own coat. "I'll wipe up the water," she said, going towards the kitchen for a rag.

"You'll do no such thing. Sit. I'll get you some tea. I'll wipe up the water," Pamela said.

But Mary was way ahead of her with the rag.

THE OTHER SIDE OF THE MOUNTAIN

No sooner had they wiped the floor when there was another knock at the door. Without thinking, Mary flung the door open to see Raquel standing there with a covered pan in her hand. She stood looking at her with her mouth open. "How... Why... Sorry. Why are you here in this storm?" She moved hesitantly away from the door. "Come in."

Raquel stepped in, placed the pan on the center table and immediately took off her raincoat.

"I heard the bridge was washed out. How did you get here?" Mary asked again.

"Oh, it's not so bad."

Pamela walked back into her living room and almost dropped the pot of tea. "Raquel!"

Myah just stood with her mouth agape.

Then all three women looked down at her full-length boots. It seemed Raquel was prepared for all contingencies.

"Oh, come on, guys, don't look so shocked. I got tired of talking with Angel and James. Plus, they left to help people with their problems. You know, flying roofs and stuff like that." She shrugged and laughed. She turned as she saw Pamela, then took the pan off the table. "I brought these for you. I made them myself."

That's what I'm afraid of. "Thank you," she said, almost pushing the words out of her mouth. "I'll take it into the kitchen." She placed the tea on the table and was about to take the pan from Raquel.

JANICE ANGELIQUE

"No," Raquel said forcefully, pulling the pan into her.

Everyone looked at her.

"I mean, there's no need. They're brownies. I made them for you. We can eat them here." She placed the pan on the table. "Do you have enough tea for one more? I could use a cup." She sat on the cushion. She had not expected to see Mary and Myah.

"Yes. I'll just get another cup. Oh, do you have enough brownies for everyone?"

"I'm not sure." She uncovered the pan. "I don't think so."

"No problem." Pamela glanced at Mary who was still standing. Mary followed her into the kitchen. "I'll take these out. She can eat hers and we'll eat ours," she whispered.

"I think she'll be insulted. She did say she made them for you."

"Oh, man." Pamela shrugged. She picked up the plate of brownies and another cup.

She placed the plate of brownies on the center table. "We must be on the same wavelength. I made brownies, too."

The look on Raquel's face was pure disappointment. "You have to taste one of mine. I made them specially for you."

Pamela pursed her lips and nodded.

THE OTHER SIDE OF THE MOUNTAIN

Without hesitation, Myah and Mary took a piece of Pamela's brownie. That didn't bother Raquel at all as she carefully watched Pamela, and then took a piece of one of her own brownies and began eating it. Pamela's eyes narrowed suspiciously. "It won't kill you," Raquel said, laughing. She got to her feet and went into the kitchen before anyone could stop her. She came back with a small plate, placed a piece of brownie on the plate for Pamela and pushed it in front of her.

Pamela didn't look at the brownie, but took a sip of her tea. "How did you cross the bridge?" she asked Raquel.

"Very carefully. It's flooded but not washed out. The water isn't muddy. At least it wasn't when I crossed, so I could actually see the bridge. I came on horseback." Speaking to the other two women in the room, she had looked away from Pamela. She looked back to see Pamela eating a brownie. She smiled. "Good, no?"

Pamela nodded. "Very good."

Raquel kept looking at Pamela as she chewed and swallowed. "I have to smoke," she said to no one in particular. Then she looked at Pamela. "Do you mind?"

"Not at all, but you'll have to go outside. I don't want the children to even smell that stuff in my house. In this little corner," she made a gesture with her hand, "no one smokes ganja."

Raquel picked up a bag she'd brought in under her arm and walked to the door.

JANICE ANGELIQUE

"Can't you wait a while? It's very windy out there, and there's no way you can light that thing," Mary said.

"I'll manage," she replied, heading for the door.

"We have to keep the door closed," Pamela said, but that didn't deter Raquel from reaching for the doorknob.

Locked inside, they could hear the howling of the wind and the rain beating on the roof and windows. As soon as Raquel opened the door, the force of the wind pushed it straight into her face. Blood gushed from her nostrils as the door slammed her against the wall. The rain blew in full force as furniture and cushions flew towards the wall. The other three women were almost blown against the wall. Pamela pushed herself to the door, but she couldn't move it without Mary and Myah's help. The heavy rain and wind had forced itself into the small cottage and had already done unimaginable damage.

Finally, they got the door off Raquel. When they got the door closed, Raquel fell to the floor crying, her face and hands covered in blood. Her nose was broken.

"Jah takes care of his children," Myah muttered, going to the kitchen to get cold compresses and a basin of water.

"I'm sorry I destroyed your house," Raquel said, still crying and holding her nose. She tried to lie down but Pamela stopped her.

THE OTHER SIDE OF THE MOUNTAIN

"You have to sit up for a while," Pam told her. She looked over at Mary. "How do we get Rita here? None of us are equipped to handle this." With Raquel screaming in her ears, Pamela ran to the kitchen to get some herbs to help with the pain. She came back and slipped a pinch under Raquel's tongue while Myah tried to wash the blood from her enemy's face and hold a cool compress on her nose. The two women seemed to have their work cut out for them, so Pamela volunteered to go and find Rita.

"You can't go out there," Mary said. "You just saw what the force of the wind can do. You cannot go out there," she stressed.

Myah removed the compress from Raquel's nose. It was still bleeding pretty bad.

"I have to," Pamela replied, getting her raincoat from the closet and slipping her feet into water boots that came up to her knees. "I'll be fine. Help me to open this door, Mary." She looked back at Myah. "Prop her up on the pillows and place her hand on the compress, this won't take long."

"I can't believe I have to take care of the one person that I hate," Myah muttered.

"Jah has a special place for you in heaven," Pamela replied. She hugged her and headed for the door. It took all three women to open the door. While the other two stood behind it holding it secure, Pamela slipped out and leaned against the wall, panting as the rain pelted her face. She pushed herself from the wall and crouched low, trying to move against the wind. She heard the crack as a palm tree broke and fell a few feet from her, missing her cottage by inches. She continued battling the wind, blinded by the rain, and pushed forward in the direction of Rita's cottage. *I am a madwoman. No one else in their right mind would be out in this storm.* Holding on to the wall, she moved slowly around the community kitchen, clutching the flimsy plastic she wore in order not to get soaking wet. As she let go of the wall, the wind pushed her back and she fell over. *No one, I say, no one would be mad enough to do this.* Not looking at the mess she'd made of her clothing, she got to her feet and continued with her quest.

She got to Rita's cottage and held onto the railing to pull herself onto the verandah. Then she pounded on the door. It took a while before Rita's husband Adam opened the door. He was more than shocked to see Pamela. He pulled her in and quickly closed the door.

"I know it must be an emergency for you to come here," he said. His dark sympathetic eyes seemed to bore into her as he scratched his bearded chin.

She was tired. "It is." Pamela stood panting with her back pressed up against door. "I need Rita. Raquel broke her nose on my door and it won't stop bleeding." She bent to catch her breath.

Rita stood listening to every word she said, then muttered, "Stupid woman. No matter what she does,

THE OTHER SIDE OF THE MOUNTAIN

it's always trouble. I'm sorry that she chose your home, Pammy." She went into her room for her medicine bag. She threw it on the floor and got dressed in her raincoat and water boots. "It's really bad out there, isn't it, Pam?"

Pamela nodded. "Yes, but we have to hurry. I don't want this woman to go into shock in my home."

"Me, neither." She kissed her husband.

With his strong arms, Adam braced against the door as he opened it. "Be very careful out there. Hold onto each other," he said as the women pushed through.

Pamela found out that holding onto each other wasn't as bad as being alone. And although they had to push through and bend low, they made it back to her cottage and pounded on the door for Mary and Myah to open it.

"How is she?" Rita asked.

"The herb that Pammy gave her seems to have worked. She's not in any pain. I don't think she gave her enough to knock her out, though, because she's still awake and crying about her broken nose."

As soon as Raquel saw Rita, she asked, "Are you the doctor? Is my nose really broken?"

"Stop talking," Rita said, her piercing brown eyes taking in the contours of the woman's face to discern the damage even before she touched her. She bent and touched the area around Raquel's nose. "It's broken, all right." Apparently no one had noticed the fine bone protruding through the skin, but Rita did. "Actually, it looks as if you splintered it. I can't reset it here. I have to go in and rebuild it." She looked up at the three women and sat on the floor. "She has to go to the caves. I need assistance to do this."

"Are you a plastic surgeon? I don't want my nose messed up."

The women looked at her and shook their heads. "If only she knew how bulbous her nose was right now," Mary said.

"I'm the closest thing to one you'll find on this island," Rita said, looking directly at Raquel.

She nodded.

In this storm, the cave was more than ten minutes away.

"I can't have her walk because of the fragments." Rita shook her head. "There's a lot of water on the path, if most of it isn't washed out."

"We have to get her there," Pamela said. "I can go on the verandah and call for any man within the sound of my voice." And before anyone could stop her, she headed for the door once more. They all opened the door and stood braced against it as Pamela went out again and braced herself against the wall, not minding the pelting of the rain against her face. As loudly as she could, she called for help again and again. She saw Tim, then Adam, and wondered where Saul and Judiah were.

THE OTHER SIDE OF THE MOUNTAIN

The two men came running and she went back into the cottage and held the door for them. They took one look at Raquel and knew why they were summoned. The only thing that could get her to the cave was the horse and buggy. The men went back through the door.

Pamela stood looking at her dirty clothes and her destroyed furniture. The broken center table had been made by her late husband. Half the paintings on her wall were now on the floor with broken frames. She went to her room to change and came back as the buggy pulled up outside. The men brought in a makeshift gurney, lifted Raquel onto it and walked out with Rita by their side, holding a cover over Raquel.

Chapter 24

Pamela took a deep breath as they pushed the door shut and walked to the kitchen. After all that, she was thirsty. She had bottles filled with water sitting on the counter. Now she poured herself a cup and took a brownie from the counter and ate and drank mindlessly. Unfortunately it was the one brownie that Raquel had made especially for her.

As soon as she swallowed, she began vomiting. She grabbed a bucket and, between heaves, called out to Mary and Myah. "Help me," she said, her face in the bucket as she vomited again and again.

"Oh, my Jah," Myah said as she saw her. "What happened?"

Pamela pointed to the half-eaten brownie on the floor. She began sweating as she held onto the bucket and retched.

Mary frantically opened cupboard after cupboard, looking for herbs to counteract whatever Pamela had ingested. She ran from the kitchen, flung the door open and headed to her own cottage.

"What do I do?" Myah asked.

Pamela sat on the floor, weak. She pressed against the cabinet, her eyes closed. She shook her head. "I

THE OTHER SIDE OF THE MOUNTAIN

wasn't thinking," she said before another wave of nausea took her breath away.

Myah pushed the bucket towards her and held it there, scooping Pamela's fallen locks away from her face. "Where are your herbs for nausea?"

Pamela pointed to a cupboard. "Up there."

Myah took down the jar, hurriedly boiled water and dumped it over the herbs, counting and cussing. Mary came back with a cup of brewed liquid in her hand. She held it to Pamela's mouth. "Drink."

Pamela took a sip.

"Drink it all," Mary ordered.

The hot liquid burned as it made its way down her throat into her stomach. Spent, Pamela leaned against Mary with her eyes closed.

Neither Myah nor Mary wanted to think of the worst. "How did you know which brownie to take when we were all in the living room?" she asked Pamela, hoping to keep her awake.

With some difficulty, Pamela opened her eyes and smiled. "I already had one in my pocket. When she wasn't looking, I exchanged it." Another wave of nausea washed over her, and once again she vomited in the bucket. She was getting weaker as the poison took hold.

Now the women were alarmed. The herb Mary had given her should have worked. Myah was still holding onto the cup she'd brewed. She pushed it in front of Pamela and she drank it. It didn't work. Again she vomited.

"Hold on, Pammy," Myah said. "Don't slip away."

"I'm holding on," she answered, out of breath. She leaned her head against Mary's shoulder.

They heard the door open and close. Myah jumped up to see who it was. "Saul," she said. "Where have you been?"

He chuckled. "You wouldn't believe all we've been up to. We've been up and down the village helping to repair roofs. Do you know how hard it is to repair roofs in this weather? What's wrong?" He'd just noticed the look on her face. He rushed forward. "Where's Pam?"

Myah moved out of his way as he rushed in the direction she'd come from. He saw Pamela on the floor and, forgetting his pain, took one giant leap to her side. He lifted her off the floor and, still limping, took her to the bedroom. "Why is she like this?" She was sweating and appeared unconscious.

"She ate one of Raquel's brownies," Mary said.

"Stay with her." He ran back to the kitchen and began mixing herbs that the women had missed. Without knowing what she'd ingested, he was flying blind. "Judiah, get Rita, now."

"She's at the cave," Myah shouted from the bedroom.

"Why?" he shouted back.

351

"Raquel broke her nose and had to be rushed there for surgery."

"Damn it. Damn it." He continued mixing. "Get Edith, please."

"Judiah has already gone to get her," Myah replied. She was beside her brother. "Give me something to do. I can't just do nothing."

He handed her the bowl. "Keep mixing." He pulled down more containers. He didn't find what he was looking for. "I'll be back in a minute." He was out the door to the community kitchen and back before she could ask another question. He poured a liquid into the bowl and continued mixing. "Water. I need boiling water."

Myah set the kettle back on the stove and stoked the fire. By the time the water was ready, Edith came in with her bag.

"Tell me what you have there?" she said to Saul.

He rattled off the names of the herbs. She reached into her bag, came up with another dried item and threw it into the mixture. "Don't stop mixing." She poured the hot water over the mixture and took it from him. His hands were trembling. "Go sit." She touched his hands. "Try to calm yourself. One way or the other we'll get the poison out."

He went into the room, knelt by the bed and watched Pamela's eyes open and close slowly. He took her hand, kissed it and then kissed her lips. She was burning up.

Edith came in with the brew. "This will have to work itself through her system. I don't know what she ingested, so it will be a slow process."

He nodded and left the room. He went through the door to the stables. He had a better chance on horseback than on foot to go to the caves. If he had to shake Raquel awake to tell him what she'd put in the brownies, he would. He got his horse and rode bareback through mud and high water, not caring how drenched he had become.

When he walked in and began looking into the compartments, he didn't see Raquel until he came to the last one. Her nose was bandaged. Rita came out and smiled. He didn't smile. She moved away as he passed her and stood looking at Raquel. She was asleep. With the herbs Rita had given her, she was feeling absolutely no pain.

Feeling as if his entire world had been turned upside down, he sat down and held his head in his hands and took a deep breath.

"What's the matter?" Rita asked.

He shook his head and explained to her what had happened.

They both sat and talked for a while until they heard Raquel moan. Saul didn't waste any time. He stood and looked down at her with a full dose of hatred. "What did you put in those brownies?" he spat as his eyes blazed with anger.

Still a bit weak from the surgery, she looked up at him. "Hi, Saul. You came to look for me."

"I didn't come here by choice. What did you put in those damn brownies, woman?"

"Did Pamela eat one?" She kept looking up at him. "I knew she would."

"If you don't tell me what you put in those brownies, I promise you won't walk out of this hospital."

She slipped her eyes from his face. "Hah! You're threatening me." She took a breath and felt her nose.

He stood seething, clenching and unclenching his fist.

She shook her head. "I told you that you belonged to me alone. The only way I'll tell you or give you the antidote is if you leave her." She looked up at him again. "Saul, we can leave this island and go someplace where we can start anew. We can send for the children in a few months, or whenever we're settled. I know we can make it this time. It won't take long for me to divorce that other man." She was fighting the sleep that threatened to overtake her.

"I have no interest in you." His voice thundered and reverberated in the small quiet room. "My only interest is Pamela and our children. I'm going to say this one more time. If you don't tell me, you won't walk out of this hospital. Now are you going to tell me what you put in those brownies?"

She took a good look at his face and was suddenly frightened by his dark, angry expression. "I don't know what it's called."

"Where is it? You must have some left over."

She shook her. "I used it all."

"How can you have something so lethal and not know what it is?" He looked directly into her face and saw something he'd never seen before. He realized Angel was right. She was demented. "Where did you get it?"

"I got it in Haiti." She didn't look at him this time.

"Then we'll go to Haiti and you'll go to wherever you got it and get the antidote."

A serious look crossed her face as she raised her head to meet him. "If I get this for you, you must never see her again. That's the deal, take it or leave it." Her head hit the pillow.

"Don't threaten me, Raquel."

"You are not in a position of power. You do as I say or she dies," she spat viciously.

She was a vindictive and conniving woman, and he knew she'd stayed on the island for this very thing. He walked to the door, turned and looked at her, at the madness in her eyes.

Rita stood by him and shook her head. "What did Edith say?"

THE OTHER SIDE OF THE MOUNTAIN

"She doesn't know what Pamela ingested. Why did Raquel choose this time to do this? We can't get off the island. The sea is too rough." He looked at Rita. "What am I going to do?" His hands washed over his face.

"If she went off the island to get this herb, no telling what it is. It may not even be a herb." She got to her feet and got her bag, and then gave instructions to the other doctor. "Let's go, Saul."

With Saul's horse walking beside the buggy, they slowly made their way back to Pamela's cottage.

It had been hours since the storm began and the force of the wind and rain had lessened somewhat, but it was still unsafe to be out because of all the flying debris.

Inside Pamela's cottage, the two doctors conversed while Saul lay beside Pamela's still-hot body. He placed his hand over her heart and closed his eyes. He loved his children to death, but if anything happened to her, he didn't want to live.

Tim stood at the door watching him with angry eyes. He could not hold back his resentment for the man any longer. "If it wasn't for you, she would not be in this position. You brought this on her."

Broken, Saul looked over at him and nodded. Yes, he'd brought this on her. He'd married and brought the witch to this island. What was happening to Pamela was all his fault. Tears rolled down his cheeks as he propped himself up on his elbow. "I love you with every fiber of my being, Pamela, and if you open your eyes and get well, I promise I will never allow anything or anyone to hurt you ever again." For a brief second he considered what Raquel had said. To save Pamela's life, he'd have to leave the island with Raquel. At this critical time in her life, he wanted to be with Pamela, but if he didn't go, Raquel would never give him the antidote. He felt heartsick.

He felt her move and heard her groan. He raised on his elbow. "Pamela. Can you hear me?"

Mary burst into the room. "She had a bag with her all the time. Even when she broke her nose, she wouldn't let go of it."

Saul got off the bed. "Did she take it with her to the caves?"

"It's not here," Mary said.

A small ray of sunshine was peeling away the dark gloom that hung over the cottage. "I'll go back and search her room," he said, heading for the door.

"All her belongings are in the footlocker in her room," Rita said.

"Did you see it? Did she have it with her?" he asked, filled with hope.

Rita nodded. "I don't know why I didn't think of it. She wouldn't let go of it until we put her under."

Saul was out the door.

THE OTHER SIDE OF THE MOUNTAIN

"Why don't you put on a coat?" Myah called after him.

"It's only water," he replied, getting on his horse.

※

Tim walked into Pamela's room and sat at her bedside holding her hand.

He took a deep breath. Was he really losing her to Saul?

Rita and Edith came into the room together with a gallon of cool water. Rita asked Tim to leave the room for a few minutes. Both women had decided to work together to find out what was in her system. The only way they'd know was to test her urine and her blood. At least they could rule out what wasn't there.

※

All the way to the cave Saul couldn't stop thinking of the possibility of losing the one woman he truly loved. If he'd tried to take her from Peter, would he have succeeded? If nothing else, he was positive of the fact that she loved him now. He reached the cave and reined in his horse. He got off and led the horse under cover. He pushed the dripping locks from his face and hurried inside. His boots squished as he walked, and he left puddles of water along the way. He stopped in front of Raquel's door. She was asleep. He moved to the locker and opened it. It was empty except for her clothes. He went to stand over her. He looked at her face and was repulsed, not because it was swollen but because he hated her. He felt under her pillow, moved her from one side to the next, but there was no bag.

The other doctor came into the room. "Did you see her with a bag?" he asked.

The man shook his head.

Saul stood looking at him until he left the room. There was a reason why Raquel could get anything she wanted from some of the men on the island. She wasn't afraid to share her body for a favor. The word had spread that since she'd returned and begun drinking heavily and smoking ganja, she was quite loose. She couldn't handle the ganja the way the women on the island could.

Saul looked around the room for something out of place, but saw nothing. He walked to the door and turned once more to look. Nothing.

It was getting dark when he mounted his horse and made his way back to Pamela's cottage. Tim was sitting at her bedside. As he entered the room, Tim grudgingly got up and left.

Mary stood at the door with a shirt and pants in her hand. "You need to change out of those wet clothes. Pamela would have your head if she saw you like that."

He turned and smiled. "Thank you." He took the clothes from her.

THE OTHER SIDE OF THE MOUNTAIN

She turned to go, but then turned back to him. "She's a strong woman."

He nodded. "I know." He peeled the wet clothes from his body, dropped them onto the floor and slipped into the dry ones. Then he crawled into bed with Pamela and held her hand. "You need to fight this thing, Pammy. I won't let you die." He placed his hand on her chest and felt the slow rise and fall. Her breathing was deep and soft and he couldn't help putting his cool lips against her hot mouth.

He gazed at her, then sat up cross-legged holding her hand.

Rita came in. He looked anxiously at her. She shook her head. "It's nothing we have on the island."

"What is it?" he asked.

"I'm not sure. Edith says there is a mixture a few Haitians know how to use to render one unconscious, to slow the heart rate close to death. Edith thinks this herb that Raquel used is mixed with that powder. Alone it can be lethal. We have less than twenty-four hours from the time it was ingested. Edith will try another combination of herbs. It would help to find that bag. I don't think Raquel would be stupid enough to get the powder without the antidote."

"Sounds like anesthesia."

"If it were only that, we would have brought her around already."

He nodded, took a long look at Pamela and got out of the bed. He looked at Rita and washed his hand over his face. He felt weak. "I may not come back, but tell her…" He shook his head and pulled out a drawer. He got pen and paper. He sat back on the bed and began writing. He wrote quickly and took deep breaths as he wrote. When he was finished, he folded the paper and handed it to Rita. "Give this to her for me. I will do everything in my power to get the antidote for her."

Rita took the note from him. She looked into his eyes. "Are you sure this is what you want to do?"

"I don't think I have a choice."

"I heard what Raquel said. I heard her request."

He nodded and left the room. Once again he got on his horse. The wind had died down and the rain had stopped completely. People were milling around assessing the damage done to property. The skies were black, a sign that although the storm had passed the rain wasn't done with them yet. He rode to the cave. This time he would agree to her terms if she would get the antidote to Pamela.

He wanted to push his horse to go faster, but that was impossible. All he heard as he rode along the hidden path was the sucking sound of the horse's hooves in the mud. His heart was breaking.

When he finally got to the cave, he walked straight to Raquel's room. She was sitting up in bed.

THE OTHER SIDE OF THE MOUNTAIN

"Have you thought about what I said?" she asked, with a degree of confidence.

He nodded. "You win."

Her voice softened. "We both win. Don't you see? We can be happy together. The only person you need is me by your side."

"Do you have the antidote with you?"

"I will send it back to her when we get to Jamaica." She got out of bed and got dressed in the same bloody clothes she'd had on before.

He didn't ask her if she was strong enough. He just watched her lift the mattress and picked up a small black bag that he was sure contained the antidote. He shook his head. Why hadn't he thought of that?

She pulled on her boots, tucked the bag securely under her arm and looked at him. "Ready?"

He nodded.

She walked ahead of him. When she got to the mouth of the cave, she stopped and waited for him to lift her onto the horse. She was an accomplished rider. He lifted her onto the horse. She looked down at him.

"Aren't you coming?"

He nodded and climbed in front of her. As they made their way back to his village he realized that this was the way she liked him to act. Docile and subdued. There was no love between them, but if he were happy with someone else she would have lost, and she hated to lose. She was willing to make his life and hers a living hell rather than see him with Pamela.

The water was under the horse's belly as he waded slowly across the reinforced bridge. The mud was soft. He tried to urge the horse up the washed-out path but found it difficult. He got off the horse and led it slowly to the village.

James and Angel were surprised to see him and doubly surprised when they saw that he was with Raquel. Atop the horse, she waited for him to help her down. She walked past James and Angel. "Come along, Saul. We have to pack," she demanded.

"I'll be in shortly." His voice was subdued and beaten.

She walked inside.

Angel was perplexed. "What's going on?" she said to Saul.

James waited for an explanation.

They got the very short, condensed version. Angel placed a hand to her mouth and shook her head.

"You're not going through with this, are you?" James said.

"It's the only way I know to save Pamela's life."

"How do you know she'll keep her word? How do you know she'll give you the right antidote?"

He took a deep breath. "I thought of all that. I know I can't trust her, but she also knows if Pamela dies, so

THE OTHER SIDE OF THE MOUNTAIN

will she." He walked into the cottage with slumped shoulders.

James had never, ever heard him talk like that before. "I'll take you both to Jamaica and bring back the antidote."

Saul didn't answer. He went into his room, picked up a small suitcase, placed a few things in it and came back out. "Let's go," he said to Raquel. He had no idea why she was taking so long.

James and Angel had a buggy waiting. They took another way down the mountain. Then the two men had to get the boat back down to the water. As they passed Nigel on his way to his cottage, Saul asked him to help get the boat into the water. He gave them a skeptical look, then saw Raquel. He shook his head and got into the buggy.

The beach was washed out and the water had come all the way up to the rocks. They all knew that if they waited until dawn the water would have receded, but there was no time to waste.

With much difficulty, the men got the boat into the water and held it for Raquel to get in. Angel had no idea what James or Saul had in mind, but somehow she didn't think Raquel would win no matter what she thought she had accomplished. She waited for Nigel, turned the buggy around and headed for his home. Then she took the buggy back to the barn. If Saul could pass the bridge, so could she.

JANICE ANGELIQUE

It began raining again. She knew the boat would be tossed, but both Saul and James were experienced sailors and swimmers. She didn't want to think of it anymore. They would be safe. She got on a horse and allowed him to take his time in getting to the village.

When she finally got to Pamela's cottage, it was filled with people. All the herbalists in the village, including those from the village she'd just left, were there conversing. She pushed her way into the room and saw Pamela lying as if she were dead. Her mother and father sat by her bed watching her breathe. Everyone felt helpless. There were herb packs on her forehead and both feet.

As the night wore on, one by one people left to go to their homes to continue praying. Only those who were there originally, along with Angel and Pamela's parents stayed. They took turns changing the herb packs on her forehead and feet.

In the early morning, James arrived with the package Raquel had given him. She and Saul were staying at the Pegasus Hotel in Kingston. Saul had told her that they would not board a plane until he was sure Pamela was all right.

Both Rita and Edith examined and tested the contents to make sure it wasn't more poison. In progression, they introduced it into Pamela's system through the syringe and packs for her forehead. All they could do now was wait.

Chapter 25

The sun threw its prisms through the trees. It was the dawning of a new day. Drenched with sweat, Pamela writhed under blankets that helped to pull the water and poison from her system.

The herb packs were removed from her forehead and her feet. Her lips were chapped, but her body was cool.

Seven adults and four children stood at her bedside. "Thank Jah, her fever has broken," Rita said. "But she's still not out of the woods." They replaced the herb packs with fresh ones.

Tim and James removed the shutters, allowing the sun's pale light to push its way into the room. The smell of fresh baked bread floated on a gentle breeze into the room, reminding everyone that they had not eaten in a while. No one had even had supper except for some of the children. Gracie had not eaten.

Pamela groaned and everyone bent over the bed to look at her. Her face was moist with beads of sweat, and Esther used a cool cloth to gently pat around her forehead and cheeks. Pamela still didn't open her eyes.

Saul went down to the hotel bar. He couldn't sit and look at Raquel's face and listen to her plans anymore. She wanted to go to the United States and start life over, to try and make a go of a marriage that had ended years ago.

He sat at the bar drinking mineral water. He wanted a drink. It wasn't forbidden in his culture to drink alcohol, and, today, he wanted to get stinking drunk. But not with Raquel in close proximity. He took a deep breath and closed his eyes. He took a sip of his water and began formulating the details of his plan then squeezed his eyes shut with deep regret as he thought of Pamela's deathlike stillness when he'd looked at her. He opened his eyes and smiled tiredly, she was so beautiful. She was the only woman who truly challenged him mentally, physically and emotionally.

He couldn't think of a time he'd seen her when he didn't want to sweep her off her feet and carry her off somewhere. He prayed to Jah that she was all right and really understood the words he'd put on paper. He hadn't spelled anything out, but the clues were there.

He spotted Raquel coming out of the elevator and quickly left the bar. He just didn't want to see her. It was enough that he'd come this far with her. She wore dark glasses and a hat pulled down low to hide the bandage on her nose.

THE OTHER SIDE OF THE MOUNTAIN

Pamela opened her eyes and looked around the room. She saw everyone except the one person she really wanted to see. "Where's Saul?" she asked.

"He ran away, the coward," Tim said.

Angel and Mary shot him a warning look.

"What? He did," he said as anger and hatred flickered across his face. Deep down he wished that Saul would never come back.

"Go away, Tim," Pamela said tiredly.

"I never left your side, Pam..."

"Go away." She glanced at him. "You must be tired."

Rita came into the room and smiled when she heard Pamela talking. "Welcome back to the land of the living. How do you feel?" She held Pamela's hand and took her pulse.

"I don't know. Hungry, I think."

"That's a very good sign," Rita said.

James came in, kissed her cheek and smiled. "It's good to look into those beautiful eyes of yours."

"Where's Saul?" she asked.

"He had to run an errand in order to save your life."

Rita took the letter out of her pocket and handed it to Pamela. Everyone saw the question in her eyes and excused themselves to give her privacy to read the letter. "I'll get you something to eat," Rita said. She fluffed Pamela's pillows and helped her to sit upright, then left the room.

Afraid to read the letter in her hand, Pamela stared at the paper. What had he written that he couldn't tell her in person? She slowly opened the folded paper and read:

My darling Pam,

As I write this letter there is a big gaping hole developing in my heart knowing that I have to be away from you when you need me the most. But please believe that I am doing this to save your life and I will be with you again. Knowing that we're not together makes me weak and split. But know that wherever I am, I'm never far from you and you're never out of my thoughts. You are always in my heart. You are my soul, a beacon to light my way back to you.

I love you forever and ever,

Saul

Tears welled up in her eyes and slid down her cheek. She didn't understand the letter. Why did he have to go away? He didn't say anything about work. Why did he have to go?

Angel walked into the room and held her hand. Pamela wiped her eyes and blew her nose. "Do you

THE OTHER SIDE OF THE MOUNTAIN

know anything about this?" she asked Angel and handed her the letter.

She nodded and told her the entire story.

"Okay." She took the letter back from Angel and re-read it. Now she understood. She wanted to think she knew Saul enough to trust what he'd said in the letter.

"Okay? Is that all you're going to say?"

She blew her nose again and nodded. "Yes." She slowly swung her legs off the bed. "I need to get out of bed. I think I've slept too much already."

Angel held her hand. "Pamela, you haven't been just lying around. You were deathly ill."

"And now I'm fine." Unsteadily, she realized she needed Angel to hold onto. "Okay, so maybe I need to take it slow for a while. But I won't stay in bed any longer."

"Do you want to talk about the letter?" Angel asked.

"No." Leaning on Angel, she walked slowly to the living room to see all her furniture gone except for the cushions. "What happened?"

"You don't remember when Raquel broke her nose…"

"Oh, yes. I have my work cut out for me in making more furniture."

"Don't worry about it. I'll replace your furniture for you," Tim said, coming through the open door. "You must feel much better, you're up and walking."

370

She nodded. "You know how much I hate to lie about."

"I don't know if I'd call what you were doing lying about."

"You're sweet."

That was a switch. She'd just flung him out of her room, now she thought he was sweet. "You mean I'm not banned from your home?"

"Only from my bedroom and when you get on my nerves." She sat on the cushion and took the tray Rita had just brought her from the kitchen. "Why don't you guys sit and eat with me."

"I have to go and see to my husband," Rita said. "But I'll be back later on to check on you. Edith will bring you some more herbs in a little while. You still need to drink the healing herb for a few days. We want to make sure all that stuff is completely out of your system. Meanwhile, please drink the herbal tea."

"Okay." She looked over at Angel.

"I'll stay, but I'll go and get my own breakfast."

Pamela looked at Tim and rolled her eyes. He laughed and sat beside her. "Together again."

She burst out crying. He made an attempt to reach for her. She shook her head while holding up one finger. "No, don't do that. I'll be fine. I'm fine." She took a deep breath, smiled and drank the entire cup of herbal tea.

THE OTHER SIDE OF THE MOUNTAIN

"Don't worry about the furniture, really. I'll make some for you."

"You've forgotten that I'm good at this kind of stuff. It takes me longer than a man, but all I need is the wood."

"Have you forgotten that you teach?"

"No. I'll do it one piece at a time."

Her mother and father walked in and sat down.

"Can I get you some tea?" Pamela asked.

"I'll get it," Tim said before anyone could answer.

She nodded. "Thanks, Tim."

Her mother looked at her and touched her hand. "Why aren't you in bed?"

"Mama, I feel strong enough not to be in bed."

"I can't say I'm all that fond of Saul, but I understand he had to leave to get the medicine for you." She kept looking into her daughter's face.

Pamela nodded.

Her father nodded. "He's a noble man." He kept nodding.

Esther sighed deeply. "Yes, but he did bring that woman to the island." On one hand, she admired Saul for going to Jamaica with Raquel in order to save Pamela's life, but deep down, she blamed him for bringing Raquel to the island in the first place.

"I know these things, woman. He took the woman from the island, didn't he? And I bet you anything she'll never come back."

Both parents looked at Pamela.

"I'm still here," Pamela said, smiling.

They both laughed. "You haven't lost your sense of humor. That's a good sign," Ishmael said. "But I'm sad for you that he's gone."

"Don't be," she said. "I have a lot to do."

Both parents looked at each other. "I thought you loved him?" Ishmael said.

"With all my heart and soul," she replied.

"Then…" Ishmael shook his head. "I don't understand you women at all."

Pamela smiled. "It's all right, Dad."

Tim came back with the tea and Esther poured a cup for herself and her husband.

The door stood ajar and Pamela realized that as bad as it was, it could have been worse. Thanks to Saul and the other men the damage was minimal. Two homes had been lost but no lives.

As long as it took to rebuild, no one would leave the village. Crops had to be replanted.

Myah came in and sat down. She hugged Pamela. "I am so glad you're feeling better." Then the smile vanished from her face. "I've decided to go back to my village."

"Oh, Myah," Pamela lamented. "I'll miss you a lot."

Myah leaned against her. "I'm just going to Twin Mountain. I'm not leaving the island. Furthermore,

I'll visit so often you'll get tired of seeing me, and I know you'll visit me, too."

"Of course." Her smile was crooked but genuine. "You're right. It will give me a chance to ride more."

"Thank you for understanding," Myah said.

"What's there to understand? You lost your home and you're reuniting with your parents. That's big. As you said, you'll only be a mountain away."

Myah poured herself a cup of tea.

Pamela couldn't help noticing that Myah didn't say anything about her brother. She didn't know if Saul had spoken to Myah before he'd left. She knew he'd spoken with James and Angel. And Angel had not kept anything from her.

Both James and Angel came in and joined the group. The conversation was all about Pamela's health until she got tired of answering questions and turned it to the rebuilding of the village. "Does anyone know the extent of the damage on Twin Mountain?"

James had come straight from Jamaica to the village. He shook his head. "When we left last night what I saw was minimal. Of course, it was very dark." He looked at Angel. "Angel and I will stay for awhile to help with the rebuilding. I spoke with Hildie and she's fine, so we don't have to worry about her."

Pamela gave a wan smile. Everyone except her parents were so careful not to mention Saul's name that she wanted to shout at the top of her lungs, "He'll be back, and I'll wait for him if it takes the rest of my life." Actually, as she rolled the thought around in her head, it sounded pretty pathetic even if it was truly how she felt.

While everyone spoke, Angel whispered in James's ear. "When will you tell Saul that Pam is all right?"

He took a deep breath. "In a couple days. No flights are leaving Jamaica now anyway."

"You're giving him time?"

He nodded.

"For what?"

"I don't know, but I want to make sure Pammy is quite out of danger before I go telling him anything."

"You know Devin could easily fly them to where Saul wants to take her."

"No, that would be too easy."

"Why do you say that?" Angel asked.

He shook his head. "I don't know. There's something about the way Saul's handling this thing that makes me think he has something up his sleeve." He looked at her.

Angel gave him a knowing look, but he just shrugged.

The children joined the group and, as Pamela finished eating, Gracie sat beside her. "Are you well now, Mama?"

Pamela nodded. "Yes, and tomorrow I'll be even better. You and I have a lot to do, young lady."

THE OTHER SIDE OF THE MOUNTAIN

"Like what?" Gracie held her mother's arm and laid her head on her shoulder.

"Replanting the flowers." From where she sat, she could see that most of her rose bushes had been uprooted. She didn't want to look any farther because she knew that even though Saul had ripped out a lot of the plants and put them in pots, the work was still there to be done. She was looking forward to it.

Edith brought her a few bottles of herbal mixture and told her to drink it twice per day without fail until it was all gone. She thanked her. "I'll put them in the kitchen on the counter," Edith said.

Pamela got to her feet, excused herself and went back to her room. She wanted to take a bath, but already knew everyone would think her mad if she even suggested going to the waterfall. Besides, she had no idea how damaged the path was or how high the river. She called Gracie into her room and asked her to bring in the bath pan.

Gracie left the room, but it was James and Angel who came back with the bath pan and water.

She sat on her bed and smiled sheepishly. "I thought I was being discreet."

"It would have worked if I hadn't asked questions," James said.

"You're not thinking of going outside today, are you?" Angel said.

Pamela looked at her and wrinkled her nose. "I thought I'd go out and see…"

Angel shook her head. "No. You will stay inside all day today. You will drink the tea and a lot of water, then tomorrow, maybe, you'll go out. Because I know that if you leave this house you'll find something to do."

"Did Rita tell you to keep an eye on me?"

"Yes," Angel said.

James laughed and they both left the room to give Pamela privacy.

⌘

After a long walk, Saul returned to the hotel. He had not eaten breakfast and now he was hungry. He took the elevator to his room and saw Raquel watching television. "Would you like to go down for supper, or would you like to have room service?" he asked, smiling, hoping she wouldn't realize his detachment.

She looked at his face and returned his smile. "I would prefer to eat up here. I hate going around like this." She touched her nose.

He nodded and took up the room service menu. "Does it hurt?" he asked without looking at her.

"Yes, and I don't have anything to take."

He put down the menu and pulled out an envelope from a small overnight case. He pushed the envelope toward her. "Just wet your finger and dip it in the herb, then place your finger under your tongue."

She looked at him suspiciously. "You're not trying to kill me, are you?"

He smiled. "If I wanted to kill you I'd have pushed you overboard last night." He shook his head. "Sorry, I shouldn't have said that."

"You wouldn't have done that because she would have died, too."

He nodded.

"I knew you'd come to your senses and realize that you still love me," she said, doing as he'd instructed.

She lay down and closed her eyes, not seeing his mouth twisted in a grimace. He replaced the envelope in his bag. "What would you like to eat?"

She opened her eyes, took the menu from him and told him she wanted steak.

He nodded, picked up the phone and ordered for both of them. He lay back on the bed and closed his eyes. Again, he hoped that the herb Raquel had given him was the antidote to whatever she'd used to poison Pamela. On the other hand, if she were any worse, James would have sent word. The one thing that rested on his mind was the hope that Pamela understood his letter. Holding onto that thought, he didn't even move when he felt Raquel's head against his arm.

JANICE ANGELIQUE

In bed that night, Pamela's thoughts turned to Saul. She was holding onto the words in the letter that she'd read repeatedly. *I will be with you again.* Those words meant more to her than anything else anyone could have said to her. She believed them and she knew he did, too. He didn't say when, but again, whatever he had to do before he came back to her, maybe *he* didn't know when.

She picked up a book and tried to read, but the herbs she'd been drinking made her sleepy. She closed her eyes and fell asleep.

Angel, Myah and Mary had decided to take turns in looking in on her. Angel slowly took the book from her arm, blew out the lamp and went to sleep in the new room.

Chapter 26

The morning sun streaked through the trees and into Pamela's bedroom. She turned on her back and opened her eyes. She felt a lot better than she had last night and was ready to conquer the task ahead. She sat up to see Myah sitting in a chair, sleeping. "You guys don't have to watch over me, you know," she said. Myah didn't budge.

Silently, Pamela got out of bed and walked to the window. She looked at the mud congealing on the ground, then at the path to the waterfall. It wasn't too bad. She turned to look at what had once been a beautiful flower garden and shook her head. She looked at the other cottages around her. They had all suffered the same fate. She shrugged. *Same as last year.*

She pulled on her robe and headed for the community kitchen.

Mary, her mother, and four other ladies were there chopping vegetables, kneading flour and cutting up plantains.

Mary rushed to pull out a chair when Pamela entered the kitchen. Pamela laughed. "Since when do you cater to me?"

"Since you're back from the dead." Mary went back to her kneading.

"The operative word there is *back*. I'm sure no one thought I'd die, especially you." She sat down anyway.

The women nodded.

"You're so right," Esther said. "Only the pure of heart die young, and I think you have a little darkness in you."

"Mother!" she gasped. "I never…"

"Oh, yes you have," Esther said with a big grin on her face.

The women said, "Ummm-hmmm," in unison

Pamela laughed. "I never claimed to be a saint. Do you need my help?"

"No, we'll bring your breakfast to you," Mary said.

"You need to stop doing that, because right now I'm going to change and do some work in my garden. The ground is soft, but not too soft to start replanting." She got up and left the kitchen.

Pamela did her toiletries, changed into old clothes and went out to begin her work. Along the circle, women who weren't going to the kitchen were already beginning to work in their gardens. Some had baskets on their heads, going to replant the fields.

Gracie came running up with a basket of mangoes. Pamela laughed. "I thought you guys were in bed."

THE OTHER SIDE OF THE MOUNTAIN

"No, we got up early to go pick up the mangoes that fell from the trees. All the children were picking up mangoes."

"Okay, take them to the kitchen. Don't you children have dance today?"

"No, Miss Daisy says it's more important to help with the rebuilding and planting."

Pamela nodded.

"We'll be back, Mama," Ruth said. They ran to the kitchen.

Pamela looked after the four children. Although it made her smile to hear Ruth and David call her mama, she couldn't help feeling a little sad. She was almost sure they'd lost their mother forever unless Saul took them off the island to see her. But that was his prerogative. All she wanted was for him to come back to her. Thinking of him, she felt an ache in the pit of her stomach and tears close behind her eyelids.

She went to the new room to begin taking out the flowers and tools to plant and discovered all that Saul had done. She saw the gramophone and vinyl records. She bent and ran her fingers along the intricate pattern on the trunk he'd made. She sat on the floor and cried. The children came to help and she quickly dried her eyes, got up and took the plants outside. She got Mary's flowers from inside her kitchen and began planting them, too. She needed to keep busy in order not to think of Saul and what he was doing.

Again, breakfast was had indoors. After breakfast it was back to work.

Soon Pamela was joined by Mary, Myah and Angel in her garden and Mary's.

Myah's home was being rebuilt, but not on this mountain. Her mother kept Isha while she helped Pamela with whatever she could. In her heart, she knew one day she and Pamela would be sisters.

The replanting and rebuilding became one big party. Palm leaves were collected. Cement was mixed and bricks laid. A lot of hammering almost drowned out the women humming and the older men beating the steel drum.

Men rolled barrels over the breakfast area to harden the dirt once more, then poured cement over it to improve the place where everyone ate and mingled. The young boys were now using their push carts and handmade trucks to carry supplies for the men.

Everyone worked and as the sun climbed higher into the sky, it got hotter and more humid. More lemonade and water were the order of the day. And instead of looking for shade trees, which were scarce, the women donned wide-brimmed hats. The men went shirtless and as their bodies glistened with sweat they were harassed by the women who whistled at them. Once again copper pipes were laid to bring water into the village. The Elders had already begun getting water in their cottages.

THE OTHER SIDE OF THE MOUNTAIN

Tim had begun making new furniture for Pamela even though she'd objected. He was doing it in his backyard. He walked now to Pamela's home and stooped beside her. "In a few days I have to resume my job at the university, but I promise I will come back every evening."

"Okay, but you do have to resume teaching here too as soon as school is back in session." She didn't look at him.

"I know. Is it all right if I have supper with you this evening?"

"I don't see why not."

Angel glanced over at them, then stood up and looked for her husband. Even though he was hard at work helping with the dining area, he was very aware of Tim's presence with Pamela. The couple trusted Pamela explicitly and knew that Tim had been friends with her from childhood, but they'd noticed his actions in Saul's absence. Angel walked to where James stood. "Do you still want to wait?"

He nodded. "He can't do anything. She won't let him into her life that way."

"Okay, you know your people." Angel sighed.

"Yes, and I know Saul and Pamela."

"Me, too."

"Then you shouldn't worry."

Angel smiled and walked back to her work.

384

The sun moved from its highest point and began its slow descent into the horizon and tomorrow. The work day was done and, once again, supper was had indoors. Both James and Angel kept an eye on Tim, but got bored when the only thing Pamela did with him was laugh. He said something close to her ear and she threw him out of her home. She walked to the new room, looked at the gramophone, and then opened the trunk, took out a record and placed it on the turntable. She slowly placed the needle on the record and turned the handle until she heard the music. She turned a little faster and closed her eyes.

Angel came into the room and smiled. "If I do that for you, you can dance."

Pamela opened her eyes and let go of the handle as Angel took hold and cranked it up then stood watching Pamela do a very sad dance to the cool sound of a young Bob Marley.

She stopped dancing and pulled her fingers against the lines of the gramophone. "He knew I'd like this. I didn't know until today that he'd brought this for me." Her eyes caught Angel's.

"He loves you very much," Angel said.

"Yes."

"You miss him a lot, don't you?"

"Yes. But he'll be back."

THE OTHER SIDE OF THE MOUNTAIN

Angel nodded and began winding the handle until James came in and showed them how to do it properly.

❧

On the fourth day, the ground was almost back to normal. The dining area was being used instead of everyone eating in their homes, and Tim presented Pamela with one very beautiful, polished mahogany rocking chair. She shook her head and hugged him.

"I told you not to do this."

"I did this just to see that smile on your face. I'll do anything for you. You know that, right?"

"Thank you very much. I do appreciate it." Frankly it made her miss Saul more than ever because she knew if he were with her he would have been doing the same thing, along with puttering with her in her garden.

"Aren't you going to try it out?"

"Why? Is it a trick chair?" She laughed boldly, trying to hide her sadness.

"Funny lady."

She sat on the chair and began rocking. She leaned her head against the back and closed her eyes. She felt his breath on her face and a kiss on her forehead before she could get a chance to protest. She stopped rocking, got up and ushered him out of her house anyway.

"Why do you keep pushing me away, Pam? Don't you want us to be close anymore?"

"Tim, I think you want more than I can give you." She looked up into his unsmiling face.

"Why? Why can't I want your love?"

"Because someone already has my heart, and you know it. I am in love with Saul. There can be nothing between us, Tim."

"He's not coming back. He left you to die, Pam."

"No, he didn't. Now you really have to go." She pushed him out and slammed the door.

He knocked softly on the door.

"Do you want your chair back?" she asked.

"No, I made it for you."

"Then go away."

In the evening, after everyone had had supper, the musical instruments were brought into the dining area and the music began.

With her sandaled feet set apart, Pamela bent her knees and slowly swayed to the rhythm of the music. With her eyes closed she moved her arms over her head and moved her head from side to side, all the while thinking of Saul. She moved her hips seductively as she thought of their love making, and the music followed her movements instead of the other way around.

Tim watched and lusted privately for what he could never have. How could he change the relation-

THE OTHER SIDE OF THE MOUNTAIN

ship? How could he get her to love him? Would she in this lifetime have him as more than just a friend? Perplexed, he shook his head and went to dance with her. Mary and Myah joined in, but they were doing it more to protect the woman who was oblivious to Tim's actions.

He went close to her. She opened her eyes, smiled, dropped her arm to her side, then cast one hand around his waist and slowly walked behind him with her hand traveling from his front to his back. Before she walked away from him, she looked into his eyes and said, "You have to find your own love. I am taken."

Mary and Myah began dancing with him, and slowly more people joined them on the dance floor, including Mary and Myah's husbands. Tim made several attempts to follow Pamela but they were foiled by Mary, whose husband was mildly amused since Mary was not a well-coordinated dancer.

No one had ever seen Pamela dance like that before and no man understood the dance unless their partners had performed it and told them what it was. It was the forbidden dance developed by an older dance teacher to show the husband or boyfriend how one felt about him. Although no one had dared to stop Pamela, the women understood that she missed Saul and did the dance for him. Unfortunately, it aroused the wrong man. They chalked it up to her being so heartbroken she forgot what it did to a man, especially when it was done by a beautiful women like her.

Pamela walked to the stables and patted her horse's nose. "Have you missed our rides, old friend?" She took her time in brushing his coat, then took him outside and jumped on his back. She took the path slowly down the mountain and sat looking at the ocean. The water had receded but the beach was filled with seaweed. She sat just looking at the water. Just a short while ago it had been spouting froth with huge angry waves and now it was as calm as the gentle wind tousling her hair. She turned the horse around and headed back to the village. She would ask the men to begin cleaning up the beach tomorrow.

☙

It was time. James was on his way back to Jamaica to give Saul the news of Pamela's recovery. He'd taken Saul's boat and used Willow's car to drive into Kingston.

When he got to the hotel, he called Saul on the hotel phone. He didn't want Raquel to overhear his conversation. As soon as Saul heard his voice on the other end, he said a few words and rushed down to speak with him in person.

"How is she?" Saul asked as soon as he saw James.

"She is completely recovered, but I have to tell you, she misses you a great deal."

THE OTHER SIDE OF THE MOUNTAIN

Saul bowed his head. "I know. I miss her more than I can put into words."

"Are you really going through with this farce?"

"I have to get Raquel far away from here."

James didn't want to pry. "If you need anything, anything at all, don't hesitate to ask."

"You've done so much already. Thank you, my brother." He hugged James and was about to go back upstairs.

"When will you leave?" James asked.

"I'll get a flight for this evening and get Raquel the hell out of Jamaica and as far away from our people as I can."

James nodded. "Good luck."

⚜

Back upstairs, Saul got a flight booked for two to Brazil. He told Raquel to pack.

"We're leaving now?" she asked with a slow, secret smile.

"Yes, I got us on a flight out this evening. We have four hours."

"I need to get some things from the shop downstairs."

"You need to go shopping? Why and for what?" he asked, annoyed.

"I need to get underwear."

JANICE ANGELIQUE

"Raquel, you have been here for a week and now that I tell you we are leaving you realize that you need underwear? You hardly wear it." He was on the brink of anger when he reminded himself to be calm. He turned, walked through the open patio door, took a few deep breaths and turned back to her. "Of course. Get whatever you have to get. I'll wait here for you."

"I need money," she said.

He took out a wad of bills, peeled off a few hundred and gave it to her.

This was the Saul she knew and wanted. A man who did her bidding without questions.

She slipped it into her purse and changed her clothes to go downstairs.

When she came back, he was ready to go. She took more time to put on more makeup before they left the room and checked out. All the while Saul never said anything to her.

The concierge called them a cab and they were on their way to the airport.

At the airport she began complaining of a headache. He gave her some powdered herb to put under her tongue. She had taken the bandage off her nose. He told her to sit while he checked them in.

They went through security and while they waited in the first class lounge, Saul spoke with one of the flight attendants. In a few minutes they were told they could board. They were the first ones to board.

THE OTHER SIDE OF THE MOUNTAIN

"Why am I so sleepy?" Raquel asked, yawning.

"I gave you something to relax you and take away your headache."

"Yes, my headache is gone."

"Then sleep," he said.

She leaned her head against him and in a few minutes was fast asleep. No longer then twenty minutes later, the flight attendant he'd spoken with nodded. He gently slipped a pillow under Raquel's head and left the seat. He gave the flight attendant a letter and told her to give it to Raquel when she woke up. He knew she'd be out for at least three or four hours.

He took his overnight bag and left the plane just before the doors closed. He smiled and hurried down the gangway. He walked to the terminal building, went back through customs and walked out of the building. James was waiting for him. He laughed. "How did you know?"

"Give me some credit, my brother. We are Rahjah. We hate being manipulated and when we say when, we really mean it. Get in."

Saul opened the car door and got in.

"How did you get away from her?"

"It wasn't hard at all. I gave her a sleeping powder and asked the flight attendant to tell me when they were about to close the door. I gave her a letter to give to Raquel and left."

"But man, where is your suitcase?"

"I guess on its way to Brazil with loads of papers and a few shirts."

"Brazil!" he said, surprised. "I thought she was going to the States."

"That's what she thinks, too. But she's on her way to her husband in Brazil."

James looked over at Saul. "You called her husband?"

"Oh, yes. Now tell me about the one woman who I'd walk through fire to see again."

As they sped away from the airport back to Kingston, James filled him in on what had been going on in the village.

⟡

The men had cleaned up the beach and tonight the moon lit Pamela's way as she led her horse down the path. She got off the horse and left him close to the rocks. She peeled off her clothes, dropped them on the sand and walked into the warm water. She floated on her back and gazed up at the moon. She saw a shooting star and closed her eyes with just one wish. The water lapped about her naked body and she sighed as a hand slipped behind her head. She held her breath and opened her eyes. His face was so close to hers she could smell the sweet nectar from the gods on his breath.

"Was that wish for me?" he asked.

THE OTHER SIDE OF THE MOUNTAIN

She smiled. "Who else could it be for?"

"This body," he said, running his fingers down the length of her smooth body as his lips touched hers.

She breathed. "It's been too long," she said as his lips moved against hers, devouring their softness.

He groaned and lifted her out of the water against his naked body. She clasped her legs behind him, pressed her body into him with reckless abandon and gave herself freely to the passion of his kiss.

"You're truly mine now?" she whispered in his ear.

"I've been all yours from the beginning."

And as passion mounted, and he pressed into her, she realized how much she'd missed their lovemaking. She opened her thighs and welcomed him into her body. Love was strong, growing with fiery embers, sparking the way to a fiery downpour as they claimed each other physically and emotionally.

Under the full moon, he pulled her close to him and held her. "Did you understand my letter?"

"I didn't at first. I had to read it three times before I was able to pick out the words that made the entire letter."

"I knew you would. I'm so sorry that I had to go away."

She placed a finger to his lips. "Shhh. You did what you had to do. You're here now, with me, the way it's supposed to be."

JANICE ANGELIQUE

They sat up together and they could see the lights from a passing ship. He looked at her. "I have us booked on a cruise to Europe in a month." He watched her eyes light up as an unbelievable smile took over her entire face.

"Really? You did that for me, for us?"

"Yes." Seeing and feeling her joy, he couldn't stop laughing. "This one is just for us. I'll take the entire family to Paris in a few months. You've been through so much in the past that…"

Again she quieted him. "None of that. Let's not go back. You have made me so happy, and I know the children will be overjoyed when we tell them. I love you with all my heart."

He pulled her into his lap. She straddled him and, as his kiss sent spirals of ecstasy through her, he leaned back on the sand and allowed her to take him to heaven's door. Again.

About the Author

Janice Angelique resides in Virginia with her husband, her daughter and three adorable dogs.

THE OTHER SIDE OF THE MOUNTAIN

2011 Mass Market Titles

January

From This Moment
Sean Young
ISBN-13: 978-1-58571-383-7
ISBN-10: 1-58571-383-X
$6.99

Nihon Nights
Trisha/Monica Haddad
ISBN-13: 978-1-58571-382-0
ISBN-10: 1-58571-382-1
$6.99

February

The Davis Years
Nicole Green
ISBN-13: 978-1-58571-390-5
ISBN-10: 1-58571-390-2
$6.99

Allegro
Adora Bennett
ISBN-13: 978-158571-391-2
ISBN-10: 1-58571-391-0
$6.99

March

Lies in Disguise
Bernice Layton
ISBN-13: 978-1-58571-392-9
ISBN-10: 1-58571-392-9
$6.99

Steady
Ruthie Robinson
ISBN-13: 978-1-58571-393-6
ISBN-10: 1-58571-393-7
$6.99

April

The Right Maneuver
LaShell Stratton-Childers
ISBN-13: 978-1-58571-394-3
ISBN-10: 1-58571-394-5
$6.99

Riding the Corporate Ladder
Keith Walker
ISBN-13: 978-1-58571-395-0
ISBN-10: 1-58571-395-3
$6.99

May

Separate Dreams
Joan Early
ISBN-13: 978-1-58571-434-6
ISBN-10: 1-58571-434-8
$6.99

I Take This Woman
Chamein Canton
ISBN-13: 978-1-58571-435-3
ISBN-10: 1-58571-435-6
$6.99

June

Inside Out
Grayson Cole
ISBN-13: 978-1-58571-437-7
ISBN-10: 1-58571-437-2
$6.99

2011 Mass Market Titles (continued)

July

The Other Side of the
Mountain
Janice Angelique
ISBN-13: 978-1-58571-442-1
ISBN-10: 1-58571-442-9
$6.99

Holding Her Breath
Nicole Green
ISBN-13: 978-1-58571-439-1
ISBN-10: 1-58571-439-9
$6.99

August

The Sea of Aaron
Kymberly Hunt
ISBN-13: 978-1-58571-440-7
ISBN-10: 1-58571-440-2
$6.99

The Finley Sisters' Oath of
Romance
Keith Thomas Walker
ISBN-13: 978-1-58571-441-4
ISBN-10: 1-58571-441-0
$6.99

September

Except on Sunday
Regena Bryant
ISBN-13: 978-1-58571-443-8
ISBN-10: 1-58571-443-7
$6.99

Light's Out
Ruthie Robinson
ISBN-13: 978-1-58571-445-2
ISBN-10: 1-58571-445-3
$6.99

October

The Heart Knows
Renee Wynn
ISBN-13: 978-1-58571-444-5
ISBN-10: 1-58571-444-5
$6.99

Best Friends; Better Lovers
Celya Bowers
ISBN-13: 978-1-58571-455-1
ISBN-10: 1-58571-455-0
$6.99

November

Caress
Grayson Cole
ISBN-13: 978-1-58571-454-4
ISBN-10: 1-58571-454-2
$6.99

A Love Built to Last
L. S. Childers
ISBN-13: 978-1-58571-448-3
ISBN-10: 1-58571-448-8
$6.99

December

Fractured
Wendy Byrne
ISBN-13: 978-1-58571-449-0
ISBN-10: 1-58571-449-6
$6.99

Everything in Between
Crystal Hubbard
ISBN-13: 978-1-58571-396-7
ISBN-10: 1-58571-396-1
$6.99

THE OTHER SIDE OF THE MOUNTAIN

Other Genesis Press, Inc. Titles

2 Good	Celya Bowers	$6.99
A Dangerous Deception	J.M. Jeffries	$8.95
A Dangerous Love	J.M. Jeffries	$8.95
A Dangerous Obsession	J.M. Jeffries	$8.95
A Drummer's Beat to Mend	Kei Swanson	$9.95
A Good Dude	Keith Walker	$6.99
A Happy Life	Charlotte Harris	$9.95
A Heart's Awakening	Veronica Parker	$9.95
A Lark on the Wing	Phyliss Hamilton	$9.95
A Love of Her Own	Cheris F. Hodges	$9.95
A Love to Cherish	Beverly Clark	$8.95
A Place Like Home	Alicia Wiggins	$6.99
A Risk of Rain	Dar Tomlinson	$8.95
A Taste of Temptation	Reneé Alexis	$9.95
A Twist of Fate	Beverly Clark	$8.95
A Voice Behind Thunder	Carrie Elizabeth Greene	$6.99
A Will to Love	Angie Daniels	$9.95
Acquisitions	Kimberley White	$8.95
Across	Carol Payne	$12.95
After the Vows (Summer Anthology)	Leslie Esdaile T.T. Henderson Jacqueline Thomas	$10.95
Again, My Love	Kayla Perrin	$10.95
Against the Wind	Gwynne Forster	$8.95
All I Ask	Barbara Keaton	$8.95
All I'll Ever Need	Mildred Riley	$6.99
Always You	Crystal Hubbard	$6.99
Ambrosia	T.T. Henderson	$8.95
An Unfinished Love Affair	Barbara Keaton	$8.95
And Then Came You	Dorothy Elizabeth Love	$8.95
Angel's Paradise	Janice Angelique	$9.95
Another Memory	Pamela Ridley	$6.99
Anything But Love	Celya Bowers	$6.99
At Last	Lisa G. Riley	$8.95
Best Foot Forward	Michele Sudler	$6.99
Best of Friends	Natalie Dunbar	$8.95
Best of Luck Elsewhere	Trisha Haddad	$6.99
Beyond the Rapture	Beverly Clark	$9.95
Blame It on Paradise	Crystal Hubbard	$6.99
Blaze	Barbara Keaton	$9.95

400

Other Genesis Press, Inc. Titles (continued)

Blindsided	Tammy Williams	$6.99
Bliss, Inc.	Chamein Canton	$6.99
Blood Lust	J.M. Jeffries	$9.95
Blood Seduction	J.M. Jeffries	$9.95
Blue Interlude	Keisha Mennefee	$6.99
Bodyguard	Andrea Jackson	$9.95
Boss of Me	Diana Nyad	$8.95
Bound by Love	Beverly Clark	$8.95
Breeze	Robin Hampton Allen	$10.95
Broken	Dar Tomlinson	$24.95
Burn	Crystal Hubbard	$6.99
By Design	Barbara Keaton	$8.95
Cajun Heat	Charlene Berry	$8.95
Careless Whispers	Rochelle Alers	$8.95
Cats & Other Tales	Marilyn Wagner	$8.95
Caught in a Trap	Andre Michelle	$8.95
Caught Up in the Rapture	Lisa G. Riley	$9.95
Cautious Heart	Cheris F. Hodges	$8.95
Chances	Pamela Leigh Starr	$8.95
Checks and Balances	Elaine Sims	$6.99
Cherish the Flame	Beverly Clark	$8.95
Choices	Tammy Williams	$6.99
Class Reunion	Irma Jenkins/ John Brown	$12.95
Code Name: Diva	J.M. Jeffries	$9.95
Conquering Dr. Wexler's Heart	Kimberley White	$9.95
Corporate Seduction	A.C. Arthur	$9.95
Crossing Paths, Tempting Memories	Dorothy Elizabeth Love	$9.95
Crossing the Line	Bernice Layton	$6.99
Crush	Crystal Hubbard	$9.95
Cypress Whisperings	Phyllis Hamilton	$8.95
Dark Embrace	Crystal Wilson Harris	$8.95
Dark Storm Rising	Chinelu Moore	$10.95
Daughter of the Wind	Joan Xian	$8.95
Dawn's Harbor	Kymberly Hunt	$6.99
Deadly Sacrifice	Jack Kean	$22.95
Designer Passion	Dar Tomlinson Diana Richeaux	$8.95

Other Genesis Press, Inc. Titles (continued)

Do Over	Celya Bowers	$9.95
Dream Keeper	Gail McFarland	$6.99
Dream Runner	Gail McFarland	$6.99
Dreamtective	Liz Swados	$5.95
Ebony Angel	Deatri King-Bey	$9.95
Ebony Butterfly II	Delilah Dawson	$14.95
Echoes of Yesterday	Beverly Clark	$9.95
Eden's Garden	Elizabeth Rose	$8.95
Eve's Prescription	Edwina Martin Arnold	$8.95
Everlastin' Love	Gay G. Gunn	$8.95
Everlasting Moments	Dorothy Elizabeth Love	$8.95
Everything and More	Sinclair Lebeau	$8.95
Everything but Love	Natalie Dunbar	$8.95
Falling	Natalie Dunbar	$9.95
Fate	Pamela Leigh Starr	$8.95
Finding Isabella	A.J. Garrotto	$8.95
Fireflies	Joan Early	$6.99
Fixin' Tyrone	Keith Walker	$6.99
Forbidden Quest	Dar Tomlinson	$10.95
Forever Love	Wanda Y. Thomas	$8.95
Friends in Need	Joan Early	$6.99
From the Ashes	Kathleen Suzanne Jeanne Sumerix	$8.95
Frost on My Window	Angela Weaver	$6.99
Gentle Yearning	Rochelle Alers	$10.95
Glory of Love	Sinclair LeBeau	$10.95
Go Gentle Into That Good Night	Malcom Boyd	$12.95
Goldengroove	Mary Beth Craft	$16.95
Groove, Bang, and Jive	Steve Cannon	$8.99
Hand in Glove	Andrea Jackson	$9.95
Hard to Love	Kimberley White	$9.95
Hart & Soul	Angie Daniels	$8.95
Heart of the Phoenix	A.C. Arthur	$9.95
Heartbeat	Stephanie Bedwell-Grime	$8.95
Hearts Remember	M. Loui Quezada	$8.95
Hidden Memories	Robin Allen	$10.95
Higher Ground	Leah Latimer	$19.95
Hitler, the War, and the Pope	Ronald Rychiak	$26.95
How to Kill Your Husband	Keith Walker	$6.99

Other Genesis Press, Inc. Titles (continued)

How to Write a Romance	Kathryn Falk	$18.95
I Married a Reclining Chair	Lisa M. Fuhs	$8.95
I'll Be Your Shelter	Giselle Carmichael	$8.95
I'll Paint a Sun	A.J. Garrotto	$9.95
Icie	Pamela Leigh Starr	$8.95
If I Were Your Woman	LaConnie Taylor-Jones	$6.99
Illusions	Pamela Leigh Starr	$8.95
Indigo After Dark Vol. I	Nia Dixon/Angelique	$10.95
Indigo After Dark Vol. II	Dolores Bundy/ Cole Riley	$10.95
Indigo After Dark Vol. III	Montana Blue/ Coco Morena	$10.95
Indigo After Dark Vol. IV	Cassandra Colt/	$14.95
Indigo After Dark Vol. V	Delilah Dawson	$14.95
Indiscretions	Donna Hill	$8.95
Intentional Mistakes	Michele Sudler	$9.95
Interlude	Donna Hill	$8.95
Intimate Intentions	Angie Daniels	$8.95
It's in the Rhythm	Sammie Ward	$6.99
It's Not Over Yet	J.J. Michael	$9.95
Jolie's Surrender	Edwina Martin-Arnold	$8.95
Kiss or Keep	Debra Phillips	$8.95
Lace	Giselle Carmichael	$9.95
Lady Preacher	K.T. Richey	$6.99
Last Train to Memphis	Elsa Cook	$12.95
Lasting Valor	Ken Olsen	$24.95
Let Us Prey	Hunter Lundy	$25.95
Let's Get It On	Dyanne Davis	$6.99
Lies Too Long	Pamela Ridley	$13.95
Life Is Never As It Seems	J.J. Michael	$12.95
Lighter Shade of Brown	Vicki Andrews	$8.95
Look Both Ways	Joan Early	$6.99
Looking for Lily	Africa Fine	$6.99
Love Always	Mildred E. Riley	$10.95
Love Doesn't Come Easy	Charlyne Dickerson	$8.95
Love Out of Order	Nicole Green	$6.99
Love Unveiled	Gloria Greene	$10.95
Love's Deception	Charlene Berry	$10.95
Love's Destiny	M. Loui Quezada	$8.95
Love's Secrets	Yolanda McVey	$6.99

Other Genesis Press, Inc. Titles (continued)

Mae's Promise	Melody Walcott	$8.95
Magnolia Sunset	Giselle Carmichael	$8.95
Many Shades of Gray	Dyanne Davis	$6.99
Matters of Life and Death	Lesego Malepe, Ph.D.	$15.95
Meant to Be	Jeanne Sumerix	$8.95
Midnight Clear (Anthology)	Leslie Esdaile	$10.95
	Gwynne Forster	
	Carmen Green	
	Monica Jackson	
Midnight Magic	Gwynne Forster	$8.95
Midnight Peril	Vicki Andrews	$10.95
Misconceptions	Pamela Leigh Starr	$9.95
Mixed Reality	Chamein Canton	$6.99
Moments of Clarity	Michele Cameron	$6.99
Montgomery's Children	Richard Perry	$14.95
Mr. Fix-It	Crystal Hubbard	$6.99
My Buffalo Soldier	Barbara B.K. Reeves	$8.95
Naked Soul	Gwynne Forster	$8.95
Never Say Never	Michele Cameron	$6.99
Next to Last Chance	Louisa Dixon	$24.95
No Apologies	Seressia Glass	$8.95
No Commitment Required	Seressia Glass	$8.95
No Regrets	Mildred E. Riley	$8.95
Not His Type	Chamein Canton	$6.99
Not Quite Right	Tammy Williams	$6.99
Nowhere to Run	Gay G. Gunn	$10.95
O Bed! O Breakfast!	Rob Kuehnle	$14.95
Oak Bluffs	Joan Early	$6.99
Object of His Desire	A.C. Arthur	$8.95
Office Policy	A.C. Arthur	$9.95
Once in a Blue Moon	Dorianne Cole	$9.95
One Day at a Time	Bella McFarland	$8.95
One of These Days	Michele Sudler	$9.95
Outside Chance	Louisa Dixon	$24.95
Passion	T.T. Henderson	$10.95
Passion's Blood	Cherif Fortin	$22.95
Passion's Furies	AlTonya Washington	$6.99
Passion's Journey	Wanda Y. Thomas	$8.95
Past Promises	Jahmel West	$8.95
Path of Fire	T.T. Henderson	$8.95

Other Genesis Press, Inc. Titles (continued)

Path of Thorns	Annetta P. Lee	$9.95
Peace Be Still	Colette Haywood	$12.95
Picture Perfect	Reon Carter	$8.95
Playing for Keeps	Stephanie Salinas	$8.95
Pride & Joi	Gay G. Gunn	$8.95
Promises Made	Bernice Layton	$6.99
Promises of Forever	Celya Bowers	$6.99
Promises to Keep	Alicia Wiggins	$8.95
Quiet Storm	Donna Hill	$10.95
Reckless Surrender	Rochelle Alers	$6.95
Red Polka Dot in a World Full of Plaid	Varian Johnson	$12.95
Red Sky	Renee Alexis	$6.99
Reluctant Captive	Joyce Jackson	$8.95
Rendezvous With Fate	Jeanne Sumerix	$8.95
Revelations	Cheris F. Hodges	$8.95
Reye's Gold	Ruthie Robinson	$6.99
Rivers of the Soul	Leslie Esdaile	$8.95
Rocky Mountain Romance	Kathleen Suzanne	$8.95
Rooms of the Heart	Donna Hill	$8.95
Rough on Rats and Tough on Cats	Chris Parker	$12.95
Save Me	Africa Fine	$6.99
Secret Library Vol. 1	Nina Sheridan	$18.95
Secret Library Vol. 2	Cassandra Colt	$8.95
Secret Thunder	Annetta P. Lee	$9.95
Shades of Brown	Denise Becker	$8.95
Shades of Desire	Monica White	$8.95
Shadows in the Moonlight	Jeanne Sumerix	$8.95
Show Me the Sun	Miriam Shumba	$6.99
Sin	Crystal Rhodes	$8.95
Singing a Song...	Crystal Rhodes	$6.99
Six O'Clock	Katrina Spencer	$6.99
Small Sensations	Crystal V. Rhodes	$6.99
Small Whispers	Annetta P. Lee	$6.99
So Amazing	Sinclair LeBeau	$8.95
Somebody's Someone	Sinclair LeBeau	$8.95
Someone to Love	Alicia Wiggins	$8.95
Song in the Park	Martin Brant	$15.95
Soul Eyes	Wayne L. Wilson	$12.95

THE OTHER SIDE OF THE MOUNTAIN

Other Genesis Press, Inc. Titles (continued)

Soul to Soul	Donna Hill	$8.95
Southern Comfort	J.M. Jeffries	$8.95
Southern Fried Standards	S.R. Maddox	$6.99
Still the Storm	Sharon Robinson	$8.95
Still Waters Run Deep	Leslie Esdaile	$8.95
Still Waters…	Crystal V. Rhodes	$6.99
Stolen Jewels	Michele Sudler	$6.99
Stolen Memories	Michele Sudler	$6.99
Stories to Excite You	Anna Forrest/Divine	$14.95
Storm	Pamela Leigh Starr	$6.99
Subtle Secrets	Wanda Y. Thomas	$8.95
Suddenly You	Crystal Hubbard	$9.95
Swan	Africa Fine	$6.99
Sweet Repercussions	Kimberley White	$9.95
Sweet Sensations	Gwyneth Bolton	$9.95
Sweet Tomorrows	Kimberly White	$8.95
Taken by You	Dorothy Elizabeth Love	$9.95
Tattooed Tears	T. T. Henderson	$8.95
Tempting Faith	Crystal Hubbard	$6.99
That Which Has Horns	Miriam Shumba	$6.99
The Business of Love	Cheris F. Hodges	$6.99
The Color Line	Lizzette Grayson Carter	$9.95
The Color of Trouble	Dyanne Davis	$8.95
The Disappearance of Allison Jones	Kayla Perrin	$5.95
The Doctor's Wife	Mildred Riley	$6.99
The Fires Within	Beverly Clark	$9.95
The Foursome	Celya Bowers	$6.99
The Honey Dipper's Legacy	Myra Pannell-Allen	$14.95
The Joker's Love Tune	Sidney Rickman	$15.95
The Little Pretender	Barbara Cartland	$10.95
The Love We Had	Natalie Dunbar	$8.95
The Man Who Could Fly	Bob & Milana Beamon	$18.95
The Missing Link	Charlyne Dickerson	$8.95
The Mission	Pamela Leigh Starr	$6.99
The More Things Change	Chamein Canton	$6.99
The Perfect Frame	Beverly Clark	$9.95
The Price of Love	Sinclair LeBeau	$8.95
The Smoking Life	Ilene Barth	$29.95
The Words of the Pitcher	Kei Swanson	$8.95

Other Genesis Press, Inc. Titles (continued)

Title	Author	Price
Things Forbidden	Maryam Diaab	$6.99
This Life Isn't Perfect Holla	Sandra Foy	$6.99
Three Doors Down	Michele Sudler	$6.99
Three Wishes	Seressia Glass	$8.95
Ties That Bind	Kathleen Suzanne	$8.95
Tiger Woods	Libby Hughes	$5.95
Time Is of the Essence	Angie Daniels	$9.95
Timeless Devotion	Bella McFarland	$9.95
Tomorrow's Promise	Leslie Esdaile	$8.95
Truly Inseparable	Wanda Y. Thomas	$8.95
Two Sides to Every Story	Dyanne Davis	$9.95
Unbeweavable	Katrina Spencer	$6.99
Unbreak My Heart	Dar Tomlinson	$8.95
Unclear and Present Danger	Michele Cameron	$6.99
Uncommon Prayer	Kenneth Swanson	$9.95
Unconditional	A.C. Arthur	$9.95
Unconditional Love	Alicia Wiggins	$8.95
Undying Love	Renee Alexis	$6.99
Until Death Do Us Part	Susan Paul	$8.95
Vows of Passion	Bella McFarland	$9.95
Waiting for Mr. Darcy	Chamein Canton	$6.99
Waiting in the Shadows	Michele Sudler	$6.99
Wayward Dreams	Gail McFarland	$6.99
Wedding Gown	Dyanne Davis	$8.95
What's Under Benjamin's Bed	Sandra Schaffer	$8.95
When a Man Loves a Woman	LaConnie Taylor-Jones	$6.99
When Dreams Float	Dorothy Elizabeth Love	$8.95
When I'm With You	LaConnie Taylor-Jones	$6.99
When Lightning Strikes	Michele Cameron	$6.99
Where I Want to Be	Maryam Diaab	$6.99
Whispers in the Night	Dorothy Elizabeth Love	$8.95
Whispers in the Sand	LaFlorya Gauthier	$10.95
Who's That Lady?	Andrea Jackson	$9.95
Wild Ravens	AlTonya Washington	$9.95
Yesterday Is Gone	Beverly Clark	$10.95
Yesterday's Dreams, Tomorrow's Promises	Reon Laudat	$8.95
Your Precious Love	Sinclair LeBeau	$8.95

ESCAPE WITH INDIGO !!!!

Join Indigo Book Club©
It's simple, easy and secure.

Sign up and receive the new releases
every month + Free shipping
and
20% off the cover price.

Visit us online at
www.genesis-press.com or
call 1-888-INDIGO-1

Order Form

Mail to: Genesis Press, Inc.
P.O. Box 101
Columbus, MS 39703

Name _____
Address _____
City/State _____ Zip _____
Telephone _____

Ship to (if different from above)
Name _____
Address _____
City/State _____ Zip _____
Telephone _____

Credit Card Information
Credit Card # _____ ☐ Visa ☐ Mastercard
Expiration Date (mm/yy) _____ ☐ AmEx ☐ Discover

Qty.	Author	Title	Price	Total

Use this order form, or call 1-888-INDIGO-1

Total for books _____
Shipping and handling:
  $5 first two books,
  $1 each additional book _____
Total S & H _____
Total amount enclosed _____

Mississippi residents add 7% sales tax

Visit www.genesis-press.com for latest releases and excerpts.